CAMELEER

Printed in Australia

Cover and internal design by Shawline Publishing Group Pty Ltd

First printing: March 2024

Shawline Publishing Group Pty Ltd

www.shawlinepublishing.com.au

Paperback ISBN 978-1-9231-0131-9

eBook ISBN 978-1-9231-0132-6

Hardback ISBN 978-1-9231-0178-4

Distributed by Shawline Distribution and Lightning Source Global

Shawline Publishing Group acknowledges the traditional owners of the land and pays respects to the Elders, past, present and future.

A catalogue record for this work is available from the National Library of Australia

CAMELEER

XAVIER PAUL

The first people of the land who lost so much, the forgotten people from other lands that survived where few did, and the children who suffered but lived in innocence.

To my Special Rainbow

Chapter 1

To catch a tadpole, patience was required, calmness was critical and a still hand essential. Charly knew all of these requirements. She would lay on this sandstone slab, not moving a muscle, waiting till a taddie, as she called them, slowly swam into the cusp of her half-closed hand. Then with no hesitation, snap, the hand was closed, and on most occasions, a tadpole was inside.

The sandstone slab sat on the water's edge of the middle of three linked waterholes, or billabongs as the local people called them. In the winter rainy season, they were simply a widened part of the river, in summer, as the river flow slowly dropped, they were the deeper sections of river that became one of the many still waters to quench the thirst of the animals, both native and domestic. But as this year, the second year of a drought, when the rain in winter had not come, when the river stopped, they were the only water for miles around.

But even in a drought, the water in the billabongs stayed, providing the life for the large trees that stood nearly down to the water's edge, up over the old tops of the riverbank, back for a hundred feet or so to where the grasslands started. The trees provided two other wonders in this harsh land, where no rain became too much rain and a normal season was one that did not cause too much devastation. These trees became a home for the local animals and, the best for Charly, lots and lots of shade that allowed the soft flow of air to cool the skin for an imaginary moment in the heat of scorching summers day.

The first billabong was back up the flood plain, providing a supply of drinking water for the cattle, the reason for the existence of Charly and her family on the edge of the dry sands to the west and north. The third billabong sat down between the sandstone low cliffs and buttresses where the river ran through a gap in the rocky spur that ran off a ridge of pinkish sandstone. These low cliffs held places sacred to the local people, caves and ledges marked over the last thousand or more years.

Charly stayed away from the lower billabong, it was a place for the men, where they gathered and did their business, while the middle waterhole was for the women, where they gave their thanks and spoke their beliefs to the younger ones. The middle billabong was also the one closest to her home, the one where she felt the happiest.

Charly lay still, enjoying the short time away from her mundane daily life on an outlying cattle station, well, more than outlying, it was the last before the start of the wild barren stones and sand of the deserts to the north and west. The faint smell of eucalyptus oil from the leaves over her head wafted past her nose as it was released in the hot sun.

Charly tensed as a tadpole swam close. This one had poorly formed legs, a special target, a prized gift she provided to the local lizards, birds or really anything else that breathed and ate tadpoles. She has this strange connection with anything that lived in the land, other than humans and tadpoles. The only thing she feared in the living world around her were the large brown snakes that also shared the edges of the billabong, she knew they were around, but while she like to feed their legged relatives, the king browns were off limits.

The tadpole was getting closer to her fingers, picking a line of travel that would place it in the grasp of her quick fingers. The soft waft of moving air caused a slight ripple on the middle of billabong, but close to the edge it was mirror calm, the shade of the big leaves providing perfect vision of what was under the surface of the water.

Suddenly, the water just in front of Charly's outstretched hand exploded, large droplets spraying in all directions. Water from the billabong landed on Charly's arms, on her head, running down her face. She reached up with her dry hand and wiped the water from her eyes with annoyance. There was no point in being still and silent now. She slowly let her breath out to calm the small fright she had experienced, knowing a quick reaction was just what the young person who'd thrown the rock wanted.

'Piss off, Harry, let me be in peace. You're nothing but a heap of cow shit when you do this to me.'

Charly pulled her legs towards her as she heard the soft rustle in the grass just past her feet up the bank a little, the sound of the big old king brown snake moving off from where he'd been sunning himself on the nice warm slab of sandstone.

'I tell Mum you are cussing again. You know she hates you doing that, saying them words,' shouted the teenage boy standing at the top edge of the embankment.

Charly looked up at him with barely hidden disgust; nice clean shirt and britches, a broad brimmed hat, which was a few sizes too big on his head and worst of all, leather boots laced tight up to wrap around his ankles. Compared to her untucked dirty plaid shirt, worn old canvas britches and very dusty bare feet, he just did not belong in her world.

'She's not my mum, I told you that a thousand times. Stop calling her my mum,' snapped Charly. 'And you are not my brother; just some dumb city kid belonging to the woman my father married, so piss off.'

Charly's stepbrother ignored her, all he really wanted was to be like his slightly older stepsister, be able to play in the edge of the lagoon, or billabong as she called it much to his mother's disgust. 'A black's name, dear, you must use proper English even living out here,' she would say.

Wanting to see what she was doing, he descended through the long dry grass that grew on the sloping bank to the stone slabs that Charly was standing on. Walking without care of what dangers were lurking in the grass, ignorant of its dangers.

Charly saw him start down from the corner of her eye as she was watching the slow movement in the grass of the big brown snake.

'Stop, stop, stand still Harry, just don't move!' she shouted, an edge of terror in her voice. 'You got the brains of a dumb poddy calf, you mutt, you are about to walk right on to a big brown snake.'

Harry stopped dead still. He recalled the first warning he'd been given just a year or so back when he'd arrived at the station with his mother: 'There is only one thing that will kill you quicker than almost anything else out here and that is a big brown snake by the water.'

Harry slowly backed up the embankment as Charly picked up a long stick and gave the king brown a little encouragement to move a bit quicker with a couple of sharp taps on the sandstone at her feet. As the brown snake slowly disappeared up towards one of the big gum trees, one with a big hollow at the base a man could crawl into, Charly gave her hand a quick wash and slowly hopped from rock to rock up the slope to the top of the bank of the billabong avoiding most of the longer grass. There was no point in staying, the splash of the stone had scared all the animals in the water, and worse it had disturbed her calmness, her moment in her own world, her sanctuary from the life she had to live every day.

She reached her stepbrother, her annoyance written on her face in a grimace. 'So what do ya want?'

'Mum wants you to finish the chores in the house she told you to do this morning, she is not happy you took off down here again.'

Charly grunted a non-committal response, knowing that the few moments of precious inner clam were about to end. She stopped at the top of the bank, picking up her old felt hat, placing it on her head, the brim pulled down to shade over her eyes. She then sat in the shorter grass and pulled on her old worn leather boots, ignoring the young man standing next to her.

'I could tell Mum I found you working out in the barn if you let me play down here with you. Please, I do not know why you keep ignoring me,' Harry pleaded.

'No!' snapped Charly as she stood. 'Just leave me alone down here, and don't tell fibs for my sake, last thing I want is that on my head.'

Charly walked through the knee length grass back to the main house some 500 yards away, positioned on a slight rise that avoided any overflow of the river when it covered the floodplains that ran away to the west and east of the river. The positioning was well-chosen, having a small cluster of gum and mulga trees to provide some protection from the winds and burning sun. The elevated ground also provided sufficient room for the main farm buildings, two storage sheds, a stable and the large timber sided barn.

The house had substantially changed since the day that Harry had arrived with his mother about two years before. The builders only left a few months back, leaving the once humble earthen floor cottage now with polished timber floors, a corrugated metal roof, real glass windows and fancy furniture. The combined proceeds of three very good years of green grass and fat cattle, all spent to satisfy a new wife rather than kept to protect against the next season of drought, thought Charly.

And now, the second year where the rains where late, just enough for some grass growth near the river, but the flooding water to satisfy the plains had not arrived. As she trudged back towards the house, Charly's thoughts did not improve, it had been three years since her mother disappeared, why, why, why, that moment had resulted in a life that turned from an almost endless happiness to a life in a black cave, with no light, no help and no love.

She looked across the plain; her father and older brothers Jessie and Bryan would be out there somewhere, herding stock closer to the homestead where there was better grass. In years past she would have helped, riding as hard as her brothers, one with her horse but at the arrival of her new mother it had all ended. Mustering was deemed an unacceptable activity for a girl, not to mention that she rode astride a horse as a man, something that appalled the new arrival. The morals of it, a woman spreading her legs over an animal. Her stepmother's mind raced, thinking what her friends would think; it would be an abomination against the Lord. But not now Charly was practically banned from riding, other than occasionally sneaking out before sunrise for an hour or so.

Harry had to run to keep up, he was a year or so younger, but a little short for his age, or was it that Charly was quite tall for hers? Regardless of which it was, a determined stride from Charly was hard to keep up with.

'Hey, Charly, why don't you worry about the snakes out here?' he asked, slightly breathless. The grass they strode through was about the same length and density as down by the billabong.

''Cause they aren't here, they live by the rocks, the trees and water, and the adders are out in the sandy areas. Nuffing here but me and you, and right now I wish you weren't here, get it,' Charly responded. She instantly regretted her snappy tone but if she was going to be miserable today, well, why be alone.

Harry had become used to Charly's irritated outbursts, he did not care, she was the only person who spoke to him as an equal, and he loved her as the sibling he had missed for all his years.

As they got closer to the house, Charly slowed to allow Harry to walk alongside her.

'Look, Harry, your mother is going to rip me a new earhole and the old man will likely give me a right flogging, so best for you to not be there. Misty needs a bit of a brush and a handful of oats, how about you just bugger off over to the stable for a while?'

Harry was excited, he rarely was allowed near Charly's favourite stock horse, one especially chosen and trained by an old stockman just for her, now gone with the rest of his people. At least she'd not been banned from riding her horse, but she felt it was coming. What did Harry's mother say? 'Not fitting for a young girl to ride like a man.' So what? That's what her real mum had done, even when she was carrying Charly's baby sister.

The thought of them cut like a knife through her heart. Both of them, one day here, the next gone, her mum and baby sister had just disappeared. No-one could find them.

She killed the thoughts of them, it hurt far too much, and she would need a thick skin and dull mind for the next few hours. She looked at the back of the running Harry, smiling that he still was left with some innocence; this place will get rid of that nonsense soon enough.

She opened the back door as she kicked off her boots, the hinges squeaked, the last oiling failing soon after the next dust blow. It was time to face the music.

'Charlotte, is that you?' called a cold voice from the front parlour room. 'Please come here this moment, I wish to speak with you before your father arrives home this evening.'

Charly let out a sigh. This place was now just a house, not a home like in the days before her mother had disappeared. Now, after the arrival of her stepmother, the old gum tree was more a home than this place, the old king brown more welcoming.

She closed the door with a thud and strode slowly up the passage to the front room, the domain of her stepmother. Charly was sure she was preparing to deliver the next tirade, a sermon of scripture to explain, rather justify, Charly's place in this world as the live-in slave. A slave to remain silent and do the housework to far below her stepmother's assumed status but be grateful for the privilege. She cautiously pushed the timber door to the parlour open and stood just inside the lavishly appointed room. Her stepmother's place of power.

'In the eyes of the generous God above, what in the world are you wearing, girl? Where is your dress?' Grace Hendricks thundered with a sneer on her lips. 'The good Reverend Griswold always considered that any woman, of any age, that wore man's clothing was little more than a harlot; is that what you are, Charlotte, a good for nothing harlot?'

Charly said nothing, this was the usual opening into the next deluge of vindictiveness. She slowed her breathing. This part was always words, expressions to reinforce her understanding of where she now stood in the greater family gathered together in God's name under this roof.

'The holy scriptures clearly show that a person with your mind is little more than a drawer of water, a gatherer of wood, in servitude of those favoured by God –' Grace took a breath to steady her godly anger, not wishing to bring celestial condemnation of her own head '– however, this time I will show forgiveness and leniency for which you are simply not deserving. However, you must complete the tasks I listed this morning. Then, only then, will you be acceptable to eat a meal at the Lord's table.'

Charly's head dropped. The punitive actions had again increased, every time just a little more to break her spirit.

'And to ensure you understand your roles, you are not to leave the house for the remaining week, except for your ablutions. We must teach you some qualities,' mocked Grace. 'And I have instructed your father that Harry is to care for your horse. It is time he learnt the things needed to manage this fine property.'

Charly's head snapped up. looking at the condescending smile her stepmother wore, she knew that she had struck home, found a way past the walls her stepdaughter had built the day that she arrived.

A look of horror crossed Charly's face as the implications became evident. 'Misty is my horse, it is my job to care for her. You can't do this.'

'Silence, girl; do not speak unless asked. Misty is your father's horse, and so she is also mine. I make the rules, Charlotte. It is time you realised this, your days of careless freedom have ended,' said Grace softly but with poison in her voice. 'So, little girl, now get changed and start those chores or you will get nothing.'

Charly did not move, a moment of defiance.

Grace Hendricks used her final weapon. 'Your mother is gone, Charlotte, no-one will protect you now.'

Charlotte stepped back like a burst of fire hit her face; she knew that she was nearly beaten. She turned and ran to her room at the back of the house, just a small room, but it was hers, secure and private. She picked up the dress from where she had thrown it earlier in the day, knowing that putting it on would almost be the final capitulation.

It was too much. To be humiliated was one thing but to be cut off from the creatures she loved, which were her life, without so much as a moment to say goodbye, Charly reacted as only she could. Flinging the dress against the wall, she rushed out of the room, slamming the door shut so it reverberated throughout the house, and ran across the yard into the stable.

Harry looked up from stroking Misty's nose, as the horse contentedly munched on a small bucket of oats. 'What are you doing here? Mum will kill you,' he warned. He'd sensed his mother's bitterness when she'd told him to find Charly. 'Get back into the house, Charly, I'll cover for you.'

'Leave me alone, Harry, I want to be with my horse,' murmured Charly. Misty lifted her head when she heard Charly's voice, turning her head to press against her shoulder. 'Please, Harry, I need peace and quiet. Time with Misty, please, Harry,' she pleaded, tears rolling down her cheeks. Charly turned her head and rubbed her forehead against Misty's neck.

Harry walked away, turning back to watch as his stepsister held her head against the forehead of her horse, slowly speaking her thoughts. Misty's ears were up and twitching, listening, almost looking like she knew what her human friend was saying. The connection between the two was obvious, Harry hoped that he would not be used by his mother to destroy what Charly felt for the lovely horse. As he opened the door to leave, he looked once more, seeing that Misty had laid down and Charly was snuggled into her side, eyes closed, at peace.

Misty stirred as she heard the stable door open, a soft shaft of light falling onto the dirt floor, showing a scattering of hay and the odd lump of manure. A hand pulled the door back, allowing enough space to walk through before softly closing it. The man, Charly's father, knew where his daughter would be, but the knowledge she was safe did not provide any solitude to his angry mind.

He slowly walked over to stand at the stall, seeing his daughter asleep next to her horse. Misty gave a welcoming snort, enough for

Charly's eyes to flick open, looking up at a glow of light, not seeing who was standing behind. Not that she was unsure of the person who held the lantern, it would be her father, she knew her peace was at an end.

'On ya feet, girl. You have caused enough commotion for one day, past time to get all this sorted so I can get to bed.'

Charly slowly got to her feet, one foot a little unstable from being slept on. Knowing what was likely to come she had no intentions to try and plead her case. She had been tried and found guilty, even before her father got off his horse this afternoon.

'Nothing to say?' he asked, not interested in a long flow of words and tears, knowing his daughter enough to know she would simply take what was given and make no sound. 'Righto, let's leave the horse alone, you and I need to discuss a few things. I've had a long day, and when I come home all I get is cold food, a long lecture of my failings, due to you, a deluge of words why I have failed God, again due to you, and why, if nothing changes, we all will perish due to his displeasure, again due to you.'

Charly walked down the stable towards the only room enclosed from the horses.

'Yep, we will go to the tack room, at least you have got that bit figured out,' her father growled in frustration.

Jedidiah Hendricks walked close behind his daughter, holding the lantern high enough to allow sufficient light for both of them to see the odd item that had been left on the floor. The lantern also cast enough light to show that the stables, as was every other farm building, was in a state of disorder. Charly reached up and pulled the solid timber door open, walking to the middle of the room before stopping, standing perfectly still, looking down at her feet.

Her father hung the lantern on a hook hanging from the roof beam, a hard look on his face; the face of the man he had become in the last few years, without love. He grabbed a chair from beside the work bench and sat it in front of his daughter. He unbuckled his belt and quickly pulled it out, the hiss of leather against denim of his trousers filled the room.

As he sat down, he looked at Charly, the anger that was building from the moment he slowly dismounted his horse this evening, reaching its peak.

'Get them off, you know what the drill is, get them off and bend over my leg, girl.'

As Charly undid the buttons on her britches and draws, letting them drop to the ground, her father released the first part of his fury in words.

'I have had it with you. Get over the issues you have; Grace is your mother now and has every right to give you work and ask you to help her. Your insolence must end, I am over having my ears flogged by her tongue every time you resist her.'

He looked at Charly, running his eyes over her body, the lower bare part topped in tight curls that affected his thoughts. He grabbed the hair on top of her head and pulled her down till she was bent over his knee and all that was up was her bare buttocks, as she was bent over his knee. Charly braced her hands on the dirt floor and waited for the first crack of leather on her skin.

The first was followed by another then another as her father swung the leather belt folded in two. Her soft skin reddened, then split, a slow trickle of blood running down her legs. After a dozen or so strikes of the belt, Jedidiah Hendricks descended into a madness, the madness that Charly feared would happen tonight, a madness that caused her father to lose all sense of reason. The madness that left her sick in stomach, in mind and in her heart. The madness that she had told her mother about just a few weeks before she walked into the desert with Charly's baby sister, never to be seen again.

Just because she could hardly walk did not mean she was excused for her chores. The demands from her stepmother started before dawn the following morning. It was now a bit over a four weeks since the episode in the tack room; she had survived the humiliation and pain once again and found ways to protect herself. Charly had submitted, her spirit broken but for a small flicker of fire, a hate she had for two people that had never existed before. A hate due to differing reasons but sufficiently entwined to keep something smouldering in her mind to force herself to keep going.

Her split skin healed soon enough, an ample coating of the liniment she kept in her room for riding sores caused by the chaffing of the saddle dealt with that issue. The hurt to her soul had not improved, it was a darkness she had found a way to endure, placing it in a small box in her heart, leaving it for a later time. The morning after the assault on her body and mind by her father, Charly picked up the dress from where she had thrown it and pulled it on. She rolled her britches and shirts, tucking them into a back corner of the cupboard in her room. Placing her riding boots over them, she knew they might come in handy one day but not for a while.

Charly hardly spoke the next day, doing what she was told, and enduring an endless tirade of verbal hectoring whenever her stepmother decided to check on her activities, which was very frequently. She quickly equated her tormentor to the ugly rock spiders that sat and watched in the crevasses of the sandstone caves, watching from their web with cold hard eyes. The next shock was when Charly placed the setting for the evening meal, one for her father, one for her oldest brother, one for Bryan, one for Harry, one for the rock spider and one for herself, on the large timber table in the dining room.

'No, girl, take yours to the scullery, you will eat there until I am satisfied you are fit to mix with people that follow the Good Lord's instructions,' ordered Grace, looking down her nose.

Later, when the men arrived and sat down at the table, Jessie looked around the table, wanting to tell his sister about the twin calves he had found today, but she was not in her usual place.

'Hey, Dad, where's Charly at, she not at the table–'

Before he could continue, his father placed his hand on his son's arm to silence him. Grace took her Harry's hand in hers and proceeded to give thanks for the meal before them, the usual staple of beef and long-lasting vegetable such as potatoes, onions and carrots they grew in a fenced-off area.

'Well? I'm not stupid, Dad, what's happening with Charly?' Jessie asked once his stepmother had finished, annoyed at the change in the table's arrangements. His father again went to place his hand on Jessie's arm to stop the discussion, but reconsidered at the last moment.

'Look, Jessie, Grace runs the house, and well, Charly has not been respectful of her authority and till she accepts it, she does not eat at the table.'

Jessie dropped his head, muttering under his breath.

'What did you say?' demanded his father.

'I need to be mucking out the ditch in the morning,' answered Jessie, starting to stand. 'I think I'll eat on the verandah; there's a smell of something unhealthy in here.'

Before Jedidiah could respond to the insult, Jessie, then his younger brother, picked up their plates and walked from the room. Jessie slowed as he past the scullery, giving his little sister a wink before exiting the back door onto the verandah.

Grace had not lifted her head through the entire episode between Jedidiah and his son, but while her head might have been down, her mind was working rapidly. Another crack had started in the original family group, a crack she could exploit.

From the scullery, Charly had a good view of her detested rock spider. She could see the evil, knowing smile creeping into the corners of Grace Hendrick's mouth.

The food was slowly consumed in silence by those remaining at the table. Charly ate in the quiet peace of the scullery, enjoying not being hectored, hoping that this would last for a little time more.

As Charly thought back to that evening, it was as if it was the first day of the new family arrangement. Grace had control; her father ran the station, but the house was not his. Jessie had lost all respect for Grace, and little more for his father; Bryan was confused, unsure what to believe; Harry was the pawn, used to hurt Charly; and as for herself, she was reliving each day, same activities, same hectoring, same humiliation.

After the first week, Grace had instituted Bible readings for one hour for Charly, replacing the previous school time where she would learn to read and write. Grace stated that a greater education was required, and Charly could learn all she needed by reading the scriptures. Other subjects were ignored; arithmetic, history, and science had no meaning, only reading passages carefully chosen to enforce Graces authority and Charly's subservience.

When Charly did not fight back, the inferences and pressures were increased. In the third week following the incident in the barn, Grace determined that Misty was to be Harry's horse. Charly was not allowed to ride, so there was no point in wasting a very good and well-trained horse. At first Jedidiah protested, saying that the horse was given to Charly by her mother, but to no effect. The next day Harry was directed to get into the saddle and he joined Jessie and Bryan working the cattle in the homestead paddocks, moving them into the enclosures with a water bore, pumped by a squeaking windmill.

But Charly did not respond, did not fight; she made no comment. In fact, had her father been around during the day he would have noticed that Charly rarely spoke, only if asked directly or when forced to read passages used to humiliate. Had he stopped thinking about his cows for one moment, he also would have noticed that his daughter never spoke to him anymore, ever; it was as if he did not exist.

A little over six weeks later, the family had reached an uneasy balance. Jessie and Bryan had returned to eat at the table but refused to speak, Jedidiah had given up trying to have Charly return to the table, mainly when she sharply told her father she preferred to eat in solitude. On this night, Jedidiah pushed his plate towards the centre of the table, after eating the thin stew, not providing the pleasure that he usually had from a meal after a day in the saddle.

'Looks like the drought will hold. I cannot see any rains this year, the floodwaters will not cover the plains again till maybe next year, maybe longer,' he said to the room, but no-one in general. 'I think that while the beasts are still in good condition and we have a little feed left in the land, we're going to sell as many as we can, all except the few good breeders.'

No-one replied. Jessie had been thinking this would happen for some time, it was the only smart option. While his father had issues running the household, without a doubt he was a good cattleman. Grace said nothing, unsure what it meant for her. Likely nothing, she had her son and that wench of a girl to help her around the house.

'We start final muster in the morning. Harry comes with us,' Jedidiah said, his tone clear that he expected no objection.

'My son? No, Jedidiah, he is far too young,' snarled Grace, missing the tone of her husband's voice. 'He can't go, he needs his mother, he is too young.'

Jedidiah looked at his wife. She had destroyed him in the few years they had been together as husband and wife. She was so different to the woman he knew for many years before, the years when a secret meeting made his heart race. He slowly pushed back his chair, standing, blotting his mouth with the fine linen napkin, before throwing it onto the middle of the table.

'Woman, the day you drove off the stockmen, you removed my support, so in return you must give one of yours. I expect he will be in the saddle before dawn tomorrow.' With that said, he knew he would never share the marital bed again. So he picked up his hat from the sideboard and walked from the room. The old bunk bed in the stables awaited, his new home.

Chapter 2

Jedidiah sat back in his saddle. The ache in his back provided the evidence of two weeks on his horse as he watched the last of the herd moving down a small rocky gully onto the large holding paddocks in front of him. From his position on a small outcrop of sandstone, he could see almost to the end of the grass filled flood plains where the curve of the earth and the distant sand hills took away his sight of what lay beyond, the scatter of gums on the horizon providing a rough edge. In the distance to his right sat his house, yards and sheds. A little past the rise in the ground beyond where his home sat were the stand of old river gums that showed where the billabongs lay, the course of the unnamed river that filled the plains one or two times every year.

Just not this year, or the one most recently past, thought Jedidiah, watching the dust rise from land covered in grass. This was a sign of the dryness in the soil that would take a number of flood events to heal. Today was the first in some time that his inner anger had begun ease out of his body. Anger at his daughter to allow herself to be used by her stepmother, anger at his wife for using him to humiliate his only daughter, and mainly anger at himself for allowing this whole situation to build to where he had been in the saddle for more than two weeks and another eight to ten weeks still sat before him.

Feeling the need to stretch his legs, Jedidiah pulled one foot out of the stirrup and lowered himself to the ground. Dropping the bridle to the ground, his horse knew this was a signal for it to stand still and wait. Taking a few steps to the edge of the rock spur overlooking the small gully that connected his best grazing areas between the rocky range he pulled the tobacco pouch from the top pocket of his calico shirt. Giving the pouch a small shake to remove any dust, he opened the leather flap and removed the makings of a hand rolled cigarette and something to light it with. After rolling the small amount of chopped tobacco in the palm of his hand, placing it into a square of light paper, Jedidiah wet the edge to make a small, slightly uneven, hand-rolled cigarette.

Poking the unlit end of the match to pack the end of the rollie, he placed the slightly dirty tube of paper into his mouth. A rapid strike of the match head on the sole of his boot provided the desired result, allowing the end of the rollie to be lit, and the first draw of the smoke into his system. Jedidiah squatted, one leg slightly out in front of him in the manner of stockmen for as long as he knew, enjoying the pleasure of a moment's peace as the king of all he could see.

Jedidiah ignored the coating that covered his skin, plastered in a mix of sweat and dust that cracked at joints or skin folds. He'd soon have to join the boys below when they started separating the unmarked animals to allow them to be branded, so for now he enjoying the moment that he as the owner should have had each day; overseeing the mustering rather than being one of the men doing the mustering. His anger rose as his thoughts returned to why this year, of all the years, he was working in the thickest of the dust, why the usual handful of experienced stockmen where not at his side as in the previous times. All over one person and her ideas as to how and what the local people should do or more rightly, be *allowed* to do.

He watched his eldest son, and his stepson Harry pushing the cattle, the boys and their horses coated in dust, the same dust that formed rings around his mouth, under his nose and eyes, anywhere moisture might, no matter how small, develop. Jessie's younger brother Bryan, was in the lead, carefully directing the leading cows towards where the other cattle were gathered. He was proud of his sons, they worked like men ten years older. As for Harry, he did well to stay on Misty. The horse knew what it was required to do, the horse teaching the boy as much as anyone else.

Looking at Misty brought his daughter to his mind. He felt shameful of what he'd done that fateful evening in the stable. What took over his mind when these things happened? Had he lost her this time? She had not spoken to him since that evening, treating him as an empty space when they crossed paths. He wished she was sitting on Misty instead of Harry; she was the best horse rider of all his children, as if Misty could read her mind. His anger grew. He'd caused the loss of her respect and love. He'd felt trapped, and struck out at the innocent, his own child.

Jedidiah slowly stood, spitting the few strands of tobacco into the dust as he flicked away the last of the rollie.

'Biggest mistake of my life, bloody stupid woman,' he snarled, his mind unsure as to which of the three women he was cursing about: his current wife, his daughter or the woman he originally married, now a distant memory but who had borne him his three children.

Jedidiah bent and picked up the bridle; his horse had been eating a few of the clumps of drying grass that had grown between the rocks. Suddenly his heart froze as he smelled the waft of extreme danger behind him. He turned. One of the other grass tussocks was burning. Swearing under his breath he rushed the few steps and stamped out the rapidly growing fire, grinding any embers into the sandy soils, finally dragging more sand over the burnt grass to kill the flames and stop air getting to it.

Mounting his horse, he looked back down at the burnt tussock, watching to see if a wisp of smoke could be seen. After a few minutes he was satisfied the fire was dead, but its rapid growth in grass that did not look that dry – the base of the tussock even looked slightly green – was a concern. Yes, he thought, they would need to be very careful with fire this year. But by the time Jedidiah reached the bottom of the spur to follow the cloud of dust, the small fire between the rocks was forgotten, he had other pressing things on his mind as he kicked his horse into a canter.

Four days later, as Jedidiah pulled his chair back to sit at the table to have his evening meal, he knew it would be the last for many weeks at this table. He had gathered as many of the cattle as he could easily find with the three others, nearly four hundred head. What was still running around in the dry sandy area past the flood plains would have to wait till next year when he might have a full complement of stockmen again to help. This was an issue he'd have to sort when he got back, an issue that would cause further conflict with his new wife.

He would be glad to be gone. The dining table had become a place of icy resentment; his wife had little to say, his daughter still ignored his presence and his sons, while relaxed and talkative while mustering, again now ate together on the verandah, refusing to communicate with him or their stepmother in the house.

'We are leaving tomorrow as I planned, Grace,' he said quietly as he sat, not wanting any conflict on this last evening. 'I thank you for preparing and packing the food and stores into the travel packs. The next shipment of supplies is due in about three or four weeks when the camel team arrive, so you'll have no issues until I get back.'

Grace looked at her husband with cold eyes, his demands over her son unforgiven. 'And Harry? You still haven't told me what *your* plans are for him,' she hissed.

Jedidiah did not reply. They'd had this discussion only a few days before, Grace simply refused to agree to what he had proposed. In silence, he cut a number of slices of roasted beef from the hind quarter of a small cow that had been butchered a few days before. When he was finished, he laid these on a serving platter for everyone to share. Not a word was spoken in the room as the meal of vegetables and beef was consumed between the three left at the table, Jedidiah, his wife, and Harry.

'As I said yesterday, Grace, I need a minimum of eight men to move four hundred head, but I have four,' Jedidiah said calmly. 'So I either have Charly or Harry.'

Cold eyes glared across the table, the answer unspoken.

'I would prefer Charly, but she… anyway, if Harry wants to live in this house and on this station he needs to learn. I agree he is young but he needs to contribute, Grace, and I need his help.' Jedidiah pushed back his chair, his appetite gone, looking at Harry. 'An hour before sunrise, Harry, at the stable and bring the spare clothes we discussed.'

Jedidiah turned and walked out of the house, across to the stable tack room where he had been sleeping for the past weeks. He was ready; he hoped that his sons were too.

In the two weeks since the menfolk left the station, driving the four hundred odd head of cattle south to the closest market town, Charly found that the daily pressures had eased a little. Yes, she was still controlled most days but as now she also had duties outside the house, a place that Grace avoided, it allowed a few hours each day without the constant feeling she was being watched. While all the horses had been taken by the men, she still had a few other animals to watch over to keep her entertained. A chain-link fenced area provided a home for a small brood of chickens, and a small vegetable garden was watered from a windmill bore that supplied the house, water sourced from a subterranean shallow basin of liquid sitting under the floodplain.

Charly clearly remembered the complaints at the cost of the chain-link fence wire by her father when her mother demanded a small enclosure for the chickens and vegetables. The complaints had ceased when the improved diet included items grown or delivered from within the enclosure. She was thankful that she was allowed a few hours each day to work in the enclosure, away from the evil eye of her stepmother.

As Charly hoed some dirt to build up the mounds for the carrots and parsnips, her mind mulled over a new concern. After they had their morning meal and a lengthy scriptural reading, Grace had demanded that all the 'unacceptable' clothes that Charly had, those worn by 'menfolk' as she put it, had to be given to her stepmother. Charly knew they would be destroyed, removed so they could never be worn by her again. Charly snorted in amusement at the thought; most were hand-me-downs from her brothers anyway, but she still did not want to lose them all. By midday, as she finished her time in the garden, she had a plan.

The next morning, as the first light softened the darkness of the night, Charly slipped out of the back of the house with a bundle in her arm. She crossed the paddock down to the billabong, moving quickly in the cold morning air to put the bundle into one of the deep hollows in a big gum tree. Knowing that the feared brown snakes were never active in the cold of the mornings and they lived deep under the sandstone rock slabs, she felt safe to tuck the bundle of clothes high in the hollow. She pushed a couple of thick sticks into the soft pithy wood of the inside of the hollow of the tree, providing a support for the bundle, ensuring that the clothes would not fall onto the ground.

Charly hoped that when her father got back, he would stand up to Grace and set matters as they had been previously. Well, that was what she hoped, but she knew in her heart that there was little chance of that ever happening. When Charly got back to the house, she made up a second bundle of the clothes almost worn-out and took them with her to the morning meal and dropped them on the floor at her stepmother's feet.

'So this is all you have is it, Charlotte? Not hiding anything in your room now, girl?' demanded Grace Hendricks, looking at the small pile of old shirts and trousers on the floor at her feet.

'No, Mrs Grace, that would be wrong, I would not be telling the truth if I be doing that,' replied Charly, shaking her head furiously.

'Not that I do not trust you, but I think I will check,' was the cutting reply. Grace strode to Charly's bedroom. A quick search found an old pair of riding boots, but a plea that she wore them out in the garden allowed them to remain.

'Not that I am happy you have these, they being part of a stockman's attire, but I imagine the Good Lord would be cross with me if I failed to allow stout footwear in the garden.'

Grace left the room in a huff, disappointed not to have found anything she could have used against the younger member of the remaining household.

Later the next day, as Charly was taking a few vegetable scraps to the chickens, a low rumble sounded from the north. She looked up at the cloudless deep blue sky, but her observations of the northern edge of the ranges was blocked by the tall stand of gum trees. Quickly throwing the scraps over the wire fence, Charly ran back past the house, throwing the battered metal bowl close to the back door. She ran as fast as she could into the open front paddock to the edge of the post and rail fence that marked out the house yard. A second low rumble issued from the north; this time Charly could see the distant billowing head of a storm cloud.

As she watched, a flash of lightning could be seen, the dark of the cloud providing enough contrast in the bright sunlight. After a short while, the resulting rumble of thunder rolled across the flood plain. As she watched, the cloud slowly increased in size, moving down along the ridge of the rocky ranges towards the heart of the station. Charly turned at the faint calling of her name; Grace was standing on the front veranda, looking at her, waving for her to return to the house.

Charly let out a slow sigh. Nothing she did was good enough, why was it a problem that she checked what the weather was doing, rain and storms meant many things, some good some bad; it was important to be prepared. Charly snorted in disgust. City people, no ideas, none! She slowly walked back to her impatient stepmother.

'You must stop running like that, it is so unladylike Charlotte,' snapped Grace. 'Even a woman with small bosoms as you so unfortunately appear to have been endowed, you must remember your decorum. You must walk as I have shown you, do not run, nothing, and I mean nothing is that important.'

'But, Mrs Grace, the storm, it was important, it...' Charly stammered, letting the cutting remark about the inadequacies of her body slide.

'Enough, girl, the storm is far to the north, it will not affect us–'

A louder rumble cut Grace's words short, a second following in quick succession, as if to enforce the threat. Grace finally walked out into the sun and looked back towards the northern ranges. A puff of breeze pushed past her face, the first on what had been a totally calm morning.

'Maybe it would be prudent to take the washing off the line, Charlotte, it would be a waste to re-clean them if they get dusty again,' conceded Grace as she turned to retrace her steps into the parlour. The preparation of her plans was important, nothing, neither a storm nor a vexed young woman were going to disturb her work for the Good Lord on this day.

As Charly headed to the outside laundry building to grab a wicker basket to bring the drying bedclothes back into the house, Grace sat at the small fold-down desk to finish her letter. A letter to her former Reverend, a man with a vision of God to bring the teachings of the Good Lord to the local native inhabitants. As much as she had not provided details of her plans to her husband, Grace was pushing ahead to establish a mission by the billabong as she had agreed with Reverend Griswold, in part as repentance for her past activities.

Before continuing writing the words to start the process of having the Reverend come to Hendricks Flats, Grace sat back and considered what she had accomplished already to bring the works of the lord to the area. She had first banned the pagan practices of the local people, especially that of the women, worshipping the false heathen water gods on the far bank of the billabong. Then forcing the men and women to wear respectable clothes, again especially the women by covering up their upper bodies that so inflamed men to lose sight of the Lord's teaching. Finally demanding that all attend a Sunday morning lecture, teaching the Lord's words, bringing their thinking away from the lost past.

She remembered with disgust the first time that Jedidiah took her down to the see the spectacle that occurred each year on the banks of the billabong. Dozens of men and women either sitting or dancing beside large fires, singing and chanting endlessly, tapping hard limbs of wood together, blowing into those horrible hollow wooden pipes. Wearing little but white and red ochre paint on their bodies, every part of their bodies to be seen. Children dancing with them. Being told by Jedidiah that the songs and chanting was for the rains to come, chanting for the animals around their feet and in the trees to thrive. She shuddered at what she remembered, her beating heart only calmed at the thought that it was now stopped and would never occur again while she existed.

Grace started writing again, ensuring she captured the full extent of her success in subjugating the Indigenous people to fulfil their role in the holy teachings, to be the drawers of water and collectors of wood. She failed to add that the local tribe had disappeared, one night all leaving the station, walking off into the wild country to the north, as her husband had simply exclaimed, 'gone walkabout' without explanation on what that meant.

Well, she had a plan for that too. How could these people fulfil their God-given role if they just walked away? No, she would work on that, maybe forcing them to stay, making it a law that they must remain at the mission. That, she thought quickly, needed to be a second letter to a man in the government that the good Reverend knew well, he would understand, he also had a love to do the Lord's work in this wild land.

She concentrated on the words being written on the pages, they had to be ready when the next supply caravan arrived, so the letters could be sent to keep her plan for this land moving forward, fulfilling her position before her Lord.

By the evening the storm had moved on, the rumblings of the thunder disappeared. The house was back on its even pace, Charly preparing the meal for them both, while Grace completed a small embroidered undershirt as a gift to be sent to Reverend Griswold. After the meal was finished, Charly took the scrap bucket and put it outside ready to feed the chickens in the morning. As she carried the bucket to the side of the house away from her bedroom, she thought she smelled smoke but then it was gone, the air clean and sweet from the trees. Putting a large rock on the lid of the bucket to discourage any scavengers, she again thought she smelled a faint waft of smoke before it again disappeared.

She walked to the back door of the house, standing for some moments before opening the door. But the faint whiff of smoke was not in the air, it was clean and sweet. Maybe some of the old local people camping up on the rocky ridge behind the house, Charly thought as she entered the house. Her thoughts were quickly extinguished by a call to her evening readings from the parlour.

The few remaining waking hours of the day remained as per the usual routine. Once the readings were finished tonight it was an hours' hand sewing and a little embroidery. The results were as usual, open to cutting critique and condemnation of her ability and skill with a needle. Charly saw no need to learn to embroider a small cluster of flowers on a blouse; for her, sewing was required for the repair of work clothes and harnesses. The annoyance allowed an early night, a chance for the escape from the evils of the parlour room, a chance for a little peace and rest in her bed.

Charly woke with a start; her bedroom was tinged with acrid smoke, smoke with a strong smell of freshly burning eucalyptus, the frightening smell of bushfire. She reached up and pulled the sash of the double hung timber window shut, closing the small opening she always had to allow a little of the cooling night air to help her sleep. Charly rolled out of bed and walked into the large central passage; a little filtered moonlight was coming through the lead-lite windows above the front door. Knowing she needed to get a good look, she walked to the front of the house and out onto the veranda. She thought she could see a slight reddish glow over the ranges to the north, to be certain she walked out onto the front yard, through the dry grass to where she stood yesterday looking at the storm by the post and rail fence.

From this vantage point she was certain the fire was where the storm ran yesterday, likely started from a lightning strike on a dead tree. While the smoke was noticeable, it only came in occasional waves from a random change of direction of the wind, most of the smoke was blowing away from the house, visible as a black column against an almost black sky.

'What are you doing, girl, letting the smoke into the house through the open door?' came an angry shout front the dark of the verandah.

Charly shook her head in annoyance at her forgetfulness, allowing another opportunity for Grace to punish her a little more. She dawdled back, getting prepared for another lashing of the sharp tongue.

'Well, what can you see?' Grace asked quickly, the voice a mix of sleepy annoyance.

'It's up north, Mrs Grace, where the storm was yesterday. Burning around the back of the range it looks like, but who would know,' replied Charly, a little stunned at the lack of spite, 'the wind is a little away from us, but I think we should prepare.'

'Prepare what, girl?' The spite was back. 'Show some faith, we are here to do the Lord's good work, he made this all happen so his faith could be spread to the wilderness, he will protect us.'

Unsure what to say, not quite believing that the Good Lord directed bushfires, Charly tried to stay silent, but her confusion betrayed her. 'Made all what happen?'

'*Everything*, girl, the Good Lord directed everything, so as to allow myself and the Reverend Griswold to start spreading the gospel to these people,' spat Grace. The moment took control of her mind and her tongue, and she turned to face Charly. 'I expect even ensuring that your foolish mother would disappear, taken by him no doubt to provide this opportunity to me to spread the word. She had clearly failed in the mission she was given.'

Charly stood stock still, her hand over her mouth, stunned by the vitriol and hate that spilled from her stepmother's mouth. Thoughts ran through her mind, but she was unsure what to say. Tears started to run down her face, she sobbed as her heart ached at the cutting words.

'Stop it, girl, know the truth and accept it, everything we do is for a purpose,' stated Grace coldly, not a slight softening of the words. 'Go back to bed, tomorrow the fire will be gone, and we can continue to prepare for His divine direction that he has so generously provided me.'

Grace turned and rapidly strode back to the parlour. Turning up the wick of the lantern, she started reading from the scriptures on the small table by the side of the chair. Charly watched, then continued down the passageway, her soul gutted at the words from her stepmother.

As she lay on her bed, Charly tried to remember the madness of the days around her mother's, and her little sister's, disappearance. When she'd woken on the morning of that fateful day, there'd been not a sound in the house, the usual rattling's in the kitchen silent. Not finding her mother inside the house, she'd run out to the chicken run and then the stables, finding her father snoring on a stretcher bed in the tack room, empty bottles of whiskey on the floor at his side. Waking her brothers, the unfruitful search of the buildings and grounds, her father little help. And finally the local people from the billabong, unusually quiet, helping but almost not, as for some reason not wishing to find her mother, passively obstructing the efforts.

Then the next day, that huge sandstorm that lasted for days, and all chance of tracking her was gone past the short distance into the desert sands, any chance of survival was dashed, everyone knew Charly's mother and sister were gone, buried, lost. From that day, the fear sat deep in Charly's heart; fear that that because she'd told her mother what her father did to her, her mother had disappeared.

Charly continued to lay on her back, staring at the ceiling of the room, her mind in knots, blaming herself for her mother's disappearance, twisting her mind into self-loathing.

Charly found the following day difficult, her mind stuck on the hurtful words of her stepmother, and the self-accusations of her guilt. On a number of occasions through the day, she walked out to the post and rail fence to look at the column of smoke slowly creeping down the back of the ranges behind the house. Towards the evening, the waves of smoke affecting the house was thicker, and the smell of fresh burnt eucalyptus was obvious as the fire had entered one of the dense forested areas.

She tried to discuss her concerns with Grace, but was again rebuffed, the inference of Charly's concerns was a clear lack of faith, something that would need to be worked on in the following weeks. Before Charly went to bed, she checked the progress of the fire. In the dark she could see that the glow was now much closer than yesterday, the air was hotter, and the winds were increasing, thankfully pushing the fire down the back of the ranges.

The shaking and rattling of the timber window sash in its frame pulled Charly from her sleep for the second time in two nights. This time, the first light of the day was evident but almost lost in the thick smoke swirling around outside the glass. The acrid stink of the freshly burnt eucalyptus filled the room, forced through the gaps between the windows and timber weatherboards. As the next gust struck, the noise inside her bedroom from the wind and items hitting the metal roof was deafening.

Clearly the wind had changed direction and was now in full storm force, rattling the house from top to bottom. Charly jumped from her bed, looking for something to wear, first finding her old riding boots next to the bed. She was bent over pulling them on when a small, burning limb hit the glass of the window, driven by a new gust. The ember had caused a crack, not quite smashing an opening in the small glass panes of the window. As she looked outside, Charly was shocked to see hundreds, thousands of burning leaves, bark and small twigs flying about.

The force of the wind increased again, the sound making it difficult to think. Charly screamed as a second, larger burning branch hit the window, shards of glass spraying in all directions. This time the branch smashed into the room, laying on the floor smoking.

She quickly grabbed the limb and threw it back outside through the broken pane in the window, but she could hardly see, as the room filled with smoke and burning, smouldering debris from the fire. Her eyes watered.

Charly rushed into the passageway to find Grace. They had to get out, the only place safe was in the water of the billabong. Charly suddenly heard crazed laughter emanating from the front parlour. Running up the passageway and opening the door she found her stepmother standing naked in the middle of the room, her arms and eyes directed towards the ceiling. Smoke flowed around the room, moved by the gusts blowing down the passageway from Charly's bedroom. Charly rapidly crossed the floor and grabbed Grace's lifted arm to get her attention.

'Come on, Grace, we have to get out. The house is on fire, we need to get to the billabong, it's our only hope.'

Grace dropped her head, staring into Charly's face. Grace's eyes were crazed, a strange look of almost pure ecstasy on her face.

'No, child, we stay. The glorious moment has come,' Grace shouted, grabbing hold of Charly, pulling her to her chest. 'We will be purified, the fires will refine us, the dross will be cleansed. You will join me in purity of God's holy spirit.'

Charly had heard enough to know that Grace was insane, the madness of her life in full evidence. All Charly wanted was to get out, but now she was held as a prisoner, to stay and die with this mad woman. Another stronger blast of wind shook the house, the sound of more windows smashing, and the smell of burning, filled the room. Charly could hardly breathe; the smoke was gagging her. Grace shouted more unintelligible words to the ceiling, for a moment lifting the arm holding Charly.

This was enough. Charly swung her arm and struck out at Grace. Though the smoke blinded her, there was a satisfying impact on something not too soft, not too hard. The grip from Grace's arm that held her lessened. It was the release she needed.

Charly flung herself towards the parlour door to escape but tripped on the rug, falling to the floor. Down here there was a small layer of air free of smoke. Taking a deep breath of the little air that was left she crawled to where the door was open. A solid thud sounded on the floor behind her, she did not look around, caring little for the madness she was trying to escape.

The front door was only a few paces from the parlour, but difficult to find. Another strong gust moved a little smoke around in the passageway, enough for Charly to see the front door and handle, allowing her to open it. As she looked out, there was nothing but flames, small patches of fire started in the grass by the flying embers. She knew where the billabong was, roughly to her left, not that she could see, but there was no option but to run for its safety.

She ran, her feet protected by her old boots but only wearing the light cotton nightdress, and no other protection from the flames and embers.

A timber post and rail fence was located about one hundred yards from the house, and Charly feared she would hit it running a full pace. She tried to keep count of her steps but the insanity of the fire, smoke and redness around her was too much. Charly had just enough time to see the fence before she ran into it, bracing a little. But it the impact of the post still knocked her breath from her lungs, knocking her to the ground.

Charly lay in the grass, gasping to get a little air back in her lungs. In the base of the clumps of grass, there was sweet air, just enough to let her recover. Suddenly there was a stinging pain up her left leg, she rolled on her side. Her night dress had caught fire. She slapped it out with her hands, the skin between her fingers blistering, but the hard work had provided tough skin on her palms, and the pain was bearable.

Charly crawled under the lowest timber rail, taking a final deep breath in the grass for her next run, knowing she had only covered less than quarter the distance. As she stood, the grass in front of her caught alight. She danced quickly to the side, but it was all aflame, there was no option but to run through it.

The skin of her lower legs above the leather of her boots screamed as the flames scorched the soft skin, but she did not stop. Her eyes watered from the acrid smoke, blurring her vision, making seeing were she was running nearly impossible. He nightdress caught alight again, forcing her to slap it out as she ran. Her hair caught the odd ember, singeing small areas down to the scalp. But she did not stop till she was out of breath. Finding some longer unburnt grass, she again buried her face as deep as it would go, drawing a few breaths before again running as fast as she could through grass, either on fire or nearly so, she did not stop.

Charly felt heat run slowly up her back, singeing the soft skin between her shoulders, the shoulder length black hair on the back of her head was getting hotter as the burning nightdress flared as she ran. Suddenly the ground dropped away, the smoke cleared slightly allowing her to just see the surface of the water. She ran past a large gum tree, jumping from sandstone outcrop to sandstone outcrop. She hoped that any slithery creature had well and truly left so she did not tread on a snake. Then just as the hair on her head finally caught alight, flaring in a ball of flame, Charly dived into the cooling water of the billabong, as deep and as far as she could go.

She surfaced in waist deep water, finding that the smoke sat a little above the water surface, allowing a good lungful of air with only a small amount of acrid smoke. As she pushed herself away from the bank, as the first clumps of grass started to burn. Then a massive thunderclap split the air above her, and what started as a single drop of water, instantly became a drenching downpour. The storm front that pushed the bushfire over the house and yards with the powerful winds, delivered the rain it carried, soaking the ground, killing the grass fire. The wind again changed direction, pushing the smoke away from the billabong, allowing Charly to breathe without choking on smoke.

For a long time, Charly did not move in the water, her mind numb from the experience, from the pain from the back of her head every time she lifted it above the water. The blast of rain had slowly dropped to a soft drizzle. After nearly an hour, the rain slowed and then finally stopped, leaving a partly cloudy sky above the silent billabong.

Small patches of grass still smouldered, but the smoke slowly died, leaving small areas of burnt grass between the sandstone rock outcrops. The big gumtrees on the bank of the billabong were unmoved, a burnt leaf here or there but not much else, as if they had gone through this type of event for a number of times in the last one, maybe two hundred years they had existed on the bank of the billabong.

Finally, Charly knew she had to do something. She could not just stay in the water, but first she started to check her body. The nightdress came away in her hands, burnt in a number of areas, the back almost missing. She looked at her hands, there were blisters on her wrists and between her fingers, but the skin had not burned away. Running her hand down her legs she found more blisters on the outside of her left leg, from the calf to her lower thigh. She guessed that the same blisters ran up her back.

Fearing what she knew she could already feel, Charly lifted one foot after the other, checking both. Her boots were badly damaged, burnt, but they had saved her feet. But her legs above ankles had copped the worst of the flames leaving blisters that were torn open by the tough stems of the grass and burning tree limbs she had brushed through. Looking at the top of the bank of the billabong, she knew there was no point in worrying what was or was not damaged. It was best for her to keep her hands and legs cool. She would stay in the billabong for now. As shock set into her mind her thinking grew unsure, her grasp on who she was or where she was drifting like the lingering smoke over the billabong's surface.

Charly woke to the sounds of the parrots and galahs that made their home on the edges of the billabong. The sun was just moving through the tops of the trees, the first rays of sun falling on the sandstone slab of rock she had been sleeping on, she had no memories, her mind was blank. She sat up, confused why she had no clothes on, other than her damaged boots. As the sun got on her burnt ankles and lower legs, the pain started, again, a brief memory, fire, pain. She slipped her legs into the water, feeling the quick relief, quickly sliding her whole body into the calm waters, soothing the burns all over her body. Her mind went blank again, only wanting to stop the pain, the burning endless pain.

The days rolled by, until the need for food cut through the fog of Charly's brain. She had no idea the length of time she had been in the billabong, but it was not just the need to eat something that drove her. As she sat up from where she had been asleep on the sandstone slab, a sharp memory cut through her thinking, her old clothes were in a hollow gumtree, close to where she sat. She slowly stood, a little wobbly with the wounds on her ankles slowly healing, but the blisters on her hands, head, legs and back were improving. She slowly walked along the sandstone, stepping carefully to avoid the hard ends of the grass on her legs as she looked in the first hollow tree, but nothing.

Something in her mind was warning her of what might be in the grass, danger, not that she could remember. Suddenly, as she took another step, the head of a large brown snake lifted itself off the next sandstone slab she was about to step on to as she moved to the next tree. The king brown lifted itself a good twelve inches off the rock, its tongue flicking in and out, testing the air. Charly's mind clicked; the thing in front of her was deadly. She stood still, trying at best to remain calm.

After a few moments, the king brown could not sense any threat from the thing that stood still in front of him, only a short strike away. Slowly he dropped his head, knowing that the thing only wanted to move past. She slowly slid up the bank to his hollow under a large sandstone slab.

Charly watched the snake move away, her breathing slowing as she took the next step onto the sandstone, heading for the biggest of the gums.

The grass was lightly burnt around the old tree, but the bark was untouched. Charly looked inside; it was big enough to let a person sleep inside the hollow. As she looked up, a bundle of material, the red plaid shirt and old calico trousers sat jammed into the top of the hollow where she had left them. After carefully removing the bundle, Charly pulled on the trousers and plaid shirt, confidence flowing through her. Being left with no clothes had been disconcerting. Now she was protected from the sharp sun and the hard-burnt ends of the grasses.

She walked over the edge of the bank of the billabong, looking to where her home was, the buildings of her youth, the structures lost deep in her memories. As she looked around to help her re-establish the gaps she felt, very little helped. As she looked at the rise above the floodplain, she only saw a slightly burnt windmill, and piles of burnt timber, twisted metal sheeting and other fire damaged debris. She could remember none of this as she walked closer. But driving her was a need to eat.

As she walked around what was her former home, a deep panic set into her mind, she could not find anything that might help her survive. There was nothing, simply nothing. Charly started screaming, turning, she ran, ran back to the one place she felt safe, the billabong and the old gum tree with its deep hollow. But before she arrived where the post and rail fence once stood, a primeval need drove deep into her, the desire to leave being overwhelmed by the greater need to get food.

Charly looked back at the destruction, her mind blank to where she could find the things to satisfy this need. A deep lying thought flicked past her conscious; a place where some things might have been protected from the flames. She slowly walked back, blood now weeping from the wounds on her thighs and lower legs.

Walking past the ruins of the house, the odd tendril of smoke still seeping out from under the twisted metal sheeting of what was once a new roof, Charly set her sights on the remains of the chain-lock fence of the vegetable garden. Passing the stables, with the horrors of the tack room now no more than a blackened and empty abyss in her brain, she was happy that her horse was not inside when the fire tore through the buildings, or any other of the creatures she so loved.

The chicken shed now emanated an evil stench, the extension of the chain-lock wire that enclosed the vegetables was only slightly damaged. Two of the posts had burnt through at ground level and had fallen as far as the wire would let it, hanging with charred ends. The rest of the posts, were scorched but standing, providing a little protection to the garden. But the security of the fence was irrelevant, anything that had been green and above the ground was now either brown or burnt.

Charly pushed the gate open, walking slowly to where the carrots and parsnip had been. She found the garden fork still standing upright where Jessie had dug the last of the potatoes before he left, the timber handle slightly burnt but sound enough for her needs. Pushing the fork into the charred soil next to the burnt tops of the carrots provided what she was desperately in need of, food, a chance to survive, for the next week or so anyway.

Chapter 3

Abdullah Rahman Khan slowed the pace of his steps until he stopped, and turned to look back at his precious four-legged children, all eight of them, and then at his beloved wife. He chuckled, knowing at times in almost frustration, that his wife called the eight camels his children. He almost loved them as much as his small brood living safely at their well-appointed home at the top of the Adelaide hills. All eight of his children had been given a name, he loved them all enough to bestow titles and names as to their character and antics. Well the mullah may not agree, and yes, he may be exceeding the strict rules of his beliefs, but he loved them as he loved the ancient stories, and so they were all named after the various characters in the old teachings of the Jews.

He cast his eyes to the clear blue skies of the heavens over his head, the sun during the day as was above him now, and the stars in the sky that helped him find his way, a night sky that took him to his destinations, and at the end of each journey, back to his home. He felt at peace; this was his world, with the people and creatures he loved.

Abdullah was dressed as his countrymen had been for as long as he could remember, the kameez, the long overshirt that almost reached his knees and underneath, a shalwar, the baggy trousers closed tight at the ankles. A wide belt that pulled the kameez tight, a belt that carried a revolving pistol in a closed holster and a knife, wonderfully engraved, a sign of his tribe. While normally he wore the rolled up woollen pakul on his head, today it was a turban of dark green wound silk, a few tassels at the end for flair.

Abdullah Rahman Khan felt at home in this land as much as his home country of Afghanistan. He was a man of the deserts and sands, this was his world, no matter the country.

The eight 'children' he overlooked with so much pleasure were his camels, a caravan of eight animals as suited as he was to this land and its dry and sandy conditions. All eight, carried supplies to distant small farms, cattle and sheep stations and the numerous telegraph outstations. His was the very process of providing support for the people who lived in these places, providing the stores to keep the people alive, in touch with the world; his eight children were their saviours.

'What ya be stopping for, Abdul? Never get to the floodplains at this rate.'

He smiled at the insistence of his beloved wife to push on. She was up before him when it was still dark and ready to leave shortly after, waiting impatiently while he still finished is prayers. Mary rarely came with him on his travels but this time she's insisted, knowing that he was to pass by Hendricks Flats, the cattle station on the furthest floodplains, the most outlying station of all they visited. The last cattle station by the three billabongs of an unnamed river.

Abdul waited till his wife of many happy and fruitful years, walk up to him past their beloved camels. Dressed almost as he was, the loose and cool clothes of the desert, only with a bright headscarf tied as a headband to manage her magnificent black wavy hair. She checked each of the heavily laden camels carefully with a skilful eye for lameness as she approached. She was a child of the ancient land, her people were of the three billabongs, a place she had not been back since her late childhood. She had a deep connection with this land and had an almost magical connection with any animal that lived there.

A second man walked to the last camel in the caravan, another of his people. As he waited, he stayed at the back of the line of camels, checking and then refastening one of the leather panniers on one the side of one of the camels. He checked all the loads and they commenced their journey.

'Tonight we will camp on this side of the low range and then by midday we will be at the station, my beloved,' Abdul stated. 'And why the sudden urgency?'

Mary looked at the sandstone low rocky range in the distance, a dip where a fault provided the pathway through to the other side where their destination lay. 'Not sure, Abdul. It is a feeling I started to get yesterday, and it is getting stronger as we get closer,' Mary replied, still staring at the range. 'Something is calling me, maybe it is the waterway and its billabongs – it is special to us women of this land.'

Abdullah smiled. He remembered parts of the strange beliefs of the people his wife belonged to, willing to accept that this was a different land from the plains and mountains of Afghanistan from where he was born. The people of his homeland too believed things and followed practices that his wife also thought were unusual, and at times little difficult to accept.

'Can you smell burnt ground?' Abdullah asked his wife. She nodded, and confirmed that she had picked up the smell in the air an hour or so before. 'The grass for the camels may be limited for their grazing tonight,' he said.

'Well, my dear man, if we stand here any longer, it will be two-foot-high and in seed by the time we arrive at the ridge...' Her remaining words were lost to him as she turned and walked back down the length of the camel train again checking their condition, a process that ensured that they always had fit animals. Abdullah laughed as he picked up the lead rope from the first camel. He enjoyed this form of communication; she may be his wife, but she was important to his business as any of the other Afghan men he employed on other supply routes they operated.

The walking pace increased to what he well remembered as a foot soldier in the Afghan army marching up to the Khyber Pass and other outposts in the mountains of the land of his birth, leading supply animals of similar grandeur. The camels' pace was steady and would cover the ground quicker than imagined without tiring man or loaded beast. The camels found this a perfect pace, allowing them to manage the great loads they carried on their backs without excessive energy use, critically useful in transporting supplies in these almost barren, sandy conditions for days and weeks without water.

Hendricks Flats was the last of a run of cattle and sheep stations that they brought supplies to in this district. They did this route maybe three or four times per year, the distance from the next station was many miles over sandy country with little vegetation. The reason for this station's existence was the loop in the river caused by the rock ranges that flooded allowing deep grass and three linked billabongs, permanent water both above and below the ground, providing life for the people that lived in this area for hundreds, or even thousands of years. But away from where the river left the water, the land surrounding these extensive river flood plains was barren, stony, or with red sandy desert.

Their imminent arrival at Hendricks Flats would allow for a few days of recovery, food and water before they headed to their next destination. The arrival and subsequent rest were keenly sought after by human and animal as they walked towards the sandstone range.

By late morning the next day, as Abdullah walked out of the gorge between the high walls of sandstone, a gorge that less than a month before, a herd of cattle had left the property for the sale yards in a distant town, his wife pulled the shawl from her head. As the land opened before him, the damage caused by the fire was visible in all directions. It was similar to the other side of the ridge, clearly the fire had been pushed by a strong, hot northerly wind down both sides, jumping from forest to grasslands, back to forest, burning but not completely devastating the environment.

Abdullah turned watched his wife with interest as she walked through the gorge with a shawl pulled tightly around her head, keeping her face partially covered. She looked down at the ground for the entire passage through the gorge.

Mary could see the lift of his eyes in question as she slowly walked her camel towards him.

'This is the land of my mother's people, the gorge is for men's business, I know of things, but I cannot look, a woman cannot not see them,' she answered quietly in respect. 'I tread with care, Abdul, I wish not to disturb the spirits of my people.'

She walked on quietly towards the burnt ground, then looked back to the mouth of the gorge. Abdul lifted the halter of the lead camel and followed. Her words did not sit well with him, but he knew even with her Christian teachings, her soul was still strongly directed by her people's ancient culture, this he had to accept. He looked to the side, at the burnt land and wondered at what had happened, and what may have survived.

Only as they carefully travelled closer to where the station homestead once stood, could the extent of the devastation be truly understood. In the distance, remained what had once been the heart of Hendricks Flats. There were no replies to the shouted greetings by the two men. They could not hear the usual calls from the local birdlife, there was nothing but silence, aside from the whistle of the gentle breeze.

Not wishing to disturb the camels with what they might find in the remains of the devastated property, Abdullah decided to stop a good few hundred yards short of the burnt buildings. The burnt grass had started to regrow, so the camels were unpacked and hobbled in a slight hollow where the grass was greenest. The three considered their actions, before deciding that the two men would check what remained of the buildings.

Mary had immediately refused, she felt uncomfortable by the intrusion of the buildings, the coming of these people on to her cultural homeland had changed many things. For Mary, the reason for being here was not in the land that held the remains of the buildings, rather the three billabongs, the river and all that lived there. She was keen that her presence was not known to the owners of the property, she was here for her own deep spiritual needs and did not wish to be disturbed by anyone not of her people until she had finished her reason for coming to this place.

'You go, Abdul. Take Wazir, check the buildings,' directed Mary. 'I will walk over to the billabongs.'

As Mary watched the two men walk towards the burnt buildings, she reached into one of the saddlebags and removed two small pieces of wood. Wood taken from the trees of the billabong by her mothers' mother. They had been shaped to remove any bark or other imperfections, rubbed on the sandstone of the valley till they were smooth, the ends rounded, the wood polished by the leathery skin and sweat of her ancestor's hands. Carrying one in each hand, she walked through the fire scorched trees on the higher side of the burnt buildings, softly singing the songs her mother, grandmother and aunties had taught her, the songs of the old people, songs of the billabong.

After some twenty minutes or so, time meaningless to Mary as she let the energy of the location soak into her soul, she arrived at the edge of the bank leading down to the water at a shallow location close to the end of the billabong. She sung with a stronger voice, tapping the two sticks to a set beat, slowly stepping over the new green tussocks of grass between the sandstone slabs with deliberate high steps. As she stopped at the water's edge, she bent forward, scooping a handful of water up to taste its sweetness before crossing to the other side of the billabong. She then continued to walk a short distance along the edge of the water to the location she remembered as a young girl, a place where her place in the tribe was confirmed, when she became a person of the land.

Mary closed her eyes. She had been away from this place for some twenty years; it was good to be back. Lifting her eyes to the tops of the trees that hung over her head, she tracked the branches back to the trunk, then down the fat base of the truck to the massive buttresses and roots that pushed up to hold the tree in place.

Just below was the circle of stones that her people used as a fire pit. The soft sand had become covered in grass, surprising Mary, knowing that it would customarily be worn away. Then she remembered that the word from the family was that the new boss woman had forced her people to stop the celebrations of the water dragon, the lizard that lived on the massive old trees around her. She had stopped their cultural needs, forcing them to leave and not come back.

Mary turned and looked down at the water in the billabong, bending to take another scoop of fresh water. The sweetness was so refreshing after the last few weeks of drinking the slightly stale water from the canvas bags. She started to sing again, this time a different song, asking for permission to take the water, giving thanks for the water they would take when the camels came to drink.

As she looked further down the billabong at the calmness of the place, a flash of colour caught her eye on the far bank. A colour that did not fit where it was located in the hollow of an old river gum.

Mary blinked and looked carefully again until she was sure. Something human was in the tree hollow. She slipped the two singing sticks into the pocket of her baggy trousers and started to walk around. Knowing the hazard of one of the local creatures from her youth, a creature that likely had little interest in the return of a native human of the area, she watched with great care the grass and sandstone slabs for the usual resident King brown snakes.

It would be much easier to walk above the bank in the shorter grass that was starting to grow back. After a little less than ten minutes, Mary slowly stepped down to the gum tree where she had seen the unusual item. As Mary walked around the edge of the massive old river gum, she saw what looked like a bundle of clothes, first a faded red plaid shirt, then some filthy calico trousers and some worn old boots.

Looking closer at the clothes, Mary took a sharp breath is surprise as she became aware that they were on a person, laying with their back to the opening of the hollow, curled tight into a foetal position. The clothes were incredibly dirty, stained with soot and the person's black hair was full of leaves, twigs and dirt. The body was skinny, where she could make out the sharpness of the hips and shoulders.

She called out but there was no reaction, first in English, then in her own tongue. The only response was silence.

Was this one of the old men of the tribe, wearing cast-off clothes? What if he'd returned to the area to curl up in the hollow, enjoying the last of his days by the billabong, before ending his days in peace? She started to draw away but a strange feeling held her, a feeling similar to the previous day.

Mary squatted closer to the body, forcing herself to go against the learnings of her youth in disturbing the dead. But she had to find out if the old man was dead or not. Mary reached for his neck, using the tips of her fingers to feel for his heartbeat. She slowly pulled the black hair way from the dirty collar of the plaid shirt, giving access she needed. She stopped completely still, not wishing to breathe, not believing what she could see.

The skin was filthy, smudged with dirt and soot, there were scabs and a few fresh scars, but the skin just below the hair was white, not like her darker brown skin. This person was white. Not of her people, a white man, not very big and very skinny. She put her fingers on his neck and felt what she thought was a faint murmur of a heartbeat. Trying a second time she was not sure, if it had been there, it was little more than a flutter. Mary slowly pulled on the man's shoulder to roll him over on his back, so she could be able to feel for his breath. The lack of any muscle or meat on his bones was obvious through the cloth.

As the man rolled back towards her, his black wavy hair fell over his face, the dirt and leaves falling to the ground. Mary reached out and brushed the hair back. Her heart stopped a second time as she saw the face.

The eyes were closed, but it was the face of a child. Well, an older child, and it looked like a girl but with all the dirt and soot she was not sure. At that moment the eyes flickered, but did not open, a soft moan emanating from the child's cracked and parched lips. Mary quickly looked at other parts of the child's body that were able to be quickly checked for injuries.

Lifting a trouser leg, she saw poorly healed burns on the lower legs, just above the boots. The burns still weeped between splits in the angry red skin and dirty scabs. She pulled the red plaid shirt up a little, finding the scabs of the burns on her back and waist.

This child had survived the fire. It raised so many questions without answers. Where were the parents, or was she the only one who survived? She thought briefly that perhaps others had survived, but having seen the buildings she had a terrible premonition. Mary slowly pulled the child from within the tree hollow, taking care not to cause any greater pain of further injury to the wounds. Once the child was out, Mary was quick to confirm that the child was a woman, a young one who had lived through what looked like hell but was now close to death.

'Was it you calling me, young lady?' asked Mary of the person before her as much to herself, thinking about the urgings she had for the last few days. 'Well, someone was. I could feel it, maybe there is something in you I need to get to know.'

Mary put her arms under the young woman and gently lifted her, surprised at the lack of weight. It was clear this young one was starving to death, a lack of food where her own people had thrived for generations. As she took a step forward with the girl in her arms, she heard the rustle in an unburnt area of grass.

'You might be sacred to my totem, old fella brown snake, but if you get in my way, I will forget everything and you will roast over my fire, so clear off.'

The brown snake slid quickly away, almost in respect for Mary, though the angry stamp of her feet on the ground was more likely the reason.

Mary carried the semiconscious young woman up the bank and towards where the camels were hobbled. Hopefully the two men had returned. Her fears now increased; the sooner this girl received help, the higher chance she would live to tell the tale of what happened.

She could see Abdullah and Wazir pulling some metal sheeting from the middle of what was once the main house, clearly interested in uncovering what was underneath the ashes and burnt timbers. As she got within shouting distances Mary called for assistance. Abdullah turned and quickly said something to his companion before walking back. He broke into a run when he saw what Mary was carrying in her arms.

'Abdul, please take her to where we will make camp – she is poorly,' said Mary, breathlessly handing her armful over. 'She has many burns, and some are becoming foul. I can get Wazir to help you.'

'No, leave him,' replied Abdul in a serious voice. 'We have found a body in the house. I have asked him to bury it so the wild dogs can not disturb it.'

'Oh. A man or woman?'

'Of that we cannot be certain, my beloved wife. The body be badly burnt and showing decay,' Abdul answered, not wishing to speak about what they found, or the gruesome memories the corpse had triggered from the frontier war in his homeland. 'We will talk later, but let the dead be done. If we can save this one it will bring blessing from Allah.'

Abdullah carried his light load down to where the camels were resting after eating their fill of the lush young grass. He laid the filthy, wasted body on the grass as Mary caught up, brushing her hair from her face. Abdullah checked the wounds. The eyes of the young woman flickered open again, this time looking up at Mary's face, then closing again.

'Yes, burns as you say, and corruption is settling in her legs,' grumbled Abdullah. He jumped up to dig in the leather pannier where he kept the important supplies. 'We need to clean them and remove the corruption.' He stopped for a moment, remembering the beliefs and feelings that his wife had around the billabong and what could occur there. 'If we will save her my beloved, we need to camp down near the water under some shade,' he stated forcefully. 'Will this affect you?'

'No, I agree. But first we need to provide her food, she is dying from the lack,' replied Mary equally as forcefully. 'Bring Sheeba, we need to get a little milk for the little one to drink.'

Abdullah walked over to one of his younger female camels and brought her closer. Mary dug out a small leather pail and squeezed out a few cupful's of milk to sit in the bottom of the container.

'So much will make her sick, it is too rich.'

'No, a little now mixed with water and little later and then a little again,' she chuckled at him. 'I do not want to milk every hour, it will stay good for a little while.'

Mary mixed the creamy milk with a little water and tipped a soft clean cloth into the liquid. She dribbled a small amount into the young woman's mouth. Her eyes fluttered open again, this time staying open while she slowly sucked in the rich liquid. After a less than cupful, Mary stopped, the young woman's eyes questioning.

'Not too much first time or it will all come straight back up. Now you just lay here while we prepare the camels and then we will move you over to some shade, okay?'

Mary quickly walked over to help Abdullah load each of the camels, moving them closer to where the carry frame and leather panniers sat on the ground. The carry frame was lifted on the camel's back and fastened like a saddle, then the panniers and other bundles lifted on and fixed to the frame. After a short while, Wazir returned to help, confiding that he could not find as much as he wanted but most of the body was now buried deep in the soil a small distance from what remained of the house.

As they started on their fourth camel, Sheeba, the young female that provided the milk lowered her head and nuzzled her nose against the young woman lying in the grass. Abdullah started to walk over, but Mary put her hand on his arm.

'Wait. This one has a powerful spirit, Sheeba knows something,' muttered Mary quietly. 'She will not bite, I assure you.'

While they watched, an arm was lifted, and the girl's hand gently rubbed Sheeba's muzzle. A deep, soft rumble rolled from Sheeba, a sound of contentment. Abdullah look at his wife in surprise; it usually took long months for a camel to accept a human, and they were usually so contrary it was often much longer. Mary smiled, a look that he could not quite read on her face.

'There is something about this girl, something precious,' murmured Mary, returning to tighten one of the carry straps on the lead camel. 'Now, how do we move the girl? You and I cannot carry her to the top of the northern billabong.'

'I have made a litter cradle on big Sampson, like we did in the wars, come and see,' replied Abdullah, a broad grin on his face, proud of his ingenuity.

Mary followed her man to one of the older male camels where Wazir was finishing the litter that would carry the young woman. It sat between two of the soft packs tied above the leather panniers. The gap between held a timber frame and a canvas trap that would act as a bed. Once all the other camels were loaded, Abdullah carried the young woman over and carefully placed her in the hollow of the litter. Two leather straps fixed over the timber frames stopped her falling out.

They commenced the short journey of nearly two miles to the northern end of the three billabongs, none wishing to be too close to the devastation of the bushfire and the horrors they had found. The devastation brought disturbance to both the people and animals. The effects of the fire made the surrounding land distressing, but the northern billabong was a sufficient distance to not be constantly reminded of the horrors of the fire.

They would camp for a most of a week in the dry riverbed, shaded by the old river gums that cast their branches widely over the dry river bed, providing shade and cool escape from the heat. The time would allow the camels to recover from the travel between the previous stations and prepare for the next push of their journey, this time through a dry and long section of desert. Their next destination was on the other side, the new telegraph line linking the north to the south of the land.

They carried supplies for a small number of the telegraph stations, isolated places where people lived, fully dependent on the good they carried on their camels. But this time, camped in recovery, would also provide a time to discuss what to do with the young woman they had found and try and help her recover from her wounds. They hoped that she would speak, but so far she had said nothing. But it was only the first day and she was gravely ill.

By late afternoon a campsite had been prepared with a round of rocks to contain the campfire, with the steel frames installed above the flames to hold the kettle and cooking pots. Swags were laid out for the three, with a fourth bed made for their newest companion from a folded canvas sheet and a couple of spare blankets. The packs and leather paniers had been removed from the camels, piled neatly in order to allow for smooth reloading when they were ready to leave. The camels had been set to graze after being watered, the hobbles on their front legs limiting the distance they could wander. The young woman was laid down in her bed of folded canvas and blankets, her eyes opening and closing as she slipped back to a deep sleep.

Mary saw that one of the large trees near the top of the riverbank had a native beehive, the small bees entering and leaving a hollow where an old dry limb had fallen off. She called Abdullah and pointed at the tree, knowing that he was addicted to the honey, a special treat when they travelled. He clapped his hands at the information, a broad smile creased his face in anticipation. Once the fire was burnt down little, Mary scraped a shovelful of coals on a large section of damp bark, which she slowly carried to the tree with the hive.

Abdul had found a large fallen branch he could use as a ladder. Leaning it on the trunk of the large eucalyptus gumtree, he then collected a large number of fresh green gum leaves, placing them carefully on the blackened coals on the bark. Mary quickly climbed the leaning branch to where the hive was, some ten feet above the ground in a large hole in the side of the tree trunk.

Abdullah lift up the coals, now starting to produce thick smoke with a rich eucalyptus fragrance as the green leaves smouldered. Mary held the bark to the bottom of the opening; the thick bark insulated her hands. She slowly blew smoke inside the opening in the tree. Abdul impatiently danced from foot to foot at the base of the tree. Honey was one of the great pleasures to his tastebuds, soundlessly clapping his hands with a little impatience.

After a few minutes of blowing smoke into the hole, Mary waved the bark around covering the immediate area in sweet smelling smoke. Quickly handing the bark down to Wazir who was now standing next to Abdul, she then reached inside to hollow in the tree, feeling the end of an enormous comb hanging from the top of the hollow in the tree. Breaking a small section off, she withdrew her hand, taking a small bite of the edge, then handing it down to her man.

The flavour exploded in her mouth, and with a smile on her face she reached in and broke off a second large piece, handing it down to Abdul again. This one he placed on a second piece of clean bark. Mary was given the smoking coals again, which she used to blow more smoke into the opening, sedating the bees a second time. She repeated the process two more times, taking only what they required, leaving the vast majority of the comb to its owners.

Mary climbed down and gave wordless thanks to the spirits of the billabong, to bounty of the honey and comb again providing the importance of this location to the culture of her people, the home of the water dragon peoples. Abdul saw the look in her eyes, knowing that while he did not understand her beliefs, her connections to this land were part of her soul and life.

They carried the honey back to the camp, Abdul and Wazir chatting excitedly in their own language, dreaming of the sweet snacks to be eaten, while Mary planned to use it to repair a burnt and broken person. She put the comb in a large metal pot, allowing the honey to slowly drain from the wax. The wax used to be used later treating the leather straps and saddles and waterproofing their boots.

Chapter 4

After organising the camp for their extended stay, Abdullah pulled his well-worn and much-loved old long-barrelled Snider-Enfield carbine from his pack and with Wazir headed onto the flood plain to bag one of the many kangaroos feeding on the grass. While fresh beef would have been preferred, and usually bought from the station owner where they stayed, the lack of a person removed that option. They would not steal, so native wildlife it would be, an acceptable second option.

As the bushfire had not burnt this far across the flood plain, the two men had only a short distance to walk to find an area where a spot fire had started but then extinguished by the following rainstorm. The fresh grass after the fire had attracted a number of these native hopping animals, hopefully allowing a quick kill.

While the men were away, Mary had taken the opportunity to strip the filthy clothes from the young woman. The young woman woke and opened her eyes after a gentle shake of her shoulder. Her eyes were sharper and looked like they were focusing on Mary as she squatted in front of her.

'I want to clean you a little, and wash your clothes too,' Mary calmly stated, 'Now you look to be a little more awake than before, what is your name? Mine is Mary.'

The young woman did not immediately answer, as if her brain was slowly readjusting to having people around her she did not know speaking to her, helping her.

'You can call me Charly,' was the slow answer. then no more, just one name.

'Just Charly? Nothing else, no other name?' asked Mary, surprised at the limited information.

'Just Charly, I don't want no other name, I don't like the other name,' Charly retorted.

'That's okay, Charly will do fine,' said Mary to soften the moment. 'And the two men with me, one is my husband, Abdul, and the other is his cousin, Wazir. Now they will be gone for a while so if you agree, I can help you get rid of all the dirt and soot.'

Charly nodded slowly, sitting up with some difficulty, before unbuttoning her shirt and britches to allow them to be washed. Mary was shocked at the condition of her skin, especially the scabs on her ankles, thighs and middle of her back and neck.

With a pail full of fresh water and a soft cotton cloth, Mary used a soft cloth to sponge all of the dirt from her face, then her back and legs, taking great care in not damaging any scabs or fresh pink skin. She let Charly clean her more private parts before she helped her to lay down and covered her with a blanket.

As Mary was washing the shirt and britches, a heavy crack of a carbine in the distance cut through the peace of the riverbed. Charly sat up quickly, a look of concern on her face that left Mary wondering why.

'It is okay, Charly. That would be Abdul trying to prove once more that he was a fine shot when he wore the uniform in his homeland,' chuckled Mary waiting for a second or third shot. 'A good man with camel he certainly is, maybe not so good with his old worn-out old gun.'

True to her word, by the time she had hung up the wet clothes to dry, two more shots had followed the first. Then nothing, indicating that there would be two hind quarters being carried back to camp before darkness covered the land.

Once the laundering of the clothes was done, Mary pulled a kameez and a shalwar from one of her bags and carried them over to where Charly was laying under the blanket. She kneeled beside Charly as a pair of questioning eyes followed her as Mary placed the clothes, similar to what she was wearing on to the top of the blanket.

'Look, they're not what you are used to, but the long overshirt and baggy trousers are really comfortable. I do not have anything else till your clothes dry, I know they will be a bit big, but with the belt you will be fine.'

A hand slid out from under the blanket, grabbed the clothes and pulled them under. A small smile spread on Charly's face.

'I have a small amount of ointment for your burns,' Mary said. 'I will apply this shortly. And tomorrow, I will look for some plants to make a poultice to put on your legs above your ankles. I know the Abdul wants to remove the corruption, but I think I remember something my mother would make, it will work, if you let me.'

Charly said nothing but nodded as she wormed her way into the baggy trousers under the blanket, then pulled the long shirt over her head. As she finished, she popped her head above the blanket, a broad smile on her face as she pulled herself into a sitting position for the first time under her own power.

'Okay by me, Mrs Mary,' Charly said. She paused. 'Say, you got more of the milk? It was really yummy.'

Mary laughed and gave Charly the cup with the remaining milk mixed with water and a little honey, then prepared a damper to put on the fire so they had fresh bread with the evening meal. Placing the dough aside to rest, she peeled a few potatoes, onions and carrots to make a stew with the kangaroo meat. Charly settled back and watched as Mary prepared the food with calm efficiency. For the first time in months she felt secure. While she did not know who these people were, she could sense they were not a threat to her.

Less than thirty minutes later, Abdul and Wazir arrived back a camp with two well butchered hind quarters of a small kangaroo. Abdul was smiling, as he always did when he proved his ability with is old rifle. As he put the carbine in the worn leather scabbard and pulled the cover over the stock and ammunition poach next to his saddlebags, he directed a smug look to his dear wife.

Mary ignored him initially, knowing the look on his face. 'So, Abdul, my dear husband, you once more have scared more than you killed,' she muttered with dubious respect for his efforts. 'Soon you will run out of ammunition for that old gun, and then what will you do.'

'Ah, my beloved, then I will hang the faithful rifle I pillaged from the English and purchase you a new one, then we will see who scares more of your land's funny hopping creatures.'

Mary and Abdullah both burst out laughing at the longstanding joke.

Working together, the pair quickly prepared the meat into small chunks that were dropped into the big pot over the fire, a little salt, some more water and the meat and vegetable slowly simmered. Abdullah retrieved a small sack of spices from his pack, the flavours he and his cousin knew so well, sprinkling a small amount into the stew.

'Calm your hand, Abdul, think of myself and the young one. I think she will have a little too,' said Mary to slow down the usual enthusiasm by Abdullah in making spicy flavoured food from his homeland's influence. 'Oh, she is called Charly, not to be confused with Charlie, as in a fella's name either.'

Abdullah looked at Mary in surprise. 'She's able to eat? Already?' he asked knowing that a person who had little to eat would take time to eat meals of solid food.

'A little broth and a few pieces of vegetables, maybe not meat. But she is recovering quickly,' noted Mary, looking at the young woman still covered in the blankets. Charly's eyes were open, now clearer, sharper, watching and learning, understanding who these people were that had saved her life. Mary did not acknowledge her, understanding that Charly still needed lots of time to recover her strength; they had only found her this morning.

As the meat cooked on the pot, a number of new aromas filled the air under the trees, smells and fragrances that the old gums of the billabong had rarely experienced. Mixed with the soft waft of eucalyptus from the oils realised by the leaves, the air became a mix of the ancient cultures from two lands. Charly smelled the air, her senses had become part of the land in the last weeks. She knew she had become something she had never been before, but these smells took her somewhere else. Her stomach was grumbling, lacking solid food for nearly a week, since the day she found that nearly all her scavenged carrots had been eaten by bunch of hungry kangaroos.

She watched in silence as Mary quietly moved around the camp, making it as comfortable for their stay. The two men pulled short mats and spare clothes from their baggage and walked down the shallow slope of the billabong. Shortly after, Charly could hear splashing and laughter from around a slight bend in the still waterway where the men were bathing far enough away from the camp that provided appropriate privacy. A while later, she could hear their rhythmic voices conversing in a language she did not understand. While she did not understand the words, she could hear the power and sanctity.

'That would be them praying. You will get used to it, they do it a bit,' explained Mary with a knowing smile on her face. The prayers often frightened people who did not know the beliefs of these men from Afghanistan.

Charly looked up at the smiling face of Mary standing beside her, Charly had not heard her approach, she had been mesmerised by the prayers.

'They be Muhammadens, they be following the words and teachings of the prophet Muhammad,' continued Mary as she squatted beside her. They both listened a little more. The words appeared to flow to all parts of the hollow of the billabong.

Charly's face crinkled in question, her forehead furrowed as her eyes stared at Mary's face, wordlessly demanding more information. Mary dropped her gaze as she untucked the blanket from around Charly's lower legs and feet.

'They may not be the teachings of the mission I was sent to, but the men are devout and believe in one God. They're both good men with kind hearts. You can be assured they will protect you like you were their sister; you need never fear them, I promise.'

Mary smeared a mix of the honey she had found in the tree hollow and a special ointment on the scarred and weeping burns around and above Charly's ankles from a small glass container. The action elicted a soft moan of pleasure as the fire in her wounds quickly eased and then nearly disappeared. The pain in Charly's eyes melted away as her face softened. She slowly relaxed, leaning back onto the blankets covering the ground.

'Ahh, good, I am glad it has doing its job. A little ointment that my mother made from a few native plants, it will help the poisoned skin and flesh to heal. And the honey I found when we arrived here in a tree close to camp,' Mary stated in a soft, compassionate tone. 'I am still very worried, but we have a chance you should be walking again very soon.'

Charly looked up at the smiling face, a small smile flickered across her face before she closed her eyes, the message that she did not wish to interact any further. Dark and confusing thoughts still rushed through her mind, the suddenness of the change in her circumstances, the newness of her companions exhausted her. Charly needed time, time to find a balance where she could comfortably interact with other humans.

Mary returned to her tasks, preparing the dough, placing it in the cast iron pot in the coals for the round of damper bread to be had with their evening meal while keeping a caring eye on her companion. She floured the round of dough and dropped it into the bottom of the heavy iron pot. As she carried it to the edge of the fire, she cast her eye across to where the young woman lay quietly.

She was concerned that the young woman was reluctant to speak, other than the time she'd wanted more milk, but since then she had not spoken. Mary opened the lid of the second pot over the flames with the simmering stew. She carefully tasted the meat and vegetables in its thick sauce, smiling. The casual injection of spices by Abdullah had provided the perfect flavours to enhance the food.

Mary placed the lid on the heavy steel pot with the dough before burying it in the ground next to the fire, placing a shovel full of coals on the thick steel lid. Another thirty minutes would be all that was needed before the food was ready to be eaten, about when the two men would be back from checking the camels.

Mary picked up Charly's clothes and took them and some of her own down to the edge of the billabong to clean the worst of the filth from them, then laid them on a large sandstone rock to dry. Mary soaked the dust out of her spare clothes before also spreading them on a second large rock. Tomorrow she would have a long soak in the cool water. At least they would not have put up with dusty clothes for a few days, until they struck out into the desert again to find their next stop at one of the stations or at a special waterhole along the telegraph line.

Mary looked up as she saw Abdullah and Wazir walking back up the bank of the billabong, both carried a long limb to be burnt in the fire throughout the night. She smiled; their timing perfect, or maybe their noses had called them back to camp.

'How is the little one?' asked Abdullah as he drew near his beloved wife. 'Wazir and I were discussing what to do, he thinks we wait till someone returns, but this is uncertain, I consider leaving on our usual course.' He looked closely at her as they started walking back to the camp. 'But being a woman of unfounded wisdom, I am thinking you may wish to have a say in this matter.'

'Maybe so, but likely your endless wisdom considered my annoyance if you had not asked, my benevolent and kindly master.'

Abdullah let out a burst of laughter, expecting little more from his wife. Mary placed her hand on his arm, stopping him as they entered the camp, the slowly cooking pot between them and Charly.

'She may appear to be sleeping, but she is always alert and has sharp ears, so I will speak with you tomorrow. I fear that, from her manner, she is carrying deeper wounds than those on her skin and flesh.'

The final preparations for the meal were undertaken. Wazir hooked the pot out of the ground, brushing of the last of the coals with a small tree limb full of green leaves he had broken off a low hanging branch. The heat from the metal scorching the leaves, provided a soft waft of burning eucalyptus into the camp. He rolled out the round of damper, the smell adding to the pleasant odours, exciting the tongues of those in the camp.

At the side of the camp, Charly's eyes popped open in fear, the smell of freshly burnt gum leaves bringing back black memories, causing her to cry out in panic, her breathing coming in rapid gasps. Mary realised what had occurred, immediately taking a few quick steps to sit down beside Charly, holding her by the shoulders, pressing the young woman into her chest. Slowly the older woman started to sing a song from her memory, a song to calm the fear, a song as old as the gums around them.

Charly's heart slowly slowed as the power of the soft song found its way into her soul. As her breathing slowed, she relaxed, finally taking a deep breath, releasing it before giving a soft shudder. Charly leaned back slightly, looking up to the person holding her. She said not a word, but her eyes sent a message a desperate plea for reassurance and support. Charly then suddenly pressed her head back into Mary's chest, breaking into quiet sobs.

Mary ran her hand down the dirty, matted hair, an action slowly repeated, the message of care and protection.

'Tomorrow, or a day after, we will talk. You and I need to find what evil ails you, you are too young and lovely to carry this pain and grief. I will be here for you, for however long you need I am here. Okay, young Charly?'

Charly, her face still buried deep between the ample breasts of Mary, nodded a few times, a bond forged between them.

'Good. Now, you need to let me go and I will get you a little broth. We need to hurry, before those two hungry men eat it all, them being men after all and rarely thinking of others but themselves...'

Charly let out a muffled snort of laughter. 'Okay, Mrs Mary, we can do that,' she mumbled.

'Ha, no not missus, call me Aunty Mary. I want you to be part of my own family. From today you are part of my life, my people, the people of this place. But now, we need to get a little tasty food for you.'

The two men had been intently watching the interchange between the two women as they quietly ate their food, mumbling thanks to whoever allowed their exceptional fortune in finding a person who provided such wonderfully tasty sustenance during their current travels. In their own language, the two men discussed the critical issues that the badly injured young woman had provided them. Finding some solutions would be easy, others more complex, but the interactions between the two women on the other side of the camp appeared to make these problems have an answer.

'I am thinking my beloved has adopted another child. Do you not think so, my good friend Wazir?' said Abdul in his tongue to his kinsman.

'She may not follow the enlightened pathway as provided by the great prophet, but the depth of her heart is a gift, my honourable companion,' replied Wazir nodding in agreement. 'I am sure that we will have Allah's approval caring for the sickly, no matter who they be, so whatever is required for the little one, we should do.'

'My heartfelt thanks for your support. Yes, we are obligated as believers of the prophet's words to care for the poorly, and this we will do without favour. The little one comes with us; we will care for her as our own.'

With Charly slightly calmer, Mary crossed to the fire and ladled a small bowl of flavoursome broth, adding a few vegetables but no meat. This she took back to Charly, who immediately held the bowl close to her chest, hungrily wolfing down the broth with the spoon, as if there were people leaning over her shoulder wanting to pull the bowl from her hands. When she was finished, Charly held out he bowl to Mary, a smile on her face. 'More please, Aunty Mary, I am still hungry.'

Mary smiled at the response, the change in the eyes putting warmth in Mary's heart, a heart torn between causing disappointment or allowing Charly to make herself sick after so many days without food. The overwhelming urge to avoid another negative allowed a small risk.

'Okay, but just a little bit more, then no more till tomorrow,' Mary said forcefully. 'But please eat it a little slower, no-one will ever take your food away.'

Charly's face dropped a little but then brightened. 'I will be careful, Aunty Mary, I know I cannot eat too much, or I will be sick.' Her voice was clear and echoed across the camp.

The two men looked at each other. Mary raised her eyebrows and gave a knowing smile. All three instantly knew that whatever affected Charly's desire to communicate, it had not affected her thought processes, they knew that this young woman possessed a very sharp mind.

Charly finished her second bowl and rolled herself into her blankets, pulling them tight under her chin. She gave Mary a smile and a quick silently worded thank you before closing her eyes and slipping off into a deep sleep.

The remaining three people in the camp quickly finished their food, cleaned the utensils, completed their ablutions and followed Charly to a night's sleep. The sounds of the camels softly filled the hollow of the billabong as they moved closer to the camp before they settled down with a quiet rumble. Mary snuggled closer to her man, listening to the hoot of an owl further down the billabong. She smiled at the calming sounds of the land, before slipping off to sleep, knowing that the next few days would either make or break the young woman sleeping on the other side of the camp.

The following morning set the slightly repetitive course for the following days, including a deal of intense and well-planned preparation for the next part of their travels. The camels were checked after a quick breakfast and any small sores provided with a salve to quicken the healing. Each was brought down to the billabong to drink, showing their enormous ability to absorb water. As they had their fill, the camels wandered slowly back to where they found good grazing, only after first investigating the camp for the treats they were accustomed to receiving on the trail.

The first camel to quietly walk into the camp was Sheba, followed by her calf. Charly was dozing and awoke to an inquisitive nose pushing the blankets to see what could be found underneath. Charly lay still, remembering the first introduction yesterday. She slowly reached out and gave the longish snout a soft rub. Sheeba gave a small rumble of pleasure, pressing her head against her hand to encourage further contact, a wish Charly was only too happy to grant.

Mary watched from the other side of the camp, pleased to see the interaction of two creatures, and the smile on Charly's face. As she watched, Moses, the big male, the powerhouse and dominate male of the group, pushed his way towards where Sheeba was, none too gently forcing his way to find the source of the rumbles of pleasure from the other camel. Mary quickly put down the cooking pot she had cleaned to move Moses away. He was well known to be a difficult and grumpy animal, with a history of nipping people.

As Mary got closer, she could hear the same soft rumbling of pleasure from the old bull, matched by Sheeba, as both were now getting their heads rubbed. A movement in the corner of her eye caught her attention. Abdul was standing a little distance away, his hands on his head unsure what to do, knowing the nasty antics of Moses. If he rushed in, Moses would react and snap, if he stayed away, the consequences were unthinkable.

Before he could find an answer, Moses rocked down and settled beside Charly, closed his eyes and began slowly chewing his cud, content as any old camel could ever be.

Abdul stared at Mary, shaking his head in disbelief. Mary responded with shrug of her shoulders. She smiled and walked over to stand with Abdul, placing her hand on his arm.

'I told you she was different. There is something about her, this one communicates in a different manner, not with words.'

'Aiii, Mary, but with Moses, it is like he is under her spell. He loves her like no other I have ever seen, even with you my kind and beloved wife.'

As Sheeba and her calf also settled near Charly, Mary and Abdul knew that there was no reason to disturb the camels. Charly had sat up a little in her blankets, still rubbing the snout of the old bull camel. Abdul sat on a fallen log at the side of the camp and started to repair a harness from one of the packs, restitching where the threads had frayed from the heavy loads, then rubbing wax to seal the cotton to the weather. Odd short words of conversation were exchanged between the two of them as they kept a wary eye on the snoozing camels and the young woman who lay contentedly between them.

Wazir wandered over and sat next to Abdul, carrying a large canvas bag that had a fresh small tear that required repairs to stop the damage becoming a bigger problem. He started stitching then looked up at the sight across the camp. He gave a small chuckle at what he observed before putting his mind back to his repairs.

'There was a man from the next village to ours who had a similar way with his camels,' Wazir finally said, continuing with his work. 'He rarely needed to work his animals as we did with all that shouting and whipping. He would simply giggle and laugh, then a few soft words and they did what he wanted; it was as if they understood his thoughts.'

The words were followed with a protracted silence from both Mary and Abdul, waiting for the Wazir to continue.

'She is similar, I feel. She has a way with these creatures that we cannot understand. It is a gift from the great one; a gift we need to respect and cherish.'

He looked across at the other side of the camp, smiling, turning to glance at his companion stitching the leather harness. These repairs were a very important process during longer stops, checking and fixing the equipment that was the core of their lives, their activities.

They continued to work, watching the relaxed camels, the camp more peaceful that for many a day past.

The early morning light filtered through the branches and leaves that were moving gently from a soft breeze blowing from the distant sands, the light brushing the ground, leaving shadows around the camp. Three of the occupants had been up and carefully preparing their day for a short time, mindful of their sleeping companion. As they finished their morning meal, Mary collected the plates as the two men prepared to leave.

'We will return by dinner, we will check if anyone has returned,' stated Abdul quietly. 'The young one needs to be cared for, best if she be with her people.'

Mary remained silent, her fears, the ones she had forcefully, yet respectfully laid out on the previous evening, had not been satisfied. There was a deep-seated ill feeling, one from her own dark memories that remained, nagging like an old hag trying to sell an unwanted item to passers-by. Her husband saw the concerned look on her face.

'My beloved, your fears are worthy but we must try, the laws require such. We cannot just take her,' stated Abdul forcefully as he could, without causing insult to Mary's feelings. He relented a small amount. 'Let us look and then when we come back we can decide. In any case, if one or more of the family returns, they will be in need of the goods we have brought.'

With a kind smile as a farewell, Abdul bent and picked up a muzzle harness and small saddle and followed Wazir to where the camels were hobbled. Both men planned to ride back to the remains of the fire burnt buildings, check for returning persons and ensuring that the remains of one of the occupants found in the house remained undisturbed.

Mary watched as her man walked over the slight bank and disappeared from her view. It was the fifth morning since they arrived at the string of billabongs and time had come for the next phase of their travels to soon commence. Tomorrow they would be leaving, the camels suitably recovered, required repairs completed and the three persons refreshed. Her major concern was Charly, still asleep, wrapped in a warm blanket that kept out the morning chill.

Mary started the process of planning for the next day's travel, preparing food, organising the cooking, sleeping and other items to be packed into the large canvas sacks. She looked at the bundle buried under the blanket; her thoughts returned to those recent concerns.

Charly had shown rapid improvement in the last two days, allowing her to spend time walking around the camp and much to her immense pleasure, taking time to help care for the camels. The basic roles she was shown did not require telling a second time, her interactions from the first days were proven again. She had an instant connection and the animals immediately responded, almost pushing each other away to get her attention.

The last two days also allowed Charly to finally have a long soak in the waters of the billabong, washing away every scrap of dirt and debris from the results of the horror of the fire. Surprising was her decision to again clothe herself in the loose robes that had been provided on the first day she was found. Her appetite knew no bounds and she was quick to have a second and even once a third helping, with no ill effects other than put a little shape on her bones.

The only issue was her reluctance to speak about her experiences. Every gentle enquiry was met with a wall of emotions: a mix of bubbling anger, pain, and most of all, fear, naked burning fear. It was the fear that concerned Mary the most. Why fear? Of all the emotions, this one would be the most difficult to overcome. Her own experience of fear provided the knowledge and desire to help this beautiful young woman.

Mary frowned as she continued to prepare the camp for their departure, her mind dwelling on the previous thoughts, and a young woman with a gift, a gift that everyone in the camp recognised, but none understood or knew what it might lead to. Suddenly a soft waft of feelings, maybe a thought brushed her mind, a sensation she instantly remembered those last few days before they arrived at the burnt remains of a once proud cattle station.

Mary dropped the pot in her hand and quickly walked over to the sleeping form under the blanket. She arrived beside Charly, looking down, the face looking up was awake, the eyes sharp and questioning, an edge of panic.

'No, I will not go back!' Charly snapped, cold determination in her voice. 'Never back, never again. I will leave you; you cannot hold me. Never... No, Mary, I can't do that; he will hurt me again... NO. NEVER.'

Charly had drawn back into her blanket, her eyes wide and filled with tears which slid down her soft cheeks. Her shaking hands held the blanket tightly under her nose. Mary realised that she had been awake and listening to the entire morning's discussions between herself and Abdul, words that had allowed a fear to build and panic to set in. Mary sat down next to Charly, carefully reaching out and stroking her shoulder.

'I will never let anyone hurt you. You have suffered too much already,' Mary said, her voice soft, as she let the words slowly soak in. She continued to provide a reassuring touch, finally saying, 'Maybe I can help you, but you need to tell me a little.'

It was as if a dam wall had shattered and the words flowed as a surge of contained water looking for freedom. Charly started with her mother, the loss of her and her younger sibling, the evils of her stepmother and then she stopped speaking. Silence flowed across the billabong, the call of a frog causing the only disturbance. Even the leaves had stopped rustling as if intently listening to the words issuing from Charly's heart. Mary sat quietly, holding the young hands of her troubled companion, tears of empathy and shared pain running down her face. Their silence kept the moment sacred until, Charly gave an angry snort.

'That man called himself my father, but I knew what he did was wrong even before I told my mother.'

Charly's words stopped again. Mary knew exactly what was being said: a young girl violated in mind and flesh was not unusual in any people. It was a situation she had unfortunately encountered in her native people and in the convent where she had learnt her English skills. She pulled the young woman closer as Charly burst into waves of sobs, shaking as never before.

Slowly the tears slowed, the sobs eased as the moments slid by. Time was of no consequence, the peace of the billabong now dictated the process the two would follow. The spirit of the location entered the hearts and souls of both, one a child of the land, the other a child in heart.

'You need say no more, I understand the meaning of your words... the evil the sins of men...' muttered Mary. 'But when you are ready, I will be here for you to listen more. I am your friend, your protector.'

Charly leaned back and smiled, taking a deep breath. The words again started, this time the inner pain was released, the words started the healing, no part was silenced. Mary sat, not listening to the words, as they were horrific, but listening as the young person beside her changed, a weight being taken away. The billabong responded, a breeze ruffled the leaves, the lorikeet's trilling a sharp message of happiness as they rushed from tree to tree. The pain of the words slowly being swept away, soaking into the ancient soils of the land.

Mary started to sing, soft words that resonated around the camp. Words her aunties taught her as child. A song old in age, words that Mary barely remembered but it was a song of healing, demanded by the land, the billabong, demanded by the ancient trees. Time ceased to exist until Charly reached up and wiped away the tears on Mary's cheeks. Grins slowly spread across their faces as an understanding passed between them, wordless and powerful.

'You may not be of our people, but you are of the land, the trees have told me,' quietly said Mary. Charly, did not truly understand the meaning of the words, nor the importance to her future. 'We will speak more when you understand but till then, let us prepare for our travels together,' Mary said.

Charly quickly climbed out of her bedding and completed her morning ablutions before enjoying a hearty breakfast. A new life had come over her, as if she was willing to be alive once more.

It became very clear to Mary that Charly had learned a great deal from watching the comings and goings in the camp for the last four days. After midday, they both checked on the camels. A number of times Charly had started to do a small task before Mary asked. Her affinity with the pack animals was obvious, Charly would quickly become a very capable cameleer.

They worked together till late afternoon when they could hear the two camels being stopped outside the riverbank to have their saddles and harnesses removed. Charly walked up the bank of the billabong, quietly walking over to the old lead camel, rubbing his nose as Abdul put the hobbles to his front legs. As he finished, he stood and watched her, a thought matching Mary's crossed his mind.

'Charly, this one likes you, but not as much as Sheeba,' he noted. Charly looked at him as he continued. 'How would you like to care for her and the calf on the next part of the travels?'

Charly's eyes widened in excitement, unsure on how to respond. The excitement stole her words, but her face told the story.

'You will be under my care, but your role is to check her when we stop, lead her as we walk. But when we ride, you can sit in the saddle, but we will put her muzzle harness on a lead.' He stopped speaking, before asking, 'Your thoughts, young lady?'

'Ohhh, really? That will be so exciting, I will care for her as never before, I promise.'

'Good, but do not spoil her, she thinks she is special as it is.'

The next day, just before mid-morning, the string of camels started their travel to the west, towards the sands of the edge of the desert. Following a pathway to their next destination. The four people sitting on the camels were surprisingly tired, a morning of the final packing of the loads into the leather panniers, watering the camels for the last time for a number of days, their humps now packed hard with liquid in the fatty tissue. Last of all, they loaded the heavy leather panniers and water bags onto the frames on the backs of the camels.

The gentle roll of the camels soon relaxed the aching muscles and tendons, a calmness overcoming the travellers. Mary looked carefully at Charly, hanging on desperately in her saddle with the hand not holding a rope from the muzzle harness, trying but not quite learning to move with the animal's rolling gait. Mary looked across to Abdul, noting his nod of satisfaction at how quickly the young woman had adapted. A snort from Wazir had them all looking back to where he was, riding one of the last camels.

'She learns quickly, dear brother. Soon she will ride better than you, if Allah wills.'

While the others laughed with free happiness, Charly had a red blush of embarrassment spread slowly across her face, smiling at the complement from a man who rarely acknowledged her, had rarely given any form of vocal support, but was clearly impressed by her efforts.

'Feel the rhythm, Miss Charly. Let your inner self move with Sheeba, she will direct you,' directed Wazir.

He smiled as the younger woman responded to his words, the awkwardness disappearing as Charly stopped fighting the unusual movements provided by the camel she was on, movement unlike any horse Charly had ever ridden. Quickly she melded into the repetitive rhythm of her camel, one that she sensed that she would experience for a long time to come.

In the distance behind them, far to the north over the end of the long sandstone ridge, dark clouds had started to build, the top rising high into the sky. By late afternoon, as the string of camels had moved to the west towards the dry windblown sands of the barren desert land, the first drops started to fall on what remained on the ground that held the remains of the burnt buildings that once was Hendricks Flats. Big, weighty drops of rain smashed into the dry, dusty ground, cooked from the years of drought. The first scattered drops caused puffs of dust to erupt, until the drops overwhelmed the dryness, causing small runs of water down any slope of the ground.

After a short time, any sign of human or animal movement had disappeared. It was as if the land wanted to erase all record of recent man's existence in the area. The rain was a solid curtain of moisture, the percentages of water to air was almost balanced. The few remaining scorched timber structures collapsed under the onslaught; all that remained were two solid stone chimneys, surrounded by twisted sheets of burnt roofing iron, oxidised a bright reddish orange. As the rain eased, the last timber to fall was a plank, burnt on its edges, with a crude cross scratched in its face that had been place upright into the soil at the base of a slight mound covered in stones. The cross was lost in the muddy surface of the ground, the last resting place of the person beneath, so despised by the one survivor of the horrors, now slowly being cleansed from the land.

Chapter 5

The rider had his waterproof poncho pulled tight around his neck, not that it helped much. Even with the wide brimmed felt hat, water still trickled down his back into the seat of his britches. His horse, his saddle and pack were soaked, but he was finally close to his home and a little water seeping down his neck provided little annoyance as he slowly moved his horse between the sandstone escarpments.

He had left his stepbrothers and stepfather early in the morning, leaving them to pack up a last wet camp. Sent on ahead, he rode on to warn the household of the men's return from a successful sale of their cattle.

As the four of them had rode over the land the last few days, fresh with belly deep grass in the land, their fathers' spirits lifted every sodden step the horses took towards the sandstone ridge before them.

'We beat it boys, we won against everything thrown at this family over the last years of drought. You bloody beauty, we are out of the other side and nothing can hurt us now,' he crowed. 'We got the best prices at the sales and now we have water and grass and still have the core of our herd.'

Harry had grown up fast on the cattle drive and now he was changed; a boy at leaving and man in returning to his home. He had volunteered to go early to ensure all preparations were completed, but he was desperate to see his mother and show her that he was now a grown man. Maybe not in years but certainly in experience. The last months had forced that issue very quickly. He smiled. A few months ago he would have complained bitterly about getting wet, now, after four days in soaking rain, it was simply part of what he did as a stockman. Yes a real cattle man, that what he was now, and a cattle man, and no-one was going to dispute that claim, ever.

Harry pushed down the last decline in the rocky gulch, excited to see his home. The water in the swollen river had just started to push over the low banks of the billabongs, the flood plain would be getting its life blood very soon. He paused his horse, he had never seen this occurrence. He had been told by Charly, but this was a first for him. As was the amount of water pushing down the river, being partially blocked by the narrow sandstone of the ridge, the billabongs now gone as a memory, only the big river gums showing where the banks had been.

He gently flicked the bridle. Misty instantly responded, a horse for the ages he thought as she started moving forward again. Misty had proven to be the best, his protector, his tutor, his horse, he could not wait to tell Charly how well her horse had looked after him. They both moved effortlessly around the last rock outcrop, bringing his home, the long-desired buildings of Hendricks Flats into view.

Harry halted Misty in disbelief. His heart raced; everything that was his home was gone. He urged Misty forward, fearful of what he would find, fearful of what had happened to the two people left behind.

A little over two hours later, the three Hendricks men sat silently on sodden horses. The three additional pack horses trailed behind them as they slowly rode amongst the burnt-out buildings. The rain had stopped as they drew up their mounts beside Harry. The young man was sitting on the ground close to where the back door of the house once was, his head in his hands, not acknowledging the men behind him. The oldest of the sons slowly dismounted while the other two remained on their mounts. There was a stunned silence, other than the deep regular sobs of grief from the young man sitting in the mud.

Jessie squatted beside Harry, putting his arm around his shoulder in support. He may not have had much respect for the boy when they left, but now he had proven himself, he was an equal of the sons, one of the men of the family.

'Harry, this does not mean they are dead, they might be around somewhere, maybe hiding from the rain in one of the caves above the river.'

'No, they're not. Look around, I don't need your bullshit!' Harry snarled. 'It's been weeks, maybe months since the fire. Tell me, what would they live on?'

Jessie didn't have a response, the truth in Harry's comment was too obvious. Bryan dismounted and walked past them, his steps dazed as he picked up the corner of a sheet of roofing. He quickly jumped back as a coiled reptile lifted its head to see what had disturbed its warm and slightly dryer abode. It was obvious that the rising waters had driven the creatures from the banks of the billabong to higher ground. Bryan turned to face his father before providing his opinion on searching the remains of the house when he heard a strange sound.

Jedidiah Hendricks, still sitting on his horse, was looking to the other side of the burnt remains. He tried to lift his arm and point at something he could see, but it was barely responding to his wishes. He again tried to form words but only a garble series of guttural sounds emanated from his mouth. Jessie and Bryan saw their father's ashen and distorted face, a look of extreme pain then unbelieving panic crossed the face as their father suddenly slumped forward, slowly toppling forward from his saddle on his horse.

His sons react as one and leaped to his assistance, but Jedidiah Hendricks hit the muddy soil with his limp arms and face before they were able to grab him. He was dragged along slightly as his horse moved forward a few steps before Bryan could take a firm hold of the dragging reins.

'Harry, quick, get Dad's feet out of the stirrups, I need to see what has happened to him!' shouted Jessie as he tried to turn him on his back to get his father's face out of the mud. 'Bry, hold the horses head away from Dad and keep him still so I can get him on the ground.'

As he spoke, the clouds darkened appreciably, the light dropping for those standing in the mud, struggling to release the ailing man from his horse. A few fine drops of rain stated falling again. Harry struggled to remove the booted foot from the stirrup, wrapped as it was around the rolled whip and rifle scabbard attached to the saddle.

A bright flash and crack of thunder shattered the moment, and a bolt of lightning struck a tree on the lower edge of the sandstone ridge behind where they were located. Jedidiah's horse reared, the sudden movement throwing Bryan backwards onto a cluster of twisted sheets of burnt roofing. He landed with a crash but had the focus to hang onto the end of the bridle with one hand. The other arm flayed backward in a vain attempt to provide balance and support. His forearm smashed into the raised corner of a rusty sheet of iron. A deep cut instantly produced a solid flow of blood down his forearm, dripping along the metal, the red flowing over the orange.

Bryan quickly regained control of the horse, ignoring the pain in his arm. His hand was sticky with blood, and a short, burst of heavy rain thundered towards them. He quickly dragged himself out of the twisted iron sheets, remembering the creatures that now lived in their midst.

Harry was picking himself out of the muddy soil where he'd landed after he was knocked backward by the rearing horse. The sudden movement had caused his stepfather's foot to slide out of his sodden leather footwear, as all he could see was a boot still stuck in the stirrup.

Jessie was laying on the ground, his father now on top of him. All he could remember was the ear-splitting blast of thunder, and being struck in the head by his father's freewheeling arm as the horse reared up. His father was a dead weight on his upper body. He grabbed his father's arm; it was limp, and provided no response to his touch. Jessie looked up at the horse, he saw that the second foot was still in a stirrup, the situation difficult in the crazy weather.

The rain flowed into his eyes, blurring his vision, but he noticed that Harry had been able to stand. With a quick push, the young man was able to remove the last foot from the stirrup, freeing his father. Jessie pushed, and with Harry's help rolled Jedidiah onto his back. A quick check of his face and breathing provided the confirmation of the darkest of possible outcome imaginable; his father, the larger than life Jedidiah Hendricks, was dead. The leader, the head of the family, was gone.

'Harry!' Jessie shouted against the noise of the next batch of thunder and rain. 'Secure the other horses best you can, not much you can do to help me here!'

Harry quickly responded to the shouted direction, tying as many of the trailing bridles and lead ropes together and then to a charred oversized timber beam on the ground. He then mounted Misty and chased after two of the pack horses that had bolted due to the first thunderclap towards the flooded paddocks, trying to stop them before they lost the supplies they carried in the rising waters.

Jessie looked at Bryan, sitting in the sodden soil, cradling his arm as he hung onto the end of the bridle from his fathers' horse. His head was down, using the wide brim of his hat to protect his face from the large drops of rain. Jessie stood from where he had been sitting next to his father, walked the handful of paces to where his brother sat and squatted next to him, putting his hand on his shoulder just as he had done to his stepbrother in what felt like a life time ago.

'Bry, I think Dad's dead,' he said in a monotone of pain and grief. 'He ain't moving none and I can't feel his breath.'

Bryan looked up, letting the rain fall on his face, his tears joining the flow of liquid down his face. He shook his head, then nodded in agreement with his brothers' devastating words.

'I know he's gone. I saw the look, just before he fell. It was a look of goodbye, I saw it, I knows I saw it,' was the disconsolate response.

'I saw it too,' replied Jessie, trying to get some order into the catastrophic situation. They had to do something, they could not stay in the pouring rain, mud and lightning. He was reminded of this by another bright flash and thunderous roll that spooked the horses. But where might shelter be? He looked at the blackened remains of the building, and was assisted by Bryan.

'Jess, how about sheltering in that windblown face in the rocks, back near the river gully? It will get us out of the rain and there should be enough room for the horses.'

Yes, thought Jessie. It was not a deep cave but would likely provide sufficient shelter from where the wind was blowing. Enough shelter to at least provide enough time for them to gather their thoughts and decide what to do.

'I had forgotten about that place. Can you sort out the horses? I'll prepare Dad.'

Bryan held up his blood-soaked arm in response, as if to question how to deal with it.

'Bloody hell, Bry. What happened, mate?'

'Hit me arm on the edge of a bit of iron sheet when I went head over arse, cut me a bit,' explained Bryan.

Jessie tied a length of cloth he had torn from his fathers' shirt around the deep wound. He wound it around a few times to slow the bleeding. Tying the ends together put pressure on the wound and stopped the flow of blood, as he had been shown by the man lying on the ground close behind him.

Rainwater ran from the brim of his hat, soaking into his shirt. He wished he had left his poncho on, but the sun had come out in the rocky gorge and he, like his brother, had pulled the sealskin poncho's off as it was too hot. Now, wet and some windchill made everything difficult, including clear thought.

'What about Dad?' asked Bryan as he stood and flicked off as much mud from his britches as he could. Another blast of thunder filled the skies.

'Leave him stretched out for now. We can come and get him later. I want to get out of this shit weather, not worth getting hit by lightning,' replied Jessie as he watched Harry bring the two packhorses back with pride. Jessie smiled slightly, he knew that the boy in him was gone, he just proved that by thinking clearly and not questioning his commands, taking the few words and acting decisively on his own.

Within fifteen minutes they were against the sandstone escarpment, a large ledge twelve or so feet above them. The rock ledge flowed back some twenty feet, enough to provide a dry and safe cover from the storm now railing in complete madness above them. The three young men slowly dismounted from their horses, pulling the pack horses close inside, under the protection of the sandstone ledge above as the storm smashed against the rocks above.

After the horses were unsaddled and the packs removed and stacked up against the rear rock face, they pulled some dry clothes from the waterproof seal skin packs and for the first time in hours felt as if they could face the issues around them. Jessie asked the other two to sit with him. It was now up to him. He had just become the man to run the family cattle station; he had to take charge and provide the directions of how they as a family would respond to the issues they faced. The other two were his responsibility.

A little over an hour later, the force of the storm had disappeared. The bright late-afternoon sun shone on the distant flood plain, glittering as the first flood water silently spread over the last areas of the flood plains. The wind had dropped, and the air temperature had stabilised, the chill now a distant memory.

Jessie walked out from under the ledge, looking at the last stingers of cloud as it moved away. He turned to look at his companions, both of them sat in a general air of disconsolation. Harry was sitting beside Bryan carefully finishing the wrapping of the deep cut on Bryans arm with a fresh bandage that he'd ferreted from one of the packs.

'Right, fellas, we have enough time to get a few things done before the night drops.' Jessie directed the other two still sitting on the packs when he had re-entered the shallow cave. 'Bry, you can organise a fire and get a bit of a camp ready for us tonight.'

Bryan snorted his agreement. This was usually his role anyway, and with a sore arm, he knew that he would be left with the lighter of the activities around the camp. Jessie then looked over to the younger of the two men.

'Harry, you come with me, we need to get Dad so the critters don't get to him tonight. Grab a blanket and one of those calico covers, you know, one of the bigger pack covers.'

Harry and Bryan slowly got their feet, the usual sharpness affected by the crisis they now faced, well aware that the next few days would be difficult.

'Tonight we'll have a bit of a chat on what we do. I have some ideas but I want your opinions, so have a think about it,' was Jessie's final request, before he set into action the things he needed done, distasteful as they might be. 'Righto, let's get this done.'

Harry followed Jessie down to the burnt house, leading one of the pack animals. Once they arrived, Jessie quickly rolled his father into a blanket with the calico tarp over the top and then secured the sad bundle with a short length of rope. The two carefully lifted the stiffening body of Jedidiah Hendricks onto the pack horse. As Harry mounted, he looked aimlessly to the other side of the burnt remains of what once was their home.

'Hey, Jessie, look over the other side. I can't remember a pile of stones over there, can you?' Harry asked. 'You might have to get on your horse and move back towards me, I think the big chimney is in your way.'

Jessie quickly mounted his horse and rode the few paces back beside Harry, looking at where the young man was pointing.

'I think that's what Dad was trying to point at,' remarked Jessie. 'I had forgotten in all the shock, I reckon that is what he saw, this is nearly where his horse was. Let's check it out.'

The two of them slowly rode around the remains of the house, Jessie trailing the horse carrying his father till they arrived at the irregular stack of small rocks. It was clear that some had sunk into the rain-softened soil. Jessie handed Harry the reins of his horse and the lead from the pack horse before dismounting. He pushed on a couple of the bigger rocks with his boot and they sunk into the wet soil. He looked up at Harry in question, then started to walk around the almost circular small mound.

He stopped at the other end and bent over, picking a slightly charred timber board out of the mud. Jessie rubbed the dirt off the face, causing him to snap his head back in surprise. He turned it to show Harry. The markings of a crude cross was slightly visible on the surface of the wood. A large dollop of mud slipped down the charred timber making the mark clearer. Harry drew a shocked breath. The silent message on that charred piece of timber was an instant challenge to his thinking.

Jessie turned the timber to allow himself to look again at what had been scratched on the face. 'This is new, Harry, since the fire. What does that tell you?'

A stunned silence followed. Harry felt slightly uncomfortable to be considered an equal, having his opinion requested, his thoughts being asked for by someone he greatly admired.

'Seriously, Harry, I want to know what came into your mind. I'm slightly at a loss, there are so many possibilities all at once. So?'

'Someone was here after the fire. Someone healthy enough to dig a grave and carry stones,' was Harry's considered response. 'But where are they now, Jessie? Who were they and where are they now?'

Jessie did not reply. This one question put a major obligation on him, it was almost overwhelming, making his response to his father passing just a few hours ago a thing of limited consequence.

'And who is buried in the mud between us?' Harry looked back at the badly burnt buildings, the ferocity of that moment plain to see. 'We may never know. I just have a bad feeling. It is either my mother or your sister in that grave, maybe even both. And that scares me.'

Jessie bent over, picking up a larger rock that sat neatly in his hand. He put the charred timber plank back at the head of the grave and hammered it deeply into the soft, wet soil. This time it stood upright where it belonged. While a name was lacking, at least it recognised that this was the resting place of a family member.

'Yep you are right, not a question we know,' he finally said. 'We need more help and a bit of time to answer that one.'

Jessie walked over to Harry's side, putting his hand on his companion's shoulder to provide his support and condolence. He simply felt empty; the day had brought too many surprises and shocks. All he wanted was a little time to think and reflect. But he already doubted that this would occur. Their lives were now on his shoulders; he was the oldest, he was now the head of the family.

Jessie took the bridle and climbed slowly onto his horse. Taking the lead of the pack horse from Harry, he knew it was role to lay his father to rest. He flicked the bridle of his horse and touched the flanks with the back of his boots, not hard, his horse was well-trained, a favourite. He moved forward, heading back to their shelter for this night and for a number to come.

The light of the day was quickly fading as they arrived at the face of the shallow cave, the sparkle of a fire provided the first warmth of the day. Bryan walked over and the two brothers lifted their father from the pack horse and laid him flat on the ground, an unspoken knowledge that this was critical if they were to bury him quickly before the heat took its unstoppable path.

A good while later, they finished the meal Bryan had prepared, the usual pot of stewed meat, a few root vegetables and the remains of the round of damper that had been cooked the night before. The night had taken hold, all that could be seen in the distance was the edge of a sliver of a moon, with a few scattered stars. Cloud had returned, blanketing out most of the night sky, the one benefit was that the night-time temperature would not be too low.

A sudden sparkle of sparks lifted towards the roof of the overhanging sandstone ledge as Jessie dropped another armful of wood on the fire. Some of the sparks met the sandstone but all died quickly as they were watched by the three occupants of the cave. In the distance, the mournful call of a dingo punctuated the still night air.

'Hunting a poddy, I bet, bugger the mongrel dog,' Bryan growled. 'Might have to sort a few out, looks like they are getting a bit too comfortable without us being around lately.'

'Might be right Bry, but we got bigger issues to decide on,' Jessie replied. 'Like what–'

'Dad would have wanted to fix the mongrels, I know that. You're failing him,' snapped back Bry, cutting off his brother's words and thoughts.

'He ain't here, Bry, he's dead.' Jessie calmly indicated at the body on the ground at the back of the cave. 'And I need to decide what–'

'So who made you the high and mighty to decide what we do now?' snarled Bryan.

Jessie stood still, looking out at the darkened sky. His thoughts were on the past, more comfortable times, the sound of another dingo calling cut the silence, bringing everything back to the moment. Jessie turned, a new hardness in his face, ready to challenge his younger brother.

'No-one made me high and mighty, Bry. But as the oldest I have a responsibility to those of us alive and those dead. I will make the final decisions that need to be made. I want to discuss them with you both, but I will make them.' Jessie looked coldly at his brother, the hardness of his father evident. 'And if ya don't like it, I am not making ya to have to stay.'

The comment took the air out of Bryan, he slumped back on the pack he was sitting on, his head dropped in resignation. He knew what had been planned by his father, it had been discussed before, the succession if anything happened. He lifted his head in partial defiance.

'This is my home too. I'm staying,' he said without emotion. 'But don't treat me like a slave; in this we are equal. We both want the same outcomes.'

An uneasy silence hung on the last words, no pathway to move forward provided by either brother, no quarter given, no agreement found.

'I like to stay too. I don't have a mother, or I don't think I now have a mother, and I lost a sister today too, you know. It was my home. So can I stay too, please?' asked Harry.

Jessie and Bryan snapped their heads to look at the youngest member of trio, shock and embarrassment on their faces.

'Ahh shit, sorry, mate, I gunna change what I said. We three are equal in wanting the same outcomes,' Bryan replied, turning to look at Jessie. 'You agree, brother? We three are equal, even if you have the final say, right?'

'I agree. I was wrong to forget we all want the same. Harry, we are equal, in this is our land, our home,' Jessie stated with a tone of conciliation and warmth. 'The three of us will have equal rights.'

The edge of anger and anxiety left the three men in the camp. All three thought over the exchange, and how quickly it had become a dangerous environment for what was left of the family unit. The three of them knew the next few days would provide dangers and moments that would change their lives, their lives would never be the same.

'We will bury Dad tomorrow. I don't think we can get him back to town to do it there, it is just too far, you all agree?' said Jessie finally.

'Yep. But where?' asked Bryan.

'Down near the other grave,' said Harry before Jessie could respond. 'Keep them all together for now. Not that we know who it is but it just feels right.'

There were no opposing arguments; that location was as good as any other. The three prepared for bed. Harry checked the secure line of horses, making sure that they would not wander during the night. Bryan tided up the immediate camp, again clearly stating that he was not the camp slave, and everyone would help tomorrow; much to everyone's laughter. Jessie walked a small circuit of the outer edge of the camp, scaring off a couple of nosy dingos, looking for a cheap meal stolen from the packs.

'Need to set watches, keep the mongrels away and keep wood on the fire,' he directed in general agreement of everyone. 'Harry, you take the first one, then Bry and then me.'

Morning brought a change in the weather. Not a cloud could be seen at daybreak, and the sky stayed blue all morning. After a breakfast of toasted damper and rich sugary jam, the three conducted a quick search of the area. They commenced at the point where the trail cut through the sandstone gorge, past the burnt property, down the edge of the fully flooded river. They rode slowly, carefully watching for any sign of recent human life and called out endlessly. Neither action provided a positive response.

They sat on their horses looking at the flow of the river as it thundered down the gorge. Any sign that might have been left of the riverbank was long gone. Looking up the river they saw one of the old river gums had succumbed to the power of the river's flow, having been washed up against a larger member of the species, a short way back up the river. Jessie climbed off his horse, handing the reigns to his brother.

'I think I'll climb up to the big cave. I know Charly played up there sometimes,' he said dejectedly, his words expressing how they all felt. 'Who knows, she might be hiding out of the weather up there.'

Not inviting anyone else to join him, he started up the narrow track towards the face of the old cave where the menfolk of the local people celebrated their beliefs and customs away from woman and child interaction. The other two in the party knew that if Charly was in the cave, it was not likely she would be alive. The lack of signs gave truth to that thought.

Harry got off his horse to stretch his legs and back, stiff from a poor sleep, the memories of his mother making the night hours on watch long. He walked down to the water's edge. A slip would be deadly, the force of the water would provide no mercy to anyone who entered the raging flow. He walked a little further, looking at the fallen old river gum, its branches interlinked with the upper part of the trunk still standing in defiance of the force being applied by the river.

Harry smiled at the strength of the roots of the tree, remembering watching Charly laying in the shade of one of these giants, maybe even this one, catching and releasing tadpoles. He walked a little closer. A strange colour flashed from the branches in an almost embarrassed manner. Harry looked again, sure that there was something in the branches of the fallen tree.

'Hey, Bryan, bring the horse over!' he shouted over the noise of the river. 'There's something stuck in the tree over there.'

Bryan heard the shout but by lifting his hand to his ear indicated that he had not understood the words. Harry waved fervently, then pointed at the tree. Bryan quickly got the message and slowly walked the horses over beside Harry.

Harry quickly repeated his previous comments. Bryan looked closely, then walked the horse a little further as Harry remounted and followed. They stopped a little back from the water's edge; the branches of the tree they were interested in was a good twenty feet out over the muddy debris strewn water of the river. The form of the object was now quite obvious, but still needed closer investigation to have it confirmed what it was and where it came from.

It was a piece of cloth, light in colour, but its origin was unknown and undecipherable. It was tangled around some branches in danger of being broken and washed away.

'I have to get it, Bry, I need to know if it belonged to Mum or Charly.'

'You're nuts, Harry. It's too dangerous, one little slip and you're gone, a memory, mate. No way.'

Harry had already dismounted and was removing his boots, hoping that bare skinned feet would provide a little better grip on the smooth bark of the gum. 'I'm going, mate, can't sleep no more anyway. I have to know. Don't try and stop me.'

'Yeah right, Harry. Not real smart but your choice. Here, tie this around your waist,' said Bryan, offering the end of the rope that was clinched around the horn of his saddle.

Harry tied it around his waist as he climbed out onto the branches. He slipped slightly but used the rope that was being slowly fed out to him to keep some control. Slowly moving along a major limb, he found that following it allowed him to head in the general direction of the cloth. At some point, he would need to get into the water, using the smaller branches as handholds to stop being swept away.

Harry chose a suitable branch as he carefully lowered himself into the water. The force just below the surface pulled his body downstream. Panicking slightly, he tried to drag himself back, but the river had him in its grasp. Knowing it was his one chance, he pushed his mind to move forward. He reached for the next branch above him and slowly drew himself forward. Hand over hand, carefully judging the strength of the branches he held. He moved more than fifteen feet through the water. Only two more changes of grip and he would be there.

Suddenly the rope around his waist went tight and stopped his progress; he only needed a few more feet.

'Give me some slack, Bry, only a bit more mate!' he yelled, only getting a muffled response. Harry turned and could see that Bryan was still on his horse, but it was now nearly belly deep into the water. His torturous path had used up all the rope they had. He could not go back now, one chance, but the cloth was just out of reach.

Harry took one hand off the branch above and reached down to untie the rope. Holding it in one hand would give him the length to reach the white material in the end of the branches. Taking a good grip, twisting it in his right hand, he reached up and took a solid grip on a smaller branch in front of him. This would give him the last little bit to get his prize.

Harry let go of his left hand and swung out as far as he could reach; his fingers brushed the white cloth. The branch he was holding in his right hand broke with a sharp snap. The momentum drove him down into the water. Catching a desperate breath, his head felt the flush of the water. His eyes stung from the silt; he could not see. His right hand tightened on the rope in desperation, there was nothing else.

Suddenly an upwelling of water pushed him up at the full stretch of the rope. His left hand took swung from memory and he felt the touch of wet material. He grabbed it as he could feel the rope in his right hand dragging him backward into the flooded branches and limbs of the fallen tree. His arms, head and face getting bruises and scrapes. Suddenly he was free of the tree, flowing with the river toward the gorge at full speed. Harry stuffed the material into the front of his shirt and tried to take hold of the rope with both hands.

He disappeared below the surface of the water again, this time getting a full mouthful of gritty water and twigs. As he finally grabbed the rope with his left hand, the rope again jerked, tightened and drew him to the bank. Harry's head popped above the water. He twisted and looked at the edge of the river with blurred vision; he was being dragged by Bryan's horse, slipping on the wet embankment. Bryan stood on the bank, holding the bridle tightly, pulling the horse out of the soft soil.

The horse got traction and Harry shot forward towards the bank, finally being dragged up onto the wet grassy bank itself. He was nearly the ropes length below where Bryan was pulling his horse forward. As Harry felt the wet grass on his back he let go of the rope, spluttering on a lungful of river.

He opened one of his eyes as a form darkened the sky above him. It was Bryan, a look of a mix of terror and anger on his face.

'Well, that was fun. You should try it.' Harry started laughing at the madness of the situation, an edge of hysteria from the sounds coming from within him. He took a breath, then descended into a bout of coughing. He tried to sit up, flopping back onto the ground to catch his breath.

'Shit, Harry, I nearly did when you went under. Old Betsy slipped and went down to her neck in the river, took everything I had to get her back out, mate.'

As Harry's horse slowly walked over to muzzle his back, he pulled out the cloth from inside his shirt. After looking at it carefully, he handed it to Bryan. Bryan flicked the cloth to open it out. He recognised the material, it was the remains of a nightdress, the pattern, and edging designating it to a female wearer. The bottom, side and back were burnt, leaving scorched edges, and numerous holes. They both knew who had worn it; they had seen it in the house numerous times.

'So tell me, Harry, how the bloody hell does Charly's burnt nighty get hooked on a tree in the river?'

As the words said by Byran ended, a large cracking sounded just below them from the riverbank. The fallen tree split under the pressure of the flooded river and slowly released from where it had been jammed against the other old eucalypt. The two watched as one of the two sections of the tree quickly gained momentum and washed into the sandstone gorge. The sounds of smashing timber added to the cacophony of noise, as the tree was shattered on the rock outcrops, to be sent on to clog some still waterway downstream. The brothers looked at each other in shock.

'That was a bit close, mate,' muttered Harry as he sat up and gave Misty a rub on the muzzle as she rubbed her head against his side. 'Hey, Misty, can you smell your old friend Charly? I bet you can.'

Misty's ears rolled forward at the question and the use of the familiar name; she shook her head and gave a brief whinny. Harry grabbed her halter, pulling himself to his feet, letting the blood flow back into his legs. Water dripped from his clothes as he reached out and accepted the offered charred nightdress. He tucked it back inside his shirt and then helped pull his stepbrother to his feet. Harry noticed that the bandages on Bryans arm were stained in red. Blood seeped through the sodden material. The wound must still be open, now soaked in filthy flood water.

'Hit it on the pommel of the saddle as Betsy slipped,' noted Bryan as he saw what Harry was looking at. 'Must have torn the wound a bit more, hurts a bit too.'

'I'll look at it when we get back to camp. I got more bandages and some salve I used yesterday,' Harry replied. 'You'll be right till then, mate?'

Bryan nodded, picking up the bridle on his horse and slowly mounting. Harry followed his lead, and both slowly rode the short distance to the base of the track from the cave on the sandstone escarpment above the river. They quietly sat there for more than ten minutes, not saying much as both contemplated what they had found and the danger they'd faced by going into the floodwaters.

Jessie finally could be heard, sliding as much as walking, back down the muddy path. As he appeared slightly above them from around a small buttress, both of the brothers, sitting on their horses could see that his face carried no good news. He quickly descended the final section and stood next to his horse, giving Harry, then Bryan a quick up and down look in question at their state of wetness.

'Well, looks like you two have been up to something I might not want to know about,' Jessie said almost laughing at the bedraggled looks they had. 'But I can say no-one's been in the big cave for a long time, no footprints, no recent fire. There is nothing marked on the walls other than the old marks the old blokes put there long before Dad arrived to make the station.'

He looked back up at the sandstone escarpments a little wistfully, knowing that one change of the station had affected the old people that once lived here, the people of the land that could have helped them now.

'Not since the old people left when Harry's mum arrived, I guess.' He shook his head, muttering to himself, 'What a stuff-up bringing her here was.'

Harry just overheard the words. He knew the pain his mother had brought to this area. He wanted to speak up but, in his heart, he knew that however painful Jessie's words were, truth sat in them.

'Shit, sorry, Harry, sorta slipped out.' Jessie apologised as he remembered that Harry was with them. 'I don't mean you, you're alright, but ya know, some things can't be denied.'

Harry could not reply at first. He turned Misty's head as he looked to ride back up to their camp, following Bryan's horse. They were a little way ahead, having left when the words on the occupancy of the cave were provided.

Finally, Harry stopped as Jessie mounted up, turning to look at him with tears in his eyes. He dragged the cloth from his shirt, holding it up for Jessie to see.

'This was Charly's. I rescued it from the river. I might have loved my mother, but I know what she did to someone I really liked. I really miss my mother but I can't forgive what she did to your sister or your family,' he snapped. 'I miss Charly more than you would believe, so just don't speak to me about my mother again. Okay?... How about we just go bury your father?'

Chapter 6

Jessie and Harry dug a grave a dozen paces from the other unknown resting place. Bryan was excused from the grim process due to his arm injury, but was given the job of making a grave marker with their father's name on the horizonal timber. When completed to suitable depth, Jedidiah Hendricks was taken on his last horse ride, from the cave to his final resting place. Jessie was first to say a few words, then Bryan recited a short drover's poem from his memory, finishing with confused words as the emotion overtook him. Harry simply shook his head when the opportunity was offered. It was not his place, Jedidiah was not his paternal father.

As Harry leaned on his shovel, watching Jessie finish the last few scrapes, making the mound tidy, a thought hit him. The thought ran around his head as the cross was tapped into position and an armful of rocks placed to stabilise it. Harry looked at the adjoining grave, his thoughts clearing into certainty.

'Hey guys, what's missing on the other grave marker?' he asked suddenly.

Both of the brothers stopped and looked at the other marker, not quite sure what Harry was thinking.

'It's got no name, not even initials. It's sort of bare,' Harry quickly noted.

'Ummm yeah, but so what?' replied Jessie.

'The person who did the burying, whoever it is, right, they did not know the name, did not know the person they were burying,' Harry enlightened them. 'So neither Mum or Charly was here when it was dug.'

The silence of agreement flowed around them, but lots of questions ran through their minds, none vocalised until Harry finished his thoughts.

'The grave likely holds both of them, Harry's mum and Charly, and they were buried by some passing person,' said Jessie quickly. 'That's why we won't find them, they're gone.'

The shock of his words hit home like a hammer; the absolute certainty of Harry's thinking could not be argued. It made perfect sense and it instantly became the truth of the matter for all of them as they stood there.

'Ya maybe, but what about the nightie? How did it get down to the river?' asked Harry, still pinning his hopes that maybe Charly was still alive.

'They dried the clothes on the hanging line, maybe it just blew down there,' replied Bryan. 'Make sense with how it was burnt. Sorry, Harry, she was our sister too, but we all have to admit to the realities.'

They looked back at the unnamed grave. Bryan's comments were hard to argue against.

With slightly confused thoughts following them, they returned to the camp to partake in a late midday meal. Harry redressed the wound on Bryan's arm, the debris and silt from the river having soiled the reopened deep cut. Harry washed it out with the last of the clean water they carried, but it did not get to the full depth. It was the best he could do, relying on the basic training provided by his stepfather on the recent cattle drive.

The rest of the day was spent searching the burnt buildings, seeing what could be found to make a crude shelter. There was the odd piece of unburnt planking of framing timbers, but the fire had been very efficient in destroying everything made of wood.

'I guess we might knock up a bit of a shelter but nothing to build a decent hut or house,' said Jessie as he kicked a small pile of charcoal that had been the side of the stables. 'There might be a few steel tools we can save but if they could be burnt, they're gone.'

Bryan lifted the steel buckles that had once been part of the harness for the wagon. Every piece of leather was gone, burnt or ash. He tossed them as he picked up the blade of an axe and threw it to a small, but growing, pile of red rusty metal items: a shovel blade, a head of a pick, a couple of big hammer heads. He finally gave a snort of satisfaction as he pulled the blade of a crosscut saw from the burnt debris at his feet.

'We can shape some handles from wood from the trees,' he grunted. 'Not as good as seasoned, but at least we'll have some tools.'

Jessie acknowledged the comment. Everything they could salvage was one thing less they needed if they were to rebuild the property. Finally, Jessie sent Bryan and Harry back to the camp to prepare their evening meal and a supply of damper for the next couple of days.

'I'll check a couple of the wind pumps to see if they still provide water. I'll be back before night,' he said. While there were enormous amounts of water on the flats, not much was drinkable, and they would need this resource very soon.

The first windmill near the remains of the house had seized, likely from the fire destroying the grease in the bearings, and the metal pump was scorched, red with rust and clearly inoperable. Jessie rode north along the edge of the floodwater to see if the second windmill that supplied the old holding yards was a better option. It appeared that the fire had not been as damaging in that area. The floodwaters lapped the base of the steel frame that held the slowly spinning blades some fifteen feet above, but water was still flowing gently into the remains of the timber trough from the small steel pipe.

Jessie dismounted and took a long drink from the end of the pipe, enjoying the sweet water he so remembered from the artesian basin under the flood plain. After splashing water on his face, Jessie filled his hat and poured it over his head, enjoying the water soaking down his shirt. It had been a long, hot day, and the evening breeze provided the cooling he so wanted.

Before leaving, he filled three canvas water bags, these would provide the fresh water needed at camp for the next day or two. He would send Harry back and fill the other three they had emptied on the last few days of the ride. As he rode back it was a relief to know that at least they had access to good, drinkable water.

They finished their meal, the usual stew supplemented with fresh damper that brought a smile to three faces for the first time today. As Jessie was picking a few strands of meat from between his teeth with a small twig, he called the other two to settle down next to him.

'Well, as much as it sounds stupid, we need to let someone know what happened here and that Dad has died,' Jessie stated.

'Why? Can't we just stay, tell them next time we take a herd to the sales,' was the expected response from Bryan.

'Nope, we gotta do it. Dad told me years ago what I needed to do if something happened to him,' Jessie counselled his brother. 'It's the law. We don't own the place or the cattle, they're not ours to sell mate.'

Harry listened. It was not his place to offer a comment, his links were too thin, he was only a stepson. Bryan was not convinced and looked for another option.

'Well, do we all need to go?' he asked.

Jessie did not immediately answer, thinking about the options. It made sense that they would stay together, it was safer, and they could bring back the extra supplies they would need. But having someone here would allow the cattle to be managed and some of the damage to be repaired.

'Let's sleep on it. We can decide tomorrow,' Jessie said. He was too tired after today, a good sleep would clear his head.

The next morning the decision was almost made for him. Bryan's arm ached, riding for a handful of days would not help the wound heal. Jessie told him to rest today as he prepared to travel tomorrow.

'I think I will ride to Cunningham's first, let them know and then ride to the Reidsville by the bend river to see the authorities.'

'You just want to see Ellie...' Bryan left the words unsaid; Jessie's affection for the Cunningham's oldest daughter was well known.

Jessie smiled. Time with Ellie would be a bonus, but more importantly, as their closest neighbours, though nearly a week's ride away, they needed to know what had happened. It would be expected. He needed to keep good relations and their help to survive, if they were to get back onto their feet.

'Yeah right, that can wait. Her dad will keep me fair busy,' replied Jessie. 'So what do ya want to do?'

'I'm staying, Jessie. This is my home.'

'What about you, Harry? It's your choice. Coming, or staying with Bry?'

Harry was surprised, expecting to be told to be on his horse first thing tomorrow. But he was able to decide what he did, that was unexpected.

'Well, now or never Harry, or I make the call.'

'I think I will like to stay at my home too. If that's okay with you?' Harry quickly said. He didn't want to miss his chance to be the person he wanted to be: a cattle man. 'I don't want to leave here just yet, I need to get some stuff sorted in my head.'

'Okay, might be a better idea. The two of you here can help each other and keep an eye out.' Not that yesterday's activities at the flooded river gave Jessie much confidence. But he knew Harry had to grieve the loss of his mother. Being here would help him find his feet.

With the decision made, they prepared the supplies Jessie would require for the next weeks' travels. Jessie pulled his father's rifle from the pack. It was still in the leather case with straps that allowed it to be tied to the saddle. He undid the enclosing flap that slowed the dust and dirt getting into the breach-works, pulling the rifle from the case, handing it to Bryan.

'I'll leave it with you. Looks like all yours and mine were burnt in the house.' He paused, then pulled the holstered revolver from the pack where the rifle came from. 'I'll hang onto this.'

Bryan looked at the dust of the breach, starting to out the clean the dust with the corner of his shirt. It was a natural response and an evening activity after being in the saddle all day. He nodded as Jessie pulled out a number of boxes of ammunition for the rifle and stacked them on a small natural shelf in the sandstone. The amount would last some months, having been purchased by his father before they left the last town they passed through before heading home.

'I'll buy a couple of new ones before I come back. We can't live out here without each of us having one.'

'I did want to take mine you know, but Dad said less weight, and in the end, I left it,' Bryan said.

'Same with me, he took mine off my horse before we left. You might find the remains of it in the stables. Well, time to move on I guess.'

Jessie stood, ready to finish the day. He watched as Harry rolled out the swag and climbed into it, totally exhausted from a day that was now just a blur of memories. Jessie walked outside the open cave, listened to the horses and then to the night sounds. Nothing unexpected could be heard. It was time to end the day.

By late morning the next day, Jessie was almost ready to depart. He had completed two tasks with Bryan's assistance that were critical to both of their survival. They had both checked out the old trapper's hut that was a few miles past the holding yards. The bush in this area had avoided the fire that had swept over the ridge a few miles to the south of them, so they were glad to find the old hut still standing. The timber-clad hut was in poor condition, but the old timber shingle roof would be serviceable with a little work. Bryan agreed that this was where they would set up their accommodation.

'Should be okay. Might have to clean out the cranky brown snakes first but better than a cave without a front door, hey?'

'Too right, Bry. Just be careful till I'm back. Harry is learning but still needs a steady hand. Okay?'

Bryan nodded his agreement as they mounted and headed back to the next task at the holding yard.

They had caught and butchered one of the calves to provide fresh meat for the next few days, a week at most. Jessie had wrapped a few cuts into waxed canvas cloth, sealing as much air as he could from the meat. It would last for a few days, after which it would be damper and dry rations until he got to the Cunningham's cattle station.

Harry had been left to prepare some airdried strips of meat, and a few cuts for the next meals. The rest would be cooked as best as they could to provide cold meat till the end of the week. The lack of a meat safe was an issue, but Jessie knew that the two had the skills to make up what they needed till he returned.

As Jessie reached out and shook his brother's hand, there were no words needed between them. All of those had been used up in the last three hours, the outcomes agreed on by both. Jessie was glad he was leaving in good spirits and agreed purpose. He put his hand on the pommel, pulling himself up and as he smoothly mounted his horse. Bryan handed up the lead rope from the pack horse which would carry everything Jessie required for the next week or longer. He nodded as Jessie carefully touched the flanks of his horse with the heels of his boots.

'Be seeing ya, Bry, and look after the little fella,' said Jessie as he looked down from his horse one last time as she slowly moved away. 'He's the last of the family that we have, and I sorta like him.'

'See ya, mate, ride careful!' shouted Bryan in reply as his brother headed for the pathway in the narrow gorge through the sandstone escarpments.

Bryan watched till his brother disappeared, the enormity of the responsibility slowly settling on his shoulders. He snorted in disgust to clear his mind. Whatever would come here, at least it was better than dealing with town-folk again. At least here, he survived on his own skills and decisions. He walked to his horse, he would ride down to where Harry was working on the meat, he was in charge, he also knew that the two were now a team to bring this cattle run back from its knees. As much as he wanted to check on the cattle, he knew their first job was to sort out their living quarters.

Harry pulled himself from his bunk, more parts of his body ached that he ever remembered. The last week had been a manic process to fix the old trappers' hut so it was livable and provide a watertight and a rodent free location for storage of their food. The first goal had been completed, the second might take a little longer as last night's shower of rain showed from the small puddles on the floor and the third was a constant problem; the mice and rats ruled the hut. During the week they had put together a small, fenced compound for the horses, made from thin tree trucks and limbs, all cut by hand, axe and saw.

He looked over to where Bryan still slept. Harry was a bit worried as his companion had lagged on the last couple of days, clearly protecting the arm that had been cut and had poorly healed. He complained of headaches and stiffness in his neck and shoulders, the odd contraction slurred his words for a few minutes.

'Feel a bit crook. Must have twisted something in me neck, stiff and hurts like hell,' he complained at the end of the day.

After relieving a full bladder against a gum tree, Harry re-entered the hut and blew on the few coals left in the old pot belly cooker that sat in the corner, adding some dry bark and a few thin sticks, blowing as the coals became a fire. He added a handful of smaller split wood and shut the top lid, waving his hands around to disperse the smoke, then putting a kettle on the top of the stove, hot water for a nice cup of tea.

Once the water boiled, he poured two cups, letting the water steep the tea leaves. He walked to the other bunk and shook Bryan on the shoulder, producing a low groan of pain. Bryan stiffened, arching his neck as he grabbed his jaw, the sound of his teeth grinding. His eyes flew wide, but as much as he tried, he could not say a word. His mouth was locked solid.

Harry held him still on the low bunk, wiping the sweat from Bryan's brow. He could feel his muscles tightening, releasing and tightening again in a cruel rhythm. Slowly the spasms eased, allowing Bryan to lay back on the bunk, his eyes closed, his breathing ragged and forced. Harry was lost. What was this illness? He could not think. All he knew is than he had to get the fever down, so he found a cloth, put it in cold water, then used it to cool Bryan's head.

An hour later, a second spasm struck as Harry was outside. He heard a muffled scream, then nothing, as if the sound had been cut off. He rushed inside the hut to see the same reaction as before, the same twisting of muscles and tendons in the neck and face. He looked closely and saw that the jaw was again locked shut and he suddenly remembered what he had been told by his mum on what had made his uncle a cripple. Harry knew what the affliction was that was affecting his companion, and it was frightening. He placed the cool cloth on Bryan's forehead, almost as a calming action for himself. He knew from what he had been told he could do nothing to help. It was all up to Bryan.

Chapter 7

Charly enjoyed the early morning, the sun casting long shadows across the plain between the two sand dunes. The cool of the air was to be enjoyed before the sting of the sun was felt as they moved along. She smiled at the land they were travelling through, a land not all that far from where she grew up, but a land she had never visited. Everyone called it the desert country, making out it was endless sand, more sand and nothing but sand. Well true, there was sand, but also lots of life, spinifex grass, the small stands of mulga and lots of lizards and other creatures that emerged in the cool of the night.

It was also surprising that there might be some life, as it was a desert, for there was no water; no small creeks, no shady billabongs. Simply no water to drink, to wash or refresh the camels. Mary showed where water could be found if they were desperate; they would dig near a small stand of mulga, slowly letting the water seep into the bottom of the hole. Water to survive rather than enjoy. On the fifth evening they stopped near an outcrop of pinkish rock, hard and rounded. At the base was a small seep surrounded by rocks and a stand of tight mulga.

The seep was busy with bird life, small finches darting out of the stand of mulga and stunted eucalypts to take a drink before flitting back to the protection of the leaves and branches. The place was stunningly peaceful, it provided an overwhelming calm that even exceeded the billabongs near Charly's old home.

'This place is sacred to my people. This is the only water for many days walk,' was all Mary said. She demanded they only took enough water to cover the basic thirsts and provided the camels with a small amount to recover some of the fluid they had used from their stores in the hump. Humps on all the camels had noticeably shrunk in the five days in the hot sandy country. They'd camped under the stand of mulga that night, and Charly noticed that Mary was withdrawn, almost silent, as if this place held a special importance to her.

Charly smiled as she walked at a steady pace. The lead for Sheeba was in her hand, the pace suited to the distance-eating stride of the camels. It was the eighth day since they'd left the billabong; she was amazed how she had quickly adapted to this form of travel. Riding a camel was now as easy as riding her beloved Misty. Walking, which was what they did for a little of each day depending on the terrain, was an activity that had become natural. The first few days were unbearable, spending much of each day on Sheeba, but very quickly, her youth and her determination expanded her stamina.

The burns on her legs and body had quickly healed, thanks to the daily application of the mixture of honey and native ointment which had killed the infections and stimulated the growth of her skin and flesh. The fresh, pink skin was becoming tougher, her body was renewing. Charly was beginning to move away from her past; in mind and body she was becoming a new person.

That morning, Abdul announced that they were less than two days travel from their next stop, a telegraph station on the line from north to south of the country. Charly watched as Abdul led his camel up the sandy face of the next large dune. Mary had pushed her way forward, moving quickly to keep up with her husband so they reached the crest together. They looked westward, both pointing with one arm, maybe three or four points of the compass in difference.

In the distance was a large rock outcrop, the largest they had encountered since leaving the billabongs. Between them and this outcrop were a handful of dunes, becoming smaller into the distance. The country changed after the outcrop, becoming more undulating, a soft, grey-blue-green colour hanging over the land.

Mary was pointing north of the outcrop, while Abdul's hand pointed slightly south of the same rock mass.

'I am not denying your extraordinary skills with that wonder of science in your hand,' stated Mary, indicating the brass encased compass Abdullah was holding, an object pilfered in the same engagement where he obtained the old rifle. 'But if you stay on that heading we will be travelling north once we reach the wire by some many hours, if not a full day.'

'I ask Allah to be kind and merciful in my understanding of your capabilities and knowledge,' argued Abdul. 'It is not normal to know your location and where we go, as you say, my beloved. My knowledge is in my hand, I say we follow what it tells me.'

'My man of great knowledge, a walker of many sands,' Mary intoned soothingly. 'While the thing in your hand that directs you is clever and knowing, I simply follow what the sands and the night sky's say. They have been here much longer.'

Abdullah wavered in the calmness of her response. While respectful, Mary's words mocked the technology in his hand, mocked the item made by man, while she relied on her oneness of the world around her.

'It would madden me if I added to our travel,' snorted Abdul in disgust, then chuckled to himself as much as anyone around him. 'We will follow your feelings, my beloved, better to enjoy the peace of our love than be reminded of my failings if such a happing should occur.'

Wazir arrived behind Charly as the interchange between the two on the crest of the dune was completed. Wazir smiled at what was a not an uncommon argument between Abdullah and his beloved wife, knowing, as did Abdul, that Mary had a way to find the correct path.

'We have been wavering to the south for some days,' Mary said without malice. While the compass was accurate, she knew the land well – she had been here as a child. 'The dunes in this land will do this easily, my dearest husband.'

Abdul smiled. It was a conversation that had been held before with other local men who had worked for him. The dune appeared to run evenly, but had crests without striking character and a person's course in the flats between them could be subtly changed without knowledge. It was a peaceful and beautiful land, but held great dangers for those who moved through it without caution.

'We go to the north of the outcrop, I expect we will camp in its shadow one more night,' said Abdul as he gave a curt tug on his camel's lead, starting the caravan on to its destination.

The small train of camels slowly descended the sand dune and commenced the crossing of the flat land. The sun caused the usual discomfort, the water was now low, they drank only enough to keep a wet mouth. Charly pulled the tail of the long cloth that was wrapped around her head over her lower face, tucking it into a fold near her ear. While not a turban as worn with such pride by Wazir or Abdul, it was worn in a manner to shield the head and face of the sun and sand.

She had rapidly adopted the clothing as worn by Abdul and his band. It was cool, loose and protective of the sun and sharp vegetation. She had discarded her britches and shirt after one day, finding them uncomfortable and hot. The clothes of her previous life were packed deeply into the leather pannier on Sheeba's back.

As they moved towards the outcrop, the spinifex became thicker, punching its needle points into their legs when they were forced to cut a path through the thicker sections. The camels were disinterested in this discomfort, they had skin as hard leather, suited to travel in this vegetation where horses or cattle suffered.

After finishing the midday meal and allowing the two men to complete their adherence to their faith, Abdul made a decision.

'We ride when we reach the next area of spiny grass.' He paused, looking at Wazir picking a few last tips of the spines from his legs. 'It will add the load on the camels but we must protect our bodies, and likely increase our pace.'

The final point had become an issue. Their pace had slowed to almost nothing as they passed through the spinifex on the last two areas. They would never reach the intended location for their evening camp at this rate. So they walked the camels to the next area of spinifex, mounted and traversed the long grasses with a great deal more comfort and speed.

By early evening they arrived at the chosen location: another small soak in the foot of the large rock outcrop, shaded by tall eucalypts. The sandy soils and spiny grass had ended a few hours before as they entered the start of a wooded area shadowed by the tall rocks, native grasses becoming commonplace. As the evening meal was concluded and chores finished – a percentage of these works demanded by Charly, claiming she was part of the team, not simply an outsider being shown a path to be rescued – the talk turned to arriving at the telegraph station.

'Charly, we need to choose what will become of you tomorrow,' stated Abdul, a tone of a father and also of a leader of the group. 'The law demands one thing, our feelings for you demand another, so what will it be?'

Charly knew what he meant. He would need to provide the alert of the fire at Hendricks Flats, the loss of the buildings and loss of life. The law demanded this, but also demanded that Charly be handed to the authorities to be cared for until family could be found. While this would not happen at the telegraph station, the information of her status would need to be sent.

Charly sat quietly. Her position was now causing compromise on those around her, causing a breaking of law; this was something she could not accept.

'The person who lived by the river died some weeks ago. I am not her,' said Charly with almost cold emotions. The reality of what she was saying were the thoughts and feelings she had felt for some time. 'I am Charly, nothing more. If you plan to announce my survival, I will not be found in your company. I will be gone; you will not find me.'

An unnerving silence descended the group of people. Wazir listened with great interest, despite having the least invested in the young woman. For Abdul, Charly had become as a daughter, her inner strength, her fighting spirit impressed him greatly, but for Mary, Charly was part of her, she felt an interweaving of spirits, there was something she could not put her finger on, but it was almost frightening.

None of the three wanted to cause pain to the fourth member of the group, but they still were required to overcome the issue spoken about by Abdul earlier. None could find an answer needed.

'Do any of you know my name other than the one name what I have told you?'

Three people shook their heads in almost unison.

'You found me, but you did not know where I am from. I am simply a person you rescued.'

More nods but now a little confused.

'So if I am not there, who would know if I was not with you?' Charly continued then stopped as Wazir finished her comment.

'And so you will leave us and re-join later, taking one camel and stores to live in the wilds for the time it takes for us to deliver the supplies to the telegraph station.'

Charly smiled. Yes, the suggestion was not totally as she had planned but the concept was accurate.

Abdul leaned back on the pack he had been sitting on, deep in thought. Mary knew that she was required by custom of his world to remain silent, allowing Abdul to make the final decision. He was concerned that they would abandon Charly, leaving her to fend for herself. This he could not accept; he had lost his family once, he would not tolerate it again.

'Charly, you have worked and helped us, but we have not been able to pay you a wage, this is unacceptable to the teachings of the prophet,' Abdul laid out in quiet words. 'As I have not the gold, and have not entered into an agreement with you, I am obligated to give you a gift of thanks.'

As before when Charly spoke, silence followed his words, the three waited to hear what he had determined was a suitable gift.

'Sheeba and her calf are yours. I will provide you later with a certificate of ownership. You are also entitled to her equipment and sufficient goods as required for you to arrive at the next town.'

Charly was stunned, unable to comprehend what Abdul had done. His camels were as his children, and he had just given one away.

'And if our paths cross again, I will be pleased to offer you and your camels meaningful employment, as your skills are of an acceptable nature.'

Abdul was finished. He stood, tears in his eyes as he walked from the camp. He walked over to where the camels were hobbled, giving Sheeba a rub under her chin, offering her few small sweet treats.

Mary rose and sat next Charly, gave her a small hug and then sat back. One hand stayed on her arm, providing the connection between them. Charly looked over the Wazir, he gave a couple of nods, providing agreement of what was said, providing agreement to an equal. Charly returned her gaze back to the person beside her, feeling the connection.

'Young lady, you will always be part of me, the land had spoken to me. Meet us in two days. Travel north of the telegraph station. There is a large billabong fed by a small river. Look for a rocky outcrop that sits partly into the billabong a short distance to the west of where the telegraph line runs. This is where our paths will again cross.'

Conversations thus ended. It had been a long day and Wazir and Charly climbed into their beds lying on the ground, slipping into sleep without effort. Mary rose and walked out to find Abdul, finding him going from camel to camel, providing his affections. The nearly full moon provided a silvery light that cast soft shadows on the ground from the overhanging trees. She took his hand and placed it on her breast in invitation, then pulled him close in a display of love. She stepped back, drawing him away from the camp, imparting her desire with her unspoken action. Abdul smiled in knowing response.

'Come, my man, you are deserving. I have something for you,' murmured Mary as she calmly walked to a secluded section of trees.

Their morning departure was somewhat delayed by the preparations decided upon the night before, a delay that did not cause consternation as it would be a shorter day's travel to their destination. Supplies, water and equipment as required were transferred to two panniers. One camel was checked, and all her harnesses either repaired or replaced with new. Abdul was in a special mood. The night's activity was the cause, reviving his love and appreciation of Mary's support of him.

Charly was the first to leave, knowing she had two days travel before finding her place to rest. As she was about to mount Sheeba, Wazir walked over, reached out and provided a handshake. He pulled her close, offering the briefest of hugs. An action that may have exceeded what his beliefs allowed but Charly had allowed him to develop a respect and consider her as he would his favourite sister.

He released her, proud to have met this person in his life. 'You will be a great camel master, young sister. I will enjoy working alongside you.'

He handed her his side-arm, a short-barrelled Remington revolver in a holster with a flap, which she slung over her shoulder, for the holster to ride low under her armpit. He had offered to show her how to use the weapon, but she had assured him she previously had been shown to use a handgun, one that was lost in her home.

'Your words are powerful, and your gift thoughtful. I am thankful to the kindness of my brother.'

He walked away as Mary stepped forward, providing a warm hug, then handing her a rolled sheet of paper. 'A rough map and instructions. Be calm, the land will lead you. Listen to what you hear.'

She stepped away as Abdullah stood before them, he handed Charly a sheet of paper, the certificate of ownership for Sheeba and her calf. He smiled; a beaming happy smile split his face.

'So, young lady, you said you have no name. If anyone asks, you are Charly, Charly Khan, my daughter, the beloved child of Abdullah Rahman Khan.' He looked at Mary. 'Yes, my beloved, our daughter. Okay?'

Charly was shocked, wordless at what was just said. She provided a stunned nod of her head before a tear settled in the corner of each of her eyes.

'Okay, Charly, time to go. I hope we meet again soon.'

Charly turned, no words required. She mounted Sheeba, pulled the lead that attached the muzzle of the calf and slowly rode away from camp. Her life was now in her hands, the issues of the past caused this necessity, but she knew she could survive. She had overcome great odds before with nothing, but now, she was armed with knowledge and opportunity.

Chapter 8

C harly slowly rode through the sparse bushland, the eucalypt trees well-spaced, the distance between the next set of roots dictated by the amount of rainfall. The occasional rock outcrop provided clusters of wallaby, the occasional open areas small mobs of kangaroos. The land was raw and untouched, there were no signs of white man presence. She rode on slowly, enjoying each step Sheeba took, the squawk from a flock of the red crested cockatoos in an adjacent stand of acacias sounded as if it was if a welcome call. The large birds squawked and screaked without fear as they ripped the dead wood from the trees, chasing fat white grubs.

Charly smirked, knowing that these grubs were favourite food for the local people, the birds enjoying being the first to a good harvest. The time with no other humans in her company, even the three she had relied on after being found, was calming. She was in a perfect environment, herself and only creatures that meant no harm.

By the evening she found a small area of grass for the camels to eat, a few rocks on the edge of the clearing to set a protected camp from a chilly evening wind. The first drops of rain had fallen from a few dark scudding clouds during the afternoon, a change in the weather. A rare blast of cooler air and showers, not the preferred accompaniment for her first night alone, however not a serious concern either.

Charly collected a large supply of dead limb wood, disturbing some smaller lizards. She was tempted to turn one or two of the larger one's into her evening meal, but as she lifted the limb to dispatch the first small reptile, she froze, unable to kill. A strange feeling flowed over her, as if the land asked that she respected the world around her. She kicked some sand in the lizard's direction as it was trying to hide beside a rotten log, it scuttled away in the sand and climbed the closest old eucalypt tree and hid in the higher branches.

The meal ended up a plate of dry damper, two slabs of preserved meat and a few spicy pickled vegetables. It lacked the usual flavours she had enjoyed; the spicy curries and stews made by Mary or Wazir, a little flavoured rice or fresh damper. As she finished the plain fare, another shower blew past, rattling the upper branches of the small trees, a few drops and another flush of colder air.

She pulled a blanket around she shoulders, dissatisfied that she did have not having a warm coat or jumper to snuggle into. She would need to obtain one if she continued with this life. While being uncomfortable, she was content, sitting as the last of the light disappeared, watching the odd spark lift into the sky before dying.

Finally as the night pulled closer, she stood, piling a small mountain of limb wood on the fire, wanting just a little warmth before she rolled into her swag for the night. The flames leaped high as the dry wood caught alight, a trail of sparks rising upwards to the gap in the clouds where a few stars glinted for the first time that evening. The flame cast an orange light around the small clearing, highlighting the trunks of the trees, the rocks and the rounded shape of her camels.

Charly noticed a set of eyes reflecting in the fire light, flitting left then slowly moving closer, then moving back and around slightly before coming closer again. A grin spread on Charly's face as she recognised the owners of those eyes: a dingo, the native dog, a very cautious and wary animal. It must be waiting till she was asleep before entering the camp to steal some food. Charly cut another slab of preserved meat and hurled it towards the dingo, landing three quarters of the way with a soft thud on the sandy soil. The dingo did the usual reaction and jumped away as it hit the ground, slowly moving back, now into the firelight. It was cautious, its nose sniffing, checking what the object was.

The dingo's yellowish fur glistened in the firelight, its long nose twitching, its ears standing up, listening for any threat. Suddenly it lurched forward, grabbing the slab of meat and bolting from the clearing, disappearing into the soft light from the waning moon through another break in the clouds. It left behind a small puff or two of dust, the only reminder of its short stay. A little while later, a mournful howl sprang out of the trees a little distance from the camp, Charly smiled again. The howl a thank you, she thought, as she bent over the last of the fire, sitting a billy of water on the coals to heat and boil for her last pleasure of the day, a hot cup of tea.

At the sound of roiling water in the billy, she used a stick to lift the handle, removing the billy from the fire. A small amount of dried tea leaves was dropped over the still bubbling water, stirring it with the stick. After a few minutes, after allowing the leaves to sink to the bottom of the narrow metal container, then giving the billy a few taps with the stick to settle the last few leaves to the bottom of the metal container, she poured the tea into an old enamelled cup. She smiled at the simple art of tea making, down to using two sticks to hold the billy, one to lift and one to tilt the small blackened pot.

She thought of the trick her brothers had shown her of swinging the billy around in a full arch over her head half-a-dozen times, but the risk was a little high to be splattered with boiling water. The tea still tasted wonderful with a touch of smoky water, the highlight the tannins in the tea. It was an act of the outback, the true indulgence at the end of a long day.

After a cup or two of black tea, sweetened with a good teaspoon of sugar, Charly went out and checked the camels. Sheeba was but a few dozen paces from the fire, settled on her haunches, chewing the cud with great contentment, her calf lying beside her, safe from the interest of the local wild dogs.

Charly returned to the fire, heaping up more wood, a couple of larger limbs that would burn for many hours, before rolling into the swag, the day done, the world was at peace. Even the clouds where clearing, promising that tomorrow would be another wonderful day.

The next day did not bring any surprises, her travels continued through open bushland, the odd changes with large grassed open areas in areas of slight hollows, but in general the land did not vary. It allowed a smooth transit until she arrived at the slightly faded path beside the line of poles with a single wire stretched between them. It was just a little after midday when she turned and followed the instruction provided by Mary, riding on while munching on a slab of dry damper crust. It was clearest of days, the previous day's showers had refreshed the air, removed the dust from the atmosphere, and the sweet smells of the vegetation provided a sharp uplift to her spirits.

It had also invigorated the wildlife, the mobs of kangaroo and the occasional small flock of emu increased, rushing across the pathway, taking Charly's breath with their sudden movement. The birdlife also increased; species that lived near water became evident. Charly knew that the large series of waterholes that Mary spoke about could not be far away.

Charly rode over a slight rise, two large, roughly rounded boulders, some ten yards apart, half buried in the soil stood out ahead on the track, standing as sentinels that she would have to pass by. Charly pulled out the rough map and checked the very basic instructions, confirming the rocks were the place to turn towards the billabong, down through the slightly denser bush, now with a well-defined understory. She saw what looked like a poorly formed path, a road made by the native animals, but this appeared to be the place. She dismounted Sheeba, walking slowly down the windy track, which twisted and required her to push through tight vegetation in places as it went about a dense thicket of flowering bushes. A sweet smell filled the air as the vegetation was disturbed, the reward for her efforts.

Finally, the path opened up to the edge of the large waterhole, many times wider than the series of billabomgs she remembered from her youth. The top and bottom of the waterhole opened into small river, which would enlarge during a flood. In the north she saw the large, rounded boulders that sat down into the water, the place that Mary said they would meet her in two or three days' time. Charly gave the halter a gentle tug, lifting Sheeba's head from where the camel and her calf had been starting to graze in the grass, and leading them along the grassed bank. The grass was green and chopped very short from the grazing of the native animals. Charly noticed the grass was eaten very evenly, and not missing the clumps of grass that were sometimes pulled out of the ground when cattle grazed in these conditions, opening the ground, slowly destroying the grass cover.

As she walked close to the edge of the water, Charly observed that the grass continued a short distance into the water. She stopped and took off her boots, then walked in the shallow water with her bare feet, holding her boots in her hand. As she headed to the boulders, the growing urge to simply jump in was almost too much. The water was crystal clear, still and smelled sweet. She cupped her hand and took a sip, and it was perfect. She could not think of a better place to stay for the next two days.

She arrived at the boulders within the hour, finding a small encampment set slightly above the water's edge, a round of stones filled with blackened charcoal and half burnt timber. The surrounds of the encampment backed onto three of the larger boulders, providing a good-sized area protected on three sides for weather and wind. Charly unpacked Sheeba, put on her hobbles and let her and her calf loose. She knew they would not stray far, there was far too much green grass and fresh water only a few steps away.

Charly lifted the holstered revolver off her head and shoulders, laying it next to the small pack of her camp goods, doubting that she would need it here. She then dug out her dirty clothes, piling them in a small heap to be washed, not that there was much, her old shirt and trousers, a spare overshirt, a few items of underwear and worn socks.

But first she knew she would need to prepare a fire. Charly collected an amount of fallen limb wood, stacking it next to the old fire pit. This time, the distance she was required to wander to find the wood was a little greater. It quickly became obvious that this camp was used on a regular occasion by other travellers, especially as she found a wider and well-worn path from the camp, looping behind the back of the granite boulders and heading back towards the telegraph line.

The fire was soon set, and the travel worn spare clothes removed from the saddlebag before being taken into the water and soaked. After a light scrub with the hand brush and then rinsing, she lay the spare overshirt on the edge of a large rock, allowing it to dry in the sun. The rest of the clothes she hung on a rope that she had strung between two trees. Once that was completed Charly re-entered the water enjoying the tingle of the fresh water on her body.

She pulled the dune coloured kameez and shalwar off herself and gave them a good scrubbing; they stunk near as much as her beloved camel. They needed cleaning as much as she did. After a second scrubbing and a good rise, the clothes were thrown onto the rocks to dry. Charly then scooped up handfuls of the wet sand that were at her feet, scrubbing her skin, feeling the dust and dirt from the last week on the trail peel away.

The tender fresh skin of her ankles, legs and back were treated with care, the sensitive skin still letting her know it would take a little more time to become hardened. Dipping her head below the water, she scrubbed her black hair, the dust and windblown sand washing out. She was clean and felt refreshed. She swam into deeper water, diving under, enjoying the cool of the deeper water, the breaststroke she had been taught by her mother long ago still able to keep her afloat.

After some fifteen minutes she swam back to the rocks, climbing onto the granite boulder, letting the sun and the heat on the rock dry her off before she put the spare overshirt on. Charly then hung the remaining wet clothes on the drying line. An armful of wood on the fire allowed her to prepare a billy of water for a refreshing cup of afternoon tea, to be enjoyed with a slab of damper, covered in sticky sweet jam.

As she finished the last of her damper, Charly sat on the boulder at the water's edge watching a kingfisher diving into the water on the other side of the waterhole. A steaming cup of tea beside her, her mind relaxed with the peace of the surrounding around her. Her knees were drawn up under her chin, the kameez overshirt pulled slightly over her knees, the rest of her legs bare, allowing her to enjoy the cool air blowing around her lower body.

She slowly ran her fingers on the scars around her ankles, happy that they had finally healed enough to withstand the chafing from the edges of her boots. They still hurt a little, the skin tingled where the fresh skin was puckered. She felt the scars on the sides of her thighs, pulling the kameez back to her waist and looking at the red and purple patches of healed but scarred skin. She would never be the beautiful woman she'd dreamed of only a few months back. She feared that no man would ever look at her again. The area around her waist not too bad, though she knew her buttocks were slightly scarred. But the front had survived as had her stomach and chest.

She closed her eyes and listened to the squawk of the crazy galahs and parrots, the chirping by the small honeyeaters from the flowering bush just behind the boulders, when the sound of metal on metal, the sound of men, shattered the peace of the waterhole.

Charly quickly yanked her kameez down to cover her lower body. She turned her head to listen. The sound came from up the main access track, a steel ring on a halter or harness; the unmistakable sound of a human about to enter her space. Where were her pants? She saw them hanging on the line at the back of the camp where the trees started. She could not get them in time to put them on, but she saw then what she really needed; it was in the leather holster laying on her small pack near the fire.

Charly jumped of the rock, sending the enamel cup clattering down the rock and falling into the water with a splash. A stain of tea slowly dribbled down the rock, where it met the water of the billabong. The noise of enamelled metal on rock echoed sharply through the trees as she ran across the short grass, snatching the holster from the pack. The sounds of the visitors to her camp were approaching as she backed away, bumping into Sheeba who was still laying on the ground.

Charly pulled the Remington from its leather home. A sudden fear struck her: was it even loaded? She flung the holster and belt to the ground behind her. Charly almost felt naked, the kameez being the only thing that covered her, falling to halfway down her thighs. Her legs bare, the breeze blowing the bottom of the material. She flicked her black wavy hair back over her shoulder with her free hand. She wanted her face unobstructed, her eyes clear.

Two men walked into view, leading a string of three camels. Charly quickly put the revolver behind her back, out of sight, holding it at the ready if required. Sheeba stood behind her, nearly knocking her off her feet. Charly took a couple of quick steps to recover her balance. When she looked up, the men had stopped, looking at the camp, then at her. The men were scruffy, roughly dressed in filthy clothes. Their hair hung long under their hats, greasy and unkempt.

'Well, lookie here, Herman. That be one good looking camel, and the boy a fair sight too,' said the man standing further back, handing the lead to the first man. 'He might be providing some good sport, I thinking.'

'Ya needing to be watching them Arabs, they ride funny I been told,' replied the first one, spitting the wad of chewing tobacco to the ground. 'Do ya speak English, boy?'

The second man walked closer. He carried an odour of a person who likely never washed, typical of a dry country prospector. Charly had a memory of the rough men who sometimes had travelled through where she had grown up, men with little kindness, unconcerned of the consequences as they took anything they wanted.

'Can we share your fire, boy? Stay in your camp for a bit?' he asked with a snigger, clearly alluding to something else more sinister. 'What do ya say? Ya can be doing with a little company... and a nice bit of conversation.'

'No, I do not need company, so please leave,' replied Charly sharply as she could. A tremor in her voice betrayed her. 'C-camp down the way, leave me alone.'

'Why, Herman, I be guessing this one's a sheila by the sound of that voice. Lots more fun than a boy,' he said, taking another few steps forward.

'Stop right there, mister. Don't come any closer.'

'And why would I be doing that, girl?' he snarled. 'Whatcha gunna do to stop me?'

Charly brought the revolver from behind her back and pointed the short barrel at him. The barrel wobbled slightly unsteady in her sweaty grip.

'I said stop. And l-leave me alone.' Again her voice trembled, showing her weakness.

The man smiled, as if the added threat was to his liking. He dropped his head as he stared at Charly's legs, slowly moving up till he reached the bottom of the kameez, then continued his perusal, pausing briefly at her groin, then slowly lifting his eyes, stopping at her chest, then lifting until he looked in her eyes.

'It's not in ya, girl. Your voice tells me so.' He laughed in an evil tone. 'I coming to get ya, and you can't stop me.'

He stepped forward again. The other man had followed down the track behind his companion; only a few steps behind but off to her right side, to close her in a well-practiced trap. Charly had two options, one frightened her, the other horrified her.

As the men approached, only ten feet away, the disgust of the desires of men rose in her mouth, the acid of revulsion sputtered up her throat.

Charly placed her second hand over the grip of the revolver, a forefinger now on the trigger. She pulled back the little lever behind the cylinder, cocking the weapon.

'I am telling you, stop. I will… back off and leave me alone.'

The man closest to Charly giggled. 'The front's mine, Herman, you get to enjoy the back.'

His words had just left his mouth when Charly dropped her aim and pulled the trigger as she had been shown. A slow, even tightening of the finger, not a jerk that would spoil the aim. The revolver proved it was loaded. The .44 bullet travelled the very short distance, cutting a rough hole through the top of the first man's boot and then cutting a second equally ragged hole through the sole, cleanly removing his middle toe as it passed. The bullet imbedded itself deeply into the sand.

The man screamed, the shock that young woman had the gumption to fire the weapon swiftly replaced by the pain in his foot. He grabbed his freshly perforated boot, the foot still inside, jumping on the other foot in agony. A red liquid oozed from the both the holes; an unwelcome object jammed between his remaining toes.

'Ya stupid bitch, what the hell did ya do that for… Arrr! Ya insane, crazy bitch. Me foot, the stupid bitch shot me foot?!' he screamed, till he tripped and fell on his face with a thud.

Herman saw his chance. He moved quickly, noticing that Charly was preoccupied with his companion's antics. He jumped forward and grabbed Charly's wrist that was holding the revolver, forcing it down. He was about to reach around and remove the revolver from her hands when a loud angry rumble sounded from behind. Herman looked up, but before he could react, a wet, slobbery mouth closed on his arm. Foamy liquid dribbled, from the camel's lips. As the teeth closed down on Herman's arm, a red patch grew as Sheeba teeth gripped his arm, closing her mouth, her teeth chopping through the skin and flesh.

Herman screamed, his scream much louder than his friend, who was now backing away, limping badly as he grabbed the lead to their three camels. Herman screamed again, frantically calling his companion to help, but he lost his lost grip on Charly's arm and then let go. Sheeba gave her head a small shake. Herman's arm followed, increasing the wound, increasing the agony.

'Hush, Sheeba, open up, come on, open up,' said Charly, using the words she used when she'd checked Sheeba's teeth during their travels.

Sheeba's mouth slowly opened. Herman fell to his knees, grabbing his torn arm with his uninjured hand, holding it tight to his chest. Blood flowed down the filthy sleave where it collected in his elbow, dripping onto the ground in front of him.

Charly re-cocked the revolver, pointed at the ground and fired, the bullet kicking sand into Herman's face. Herman flinched, lifting his head, his face grey, fearing what the woman would do next.

'I said, leave me alone. So get up and piss-off, or the next one will be a lot higher,' Charly sad. This time the tremor was gone, her voice cold as she cocked the Remington again.

Herman squirmed backwards as quickly as his damaged arm would allow and then hauled himself to his feet. He ran after his companion, still holding his damaged arm. His companion was already leading their three camel's back up the pathway past the granite boulders towards the telegraph line. Herman stumbled a few times in his haste, but each time quickly got to his feet again, running low, fearing she would change her mind and shoot again. He soon joined his companion who was limping a little less, both men happy to leave the mad woman and her crazy camel.

As they disappeared up the path, Charly sagged to the ground. Sheeba lowered her head and let out a low rumble, the camel's usual comment of contentment. Charly reached up and patted Sheeba's head. She had just been saved by her four-legged companion.

Charly did not move for some time, staring at the top of the path, the fear of their return not leaving her mind until the arrival of evening light became noticeable. Charly slowly stood and stretched her legs. She had collapsed to the ground an hour or so before. It was enough time to slow her racing mind, find where she needed to strengthen herself to survive such incident in the future. She let the thoughts ferment into an understanding: this would happen again. Given what she planned to do in the future, operating her own camel team, it was to be expected she would be threatened, be in jest or intent. Charly knew that she needed to find an answer to one real problem, how to manage the unwanted attentions from the likes of men who wished her harm.

She stood, noticing that the fire had burnt down. First, she picked up the holster, lifting the strap over her head. It would always be with her now. She reloaded the two cartridges she had fired, noting that she would need to keep a regular check if the revolver was loaded, not make a desperate guess at the moment it was required. An armful of wood thrown into the coals and the fire sprung to life. Sheeba's calf moved closer to the camp from where it had been grazing a little way back up the banks of the waterhole, laying down next to her mother. Their company was reassuring. They might look ungainly but she trusted their sharp ears and reactions to things being out of place.

Pulling her clothes from the line, now dry and soft, she knew she needed to be more cautious when she washed and cleaned clothes when alone. Had the men arrived half an hour earlier when she was swimming, she would have been unable to respond.

Charly pulled on her baggy pants, enjoying the last of the evening air before the temperature fell. She was ready for the night as she prepared to make her evening meal, suddenly realising that her enamelled cup was in the water, waist deep at the front of the rock.

Annoyed at her carelessness, she stripped of her baggy trousers and waded into the water, holding the kameez high around her chest. As she found the cup with her toes, she now understood that the kameez had to either come off or get wet, her irritation at herself increased. She was not going to take that part of the clothing off.

She finally put her toe through the metal handle and slowly walked back until she could lift it with her foot, balancing with one hand on the boulder. She was still holding the bunched up kameez in her other hand, but as she reached out to grab the cup from her toes, she lost the grip on the cloth and the bottom of it dropped into the water. She looked at the wet kameez, shook her head, wondering if she could have made the process any more complex, all because of her fears, and uncertainties. She walked up to the pile of dry clothes, stripped off, her annoyance dissolving any inhabitation before she dressed in the fresh and dry kameez and the pair of baggy trousers she had left before rescuing the cup.

After quickly preparing, then completing her meal, the first fears crept up to her. The darkness, the sounds of the night, though ones she knew so well, suddenly held new threats. It would be a long night.

The following morning Charly awoke with a start, the first rays of the sun trickling over the tops of the trees, touching her face as she slept leaning against one of the rounded boulders. As she opened her eyes, she was surprised, as she had been determined to stay awake during the night. The fears had taken her mind as she rolled into her swag, every sound becoming someone sneaking up to take her.

She had dragged the swag from the edge of the fire, placing it into the small recess between the granite boulders, feeling slightly safer but her mind still had refused to sleep. Now as she awoke, the knowledge she had been asleep for many hours, untouched and unharmed provided a further feeling of shame and foolishness. She had to sleep sometime, but what she had done on the previous night was not going to work. She needed to consider her welfare as well as her obvious needs.

Charly stood, stretching out the stiffness, then rolled up the swag and carried it back to where it had originally been located next to the fire. Tonight, this is where she would sleep, she decided, dropping the swag where it had been previously. At least it would be warm and she would not feel so stiff from the cold when she awoke. She knew that she would have to rely on her camels to alert her to unwelcome strangers, but in any case, in the future she would rarely find granite boulders that provided such protection on the trail. After re-lighting the fire, she made a hot meal as breakfast, with a cup or two of hot tea. She ate slowly, she was in no hurry, as she was staying in the camp for one or more days.

She passed the remainder of the morning checking the camels, rubbing them down in the water to clean their hides of all manner of burrowing insects, dirt and other debris. Sheeba and her calf enjoyed the process, though for Charly, she and her clothes were wet through yet again. As she led the two camels out of the water, she understood that she could do a number of things at the same time, clean the camel, clean herself and her clothes, a way to limit her exposure to risks of being caught out.

By mid-afternoon, Charly climbed onto the rock again and sat for some time looking across the billabong, thinking on her future. Then she heard the clank of metal on metal, again the sounds of steel rings on a camel's head harness. Charly pulled herself to her feet, and climbed down off the rock, pulling the Remington from the holster, giving the loaded cylinder a quick check, before placing it back in its leather home. If the men had returned, this time there would only be one outcome.

As she waited, the fear rose again, the bitter taste was back in her mouth. She would need to quash her fears if she was to survive.

The first movement through the trees showed two people walking, then a third, leading a string of camels. Charly was terrified that the two from yesterday had a friend. Three was too much for her and Sheeba to overcome.

Then the first person in the group stepped around the corner of the boulder and there stood Abdullah Rahman Khan in all his glory, with a huge smile and jaunty tilt of his head. Mary gently pushed him forward. Wazir followed, leading the caravan of camels.

Charly was safe, her people had arrived. They were her new family, and she was determined not to let them go again.

Chapter 9

Charly dropped the canvas carry bags that held her personal travel items on the floor of the back verandah of the building, leaving a small cloud of dust. Dust that had travelled with her from many places in the last four weeks she had been on the trail. Dust that had entered every part of the clothing she wore, dust that caused a small cloud down the front of her as she unbuttoned the leather vest that had provided a small amount of protection to her clothes, and the Remington in the shoulder holster.

It had been four weeks since she had slept in a bed, four weeks since she had a soak in steaming hot water, four weeks since a less than warm beer, actually any beer.

She grinned slightly as she pushed open the door. This was the life of a cameleer, the life she had chosen two and a bit years prior, when she agreed to the terms required to work for Abdullah and Mary Khan.

A life then with just one camel and her calf, in employment; now with enough camels to run two caravans of her own, with men to care for them. A life she so loved every day when on the trail.

She pushed the door open and entered into a large, timber floored room, bare in decoration. The few occupants, all men, stood with their backs to her. The smell was uncomfortable, a mix of dried sweat and stale beer, a smell that had soaked deeply into the bare timber of the floor and panelling on the walls. The concentration of the occupants was fixated on one place, the place that one item was commonly sold and consumed: the long timber bar. Charly had opened the door to the one building in the town that could provide the three things she had so missed for four weeks: a bed, a bath and a beer. Those three may not be in that order.

Charly walked slowly, with deliberate confidence over to the bar. The man who watched her enter sat on a hard stool at the door to his small office, ready to provide another glass to the men facing him when it was indicated by word or a raised hand. He knew Charly well, she was a regular and good customer, caused no disturbance, and paid with hard coin on time, every time. He had no dispute with the young woman, though he was sure the same could not be said for the others in the room, most who had never met a camel driver, especially a female camel driver and a young, good-looking female camel driver at that.

He smiled as he left his seat, the timber well-loved and polished due to the cloth of his britches. He had no doubt that the next few minutes would lighten the day, as generally happened when Charly arrived in his establishment. He stood expectantly in front of her as she reached the bar, standing between two men who were unaware of her approach, both equally engrossed in the glass in their hands and its contents.

'Giday, Baz. Usual room, some hot water in the tub and a nice glass of your finest, please.'

Baz Murphy smiled as he turned and reached for the key to Charly's usual room, one rarely used by other patrons even when the hotel was full.

'What the hell is that smell?' said the man beside her. He turned and looked Charly up and down in disgust. He did not comprehend that the person beside him had shape that was not entirely male, and in unusual clothes – only the smell and the fact he was looking at a someone coated in trail dust with a darkened sun burnt face and wavy black hair that casually hung just over the shoulders in a loose ponytail from under a sweat stained hat. The form of dress was disconcerting, but he only saw one thing.

'What in blazes is a black doing in here? Someone chuck it out before I puke,' the man said turning back to the bartender. 'You gunna do something or what, mate?'

The man on the other side of Charly also turned and looked, putting his glass down ready to assist the request of the other man. A number of the men turned and looked, a mixture of shock and annoyance. One of the local men who knew Charly well was unsurprised at the situation. Knowing the possible outcome of what was about to occur, he quickly rushed to the door, with a curt nod from the bartender as encouragement.

'Gentlemen,' said the bartender, addressing all in the room other than Charly. 'I don't want a fuss, I am sure that we don't need to cause any issues that might lead to unpleasantries.'

Charly turned and looked at the first man who had taken offence at her arrival, lifted one eyebrow in question as to his comments. She gave an unsurprised shake of her head and turned back to speak to the man behind the old wooden bar. Before she could open her mouth, another man walked behind Charly, then spoke forcibly at the bartender.

'We got rules in this part of the country. No blacks,' he said. He reached out and squeezed Charly's bottom with force to prove his point. 'And no sheilas, especially black ones. Either she goes, or the boys will have some fun. Even if they have to hold their nose as they do her over.'

As he finished speaking, a large hand settled none to gently on the man's shoulder, then squeezed with much greater force than the former had applied to a firm buttcheek in that loose pair of very dusty britches tied at the ankle.

'Be moving me hand off that piece of female appendage if you be one very smart cove,' said the owner of the hand grasping the shoulder, now forcing the shoulder down as further immense pressure was applied. 'No-one, and I truly mean no-one, in this town threatens a woman, any woman, with violence or other vile activities. Got it?'

The man whose shoulder was now screaming in pain nodded, with a vigour that unsettled his hat, allowing it to fall to the ground, showing a balding head with sparse greasy hair.

'Agreed, no question,' responded the man having his shoulder crushed, eliciting response of vigorous head nodding, this time with groans of pain.

The big hand released the shoulder and the man slumped to the floor. He slowly picked himself up. The room was silent, the man's friends had backed away, an air of fear in the room. Charly had not moved; only her right hand had made a slight repositioning, the squeeze of her well-rounded bottom had been an annoyance, but little more. She let out a sigh of exasperation as she turned to face the owner of the powerful hand. Looking up at the bright red thick square cut beard, well cropped hair, and greenish eyes. The man had an unquestionable heritage, the dark blue uniform with three large chevrons on his sleeves provided the unquestionable authority he carried.

'Let the bugger go, Macca, he obviously ain't been around these parts long enough to listen and understand the warning words from Bazz.'

'And you, young lady, know better than come in here. Just makes men do stupid stuff, like this fool,' growled Sergeant Angus MacDonald, the head of the local territorial police force.

He turned to the gathered throng of men.

'You blokes going to the Tamimi goldfields?' he asked them generally, receiving a few nods in return. 'Well, think yourselves lucky, it will be this dusty, but rather pleasant looking and smelling, be it after a good wash, woman who will be taking your digging gear,' he announced. 'This be Charly Khan, she'll be taking the next load of goods to the Tamimi field.'

The men looked closer, shocked at the comments by the well-muscled sergeant. One and then more of them suddenly realising she had a firearm slung under her shoulder, the holster under her left arm. Her right hand was slowly sliding the short-barrelled Remington revolver back where it belonged. They knew who the fools really were then, taking a serious risk to their wellbeing, reinforced by the sergeant's words to the man slowly regaining his composure.

'You be lucky you still have a hand, you idiot. If she blew a hole in it, I would jail you for the disturbance of the peace and make you pay for Baz to clean up the mess.' He grunted in warning. 'So git back to what you were doing and leave this one alone.'

Charly reached out and received the key to her room from Baz the bartender.

'Can you get the girls to heat me some water?' Charly asked the bartender as if nothing was unusual. 'And what about it? Can I have a beer now? Just one and I be going.'

The bartender shook his head. Normally one or two would slip over the bar, but not with present company.

Angus MacDonald cleared his throat. 'Pour me a couple in tall glasses, Baz, if you be so good and bring them outside. Stick them on my tab.' He turned to Charly. 'Right, outside, missy. You be upsetting the menfolk. Let's go and have a chat under the tree about your manners.'

The tree in question was an ancient gum tree, which for some unknown reason had not been felled as every other standing tree in what was once a small patch of bush as the town had grown. The old gum stood in the rear yard of the Imperial Hotel, or King's Pub as the locals called it. A table or two and some benches were randomly placed under the tight canopy of leaves that provided the back yard of the pub a circle of agreeable shade. Sergeant MacDonald led the way, followed by Charly without word, knowing that they had a few business details to discuss before the more personal exchanges that would inevitably follow between two persons who had developed a deep professional relationship over the years.

MacDonald picked the table furthest from another couple of people sitting under the tree and sat with his back to them. A third table had a stockman who appeared to be asleep, his head in his arms on the table, a half-finished glass of beer beside his head, the sounds of snoring occasionally heard. Charly sat on the other side of the table from MacDonald, her back to the sleeping stockman, settling in before replying to a general question on her last trip and news from the mining camp at Tamimi field.

'I've had word that you'll be bringing back a shipment on your next trip, that be right?' he asked, regarding the message that had reached him a few days before.

'So I have been told by the management at the bigger show. They asked if I could organise a bit of extra cover,' Charly replied casually, as if carrying the unprocessed gold ore and nuggets was just another load to transport.

A quick flick of his eyes stopped the discussion on the subject as one of the other hotel staff walked to the table with the two glasses of beer that were put before the policeman. MacDonald nodded his thanks, before pushing one of them over the table surface to Charly. The glass nearly tipped as the bottom stuck to some previous uncleaned semi-dried liquid. Charly grabbed the glass before it tipped over, beer splashing and adding to the sticky mass.

'Bloody oath, Macca, have some respect for the grog,' she snorted. 'Been too long to have it wasted with your lack of care.'

Charly lifted the glass to her lips and savoured the slightly warm liquid. Smacking her lips in pleasure she put the glass down, looking at MacDonald to continue the discussion.

'Tamimi field gone dry? I was told there is some bloke making sly grog.'

'Nah, that place might be dry cause it got almost no water, but there is always grog out there.' She laughed. 'Just ya don't want to be drinking it. It cleans gold better than anything I ever seen, not sure what it does with your gizzards.'

'Might head out and catch the bugger, not showing much respect to me doing what he be doing.'

'So ya want a riot? The couple of constables of yours out that way not gunna help much, closing their eyes are like they're doing now,' Charly muttered. It was well known some were aiding and abetting the sly grog market in the mining fields. 'Let them be. It keeps the blokes happy, they've got not much else in that dry windy valley.'

Charly was right, thought MacDonald, the Tamimi field was about as harsh an environment could be for a man to survive. To the northwest of their current location, a bit over a week by camel caravan, deep into the sandy desert country. Three years ago, four prospectors left the same hotel they were now drinking at the back off, one came back. Three did not, died from a desperate lack of water.

The man who returned gave most of the gold he carried for a drink. He never went back, just left a rambling story of insanity and madness, and a possible location for the treasures he carried. He only survived to tell the tale because his mates died, their dying leaving just enough water to get back. That thought drove him mad in twelve months.

But the story was out, driving a crazed stampede of the dry sands until two men found gold sitting in the sands of a windblown gully. How many died in the red desert sands looking the second time, a good dozen, maybe twenty. But while two found gold, one man also found a small spring in the sands on the edge of some rocks not far from the Tamimi field, just enough for the barest of survival. Gold was worked from the ground without water, dry blowing, techniques akin to winnowing, but the prize was a yellow metal rather than grain.

Charly had started taking supplies to the goldfield nearly six months before, an enterprise at first organised by Abdul and Mary, but the two camel caravans that Charly owned, provided a regular transport of food, equipment and occasionally passengers. They also brought the gold back, on special trips, well managed and guarded. Charly had soon taken over the regular run under her authority with agreement from Abdul and Mary, providing an opportunity for her to progress in her life.

Then two months ago, a dirty and rust coloured quartz reef was found under the surface of the sands at the head of the windblown valley, the host for the riches in the sands. The owner of the squares of ground that had the reef was instantly wealthy but had little money to prove the reef; wealthy but left with enormous issues to work it, to make it pay. A few sacks of gold in quartz had been brought out to prove it richness, but there was almost no way of transporting that amount of rock on a regular basis. The next trip by Charly would bring another shipment. This time it had been crudely sorted, ready to be sent to the mill down south by wagon to test its worth and raise much needed funds.

'Yeah, guess you be right, but I might swap over my lads, put a couple of new ones in who have better opinions of the law,' noted MacDonald, as much to himself as Charly. 'So do you think we need extra escorts?'

'Maybe on the last day or so, close to town, not out in the soft sands of the dunes, no horse will carry loads like the what the camels carry in that country.' Charly contemplated. 'The two constables will do what I need. Doing the swap over will be enough cover.'

The discussion went on from some minutes more, Charly now enjoying the second glass. She'd known it was not for Angus MacDonald, he never drank while on duty. Finally, they developed a plan to be enacted in approximately one weeks' time, allowing time to rest the camels and Charly and her two Afghan cameleers. As Charly pushed back the second glass, now empty but for the remains of a ring just below the lip, Angus suddenly cleared his throat.

'The aunties have been asking after you.'

'Where? Are they here?' asked Charly, knowing they were the older women from Mary's people, the ones who had taken her as family, taught her the secrets of how to live in the bush and respect that land and its spirit.

'Down by the river, usual place. They arrived about a week back. Emmie came up to see me. She was very insistent that I tell you they want to see you.'

'They left or still around?'

'They're not leaving till you see them, so I been told. Peeved off some of the old boys who want to get back bush, away from town,' MacDonald replied, with a slight interest in Charly's relationship with the local people and the reasons for the unusual actions of the older women.

Charly chuckled. 'Yep, that would be right, Macca. The old blokes think they make all the decisions, until the aunties have a reason and then the truth pops out who actually has the final call.'

With that information provided, MacDonald stood. As much as he would like to finally know more about this young woman, she would remain an enigma. Of Anglo-Saxon descent, but an Afghan name, a skilled cameleer and tough as he'd ever found a woman, having deep interactions with the local people who lived on the riverbank long before white man arrived – well maybe one day he would find out.

Charly watched him walk away, back to his small single-roomed police station with a stone walled jail at the rear. He was a friend, but she always was cautious, knowing that one Sergeant Angus 'Macca' MacDonald would enjoy digging deeper into her past, a past she worked very hard at keeping buried.

A movement at her side snapped her out of her thoughts. One of the staff from the hotel was standing quietly at her side. *New one*, thought Charly. Another with some form of oriental parentage from the north coast.

'The bath is ready, Mrs Charly Khan. We take your clothes and wash them when you in bath. Okay?'

Charly smiled as she stood, picking up the glasses from the wooden table, a special level of treatment as the hotel's favoured guest. Services that she paid for, but she was sure not to its full cost. The maid took the glasses carefully; the cost of breakage was unthinkable, so they were treated as precious items.

'Thank you. Say, I do not think we have met before. Are you new?'

'Yes, Mrs Charly Khan. I am new, very pleased to be serving you. You considered special with us girls,' was the instant and loud reply.

At the adjacent table, the previously sleeping stockman woke, his back to the interaction between Charly and the hotel maid, his head still on the folded arms laying on the surface of the rough wooden table. He was exhausted from weeks of being in the saddle, mustering a herd of grumpy steers to the stock yards just outside town. He had been enjoying a beer or three waiting for his companions to arrive, having been sent ahead to obtain some accommodation in the back rooms as they made the last arrangement to sell the cattle. His head jerked up from his folded arms as he heard the name, it was a first name he so had missed for last nearly three years.

The stockman slowly turned and looked at the person with the first name he knew so well, but all he saw was the back of a tallish, slim woman in a unique, very dusty matching tunic top and loose britches. She had very dark almost black hair, slightly longer than shoulder length, which flowed from under a sweat-soaked hat. The tunic top she was wore was loose, falling almost half thigh length, but he could see she was exceptionally muscular and broad shouldered. A leather holster for a revolver was slung over one shoulder in a wide leather band, the leather nearly the same colour as the tunic and just as dusty.

While the hair colour was about right, not much else was, but for the stockman, any hope of finding the young lady he'd once loved meant that he had to ask. As the maid entered the back door of the hotel building, she turned and looked back at the tree. The stockman lifted his glass to indicate he would like another. The maid acknowledged this with a quick nod of the head before entering the building.

A little while later the maid returned with the glass of beer in her hand, placing it on the table in front of the stockman, his head again resting on his folded forearms in the table surface. The stockman lifted his head, giving a word of thanks as he placed a few coins in the maid's hand.

'Tell me, please, the woman just before, at the next table with the policeman, who is she?' he asked quickly, in as disinterested tone as was possible for him to muster.

'Oh, that be Charly Khan. She important and rich. She run a real big camel transport business,' the maid said with utter pride without need of any additional coercion for the information. 'She take goods to the goldfield in the desert. She is the best camel driver in the town.'

Harry's heart sank. The Charly he'd known and so missed from his childhood would never have managed a transport business and certainly never gone within a mile of owning a camel. As he feared, the Charly from his past had died in the fire or flood in the place that gave him no joy in his heart. Harry picked up the full glass and drained it, thanking the maid again, then asked for a refill, his mind quickly moving to other problems he faced.

An hour or so later, still soaking in the bath as the water cooled, Charly lifted a leg, looking at the scars that circled both her ankles and legs, a puckered and pink ring of scarred skin that reminded of what it had taken to make her life. She snorted as she dropped her leg with a splash, happy that she was able to enjoy all the things she loved, the peace of the land, the ability to prove herself and to spend time with the beloved camels, the nearly twenty, grumpy, smelly and beautiful creatures she now owned. She laughed to herself at the madness. She now made the kind of money that her father could have only dreamed about, and with what he would have considered to be very ugly four-legged animals with humps.

She ran her hands over her body, the sensation causing a tingle in her clean skin. But she was emotionally torn. She had no lover, no man; the very concept terrified her, even if her body craved something other than business and similar professional interactions with the other side of the gender fence. Letting out an grunt of annoyance at her thoughts, she finally stood in the bath. Water cascaded from her body, and she looked at the mirror. She was slightly taller than most women, definitely more powerful in build, not particularly busty and hips not all that wide. More a bloke than a sheila. She snorted, clearing her mind as she stepped out and dried herself.

Her face, neck and arms were a deep bronzed brown, the rest of her skin was as she had been born, as those parts never saw the sun. Clothed, she was often mistaken for someone from the land of her adopted father, unclothed, well no-one saw that, but she was very very white. Laughing again she continued to dry herself and then slipped into a set of clean clothes that had not been worn since before her last trip, kept ready for her return. She would have a quick dinner and then head down to see the aunties. It was a solid hour's walk to the riverbank, but walking was what she did; it would be enjoyable.

She could smell the sweet smoke of eucalyptus leaves burning on the smouldering fire as she reached the top of the riverbank, stopping to look at the camp below. The riverbank gently sloped down to the water's edge, in places having large flat areas with fire pits of rocks that had obviously been used for camps for a long time, a very, very, long time by the local people. Seven woman sat around the fire, making talk as they fixed up the reed carry baskets they used as they moved between camps. Charly knew two or three immediately, a couple more were screened by the smoke, keeping the small annoying river insects away. Two of the women she could not remember; Charly wondered if she had ever met them before.

There were no men, this was clearly a women's only affair. This occurred when specific subjects were discussed that their culture considered to be outside the knowledge of men. But why the urgency for her inclusion? She had been brought to this camp when she first was accepted by the people due to Mary's influence, but had not been in over four months, the schedule of her works leaving little time of late, the invitations not often coming as today.

Charly called out to obtain the invitation to join the group by the fire, a critical cultural need to show respect to the older women.

'Charly girl, that you? Come sit with us old ones,' called the oldest of the women, Charly's special friend, Emmie, a close relative of Mary, a cousin, whatever that meant. 'You been missed, girl of the water dragon. Come spend time with us old crows.'

In the few minutes it took for Charly to walk down the bank and enter the ring of women sitting around the fire, Emmie had quickly spoke to the women in her native tongue, providing a quick description of Charly's position to the women who did not know her. One or two comments were returned, in a dialect that Charly could not understand, not that her grasp of the language spoken by Mary's people was great.

'Charly, cousin of mine, you know most of the other cousins from our people, but this and this auntie be from the people out in the desert. You been travelling with your camels out way from here,' said Emmie as Charly sat next to her, brushing a few sticks away that poked into her bottom.

Charly provided a respectful greeting in the local language to the strangers, and a warmer joiner to the women that she knew well.

'You been missing us last time we come and camp here, you been away too much. We miss you,' noted Emmie. It was a firm but gentle reminder that Charly should not forget her greater family.

'Sorry, Auntie Emmie, timing was wrong. The camel work keeps me too busy now, but I will never forget the land or the people of the land,' replied Charly, knowing that a respectful words were needed to re-establish the important ties.

For the next half an hour, there was more gossip between the women, who wanted to know all of Charly's exploits. At one point, the older woman on the other side poked the lower part of Charly's belly.

'You got a child in there yet?' she asked seriously. 'Got a man doing the job yet? Can't wait too long, you know.'

'No, it's… I don't have a… No I don't – can't,' stammered Charly, a little upset and hurt by the words. Sh was unable to clearly reply to the question, even though she knew it was asked without malice.

'Hey, Ginny, you be holding your tongue. Charly been treated bad, like some of them children at that mission, hey, think about that,' snarled Emmie in immediate defense.

Charly was slightly annoyed that something so painful and private to her was open discussion, but that how this group discussed matters.

'Hey, Charly, these women from the desert want to ask you something,' Emmie said, turning the conversation away from Charly's painful memories of her past. 'Something about their special places.'

'No worries, Emmie, not sure I know much about their land.'

Emmie rattled away in the other women's dialect. Charly caught an odd word, grasping it was something to do with the Tamimi mining field.

The older of the desert women asked the first question.

'They want to know if the spring near the goldfield is still giving water and has not been changed,' asked Emmie on behalf of the women from the desert country.

Charly knew it was a place sacred to them, any place with water was special, most in the deep desert lands were sacred, as that spring was known to always provide water, any time in any year. Her reply saddened the women; the spring had been dug out, a small well dropped to the full depth of the soak, into the sands that sat as a bowl in the rocks that held water.

The level of the well had dropped, even with the most careful of use, the soak just was not big enough. Even her camels were limited how much they could drink at each trip, but the levels still dropped. For the local people, its removal from their access meant they could no longer visit or hunt in that area for large parts of the year. Customs and processes going back longer than anyone could remember had suddenly been changed, taken away.

When Charly had finished answering the questions, the two desert women had tears in their eyes. The younger was silently chanting to herself and the mood in the camp had become sombre. Charly felt guilt for taking this water.

The older of the women quickly looked at Emmie, providing a sharp string of words, her tone angry. Emmie nodded, sitting quietly before speaking to Charly.

'They have no anger for you. It is not you that has done that bad thing to that spring.'

'I know that, Emmie, but I have my camels drink the water, I use more in one trip than their people in a year.'

The older woman asked Emmie what Charly had said, the reply causing a hearty chuckle before the younger of the desert people replied. Charly was at a loss as to the words, failing to understand how they would find anything that would provide a little levity; she certainly could not find anything.

'They think that your camels should be drinking all the water, then maybe they all leave and give their springs back.'

Charly knew this would never occur while there were soft yellow minerals in the rock to be dug. It was the way of white man, to take and leave nothing. The conversation had upset her to the point where she knew she had to leave. She slowly stood, turning to Emmie to pass on her words of parting. The older woman from the desert people fired a short string of words at Emmie, then at the Ginny, who had been silent for some time.

Emmie lifted her hand, in slight rebuke at all of them still sitting, however Ginny replied to Emmie's action. 'She needs to know one day. I agree with Lowetha.'

'I need to know what? Why does she know and not me?' snapped Charly, annoyed she had been left out of something others thought were important to her. 'Well, what is it? What should I know?'

Emmie let out a long sigh, indicating that Charly should sit down. Charly did not move, her response sending a message of annoyance.

'Okay. Your mother lives,' said Emmie flatly.

'I know, I saw her a month or so ago,' snapped Charly in annoyance.

'Not my cousin Mary, I mean the person who carried you. We are talking about your birth mother,' Emmie said quietly, a little concerned what the response would be.

'Sorry, ummm, you must be pulling my leg, Emmie. My mother, who went missing in the desert with my little sister, might be alive?'

'No, *is* alive, she *is* alive.'

Charly was in shock. Her mind raced. She felt as if she had been violated once more by the keeping of secrets. She turned to walk away, starting up the slope. Then she stopped and walked the dozen steps back. Her anger was now palatable; the older women knew they had failed a person they respected greatly.

'Did Mary know?' she demanded calmly.

'No. Mary never knew, and she not know now. Only me, Ginny and some the other women at this camp.'

Charly opened her mouth to reply, but said nothing. Sensing she was too angry, she walked away. This time, she kept going, she needed to think and burn off the madness in her mind. She could not think, the fact that someone that had deserted her – left her to the cruel abuse she had suffered by the hands of her father, that she believed was gone from her life forever and now she was somehow alive – had left her unable to find a suitable emotion.

It took two days before she had settled her mind, until questions developed that needed answers: where was she? What about Charly's sister? How did the aunties know with such certainty that she was alive? By the end of the day it all got too much, these questions had to be answered.

She instructed the three Afghan cameleers she employed to finish the tasks in preparation to their departure in two days' time, and Charly headed to the camp by the river. As she walked, she worked her mind through an endless number of questions that she could ask, sifting out the ones that would fail to provide the answer she craved; but how could she ask without causing any offence?

The hour of the walk passed before she realised, suddenly she was standing on the bank of the river, looking down to the camp. There was no fire, no smoke and no aunties. Charly ran the last steps down to the camp. But there was no doubt they were gone. They had left with no message, no help, gone. Charly knew in her soul there was a reason that they had left no message to her. It was the way of the old people. If she wanted to find out where her mother was living, she would get no help from the aunties.

Chapter 10

The noise, the activity, the madness of departure never changed. Ten camels fully loaded, two camel drivers, and another six men on foot, prepared to leave the Khan family transport compound that Charly Khan had originally managed for her adopted father and mother. Now it was hers. Dust rose in billowing clouds, and the usual mangy dogs that hung around the compound barked, adding to the madness.

She looked at the six men who had brokered passage with Charly and her caravan. It was safer for them to join the camel caravan, walking on foot and allowing their water and supplies to be carried by the camels. She recognised a few of them as they stood waiting, small packs on their backs; they'd been in the hotel bar when she had arrived nearly a week ago. However, the two men who'd caused the trouble that day in the bar were missing, which did not surprise her. They were likely stupid enough to try the crossing alone. Charly snorted, they would likley be picked up dead or barely alive somewhere on the well-marked track the caravan used.

Charly calmly nodded at the senior Afghan, Qadir, a cousin of her old friend Wazir, who took the halter of his camel and headed at a good pace for the open gate. While Charly usually took the lead, she had recently allowed Qadir to take to lead in the movement of the camel caravans. She pulled the end of the long, green silk scarf around her mouth and nose, tucking it into the wrapped material behind her ear to filter the dust. She had held back before leaving the compound to ensure that if an issue happened, she would be around to sort out the problem.

As the last camel left the compound, she walked behind it to close the gate and seal off the compound until they returned. As she arrived at the gate, a tall man walked through. The dust obscured his features initially, until the deep red beard informed all that it was Sergeant Angus 'Macca' MacDonald of the South Australian Police.

'Bloody dusty place. Can't see to find me own shoes,' he growled at Charly. 'I've no idea how you can like this for weeks on end.'

Charly laughed. She'd heard the words many times previously. She looked at what the sergeant was carrying under his arm. The two constables who would accompany the camel caravan where standing behind him, holding the halters of the special bred camels they used for their police work, camels supplied by one of Abdul's competitors. Both men had a small packs hanging on both sides of a small frame just behind the saddle.

'Right, thought you might find a use for this thing,' he said. He opened the leather flap and pulled out a rifle in a design she had heard about but never seen. 'Repeating rifle, fifteen or so shots before you reload.'

Charly looked at the rifle, as Sergeant 'Macca' MacDonald held it for her to take. The near new condition and well-made metal workings were striking.

'Winchester, lever action,' he said, showing how quickly it worked to reload. 'Might be useful, better than that old single barrel shotgun Abdul left you, so take it. Was left by one of my guests a month or so ago. He'll not be needing it again.'

By 'guest' Charly knew Macca meant someone he'd arrested and who had been sent to the jail down in Adelaide for a long visit. She was surprised, but knew Macca had concerns about the security and safety of the shipment they were bringing back from the goldfields. It was the biggest to date and they'd all been alerted that word was out.

A leather pouch was handed to Sergeant MacDonald by one of the constables behind him. Macca held out the leather pouch to Charly; judging by how he held it in one hand, it contained a bit of weight.

'Around two hundred rounds, .44 calibre, same as the Remington,' he said pointing at the hand gun in the holster under her arm. 'Been told you tend to use lots in a hurry. Take them, it was all the bugger had in his pack. I'll get some more for you when you get back.'

Both the rifle and leather pouch with the ammunition were handed to Charly, who gave her thanks quickly, not wanting to delay the departure. She strode to where Sheeba was sitting on the ground waiting to be mounted, tying the leather pouch to the back of the saddle. Charly pulled the old rifle she carried out of the saddle pouch and handed it to Sergeant MacDonald, siding the new Winchester in as a replacement.

'Thanks, Macca, hope to hell I don't need it. But I was thinking about getting one of these one day. You've saved me the trouble.'

Charly climbed onto the saddle. Sheeba stood, lurching forward, her rear legs straightening, then the front, one at a time, till she was on her four feet. Charly gently flicked the halter that was fastened to Sheeba's nose ring, starting the slow amble out of the yard.

'Shut the gate for me please, Macca!' she shouted. His nodded response satisfied her and she turned to the two constables. 'Right, gents, let's go catch the caravan and get out of the dust.'

Sheeba increased speed to a slow rolling trot. Charly knew that they soon would catch the others. Sheeba was her first and favourite camel, but this would be her last trip. Charly had already decided that Sheeba would become one of her first breeding stock, a version of a brood mare, as so-called among the horse breeders. Though she did wonder how long they would be using camels. While consistently needed in the desert country, their roles were dropping in other areas, such as along the telegraph routes where the trainline was slowly progressing from the south, now only months from the Springs.

Charly slowed the camels as she and Qadir crested the last rise before the track slowly wound down through the red coloured sand, sending spinifex and loose rocks tumbling into the shallow valley below. The wind was enough to pick up some sand and blow it over the crest, stinging their eyes, the only part of their face which was uncovered. As the rest of the small caravan slowly moved up behind them, Charly, then Qadir, flicked the halters. Their camels slowly commenced moving, the pads of their feet flicking up puffs of dust that quickly were blown back toward those following.

It had been a little over two weeks since they had left the Springs, a slower than usual trip, not because of the loads on the camels, but due to the feet weary men who had joined the caravan. Charly smiled. Walking thirty-five to forty miles a day might sound easy for most, but in these hot, sand dry conditions it soon took a toll on someone walking, even without the weight of a pack on their back.. These men were to work at the mine, and she would be in a difficult position if they arrived for work at the mine foot weary and exhausted, so she slowed the pace to suit the men's foot speed.

The scene in the valley below had changed again, more of the valley had been riddled with shallow mine shafts and small test workings. The timber and metal sheeting transported to the valley recently had been turned into a new building close to where she knew the quartz vein was in the rock outcrop. A few new crude lean-to shelters, large part tent, small part timber or metal structure, had been added where the workmen of the mine and individual prospects lived, the place was looking more and more established.

She looked further down the valley that slowly widened into the distance until it was defined by two sentinels, two large rock outcrops on either side of the valley. The words from the aunties cut through her, but she knew that the land they knew would never be the same, the soak with the precious spring of sweet fresh cool water had been changed forever. The dust from the valley got a little worse as they closed to the floor of the valley, dust blowing from all the working men, dry sifting the sand and gravels, using the wind to separate the gold from the other sand and rocks.

The caravan of camels quickly moved down the last of the track to the main building where the office was located, the only building where the stores could be held, kept out of the sun and the odd rain shower. The few personal items that belonged to the men who had joined the caravan were taken off and handed over to allow them to organise themselves. Nearly all that remained belonged to the main mine or for one or two of the independent small miners.

Charly left the unloading to the capable hands of Qadir, who quickly organised to have the large loads removed and placed into storage. As this was happening, Charly spoke to the two constables before they rode off to their small police office, a couple of slightly battered tents not far from the main office. As she watched them, a man walked towards her. Charly gave a quick wave of acknowledgment, recognising him as one of the senior managers.

'Good day, Mrs Khan. Good to see you have made the crossing in good order.'

'Hello, Oswald. A slower than usual run but without any issues,' Charly replied warmly. 'Let's hope the return journey is as trouble free.'

'Agreed, in that matter, we will be ready to load from early morning tomorrow. I assume a mid-morning departure is planned?'

'Sound good to me,' she said. 'Can you have the watering trays set up for the camels? I think we have time to give them a quick drink ready to head off in the morning.'

'All done and ready as usual, I have men filling them as we speak. I'll tell Qadir as soon as we're finished.'

'Anything else? I can just about hear it bursting from you.'

'Not much that I can say, other than the boss wants to see you at the first chance. It's about the supply program.'

'Wants to cut my rates,' snorted Charly, always wary when being called to the mines owner at short notice. 'He won't get anywhere as good with anyone else.'

'We know your rates are good. What he wants to speak to you about is something you might not be expecting, but I am sure it will get you thinking,' Oswald replied with a cheeky grin, showing he was very much aware of what the subject that the discussion would be. 'Best get going, the boss will be expecting you.'

Charly crossed to Sheeba and opened one of the water bags, taking a short drink and washing her hands and face, drying them on the long end of the scarf that was wound around her head. As she rinsed her mouth with the tepid water, slightly cooled by the air blowing past, she was glad to get the taste of the dust and sand out of her mouth, it almost made her feel human again. She gave her kameez a quick brush down to get rid of the worst of the dirt from the trail before heading to the mine office to see the manager.

'Charly, it is wonderful to see you again,' Derek Burrows said smoothly with obvious warmth. 'I take it you are ready for tomorrow, a very big day for us.'

'Not a problem, Derek. We've done all we can.'

'Good. But that's not what I wanted to ask you. I'll get right to the point as we have little time,' he said, transitioning the conversation to the matter that was of greatest importance to him. 'We have a three head battery, most of a big shed and a stationary engine arriving on the train once the line has been finished into the Springs, say hopefully in a month or so. It will be all in one big load on the train from Augusta.'

Charly's ears tuned in; this would change a number of things, including moving the refined ore, equipment and stores. The opportunity to either gain from the changes or lose the business.

'We are talking some big loads, and we need them brought out here without too much delay,' Derek stated. 'We'll be making the track a bit better; I've organised a team of workers to start on that very soon. You might meet some of the surveyors on the way back.'

'So you don't need my camels, is that what you are saying?' replied Charly cautiously.

'No! On the contrary, the first issue, I need you to find a way to bring the battery and engine out here. Can you do it?'

Charly thought for a moment. She remembered that Abdul had moved some similar loads to a copper mine down south with a massive dray and twenty camels on harnesses. She could use oxen, but the heat and lack of water would risk finishing some of them off before they arrived, leaving the load stranded.

'We can do it, but it will cost a bit. I'd need some payment up front, likely four, maybe five trips. Yep, it's going to cost a bucket.'

'I was expecting you might say that. Well that may be an issue as we are short of ready cash till we produce and sell a bit more gold, so we need to get the mill running,' Derek answered. 'Are there any other options?'

Charly thought. There was one option; it would be a risk but the rewards would be great. Opportunities like this, where she was in the box seat, did not come every day but it had its risks.

'Okay,' she said at last. 'You pay the half the standard rate per trip with the equipment,' she said carefully, then the cruncher. 'And five per cent of the mine income for the next five years if I get the equipment here without damage and within three weeks of leaving the Springs. That will cover all other supply crossings for the next six months, my risk if I fail.'

'Mmm, interesting,' came the non-committed reply. 'Then my second issue, the building of the track. It will be dray strength and width. I need you to provide the supplies, materials and one extra feature.'

'And what might that be?'

'I need you to purchase and operate two or three water carts and some wagons, camel drawn, to bring water and materials to the workers and use when they have to building culverts, etc.'

'My cost, what securities?'

'Your contract will be for the life of the build, and then we purchase them at the end at half cost,' Derek said.

'Maybe. Well, okay, we purchase, operate at our cost and at the end of the road build, we hire to you at a set rate for five years and then you own them at ten per cent cost.'

'That is interesting. I'll think about that tonight and we'll speak at sunrise tomorrow.'

'No worries, Derek, but I have a proposal for you.'

Derek smiled. This young woman, with no formal business training was doing deals that could be considered exemplary in process and negotiation. She was likely about to make a fortune as he had already agreed to the proposals in his mind as both were fair to both parties, but did not want to appear too eager. He simply nodded his approval for Charly to start her proposal.

'Water, that's your biggest issue out here, right?' Charly asked. Derek nodded again. 'So what if I provided two, three, four times what you have out of the old soaker spring out there?'

Derek said nothing. No answer was necessary; they both knew that amount of water would change everything, how the mine was planned, operated and staffed.

'At my cost, I'll drill some wells in the valley, the number depending on depth and ground. If I hit water, I'll sell it to you at an agreed gallon rate for–'

'Five years,' said Derek, finishing her sentence with a laugh.

'Err, no, actually for ten years and an option for ten more,' replied Charly. 'Water is the real gold out here, I'm not giving it way for free.'

'If you hit water, Charly, you just might get ten per cent of the shares in the mine. But let me think about it.'

They agreed that the subject was closed, though the last comment fairly summed up what would be agreed tomorrow. Derek invited Charly to have supper with him and one or two rather warm glasses of beer to watch the sun go down.

'Yep, that would be nice. But Derek – I will be sleeping with my camel,' she said with humour; a gentle hint to kill any ideas.

Derek laughed again; he enjoyed the byplay. A comment like that would never occur in the circles he normally ran in, back in his wonderful home in Adelaide that accommodated his wife and children. Charly was a woman that lifted the spirits and his heartrate, but most importantly to him provided a loyal and trusted comfort in their business dealings.

The morning was crisp, the usual cold air just slightly before sunrise. Charly walked among the camels crouched on the sand, carefully checking each one in the soft predawn light.

'You are like a mother hen with her chicks,' came the accented comment from behind her. Charly did not turn, it would be Qadir. Also checking their camels, only he was required to do this as part of his role. 'Wazir always said you were special with the camels, and I agree, you pick up things even I cannot find first or second time looking.'

Charly smiled. Wazir always had been in wonderment at her connections with her animals, right from day one when that old grumpy bull had settled down next to her by the banks of the billabong. She'd soon realised was simply because the old camel had wanted to watch over her.

'Your words are too kind. I simply relate well to them, much better that my own species,' she chuckled. 'One day you will also reach my position, and then we can be mother hens together.'

Qadir laughed, to have a woman as his boss was difficult in his culture, but with Charly, it would never be a problem. His respect was as required by the prophet for a capable leader.

'Five hundred pounds per male camel, four hundred for the females, each split between two side panniers. The rock with gold in sacks we can load with two men. That will allow us to ride, I do not wish to travel long periods by foot.' Qadir knew that when Charly said men, it also included her. She could lift sacks like most men.

'Can you organise with Oswald?'

'Already done. I anticipated this, the camels and carry packs will be ready to load in an hour.'

Charly smiled. Qadir was well in front of her, they both thought alike. She nodded her approval and walked towards the mine a mangers office, seeing the yellowy light of a hurricane lantern in the only glass window in the building, for that matter, the only glass window in the valley.

After been shown inside the main office, Charly pulled up a chair on the opposite side of Dereck's desk. An ever-present layer of fine dust coated everything that had been still for more than a day. Derek lifted a sheet of paper and gave it a gentle shake. A small cloud formed, illuminated by the yellow light of the lantern, drifting to find another place to deposit itself. The sheet of paper was slid across the desk, stopping almost carelessly in front of Charly, as if a page from a newspaper.

'Well, you gave me a few sleepless hours, I'll give you that,' said Derek sincerely. 'But I believe in you. How you've kept supplying us for the last year I will never know, but you have.'

Charly remained silent. It was not her place to add comment at this point. Derek was simply providing reason for his decision, as mad as it might have sounded.

'So, for your loyalty, your doggedness, I agree to what you have suggested as your conditions and rates. A bit over the pail in some things but I can't see any other sensible options that would provide a good outcome for both of us–' He stopped almost in mid-sentence, a palatable fear as to what he would say next, knowing the risks to both of them. 'Sign that paper in front of you and you will be part of my company, this mine, our future.'

Charly looked down for the first time at what was written on the paper. It was a very basic agreement, but one that would make or break her. She accepted the fountain pen that was offered.

'Hang on, I'll get Oswald to witness. You should get Qadir to do the same.' He suddenly laughed. 'We might be talking a fortune, we should at least make this look right.'

Once their two men were dragged away from the preparations in loading the camels, the page was quickly signed by all four. As Oswald and Qadir rushed back to their task, Derek stuck his hand out. Charly grasped it. Both of them understood the mutual recognition of what had just occurred, they were now business partners

'Welcome, partner, let us make this work.' Derek looked down at the signed page on the desk. 'I'll bring it back to the Springs on my next trip home in a month or so. Until then, I think we have enough trust in each other.'

Charly nodded her agreement, dumbstruck at her change in fortune, and the challenges ahead. She sat for a moment as Derek poured two small glasses of whiskey, handing one to Charly then raising his silently in toast. Charly raised her glass, then swallowed the majority in one gulp.

'Agreed. And make it work we will. You dig the rock and I will move the stuff,' Charly replied, causing a quick chuckle from the man at her side. She finished the glass, setting it back on the table, only to have a refill offered.

'Thanks for the offer, but sadly no, I have work to do.' She smiled in an almost cold humour. 'Moving our stuff.'

The manic preparation gained new urgency as the final packs were loaded. Just as Charly and the mine were starting to be unsure if the two men would turn up before the camels were ready to leave, the two constables who had been stationed in the valley walked up to the group, carrying a few bags and their carbines sealed in leather scabbards on their shoulders. Both had a disconsolate look, their uniforms somewhat dishevelled and dirty. They introduced themselves as George Cullen and Lachlan Goodwood. Oswald showed his feeling towards the two men by walking away. Cullen and Goodwood were not liked by management; their departure would not be opposed.

'Where are your camels?' asked Charly in surprise at them being on foot.

'Well, we never had any and the other blokes don't want to hand theirs over,' Cullen stated. 'So your camel's gotta carry us and our stuff, cause we ain't walking.'

The disrespectful demand threw everything into disarray, especially when it was found that the two constables who had travelled in the caravan had left to check other parts of the valley mining field last evening, so the availability of their camels was definitely not an option. The actions of the newly arrived constables was clearly a process in pushing their wants. And the current pair had left their appearance for departure till the last when everything was loaded, on the chance they would be told to stay and wait till the next caravan in a month or so's time.

It was well known that Cullen had protected, if not encouraged, the sly grog arrangements in the valley. Goodwood likely assisted. They both had very good reason to be left behind for some months, it would financially be very productive for them and the sly grog makers.

Their game was obvious, but a solution was beyond Charly's grasp. Oswald quickly walked over to see Derek, who returned to stand beside Charly. He was not going to miss a chance to remove a problem from the valley.

'Take a hundred pounds of the poorer ore off a couple of the camels to allow these two to ride. We can get by,' he said to Oswald and Qadir, as he then turned to look directly at the two constables. 'Anything to be rid of the both of you. I might have a bit of a chat to the commissioner next when I am in Adelaide, he being from my wife's family.'

The two men paled, the threat was instant; the commissioner was a man to be feared. Cullen started to stammer a form of justification and apology but was stopped when Derek raised his hand.

'But, if Mrs Charly Khan here tells me you both were on your best behaviour and showed some pride in the uniform you men wear, I might reconsider what I say.'

That brought two very quick, 'Thank you, sir,' and an instantaneous change in their demeanour. They rushed to assist the redistribution of the loads and organise themselves ready for departure. Charly watched them, muttering a few choice words under her breath about the quality of these men that would supposedly provide the caravan's security and protection.

'Not the best outcome, but they should at least provide some deterrence to those watching your travels,' he grumbled in agreement. 'But I doubt anyone will trouble you, not in the sands. Now where they gunna go if they pinch the rock, hey, Charly?'

Charly did not answer; she just had a dark feeling. All the rest of the shipments went without hitch, it was just too good, and this one held a goodly number of high-grade nuggets. She softly slapped Derek on the arm in thanks and shouted to Qadir that he should take the lead and start the crossing back to the Springs.

'See you soon, Derek. I'll start on the plans we discussed as soon as I get back,' she said as she climbed on the back of Sheeba. 'I'll bring you a nice bottle so we can celebrate next trip – but I'm still gunna sleep with the camels.'

With shared laughter, Charly twitched the halter and kicked her camel to ride to the front of the caravan with Qadir and set their path for their home at the Springs.

Chapter 11

The first three days passed as could be expected in the circumstances, no serious issues and no real problems. However, a portent of the future was hinted at when on the first night the two constables made their own fire and sat away from the rest as they ate their meal. Afterwards, as they cleaned the day's dust from the Martini–Henry rifles they carried, and checked the workings, there was little more than a bare acknowledgment of the offer of company and conversation. Shortly afterwards the two policemen men rolled into their bedrolls, feigning sleep and turning their backs on the remaining three.

Next morning, there was a little more willingness to engage, but for Qadir, Ismael and Mohamad, the reaction was not unusual. They shrugged to each other and did what their master required of them. For Charly, the actions of the constables were an annoyance, but she knew that the two had a somewhat questionable reputation. Given their actions, they were obviously dreading being called back to face the big, red headed Sergeant awaiting them at the Springs.

There was an uneasy air in the camp, but each of the first three days travels were comfortably completed. But on the fourth day, the poison bubbling under the surface flowed over the edge. It started with a complaint. A complaint that was needless and set the tone for the next day, and the one after.

'Can you stop the howling and chanting from that lot five times a day?' Cullen demanded in a superior tone, knowing Charly was not an Afghan and did not participate in the prayers. Perhaps he was hoping to elicit some sympathy. 'They should keep their beliefs where they come from, makes my guts churn.'

Charly stared at him, knowing a wrong answer could upset the balance and lose her the respect of her men. She glanced at Goodwood, who gave his head a quick shake, suggesting he had no part of the complains that Cullen was making.

'If they don't disturb the camels then they can believe in what they want. There's no law against it. And Constable Cullen, if I be remembering correctly, you might be wanting to keep me a bit happy.'

The calmly presented words struck Cullen, reminding him of the consequences should he not comply, but it did not stop the grumbles and sniping at the Afghans as they stopped to pray for the next few days. The petulance continued to a point that the Afghans avoided the two constables. A serious rift was appearing in the travelling group. The final moment before possible conflict was fast approaching; it was not a happy time on the trail.

They still made good time. Being able to ride most of the day allowed a normal two week crossing to have a number of days cut from the length of the trip. But it was clear that the crossing could not come fast enough for Charly or the Afghans. As the standard evening meal was prepared, consisting of mainly rice and a little meat in a spicy sauce, the moment was about to arrives as the sun dropped, leaving only the light of the fire.

'I want some real food. This is crap,' Cullen snarled as his dinner was handed to him by one of the Afghans. 'Who would eat this? Only pigs, I be thinking.'

The cameleer, a Pashtun from a warrior tribe, had been walking away. Now, he slowly turned, hands clenching as the fury that had built for days threatened to be released. Cullen put the plate down, starting to stand, readying himself for what he had been trying to instigate. A shout from Qadir stopped the movement of both men for a moment before they again started, moving slowly looking for an opening to attack.

The sand between them suddenly spat in a small eruption with the noise of a rifle firing. The clear metallic sound of the next round being loaded, ready to be fired, cracked through the gathering. Everyone stopped stock still, turning towards the source of the sound.

Charly stood still, the new Winchester in her hands, pointing in their general direction.

'Mohamad, enough. He plays with you, show your greatness and treat him as a fool child who shouts foolish words,' she said in the Pashtun's tongue she had learned over the last years, offering what action would please the prophet.

'Aiiee, your words are wisdom, the prophet be praised,' he replied, his anger cooling as quickly as it had rose. Turning he looked at Cullen, and spoke in accented English. 'Not today, in respect for my master and Allah, I have no wish to cause you humiliation.'

Mohamad continued his initial path, as if nothing had occurred. He'd seen the wisdom of Charly words; there was no benefit for a conflict with an official of the law, while he may win today, his existence in this land would be finished.

Cullen stood still, his anger unabated, his need to engage in a conflict had been satisfied. Looking at the rifle in Charly's hands all he saw was the indignity of a woman in a role he felt were reserved for men alone. He moved towards her, staring at her face, fury and hate oozing from him. He expected she would step backward, surrendering her position of authority. A single step back would be all he needed to prove his power.

Charly looked at him quizzingly, surprised at his stupidity of trying to intimidate her, the head of the caravan, the boss of the camels. There was no chance that would happen.

'Constable Cullen, are you threatening me?' she asked in a mild disarming tone, her head slightly tilted to one side.

There was no response, but his pacing continued. A second shot echoed around the camp, sand again spitting where the bullet entered the ground some six inches from the inside of his front boot. She fed another round into the breach of the Winchester being held at her side, the metallic scrape sounding once more.

'The next one will be on the same line, Cullen, just three feet higher,' she said. But this time her tone was cold, chilling the warm evening air.

Cullen stopped; the threat finally sinking home. Goodwood jumped out and stood between the two, facing Cullen. He grabbed the end of Cullen's beard and his shoulder with his other hand, giving both a shake.

'What's wrong with you, George? You know she's the boss, her words are the law in the camp. Macca will kill you if you hurt her.'

Something clicked in Cullen's mind. His eyes slowly cleared, he looked at Goodwood with a little recognition. He was given another shake and then pushed slowly back where he came from to sit by his pack and the dirty service rifle. Goodwood sat beside him, slowly calming his fellow constable down to see reason.

'That bloke was a Pashtun, friend. I fought them in the mountains where he comes from, he would have cut you into small bits before you had two good swings at him,' Goodwood said. 'Just forget it, we'll be back to the Springs in a few days.'

'Yeah, just sick of them, they annoy me,' Cullen replied. 'And that bitch, she needs it bent over, show her where she belongs. Dresses like them, eats like them and speaks like them.'

'Forget it, she has people protecting her, let her be from your mind.'

Cullen laid back, closed his eyes and tried to sleep, but his mind was working, planning, finding answers till the tiredness took over and sleep filled his brain. Goodwood sat beside him, a little concerned. He'd never agreed with Cullen and his activities, but it was easier to accept a passive agreement rather than be bullied out in the wilds of the dry valley. He was unsure where the next few days would lead but he knew Cullen would not rollover. It was not in his makeup.

Sitting on the other side of the camp, Charly quietly spoke with Qadir to receive his council. She still had the rifle over her knees, as she looked at where the two constables had slightly removed themselves. In reality, the Afghans had moved aside, to show the division that had been building for some days.

'I agree. Keep a watch for the next nights, but one that is not too obvious but is obvious enough that they know we do not trust them. I am sure you have the knowledge for this,' Charly said. 'And speak with Mohamad privately, his Pashtun blood will not be calm yet. Explain I am pleased in his response, he has proven himself the man he is.'

Qadir made a quick reply of agreement and walked to where his fellow countrymen and their neighbours were seated. They engaged in a soft discussion in their own tongue as was their want at the end of the day, intermixed with the words was the occasional laughter. Cullen and Goodwood were not included, today had been the last step. Charly laid back and watched, concerned. Finally she gave up, what would be would be, trying to prepare for any specific possibility was a waste of energy. She closed her eyes and slipped off to sleep.

The next day provided no exceptions to the usual activity. Cullen and Goodwood said little other than curt responses to commands, if they thought a response was at all necessary. They knew that there was only one way back to camp, and it was part of this caravan. The mood was sullen, but the common need had calmed the words and actions.

The following day was no different, another day moving slowly along the worn trail. The only change was meeting the second caravan heading to the mining field with further supplies, an amount of iron sheeting on four camels. Both caravans stopped to exchange words and encouragement. Charly spent a little time with another of her cameleers, a long distant cousin of Wazir who was the leader of the second caravan.

'Mustafa, the prophet be praised at the health of the camels and men, there are no words for your skills,' she remarked. He was man of great integrity but loved a little commendation from his boss, especially a young female. 'You have made good time, when you return I wish to have a meeting with you and Qadir over a new enterprise.'

'Allah be praised I have such a kind and observant overseer,' he chortled in glee at her comments, knowing that she was having a subtle play of humour at his ego. 'I will return as quickly as possible without harm to those creatures in my care.'

Soon after, the two caravans departed, each heading to their original destination, a smooth and efficient operation to keep the mining district alive. The path a little more worn with each crossing, the basis of the planned road.

The day again went without incident, the evening meal a little less tense as Goodwood sat beside Charly and Qadir to make general conversation on the day and the speed of their crossing. Charly was a little reserved, but softened as Constable Goodwood's demeaner was nothing but pleasant.

The following day followed the same path, the endless low dunes on both sides as they followed the flat base between them. As they moved away from the desert, the vegetation was a little thicker, the occasional stand of mulga breaking up the monotony of the land around them. The only change was the heat, today it was brutal as a wind change pulled hot air from the centre of the desert to the north-west.

As they pulled up alongside a larger stand for their midday meal, all enjoyed the shade provided, and the instant cooling of the shaded air, if only by a few degrees. A meal of flat bread, pickles and cold meat was washed down by barely palatable water. No-one spoke, the heat of the last few days was sapping the very core of the men. Constables Cullen and Goodwood had stripped down, letting the breeze blow over their bodies, the sweat barely staying on their skin long enough to have a cooling effect. The Afghans watched in amazement. They had learned in generations past, that loose clothing worked best, allowing the sweat to naturally provide a cooling effect as it evaporated off the skin. In these conditions they were in their element, and they were careful to protect themselves from the harshness of the hot sands.

As Qadir called the finish of the meal, the response from Cullen was belligerent as he lay in the shade of the mulga. 'Not moving till it cools. I'll wait for the night air, this heat is killing me, I not going anywhere.'

Qadir looked in surprise at the man spreadeagled on the ground, his shirt unbuttoned, his boots off in the sand.

'We go, Constable, we not waiting till evening. It is too dangerous, we must be moving quickly.'

Cullen sat up slowly, looked in contempt, his disrespectful attitude re-emerging. 'Piss off! Ain't moving an inch, too bloody hot.'

Qadir shook his head. He shouted to his fellow Afghan to prepare to leave as he walked over to Charly, providing a quick assessment of the situation. Charly said nothing, gave a nod to Qadir to keep his preparations and slowly walked over to stand a little way in front of the sprawled figure of Cullen.

'So you are staying, I am told. Not sure how that works when we leave,' she said calmly.

'You're so smart. Leave me a camel and I'll catch up tonight.'

Charly smiled at the poor attempt by Cullen the split the group, to give himself a little power by questioning her decisions and authority.

'Well, Constable, you must have a camel that does not belong to me. Let me see,' she said as she slowly made a play at counting the animals in her sight. 'Nope, that's ten, and they're all mine, so where's the one you'll be using? Is it around the back of the mulga?'

Hatred filled Cullen's eyes as he looked up at her. She was mocking him, treating him as a stupid new chum that arrived off the coach with no ideas. Her comments were clear, all the camels would be leaving, and leaving him if he did not get on the one he was allocated to ride.

'Bitch, reason you got no man because no-one can stand the smell. Only thing that will root you is a camel, and they have better taste in women!' he spat at her with venom.

'Well, Cullen, we all have our opinions,' Charly replied calmly, though her anger was detectable in her tone. 'You are welcome to vent yours as much as you like if you get on the bloody camel. Your choice, ride or stay and walk.'

She walked away, her anger as much from his insult as was the fact that the words cut deep. She knew that she could not form a relationship with a man. As much as they tried, as much as some would be wonderful partners, she withdrew into herself every time, fearing the next step: intimacy. Three or four more days, she considered, three more days and she would be rid of one of the most unpleasant humans that she had ever met, a man who kept reminding her of the worst traits of her father.

The rest of the day was exhausting. The heat only built as the hot air ravaged their throats and lungs. The sand dunes shimmered in the distance; the environment was surreal, unnatural for humans. The Afghan's did what they could to beat off the sun and heat, pulling the ends of the silk turbans around their faces, peaking them to provide shade to the eyes from the direct sun. But the heat, nothing could be done for the heat but to keep riding.

By the day's end another large stand of mulga with a few scatted eucalypts was found that allowed everyone, including the camels, to be in the shade. It was an hour before the usual time to stop, but the day's conditions and the relief from this stand of vegetation demanded that the travels for the day would end. A small area of dry grass with small green shoots formed a base to the taller eucalypts, a perfect place to allow the camels to graze, the first good feed that they had eaten in the last two days, it would be enough to get them home.

The start for the next day was without incident, the evening before had been equally without issues, but the heat of the day had burnt-out each person, leaving only enough remaining energy to prepare an evening meal and collapse into their swags. Unusually, the hour or two of quiet chatting between the Afghans did not occur, even the two with long experience in the heat and dry of the high plains were exhausted.

During the night a change blew past, the temperatures dropping quickly. A small amount of rain fell, the cool air and rain making the men pull the blankets a little tighter around their necks. A one point in the poor light of a half-moon as the clouds blew away, Charly woke to an odd sound and movement, but when she looked around the camp, her Winchester in her hand, she decided that the cause of noise did not pose a risk to the safety of the camp and she returned to her swag.

As they rode from the overnight camp, the temperature had dropped noticeably from the previous three days lifting the spirits of the group. Even constable Cullen let out the occasional smile, and engaged with the Afghans in a little verbal byplay as they covered their first miles. Charly slowly rode her camel up beside the camel that Cullen was riding.

'Feeling better today, George? You are looking a bit more refreshed,' said Charly, showing concern, waiting to see what the response was from her most recent adversary.

'The cooler air makes me feel much better. Yesterday near killed me,' he replied without anger. 'I'll make it now the weather is with us.'

'Is that what changed your mind last night?'

'Err, not sure what you mean,' he replied, a little reserved.

'When you slipped away to the back of the grove to leave on a camel that was not yours,' Charly replied in an almost disinterested tone. 'I saw. I was up, watching, but I was relieved that you changed your mind and went back to camp.'

'Aiiee, you are the spirit of the night. I saw and heard nothing, and I was being very careful,' he said almost laughing at his own foolishness, 'Well, whatever I am and have done recently, I am charged to protect the caravan. So, I could not do it. Leave, I mean.'

'Mmmm, and steal one of my camels.'

'Well, yeah, that too. That would be wrong,' Cullen stated earnestly. 'Look, I don't like these blokes, what they believe and eat but sometimes I just go off half cocked.'

'And perhaps the fact you've not had a drink in nearly two weeks?' noted Charly, knowing the condition that affected Cullen, one of the reasons for the sly grog. 'Well, I think you're doing okay.'

Constable Cullen almost laughed at the predicament, to have been making a goodly amount of sly grog and only to not bring any on the journey. He'd sold all he had for an inflated price to a handful of desperate men at Tamimi mining field. The glitter of gold had been the only thing overcoming his desire to keep the last bottles of booze. The gold now sat in his pack.

'Tell you what, Cullen, you get this caravan to the Springs safely, I'll buy you a few rounds at the hotel I stay at.'

Cullen turned his head in surprise, a warm smile spreading across his face. Everything that had happened would be left in the sands. He gave a small kick to push his camel to the front of the caravan to take his place leading the group as he drew his rifle from it pouch to sit across his legs.

'You're on – see you at the Imperial.' He laughed as he rode away.

Chapter 12

The caravan slowly moved through the spinifex, staying close to the well-worn narrow pathway, crossing two dunes, but now travelling more along the widening plains, rather than across them. In the distance was the gap in the last dune they would cross before travelling in more vegetated grassed plains till they reached the Springs on the banks of the river that flowed intermittently depending on the seasons. That last crossing was not much a crossing of a dune, but rather passing through the gap that had formed when one part of the dune had moved forward, and the other part had stayed put because of the vegetation on its sides.

The offset in the dunes could be seen a long way in the distance, more than an hour's travel away. Charly looked at the sun, thinking they would stop for their midday meal on the other side of the gap. There was an agreeable stand of trees and a small soak where they could cool off and get a bit of the trail dust from their faces. She called to the others, all agreed in response to extend the travel by an hour or so to stop at such an enjoyable location.

A little short of the hour, they were a few hundred yards from the opening of the dunes. The gap was a little over one fifty yards wide. The end of the dune on the southern side was stable, stands of spinifex and a few clumps of low windswept mulga had taken root, slowing downs its movement. On the opposite side, the dune was sandy, windswept with small ridges and crests. The odd clump of grass grew but provided little stability in the shifting sands. The peaks of the dune were little more than fifty feet above the plain below, enough to be annoying to climb, so passing through the gap was much preferred, a landmark well remembered by of the travellers on the trail.

Cullen turned in the saddle, looking at Charly behind him with a broad smile. His demeanour had improved with each mile, seeing the last of the dunes was a lift to his spirits.

'Last one! Hey, I can taste the beer on my–'

His words were cut off as his body jerked backward, as if a string was pulled, flicking his body in an unnatural stance on the camel. The reverberation of powerful gunshot filled the plain, echoing of the sides of the dunes, a brief moment after the bullet struck Cullen in the chest. Before anyone could move, a second shot could be heard as Goodwood sagged on his camel, holding his side as he toppled from his seat as if in in slow motion, landing heavily in the sand.

'Down, off the camels, take cover!' shouted a voice in a language immediately understood by the Afghans, the voice of an old warrior. A third shot plucked the inside of the upper sleave of Charly's arm as she struggled to understand to what was happening. The searing pain as the bullet tore a track through skin and flesh of her inner arm snapped her mind into action. She had enough foresight to pull her camel, the wonderful Sheeba, down laying behind her, as she tried to stop the blood running down her arm.

A fourth shot closely followed the third, the bullet catching Qadir in a leg as he dived from his camel. He landed with a thud, but he held onto the halter, also pulling his camel down. Momentarily safe, but without a way to fight back, Qadir looked at his leg, bleeding but not serious. He wound his turban around the wound, stabilising his leg enough to move if required.

The two men who had engaged in battle with camels in the land of their forefathers had dismounted and pulled their camels down, providing cover from the gunfire. Mohamod and Ishmael were unarmed but immediately assessed the situation, planning a response. Mohamod looked to his left and saw that Goodwood was laying in the sand some twenty feet away, trying to move but was struggling with his wound. The camel that the constable had been riding had walked some ten feet further, looking around, skittish in the noise of the gunfire.

'Two, one on either dune. Second clump grass on sandy dune to this side. Another in the small trees on the other side!' shouted Ishmael, taking on the role as observer.

'Good, Ishmael, cause a distraction and I'll get some weapons.'

After Ishmael stripped off the hooded over-cloak he was wearing, he waved it as a man moving behind the camel. Immediately two shots sounded as one, the cloth was almost plucked from his hands. Mohamod jumped to his feet and ran to Goodwood's camel, dragging it by the halter back to where Goodwood was laying on the ground, forcing it to lay down as a barrier. A bullet ripped into the laden leather pannier, but Mohamod and Goodwood were safe.

'Show me the wound quickly,' demanded the Afghan.

Goodwood pulled his tunic up and unbuttoned his underwear, pulling it open. Mohamod ran his hand around his lower chest, finding both the entry and exit wounds.

'Good. It has passed through without hitting bone or organ, the blood is a good red.' Mohamod grunted in satisfaction. 'You will bleed a little, but not die from this. The bleeding is slowing already.'

Goodwood slowly buttoned up the underwear, pulling his tunic top down, the pain from the wound affecting his actions but not his thinking. He pointed to his service rifle in the scabbard tied to his saddle.

'Take it. The cartridges are in a small pouch in the pannier on this side.'

Mohamod quickly retrieved the weapon and pulled out the small pouch, holding around fifty rounds for the well maintained and relatively new Snider-Enfield rifle.

'I know this weapon, it will serve us well. Stay by the camel, do not move,' he told Goodwood. 'Now it is time watch the Pashtun way to fight.'

Even with the pain, Goodwood smiled. He had been on the receiving end of the Pashtuns' fighting skills in the mountains of the tribal areas of Afghanistan. He was happy to have them on his side this time.

'Again, Ishmael!' Mohamod shouted sharply.

Again, the distraction, again two shots. Again Mohamad was able to scuttle back to quickly lay down beside his countryman. One of the shots from the sand dune hit the camel in the head. It let out a snort and died, settling slightly as its life drained away but remaining in place to provide the men protection from its body.

'Well done, countryman. Here, enjoy, you always could shoot the eye from a flea,' he said as he handed over the Snider-Enfield rifle and ammunition pouch to Ishmael. 'Now, let us make them think we have teeth.'

Ishmael checked the service carbine, nodding appreciatively at its excellent condition. He pulled back the backsight to select a distance. It was an educated guess, informed by experience. He wiped the foresight, nodding with agreement as to his selections. He pulled a handful of cartridges from the pouch, loading one. He pulled his hood over his head and over the rifle, then slowly looked over the immobile camel at the sandy ridge with calm intent.

'Now, old friend, give that one something to shoot at.'

Mohamod had no cloak to wave, he wanted to do something else anyway. He stood, hunched over, and ran as fast as he could. There were two shots, both snatched at his clothing before throwing up a spit of sand. The third shot, this one from the camel behind him, then a fourth and a fifth that were fired in a regular cycle at the top of the ridge.

Mohamod slid in beside Charly. 'Are you hurt?' he asked quickly, seeing a long smudge of blood down her sleeve.

'My arm. It's painful but I can use it.'

He unwound Charly's scarf from her head, quickly winding it around her arm, stopping the bleeding, and giving the wound support as he tied it tight. Mohamod reached over Sheeba to get a grip on the butt of the Winchester. The gun in the mulga responded, a bullet hitting the leather pannier. Mohamod took the chance that the other gun on the sandy hill was occupied by Ishmael, and stood slightly, pulling the rifle from the scabbard, grabbing the leather pouch hanging below.

Another shot from the mulga fired as Mohamod dropped behind Sheeba. Sheeba convulsed, her head dropping lifelessly to the sand. Charly screamed. Her beloved camel was gone, finished from the world. She went to grab the rifle from Mohamad's hands, her anger making her want to rush the person in the mulga.

'Stop, woman!' shouted Mohamod, spittle spraying into her eyes. 'She was wonderful, but would she want you to die for her? No! Now is a time to think, to win, because of wisdom, not lose from foolishness.'

His harsh words hit home. She knew what pain was, what needed to be done to survive, to be cold, to be calculating, to be strong. She gave Mohamod a nod. She was back in control, she would cry over her best friend later, now it was to fight.

'Can you shoot? Can you hit that dune? Hit the crest, hit those bushes.'

'Any and all, Mohamod, what is it you want from me?' she asked.

'Keep that one busy with lead. You have bullets, shoot as fast and accurately as you can, then reload and repeat, and repeat until you have no more.'

He wanted a distraction. Another series of shots sounded from behind them. This time, a muffled scream emanated from the other dune, the gun from that sandy crest went silent.

'Ahh good, Ishmael is a master with a good English long-barrelled rifle,' he said almost with disinterest, as if he had forgotten about the other adversary. 'Okay, Charly, shoot.'

Charly fired as many rounds as she could with minimal sighting at the stand of mulga. Mohamod stood and ran, this time forward to Cullen's camel that had wandered towards the dune. He reached it as

Charly emptied the magazine. Pulling the large service revolver from the saddlebag where Cullen always kept it, he knew that he had the advantage when he found it was loaded.

Another handful of shots emanated behind him with a deeper bark from the Snider-Enfield. A shot resonated from the mulga, aimed at Charly but harmlessly imbedding itself in the body of Sheeba. Mohamod smiled, knowing that the person on the dune had a problem, unable to choose which target to shoot at. After a short time, another shot, but at Charly again. Mohamod had counted the seconds, knowing that it was from a single shot, with rear feed breach.

Charly commenced the cyclic firing from the Winchester, all seventeen rounds in a steady rate, ripping through the stand of mulga bushes. Mohamod ran again, diagonally, away from the front of the dune, back towards the side some small distance away from the gap.

As he counted fifteen shots, he lay down, as flat and still as he could, the dirty sandy coloured cloth of his clothes merging into the spinifex. More shots from Ishmael, and a responding shot from the person in the mulga, but nothing from the other dune. Mohamed waited, not moving until Charly started her third fusillade. As it commenced, Mohamod ran again, this time making it close to the dune but in a small stand of mulga. He waited one more time.

The fourth burst of shooting from Charly allowed Mohamod to climb the dune, he was in his element now. The man in the mulga was in danger, he had become the hunted and his position was known. Mohamod slowly moved along the far side of the ridge. He saw two horses tied and hobbled, a small camp, the remains of a small fire. He moved on, guessing where the person who attacked him was located.

The sound of the rifle directly above him was all he needed as he slowly climbed the last of the sand dune, remaining no higher than the spinifex and stunted mulga. Finally, he found his target, and swiftly, without remorse, eliminated the threat with a quick, well-aimed shot of the service revolver.

He saw no need for pleasantries. That was the way of the English, he thought. This person had attacked them without warning, so he also gave no quarter. The person was dead from the first shot, but a second ensured Mohamod's safety. He walked forward and turned him over. A white man, as he'd expected, but not one he knew from the Springs; he was a stranger. He pulled the rifle from the dead man's hands, a Sharps, a hunter's weapon. With his other hand he grabbed a leg, then pulled the man from the stand of mulga, the man's arms dragging, a smear of blood on the dry sand.

Suddenly the mulga around him exploded in splinters from flying bullets. Mohamod dropped to the ground, chastising himself for his foolishness. There was a young angry woman down on the plain, and she just wanted to shoot anything that lived on this sandy ridge. He counted the shots till he reached the magazine capacity of seventeen, he then stood and walked to the front of the dune, waving his free arm above his head. They had survived, hurt, wounded with some dead, but as a group they had won.

Charly lifted her rifle after reloading one more time. This was it, she thought, there were only a handful of cartridges left in the bottom of the pouch. Her eyes were wet with tears, making seeing anything difficult. She took aim at the clump of mulga, then she saw a shape, a person walking quickly over the crest of the dune, and what looked like a rifle in his hand. Anything on that place was hated, she changed her aim slightly and prepared to provide one last surprise to that person.

She felt the first stage on her finger as it pulled the trigger, the next would release the firing pin. Her mind swam with a mix of anger and jubilation that she finally had a chance to kill the person who'd caused such pain to her, her friends and her beloved animals. They would suffer. She held for a moment, blinking her eyes to clear them, then taking a steely aim at the person descending the dune.

A moment before her finger pulled against the final pressure, as the firing pin released, a hand struck the barrel. A body crashed into her side, knocking the aim and firing the bullet into the sandy dirt.

'No, miss, stop, stop!' Ishmael's voice screamed in her ear. 'That be Mohamod, he be holy unhappy if you shoot him.'

Charly lowered her rifle, looked at the person and with a clear mind saw her larger than life Pashtun cameleer. She let out a deep long breath. She'd been a moment away from an unspeakable outcome. Charly looked at Ishmael, who had a huge grin on his face, clearly the last few minutes had been to his liking, the dangers bringing back a feeling of exhilaration he enjoyed. Charly could not resist the boyish grin, replicating it as they both laughed.

'I go and check the other dune. Not want bad surprise, okay, Miss Charly Khan?' said Ishmael as he stood and walked over to pick up Cullen's rifle that lay in the sand. He brushed it off, checking if it was loaded, before striding towards the sandy dune to check what had occurred to that attacker. He stopped next to Cullen's camel, now grazing in a small clump of grass halfway to the dune. He pulled the ammunition pouch from the saddle and lifted the strap over his shoulder.

He had returned to his youthful past fighting the British in his homelands, armed and at war. He, and Mohamod, were warriors again and that was to his liking.

Charly stood slowly, seeing the mass of empty brass cartridges laying in the sand to the right of where she had crouched over Sheeba. Macca was right, she thought to herself, you tend to run through them fairly fast.

She walked quickly the two dozen or so paces to where Cullen lay, carrying her weapon in her good hand. A quick check confirmed he was likely dead well before he hit the ground; a massive pool of blood spread from the centre of his chest. She turned to see how the rest of the group were. She found Qadir sitting next to Goodwood tying a length of bandage around the constable's bare chest, two well soaked pads of cloth underneath.

While the wounds looked serious, the rosy colour of his face showed that he was not next to death's door from a loss of blood. Qadir sat with one leg outstretched, the lower part of his leg soaked in blood that had leaked from where his turban was wrapped. Charly squatted down beside them.

'Goodwood will be living, Charly Khan. Ishmael told him that to die here would upset him greatly, so Allah willing he will live,' stated Qadir nonchalantly, as if the last moments they had survived were of no great concerns. 'My leg, it may be broken by the bullet I think, but no problem, I can still ride Zeeja.'

'Qadir is right, just a fair hole. Maybe a crack in a rib but the slug passed on through,' affirmed Goodwood, a half smile and grimace on his face as he sat up slightly, 'us territorials are made of tough material.'

Charly shook her head at the boy bravado of the two of them, but it lifted her spirits, knowing that no more of her group would die just yet.

'Cullen… I am sorry, Lachlan, but–'

'Yeah, I know. I saw him hit just before I was,' said Goodwood, cutting off Charly's comments. 'I have seen that before. Men don't stand after that damage.'

Silence lingered between the two of them, neither wishing to speak, avoiding thinking of the fallen constable's bad parts, wanting to simply remember the man as he was at the end. They knew his last regret would have been that he had no opportunity to protect the caravan.

'Don't worry, he went as he would have wanted to, as we would prefer: quick and painless,' Goodwood said, his final comment on the subject before he slowly slumped back against the dead camel's side. He had lived, his fellow constable had not. Goodwood smiled; two policemen: one a man who stood up for right after years not honouring his pledge now a memory, remembered as a hero by simply being killed, and the other a man who honoured the badge, alive but likely a cripple if he survived the seriousness of his wound, who would be forgotten because he lived

Charly stood and looked around her, the camels still standing were scatted but all within sight. Ishmael was nearly at the top of the other dune, finishing the last part with clear caution. She turned towards the bigger dune and saw that Mohamod was nearly back, carrying a large rifle in his hand. She decided to walk over to him, Charly knew they had much to discuss and decide of what to do next, this was situation outside her experience and knowledge.

It took another three hours before their quickly drawn up plans materialised into a positive action of leaving the killing field, now called 'Casing Gap' by Goodwood when he saw the mass of spent cartridge casings glittering in the sun where Charly had been shooting from. He was wrapped in a makeshift stretcher, a sight that brought back vivid memories for Charly. Qadir somehow hobbled to his camel, climbing on the saddle and with a few bloodcurdling screams of pain, urged the camel to stand and move forward.

Charly refused any attention to her wound. She would need to strip off her overshirt for it to be bandaged, and her lack of underclothing under her kameez would likely cause an issue for her Afghan cameleers. While she knew they would gladly ignore the issues to care for her, she preferred to avoid placing them in a position that may compromise their beliefs. She grunted at the annoyance of being a woman in a man's world. Not that she had much in the way of breasts anyway, but she also had her inner fears to manage.

She was confident that the bound turban had done the trick for now, she would check it and bandage it later in her own privacy. She had survived worse. Her mind now set, she waved away any requests or demands to check her wounds. She was the boss, her words mattered, her toughness was without question.

They arrived at their planned midday destination a few hours before dark. This allowed a considered and well-prepared camp to be made for the night and possibly a few days. They had left the three dead camels where they'd fallen, moving their loads away from the path next to the base of a dune, covering them with brush to be collected at a later date. Only the poorest rock ore was left, any smaller bags with pure nuggets were redistributed among the remaining camels.

The three bodies, that of Cullen and the two attackers, were bound over the horses Mohamod had retrieved from behind the dune. While both of the attackers had massive wounds to their heads, Charly immediately recognised them as the two men who had taken a dislike to her presence at the hotel bar room some many weeks before. While she had repaid them their hate and abuse, the loss of three camels in the ambush, including the one she'd first so loved, cut deeply into her soul.

The discussion around the fire ended without finding a clear outcome, rather leaving it till the morning after a night sleep and rest, when the extent of the damage could be truly discerned and plan as to how they could travel. Goodwood and Ishmael had suddenly become the closest of companions, with Mohamod not far behind. Qadir had smiled at Charly, nodding at them as they discussed the action as warriors do after a battle. Dissecting each moment, each element of the actions, the flaws and the strategic victories. Goodwood finally declared that Ishmael and Mohamod would have been welcome in his regiment due to their skills and bravery, to him there was no greater compliment. They laughed with pure joy and extended their compliments and a similar welcome to their tribes but noted his camel riding skills would need to improve, especially dismounting under fire.

The sun rose on another day, a day that quickly showed they were in no shape for travel. It was decided that they would rest one day and then push to reach the Spring in two days. The provision of shade and a little fresh water in a soak would allow then to clean and redress their wounds before two dusty days on the trail. Both of the older Afghans and Goodwood were concerned about infection from dirty deep wounds, an experience they had suffered in older battles, and not something they wished to occur in their group.

It was noted by all that the camels were still agitated from the noise and smells of the ambush, and a day's rest with a little water would calm them. A camel that spooked with Goodwood as a passenger could be disastrous. As they had little more than forty or so miles to travel to the destination, a cautious approach would provide little disadvantage and limit most of the risks.

On the morning of the following day, they made slow preparations to leave; the loading of the camels took double the usual time, as it was left to only two men. The caravan moved off slowly, taking no chances. Thankfully the path was clear and wide. By midday they all were exhausted as they stopped in a small shelter of sparse eucalypt trees. Goodwood was slightly feverish, the jolting of the camels not helping his wounds. A check once he was lowered to the ground under the shade showed that the two wounds had started bleeding again. Mohamod replaced the bandages and pads, giving the two holes a good looking over.

'The bruising is now yellow and green, but fading. I cannot smell or see any corruption,' he stated contentedly as he re-wrapped Goodwood's chest with the last of the bandages. 'He fights the sickness and he will win this, he is strong this one.'

Qadir's leg ached. He had refused to move once he was helped from the saddle. The ride had taken all his youthful bravo and exhausted his boundless energy. He feared the next part of the ride, almost asking to be left behind.

The stop had lost much of the usual enjoyment provided after a few hard hours in the saddle or walking the dry red sands. The stop was little more than a drink of warm water from the water bags and small meal of dried dates, bread and dried meat to quench a dry throat and feed craving of their stomachs. Most of them closed their eyes and enjoyed a short sleep as the camels munched contentedly on some small clumps of dry grass among the trees.

The usually silent birdlife during the heat of the day exploded into noise. Charly pulled herself upright in time to hear the sound of steel shod hooves on the rocks near there midday camp. As she rose, Mohamad picked up one of the service rifles, now suspicious of any unusual activity. He motioned for Charly to get her rifle before they showed themselves to the approaching horses and their riders.

Within ten minutes the riders were evident, moving quickly but very alert, four men in uniform of the territorial police. One of the man lead, the other three rode a short distance behind, all were carrying their weapons in easy reach. Charly recognised the man at the front, wondering why he was here, why he had so many of his constables with him.

'Macca, over here,' called Charly, waving one arm above her head, thankful she had no need of the Winchester in the other.

As the horsemen rode into their sparse midday camp, Charly and Mohamod stood and walked out into the open.

'What you doing here, Macca?' she asked as he stopped his horse next to her and Mohamod. 'Whatever the reason, boy are we glad to see you.'

It took two further days to reach the Springs, the last few miles a mixture of euphoria and maddening pain for Qadir and Goodwood. One of the Constables that rode with Sergeant MacDonald had ridden back and brought the town doctor out to meet them the evening before. All wounds were cleaned, sterilised and bound. Doc Burgess gave Qadir and Goodwood an excellent chance of recovery, commending whoever cared for the wounds.

He looked at Charly and over her arguments, explained in clear detail he had seen every type, shape and form of human body, so she had no options but show him the wound that needed to be cleaned and bandaged. She pulled off her overshirt, much to her reluctance exposing her upper body to the gaze of a man. It was not the front she wished to hide, but the scarring on her back that provided a short whistle of amazement from Doc Burgess.

He looked at the skin on her back that had been burned and was left with puckered scars but said nothing, keeping the information to himself. Burgess quickly cleaned the wound where the bullet had torn a deep furrow across the inside of her upper arm.

'You're bloody lucky. A little one way or the other it could have smashed your arm bone, shoulder or chest,' he suggested as he cleaned it and bound it in a new bandage. 'It looks okay, should be no long term issues thankfully.' He then stopped and looked at the wound.

'Bloody big calibre too. Low-life mongrel shooting at a woman, hope he paid.'

'Thanks, Doc,' Charly replied, self-conscious of being semi naked in front of a man. 'Say, do ya think you can forget what you saw on my back? And yeah, he paid. He's on that horse over there.'

Doc Burgess looked at the body tied over the horse and snorted his satisfaction before changing back to the original conversation.

'Not a problem, Miss Khan. But maybe you need to come and see me occasionally, I am sure my wife would enjoy a little female company.'

As they all sat around the fire that last night before the final days journey, one thing eating at Charly, one question gnawed at her mind.

'Tell me, Macca,' she asked Sergeant MacDonald as she sipped on a cup of tea. 'What brought you out here? Not a golly into the bush with your boys, I would be guessing.'

'You're right, it's no coincidence we came up the trail,' he replied. 'The mine had a surveyor setting out the new road. He was maybe ten or so miles away and heard a shit load of gunfire. He was a bit scared and shot through back to the Springs.' Macca laughed at his memories of the man's arrival at his office. 'At least he had the sense to come and see me. I knew your caravan was not too far away and what you were carrying, so I got some of the blokes and hightailed it your way a day or so early than we expected to ride out.'

He looked in the general direction where the bodies lay. 'Knew something was fishy about those two, they kept disappearing into the wilds and then arriving back, keeping to themselves. I reckon they were staking out the ambush site.'

Charly nodded, satisfied by his explanation and lay back in her swag. Sleep suddenly overwhelmed her. Her eyes closed and she instantly fell into a deep sleep, for the first time in weeks she relaxed, knowing that she was safe.

As the caravan rode into the small town, every person stood on the sides of the main street, on the verandahs and walkways, watching the caravan. They were pleased to see it had arrived, infuriated that it had been attacked and thrilled that the men who'd done the vile act were dead. Charly rode slowly at the front with Sergeant MacDonald, a message that law and order had been maintained, that the future of the town would not be disturbed by violence.

Charly rode her camel into the compound once the gates were opened, wishing she was on Sheeba. She knew in her heart that with Sheeba's passing, a new page in her life would begin. She was not linked to a project, she had obligations, she had no time to fret, life went on.

Chapter 13

The locomotive belched thick clouds of smoke as it slowly climbed the last small incline to the rail yards at the Springs, the terminus of this trip for the passengers and freight. Most of the passengers had started outside Adelaide on spur line before catching the train they were on. Most of the freight, was loaded at Augusta, direct from the ports of England or elsewhere in the country.

This particular load of freight was highly anticipated. It had been expected for months before but delayed on the sea as it was shipped from England, it had finally arrived in a cloud of dust, coal smoke and steam. Once the handful of passengers disembarked from the first carriage, the train would be slowly moved to the goods yard, there the important things to be unloaded and the rail lines true reason for existence could be exercised.

Charly stood on the siding as the passengers climbed down the two steps onto the roughly cobbled platform. Her eyes were not on the passengers, but on the large metal objects of the following flatbed carriages. The three headed stamping mill, the stationary engine and other infrastructure that would be taken to the mine, hundreds of miles away in the desert on her newest transports, large wooden drays to be hauled by teams of camels.

It was a little over five months since she had returned on that fateful trip with her camel caravan. It had been her last till now, as these loads would require her supervision, they would test all the work that had occurred since that time. The delivery of water carts had quickly increased the rudimentary forming of what one day would be the well-made road to the mine. A couple of road works teams were now constantly provided with water and supplies with Charly's camel teams. The number of teams had trebled in the last months with more to come.

The surveyors had found a route that had removed nearly all the larger dune crossings, making the distance not quite a quarter longer, but almost a few days shorter. The new roadway was required as heavy-laden drays do not cross dunes like camel caravans in single file. The transport of two smaller loads on the drays had been completed the month before, taking building materials for the sheds and the concrete structures for the stamper mills. These loads were used to test the route and test the transports.

Charly walked over to the goods yards where the large equipment would be unloaded. A large derrick driven by a small steam engine had been installed only a few weeks before in preparation of the arrival of the heavy equipment for the mine. The derrick stood beside the shunting tracks, allowing the load to be lifted and quickly transferred to the waiting drays. Two of the special oversized drays stood ready for use beside the derrick. All that was required was a team of camels to be harnessed to the stout tongue for the load to be sent on its way.

By the end of the day, one of the drays were loaded with all the components of three headed stamp battery while the stationary engine had arrived with large steel spoked wheels. It was quickly decided that it could simply be towed by the second team of camels. There was a great deal of huffing and puffing, both from the steam powered derrick and from the men manoeuvring the two objects to their next forms of transport.

They had dismantled the majority of the stamp battery to make the lifts easier, slowly transferring the three immensely heavy stamping heads one by one. The large pully wheels and drive shaft followed with the lifting cam, finally stout timbers that provided the support frame for the battery. All carefully loaded then strapped down onto the bed of the dray. It would be the biggest load Charly had ever moved.

A large timber ramp had been quickly built to allow the removal the stationary engine from the flat bed railcar. It was slowly rolled down to solid ground, all its equipment strapped to the sides, ready for installation when it reached its destination.

Charly had watched with interest and concern, nearly leaving the yards in fear after hearing the stresses on the riveted steel frame of the derrick. Finally, when everything was unloaded and then reloaded, she slowly released a sigh of relief; the first difficult step was done, now to test the barely built road. She smiled as she walked back to her compound, a problem for tomorrow, not before.

The last five months had been a hive of planning, started by a train ride to visit her adopted parents to organise additional camels, drivers and equipment. The change in transport required different skills, forcing her to employ two experienced teamsters, both non-Afghan, to manage the large camel teams that would pull the drays. Her yards now held over one hundred camels, including the two special teams of twenty, trained to be hitched to the oversized drays and on this occasion the stationary engine.

Abdul had provided two drays from his unused equipment, previously required to take equipment to copper mines, but now rarely used. These had arrived by train with the two steel water carts being used on the road works. Every cent that Charly had saved and with a supportive loan from Abdul and Mary funded the rapid expansion. Any failure would be her financial ruin, but the risk provided opportunity. As she walked back to her compound, her fear was that the risks were too great, the incident five months before had proven how quickly the unexpected could cause disaster.

Charly pushed back the door to the operations office as she arrived at the compound, the door opened with a small crash of boxes loaded for departure. Additional materials and stores that would go on a caravan with the two drays. A single face looked up at the noise, a face Charly had come to know very well in the last month.

Lachlan Goodwood smiled at the flustered and slightly frayed look on his boss's face. 'Will ya stop worrying for five minutes? You've moved stuff to that place for years, this is no different,' he stated calmly.

'Maybe, but this is all a bit new, and I am over all the bloody changes this week,' she grumbled. 'Ten camels in a string for four weeks was easy, just load them and ride away. Wagons, twenty, maybe thirty camels in a team, harnesses, and self-opinionated teamsters... blah, stop worrying you say, well maybe you should do it.'

Lachlan Goodwood leaned back in his chair; his ribs still tender even after the damage from the bullet wound had healed. He'd quickly accepted his new position as logistics manager of the expanded transport operation for Charly, a similar role to the one he'd had in the British military forces in the border wars in Afghanistan. While his position provided instant financial benefits, he also provided a steadying voice of council for Charly to rely on.

'Maybe I should.' He laughed at the exasperation evident in Charly the last few days. 'Or maybe I am already. Or maybe you need to let some of the worries stay with others that you pay.'

Charly smiled, knowing full well that Goodwood was right, she needed to relax a little.

'You still going with the two teams?'

'Yep, I am. I'll lead the support caravan,' she replied, knowing Lachlan recommended that this could be done by Qadir who now had responsibility to all supply caravans, with Ishmael and Mohamod as his trusted lieutenants. 'I want to check on the water carriers anyway.'

They were both silent for a while as Goodwood returned to his ledger spread on the desk before him.

'And I need to see what the dilatory fool that is driving the wells is doing,' she mumbled. 'Took his gear out there two months ago and not heard anything back how he is doing.'

Goodwood looked back up from the desk, a small frown on his forehead as he thought about the only well driver they could get in the district.

'Fair point. That bloke may not be your best business choice. But I guess that you did not have much option.'

The discussion flowed back and forwards for a short time until frustration and impatience finally got to Charly. She stood, wishing Lachlan a good evening and headed to her accommodation, desiring a warm bath and clean skin. The last time she would enjoy such pleasures for the next four or six weeks. Just to be moving tomorrow would remove much of the anxiety that was in her system.

As she walked into the hotel, avoiding the main bar, one of the women who cleaned and cared for the residents chased her to the door of her room.

'Baz say the aunties want to see you, they down by the camp at river.'

'Arrh, why today?' snapped Charly, her mind on the pleasures of clean warm water, sweet smelling soap and tingly skin. 'Thanks, Fay, please put off my bath. Maybe later when I get back.'

Charly spun on her heals and walked down the long passageway between the rooms. Her steps were a mix of annoyance and a determined impatience. She had been waiting for months for them to return. It was one of the reasons for travelling to see Mary, to send a message that the previous conversation was unfinished, that she wanted more information on her birth mother.

Within the hour, Charly arrived at the top of the riverbank. A smoky fire smouldered in the usual camp. Three older women sat together, as usual, working on repairs to the small baskets they used when moving from place to place. Charly recognised only one of them, Ginny, the other two were unknown to her. She continued to walk down, calling out as per custom to request joining the group. A request that was quickly provided by Ginny as she stood and walked over to warmly embrace Charly.

'Welcome, child, I have missed you. We parted in difficult circumstances when I last saw you,' Ginny said with warm affection. 'These are cousins from the north of your birthlands.'

Introductions were provided and then both sat, the usual conversation of general activities and wellness of family was undertaken at the slight impatience of Charly who want to only ask a few questions. The conversations required the fulfilment of custom and dignity expected when a visitor to the camp, but time was ticking, her bath was awaiting.

'Emmie did not come this time?' asked Charly, trying to steer the discussion.

The two other ladies looked shocked at the words.

Ginny replied quietly, 'I not speak that name now, Charly, that cousin not with us now.'

The implications were clear; Auntie Emmie had died, and a dead person's name was not spoken.

'Ohhh, I am sorry. I did not know, no-one has spoken to me from the tribe since last visit here.'

'It okay, Charly, you not at fault. It our fault,' said Ginny in sadness, knowing that words from the last visit had damaged an old friendship. 'Things said then that need to be forgotten, friends and family should not stay apart.'

'I agree but I cannot forget all that was said. My life, my blood, my other family, no, I cannot forget.'

Ginny sighed, looked at the far bank of the nearly dry river. 'Best you forget. No good come of wanting this,' stated Ginny firmly. 'She told me that she does not want what you want.'

'When? When did she say that?'

'Spoke to her since last meeting, Charly, she not happy we tell you.'

'So you won't be telling me where she is then, Ginny?'

'Not happening. I gave my word,' Ginny replied in annoyance, 'These cousin here to make sure I do as I was asked, or they tell her.'

Charly looked at the two of them, a hardness in their eyes confirming the words spoken were true. Charly knew that nothing would be said to answer her pressing questions, there was no point in asking, this would only cause greater insult. She knew Ginny had come to mend fences, but only if respect was shown for her wishes.

'Okay, Ginny. My love and respect for you and the people of your tribe remains,' said Charly quietly. 'But my hurt also remains and is now greater. This will take time to heal.'

With that said, Charly respectfully requested her leave from the camp and walked away without waiting for a response. The visit had opened new cuts, new questions and new disappointments. She did not know why she was being shunned in this manner. At least she had a few weeks to consider her thoughts, Charly contemplated. There was nothing quite like swaying to the rhythmic stride of a camel to clear one's mind of the many confused thoughts that were rattling around.

Chapter 14

The roll of the dray and engine had been effortless on the first day's travel over the reasonable roadway. Powerful beasts and skilled teamsters had brought the slow convoy to the first night's camp without incident. The camp locations had been chosen before they left, the sites identified during the first two deliveries to the mining camp and Tamimi field. The planning by Lachlan Goodwood provided additional benefits, allowing the support caravan to pull ahead late in the day and prepare before the drays arrived.

The second and third days followed the rhythm of the first. The gentle sway of the camel slowly bled the anger, frustration and anxiety from her body. By the morning of the fourth day Charly had found her old calmness. The countryside slowly changed as they moved from the taller open eucalypt bush to the lower, hardy stands of mulga and clumps of the various grasses, providing a fresh energy. For the first time in weeks she was happy with herself, providing a confidence that had almost disappeared at Casing Gap.

The road was little more than a sandy track, but with the rocks, roots and bumps removed to accommodate the big drays, their pace was good. The large wheels occasionally sank into the softer sand, but the combined power and weight of the camels dragged the dray onwards. The reason for the oversized wheels soon became apparent, they provided a larger curved surface on the ground, spreading the weight, transferring the load. Combined, all the parts allowed the weight of the mining equipment to continue towards its destination.

On the fifth day they met a water cart, one of the works team and small caravan preparing to return to the Springs. Qadir rode his camel at the head, clearly content with his world.

'Ah, it is wonderful to meet you, Miss Charly Khan!' he exclaimed as the stopped beside each other face in opposite directions. 'I trust the path is smooth and the camels have moved without problems.'

'Yes, Qadir, the road workmen have done well,' replied Charly, laughing at his endless boyish enthusiasm. 'I am without complaint in these matters.'

As the rest of the camel caravan passed, the discussion between Charly and Qadir revolved around any issues he had and how they would be resolved. Charly was pleased with Qadir's plans, he was a step or two ahead, she had no complaints or suggestions.

'So what of the road for our transit? Where are the last problems we face?' she asked.

'Two places,' he replied, knowing exactly what she was after. 'A little over a day's journey past the Gap there is soft sand. There are two locations in the middle of the plain between two dunes. On the first we have tried to bring in rock as a base. Unfortunately, there is little of this material, but the corduroy is completed. We are working on the second area, some two or three hours by camel past the first, but we need to lay more small logs, but the men have not had the time to finish this by the time you arrive.'

Charly had been told this area was a problem last time with lighter loads, this time would be more difficult. Hopefully the rocks and corduroying of the track would help. 'And the dunes?'

'The last two dunes remain an issue, we have not found a way around or over. As before, it is your greatest challenge and danger.' He paused. 'Both up and down.'

Charly knew the surveyor had tried to find a way around the last two sand dunes before the valley where the mine was located but had found nothing. The workers had considered digging a pass, a cut through the sand, but the logistics were overwhelming. With a quick farewell both parties moved in separate directions, leaving Charly with her worries and plans, all of which could only be proven accurate when the challenge was encountered.

A few days later they camped at the old camp site with the trees and small soak just short of Casing Gap. Tomorrow would be the first big test, the windblown sands at the Gap and then the area of built up track, with the sections of poor bearing ground. The location brought back many memories, causing a melancholy in her emotions, an air that quickly permeated the group as they sat around the fire that evening. All knew of the events of that incident, but few understood the reasons why Charly was so sad.

'That copper, Cullen, he die near here?' asked Jamison, one of the teamster drivers. 'That why you looking so glum?'

Charly smiled at the blunt words, both the teamster drivers were similar, short on words, clear in meaning. 'Sort of, Jammie. Yeah, he died at the start of the ambush, and it hurt lots, but I lost animals I had with me for years. One was my first camel,' Charly replied.

The teamster drivers nodded, they understood perfectly. They had deep appreciation if not love for their animals.

'Aye, be knowing what you say. When I lost my first bullock hauling into Burra mine, it ripped me heart too.' He looked at his compatriot. 'Same with you, Smithy, hey?'

They both nodded and the conversation ended. No words could be said to express this emotions on the subject.

'Hey, missy,' Jamison finally said. 'We been watching you on the track, you be okay to us. You know your stuff better than most.'

The compliment almost shocked her, these were very tough, hardened drivers, they did not give praise ever, it did not happen. Charly looked at them in surprise.

A smile was on Smithy's face. Nodding he replied, 'Bloody right he is, bloody right.'

Charly retuned the smile, a lift in her spirits. She only hoped that she could prove them right in the next difficult days.

The first dray had almost crossed half of the corduroy track before a wheel broke through the timbers. It quickly tore up the small logs, jamming timber under the frame and the left side wheels sank, tipping the dray dangerously.

'Be fucked, Smithy, gunna be a bit of fun to get this one out!' shouted Jamison back to the other teamster walking close behind him, his teams and dray waiting on the last firm ground before the softer sandy area. The camel team halted as the two experienced men looked at the issues.

As Charly rode her camel back from her earlier crossing of the area with the supply caravan, to stop beside the two men.

'Jammie, Smithy, I guess you know how to get out of this?' asked Charly. Both nodded at the question. 'Good, I won't interfere then,' she said calmly. 'You let me know what to get you, how to help and I will sort it out. You worry about the problem; I will worry about getting you the stuff you need.'

Both men smiled, they had spent too many hours removing stuck wagons and drays and being harried and shouted at by people who knew nothing. To have a boss who knew the ropes and stayed out of the way was a blessed moment. While it might take a few hours or more, the process was not that difficult.

'Four issues really, boss. Need to stop the dray tipping, then clear the jammed logs under, fix the rest of the damaged corduroy and then pull the old girl out,' Jamison stated, smiling at the surprise on Charly's face. 'Done it before, will be doing it again, I be thinking, boss. No dramas.'

Charly stood back and watched as the two canny teamsters went about the task. As they started the process of clearing the damaged roadway from under the dray, the rest of the camel drivers with the supply caravan were given orders that they quickly followed. Two long ropes were tied to the axles on the side of the dray that had sunk into the sand. They were looped over the dray and its cargo and pulled taut, then tied to stakes driven into the sand to stabilise the dray from tipping further. Two short poles were also propped under the low side of the dray to assist the problem. Issue one was resolved.

Issue two required the remains of the corduroy poles be cut or dug out. This was a simple process, it just took time, it took manpower. Manpower they did not have. But Charly thought she knew where the manpower they needed was and how to get it. Charly walked to the end of the dray.

'Hey, Jamison, you got a moment? I have a question.'

A filthy face popped out from under the dray as he dragged a rock out with him. 'I know the problem, the silly buggers did not take the rocks out to the edge of the track,' he grunted in annoyance. 'So when the wheels got on the logs, they snapped over the rocks.'

'Is that good news or worse?'

'Narr, good me and Smithy thinking,' he said. 'Once we get out of here, we pull the corduroy up, move the rocks to the right places and we should be okay when the logs are put back. But it will be a slow. Might take a half a week to cross this.'

'If we had more men, would it be quicker?'

'Sure, lot quicker, but we go none.'

'But I have. A works team is about two or so hours from here, working on the other soft area,' Charly said. 'So my question to you is should I get them to help here or keep them working on that area ready for when we get there?'

'A road works team! Shit, no question, missy, get them.' He suddenly laughed, his worries evaporating. 'May your camel have wings, girl. Get them for me and I will show these idiots how to build a dray quality road.'

Leaving Jamison in charge of the retrieval, Charly removed everything from her camel that would slow her travels before departing, only a pouch and water bag hanging from one side of the saddle, the now famous Winchester on the other. The trip was via the flat of the valley along a well-worn path, allowing a good pace, somewhere between a fast walk and a slow canter, a pace that a camel could manage for hours on end.

A little over an hour later, Charly rode up to the road work team. The men looks of shock on their faces, concerned by the arrival of a single rider. It was a possible poor portent of what may have occurred back down the road. She rode up to the supervisor, a huge man she had met once before, but unfortunately she was unable to remember his name. She climbed down from the camel, glad to be out of the saddle, if only for a few minutes.

'Mrs Khan, welcome. I'm concerned with your arrival there may be a problem,' he said with little enthusiasm.

'Yes, one of our drays have broken through the corduroy and has become deeply bogged, ummm Mr ah–?'

'Patterson.' He smiled. 'Thought you may have forgotten, not that we really ever have met.'

'Thank you, Mr Patterson. I do apologise, but can you organise to bring your team to where we are bogged, help us move forward?'

'Well, we probably could but we are employed by the mine, and they want us to build the road,' he said, towering over Charly. 'Now, you get permission from someone at the mine, well, we'll be right there.'

Charly looked incredulously at the man, the rules of the outback was to help, friend or foe, no matter what the circumstance, someone in distress was always assisted. She looked at the other ten men. All had stopped work, some had even started to pack up their equipment, ready to leave.

'Well that might be a problem for you, Mr Patterson, because I am one of the mine owners and you, at this moment, are ignoring the orders from management.'

'Nah, girly, you be trying to pull me leg,' he snarled, turning to walk away. 'Dig ya fucking wagons out yourselves.'

Charly shook her head at his response. She looked at one of the other men she knew well from her previous supply activities of the Tamimi mining field.

'Hey, Jacko, ya might want to let this idiot know his job is finished and then I will have him charged with refusing to assist stranded travellers if he does not get you lot moving,' she snapped in frustration.

Everyone in the bush knew that the territorial police did not have a high opinion of people that left travellers to fend for themselves. The man she had spoken to, Jacko, had been part of the big mine since the first days and knew well of Charly's connections. Gossip tended to spread quickly travelled through the Tamimi field on the new arrangement, she was a little surprised Patterson had not known of her involvement in management. Jacko rushed over and had a short and very animated conversation with the supervisor.

After a few minutes, Patterson strode back, his hands slightly clenched, his face hard. He stopped, his body too close to hers, trying to get Charly to take a step backward.

'Jacko tells me you might be telling the truth. Not that I am inclined to believe him.'

'Tell you what, Patterson,' she said quietly. 'You get half of the blokes on the wagon headed our way right now, I will forget our last conversation.'

He said nothing, still contemplating ignoring this woman, acting like she owned the world.

'If the rest get packed, ready to join the others when the wagon gets back for them.' She then smiled. 'I might put in a good word for you.' Charly turned and walked back to her camel. After mounting she looked down at Patterson. 'Defy me and you might not enjoy the outcome.'

Charly looked over at Jacko, standing with the others, watching who would buckle, who take the backward step and cede authority.

'Jacko, get the camels hitched on the wagon first thing in the morning, five men and light digging equipment, then come back and get the rest. Bring the water cart on the second trip,' she ordered without providing any options to the men.

She did not want to put the men in a difficult position, but she had no time to waste. Damn Patterson, stupidity in these parts lead to deaths, either his own or his men. She did not have time for him. He would be gone when they reached the mine site. She kicked her heels softly into the camel's side, leaving at the pace she'd arrived. There would be an argument left in her wake, but men knew the rules.

A little less than an hour after Charly had arrived back at the bogged dray, the sound of a wagon rumbling down the corduroy track made everyone look up. Sitting on the driver's seat was Patterson, his face expressionless as he pulled up. His men hopped off the back with their equipment.

'Great to see you, Patterson. Change of heart?' asked Charly quietly.

'Yeah, well, the blokes just did their thing and got ready, then they politely told me to piss off and not come back,' he replied earnestly. 'I then understood you and how you motivate men. I asked if I could come, they said only if I drove.'

Charly smiled. The men had shown that not to assist was against all they stood for, and making Patterson drive the wagon, while they rested, showed what they thought of him.

'You can stay for the night, head back for the rest in the morning.'

'Nah, I got enough light. The rest would be pissed right off if I delayed them coming to help,' Patterson replied. 'Got just enough time to get back before dark sets in, see ya tomorrow.'

With the extra five sets of experienced hands, powerful men who worked the earth, the dray was freed of broken and jammed timbers, and the first section of corduroy roadway prepared. Everyone agreed to not try and move the dray till the next morning. The camels had been removed some hours before, all fifty of them now hobbled and quietly grazing on the soft, native grass.

The work of the day had been exhausting, and after a quick meal, most unrolled their swags and were sound asleep. Charly walked out to where the camels were settled down, some asleep, some chewing cud. A soft quarter moon just providing a little light, but the intensity of the stars in the clear night allowing safe steps.

Charly saw the shape of the teamster off to her left. She suddenly smiled, knowing what it was. She walked over and sat down beside

Jamison. He stuffed tobacco in his pipe and lit it, a small cloud of smoke covered his face as he puffed to set the embers inside.

'You need your sleep, Jammie. Long day tomorrow.'

'Yeah, but needed to check the boys and girls, they be my family and children.'

Charly smiled, knowing exactly what he meant. They chatted about what the animals meant to them for a short time. Finally both wandered back to their bedrolls, sleep called.

The following day, the wagon with the rest of the road team rumbled to the camp shortly after dawn, travelling in early half-light and eating cold rations to ensure they arrived without delay. Charly insisted they had a hot cup of tea and warm fresh damper with tasty dripping before they did anything. She immediately took up organising the camp duties, staying away from the road repairs, knowing this was work for powerful men. One of the road crew spoke with Patterson, then walked over, informing Charly he was the cook for the road works team and would run the camp and kitchen to ensure everyone had hot food at the midday break.

The team of twenty camels were harnessed to the bogged dray. The second team of camels were harnessed to the two long ropes used to stabilise the dray, positioned to pull at a forty-five-degree angle, slightly lifting and pulling the bogged side.

In front of them, the road work crew were already repositioning the rock under the outside edges of the logs, under the line of the wheels. They were progressing remarkably quickly, Patterson in the middle of the action, his extraordinary power making the heavy lifts look easy. Jamison waited until he had enough room to pull the dray out and then move it to a stable section of the rebuilt roadway.

After two hours he was satisfied. Jamison called all the men away from the roadway, he did not wish to hurt anyone if the camels bolted when the harness broke, an issue that had happened to him once before. Everyone moved away and stood watching. Jamison had rejected the thoughts of pushing, then changed his mind after watching Patterson and two of the other large framed men working this morning.

'Oi, Patterson, changed me tune a bit. Can I get you and them two big blokes of yours to give the old dray a bit of a shove? Just when she starts to move, stop the bugger rolling back if the camels slip on the logs.'

With the three men positioned, Jamison called his camels in the softest voice, a call Charly had not heard. The camels reacted, taking the strain as Jamison touched the leaders back with end of his long whip. Then with a different call, again one not clearly heard but just a little sharper, the camels put power into the harness. Smithy also applied force via his team. The dray started to quiver, then rolled back ever so slightly. Three powerful bodies lifted the back of the dray, their slightly crouched legs straining, slowly straightening. The timbers they pushed off the dray creaked and groaned from the applied force.

Jamison called again, this time it was roar of energy and excitement, urging power from his team. The dray did not move. It quivered slightly as the power was applied, then suddenly the grip of the sand was no more. The dray moved, and inch, five, ten, a foot, two feet, then there was no resistance. The dray rolled up on top of the logs of the repaired corduroy. They were free.

The team stopped, allowing them to rest, as Jamison knew the simple process of dragging the dray from the sand took a great deal from them. Smithy loosened the two ropes, a broad smile on his face as he came over to slap his mate on the back.

'Nahh, Smithy, it was them three blokes. Shit, mate, they nearly lifted the bugger out of the sand. All we did was roll it forward,' he said pointing to the three men laying on their backs, their chests heaving but all laughing as their road team stood around cheering them on.

Patterson sat up, took a final deep breath. 'Right, blokes, enough, now let's fix our stuff up and get this load to the mine.'

The repair to the damaged roadway was quickly fixed, logs and rock having been already stacked beside the damaged area. All the available people, including the two teamsters worked on the repair of the roadway for the remaining part of the day, and through the next, before Jamison slowly brought the team of camels and the dray across to solid ground late the second day. The steel wheeled engine followed shortly after, stopping beside the loaded wooden dray.

It had taken more than two days to move just a few hundred yards. Jamison, Smithy, Patterson and Charly had a quick conference to plan their next move as they watched the men unharness the camel teams.

'Leave the dray and engine here tonight, let the camels rest for the night. We attack the next section tomorrow.'

'Patterson, do you think we will get across in one day?' asked Charly.

'No, the corduroy is twice as long, and we aren't quite finished yet. After seeing what we did today, maybe three or four days.'

The following days were a repetition of the first two, after reaching the second soft sand area a few hours after leaving the camp. The first activity was the rebuilding of the road to the new standards required by the teamsters, then extending the last section to ground that could bear the weight of the drays. Finally, on the evening of the fourth day they were ready to go, but everyone knew that tomorrow would be the test. They were too tired to try, one error and then it would be two days or more days longer.

As they waited for the evening to close in on the fourth day, Charly took two of the workmen a little way from the edge of the corduroy roadway and asked them to dig a hole about four feet deep, deeper than any of the road works. The hole was quickly dug in the sand, and to everyone's surprise, water filled the bottom quarter of the hole, sweet, clear water.

A second hole was dug a short distance from the first, little deeper, again filling with water. They had a soak, they had water on the trail, and it was cool and clean, much better than what was in the metal water cart.

'How the hell did ya know?' asked Patterson after taking a long drink and washing his face from a bucket of water. 'You some sort of water witch or something?'

Charly smiled, shaking her head. 'Nope, just that this place reminded me of somewhere else we found water, it had soft sand too that did not provide much bearing.'

As she walked away, she suddenly thought of another place she knew like this, a place she would see very soon in a long windblown valley.

As they sat around the fire after the evening meal, all the men either laying back enjoying a quite smoke or discussing the day's activity, Patterson suddenly asked a question that had been making the rounds of the roadworks team.

'Jamison, got one question that the boys want to know.' His words brought a hushed silence to the camp. 'What's the longest you been bogged? Like, days or weeks?'

Jamison chewed on the ball of tobacco for a while before looking over at his fellow with a cheeky grin before replying. 'Not as long as you, hey, Smithy, you being a bloke that likes to stay put when the occasion calls,' he said, laughing. 'Me, well the worst, about a few days short of two months, I reasoning. Smithy, well, his dray was still there last time I saw. That would be about two years ago.'

Everyone looked stunned, imagining spending two months digging out a bogged wagon.

'When I had a bullocky team, deep in the country near the Murray, bloody soft black soils after lots a rain and the roads collapsed into muddy goo below.' He looked at Patterson and the rest of the road team. 'That's why I be so particular on how ya build them.'

He let his words sink in.

'Not that we dug for two months, but that was how long before we got the big dray out. Bullocks more than belly deep in the crap, lost a couple that time. Smithy's drays sunk, only one front corner above the muck by the time we got his load off, lost half his team.'

By the time Jamison finished his words, his eyes glinted with the formation of tears. He stood to take his late evening walk before heading to his bed roll for sleep. Charly watched him leave the edge of the fire's flickering light, knowing that just the thought of his lost animals was distressing. She rolled over and pulled the edge of the blanket and waterproof canvas over herself to keep out the nights cold, knowing that she too would remember the animals she had and would lose with similar emotional pain.

The crossing the next day was not without incident. The steel rear wheel of the engine slipped off the side of the corduroy, sinking deeply into the sand as part of the corduroy sagged. Again, it looked as if the engine would tip over, but a quick reaction allowed the large wheel to be dragged from the grip of the sand back onto the edge of the logs. Two or three logs kicked up as they snapped on the ends, with one smashing against the side of the engine, splintering and denting some of the equipment strapped to the side.

But the engine was out, continuing slowly along a slow walking pace, following where the wooden dray had travelled an hour before. A little after midday both the dray, engine and both teams were on the other side of the first major challenges of the trip, the soft boggy sands. The next and last of the challenges was a little over a week away, plenty of time to think about a solution to that problem of two sand dune crossings before they dropped down into the valley that was their destination.

With the support caravan and the two teams drawing the dray and the metal engine slowly disappearing into the distance along the roadway, Charly finalised her discussion, making her farewell to Patterson and his team.

'Look, Mrs Khan,' – as Patterson now tended to call Charly, a tone of respect in his voice – 'I can leave half the team here, working on this and I can follow with rest later today. Never know what might happen. I be thinking that you'll likely need our help at the dune crossings.'

Charly was unsure. She knew that added manpower would be helpful, but finishing the road was also a priority. The safety of the men who remained also sat on her mind, pushing her one way, while the importance of getting the equipment to the mine was both a personal and financial profit.

'If you be worrying about the boys staying, well, the team is set up to work in two groups, and they'll be supplied by your caravans anyway,' Patterson stated, sensing what was causing the uncertainty in Charly's mind.

'Okay, Patterson, your final choice but having your team's assistance would be very welcome,' Charly finally replied, knowing that the operations of the mine, and the safe, timely arrival of the machinery was critical. No-one would complain. 'Actually, bring them all. See you at the camp tonight, your team would be most welcome, I'm sure.'

Charly followed the teamsters and their wheeled burdens, slowly disappearing into the distance. She rode at a steady rate that would catch them up in an hour or so, enjoying the time alone, just herself and the surrounding environment. The wheels had barely cut into the surface more than a width of her hand she noted as she rode, then the odd softer section, the power of the camels had pulled the loads clear. As the miles dropped by, she knew that the next few days would be a steady plodding till the next challenge awaited.

Chapter 15

C harly sat and stared ahead. Before her was the barrier of sand and
grass she had dreaded for the last two days. Maybe two or three
hundred yards to the top, not too steep but the grade was challenging
at around twenty-degree up the long slope. She squirmed in her old
saddle, worn to a finite level of comfort, a level of comfort as could
be possible when perched on a long-legged, hairy animal. The tracks
of the last trip by the drays with substantially lighter loads still were
still cut deep into the sandy slope between the tussocks of grass. For
the two teamsters, the memory was fresh of the agonised crossing: the
frantic climb, followed by the heart stopping decent, barely controlled
by the large wooden brake on the drays.

This time, the weight was more than double, close to treble on the
dray. And the engine did not have a brake, the wheels simply provided
motion to the heavy steel frame and boiler. To get up one side was one
thing, getting down without the dray or engine rolling through the
team of camels was another much larger issue to be resolved.

Charly snorted her annoyance at not having a clear answer. Whatever
the answer was lay in the minds of some very strong men, men who
rarely confided what they thought, enjoying the small amount of
private knowledge, provided willingly only when she was truly at her
wit's end. She knew it was a game they played, she knew they would

never risk her mission, rather waiting until she asked, allowing them to show their, at times questionable, superior knowledge.

She rode back to where the support caravan was setting camp for the night, a short thirty minutes travel from the foot of the first dune crossing. Just enough time to warm the animals, without causing any loss of energy from excessive activity. The two teams were about an hour behind, the last few miles being difficult as the sand was not as firm as on the flats. Patterson's teams rode behind them on the last wagon, fixing the track as they moved forward or helping the teams keep moving.

As the dray pulled in and Jamison started to remove the camels from the harnesses, Charly assisted as had become the norm, putting the hobbles on the forelegs as they were freed. Taking time to discuss the days travel, issues with the track and camels, simply enjoying being with the animals.

'So, Jammie, you have travelled it once, and now seeing the bugger of this sand bar again, what are your thoughts?' Charly finally asked, getting to the subject she had wanted to discuss since Jamison arrived.

'Be thinking I unbuckle the harness and take my team home. I be a flat land teamster. If I cannot be seeing over it and can't be getting around it, then I will avoid it,' Jamison answered, knowing what Charly had wanted to discuss, dragging out his other comments to heighten the tension.

'Shit, Jammie, you're not helping me much,' Charly grumped. 'Take a little pity on a poor young woman, my emotions will overwhelm me if I do not know soon.'

'I be thinking the poor young woman swears too much. One would think she be a driver or something worse, maybe one of them cameleers, hey.' He laughed. 'And a tough one at that.'

'Jamison, enough for goodness sake man, give me something so I can sleep at least.'

Jamison kept unbuckling the team, chuckling to himself, taking his time checking the condition of his camels as he went. At one point he called to one of the Afghan drivers in the support convoy to have a closer look at a foot pad that had been cut deeper than usual on a rock.

'Bloody quartz, the odd bit of rock on the track, edges like knives. Have to watch for this tomorrow.'

'I agree, but I am also giving up,' retorted Charly.

'Already, girl? You got no stamina for a little word jousting.' He chuckled again, this time in a warm tone between people of deep respect. 'Okay, Smithy and I have some ideas. Might be difficult, but I know we can do it, with a little luck and Patterson's burly blokes.'

'And, pray tell, what would that be?' she retorted.

Chuckling at her response, he explained the plan, a mix of clever use of the two teams and a couple of items brought on the wagon with Patterson's men. The plan was simple. Complexity led to issues that escalated to major failure, growled Jamison, a simple plan for simple creature.

'Speaking about us blokes only, them camels are smarter than most think.'

'How so?' replied Charly, knowing that this would lead to another of his word riddles.

'Well, they act dumb, right? Then they make us think they are dumb, and so we treat them as dumb. Ya following?' Charly nodded, wondering where all this was going. 'So we don't ask them to do stuff like horses, just mosey around and occasionally carry stuff at walking pace, and get cared for like babies. Now I have to be asking ya, who be the smart critters?'

Charly laughed. *Yep, only they had to do this in the heat and dry of the desert*, she thought as she walked back to the camp. But it was better than the wet and cold, that's for sure. A hill of sand might be difficult, but a hill of slippery wet dirt and mud would be impossible.

The morning started earlier than usual. Hot sweet tea and toasted damper left over from last night's dinner, liberally coated in sweet jam, filled the bellies of the men as they stood around gazing at the top of the dune not yet provided with a first rays of sun, simply a dark ominous mass.

Jamison hitched up his team first, Smithy then pulled out a special braided rope with shackles that he linked to the tongue of the dray, then the back of the harness of his own team, putting his in front of Jamison's by some twenty yards. The dray now had a team of forty animals, a dangerous and unwieldy mass of animals connected by a braided rope. Two ropes were tied to the rear corners and spread out to each side. Ready for five men on each side to stabilise the dray.

The two thin poles, a little longer than the width of the dray, were tied to the load. Jamison was disinterested in the small additional weight, knowing their importance when they reached the top of the dune.

'Right, Smithy, you lead and set the pace. And for the sake of angels, don't be slowing or my boys will drive right up their arses, and that will cause a commotion.'

Smithy laughed lightly, but he had a steely look on his face. He knew his team was critical to find the top with an even rhythm, Jamison's team only provided power to keep the dray moving. Without a word, just a slight nod, Smithy tapped the back of his lead camel. It took the first strain, slowly transferring it to the next and so on until the dray slowly inched forward. The ten men carried the ropes, five to a side, knowing they had to take the sharpness out of the sideways movement as this killed forward motion.

The first team arrived at the sandy base of the dune, the slightly softer sand allowing for a deeper print of each pad, but the pace did not change. The full length of Smithy's team was on the dune by some distance when the lead camel from the second dune started up. The men had run out and now slowly walked at the smooth, even pace of the camels.

The dray finally arrived at the first change of the incline of the sand. The wheels sank in a little more, but the pace did not change. If a camel slipped slightly, the overall energy of the forty camels swallowed the loss. The pace continued as the lead camel from the first team reached the halfway point. The dray sagged as one side slipped into a soft patch of windblown sand, the men of the opposite side strained against the pull, lifting the drays slightly, allowing the wheels to keep momentum.

Each step by the lead camel was another to winning the battle. Smithy called quietly to his team, urging power but keeping calm. Smooth rhythm would be the winner, and surging would hurt, then kill their momentum. In the second team Jamison was doing the same, calm and smooth, but he could feel the power being applied. Ever so gradually, the pace dropped as the gradient sucked the energy from the teams.

They required some forward movement as the first team reached the summit, or they would never be able to restart on the upslope, they just needed some pace. The lead camels from the first team reached three quarters of the climb. The pace was still good, until two of Jamison's camels slipped at the same time that the right side of the dray sank into another soft hollow of windblown sand. The pace collapsed, leaving a little movement that appeared to be about to falter, when both rope teams surged forward, the big men straining, providing the small spark to keep rolling.

With this minimal pace, the camels digging deep, the lead camels from the first team breasted the crest, then the next two, and then the two after. The camels leading suddenly were facing downhill, their body weight adding to the power pulling the dray higher. As the entire of the first team went over the crest, Jamison waved to Patterson's men, who rushed in and pulled out the poles, slipping, running, falling but reaching the crest as the long-braided rope touched the sand. The poles were laid across the sand, the ropes sliding over them, stopping them burying into the sandy surface of the dune.

With a full team pulling downhill on the other side of the dune, the second team quickly reached the top, coming to a stop when the dray sat perfectly on the crest. The first step was complete, now to safely descend to the flat ground below.

Jamison quickly disconnected the braided rope from the dray's tongue, allowing Smithy to slowly turn his team, bringing them back to the top of the crest. Jamison had locked the brake on his side of the dray's front wheel, providing just enough holding power to stop it rolling, but not to slow its decent. The two teamsters had a quick word and shook hands. Their well-planned ascent of the first dune had worked within their expectations, now for the decent.

Two of Patterson's men were called over and asked to lift one of the poles laying in the sand under the dray. The pole was slipped into the rear wheels of the dray and securely fastened to the thick spokes with leather thongs, just below the tray framework of the dray. A small turn of both wheels would lock them tight, stopping the rotation. The rear wheels had become skids, allowing them to dig into the sand enough to provide resistance. The resistance from the sand was just enough to cause the skid, but not enough to damage the large, sturdy spokes.

With the two teams of men taking up the ropes on either side, Jamison walked to the front of his team. He took the head halter from the one of the lead camels and started walking down the slope. As the dray moved forward, the rear wheels sank slightly into the sand, forcing the camels to pull sightly.

At a calm, even walking pace the team of camels moved at a steady rhythm and the dray slowly slid slowly down the sandy slope. Occasionally it dug in more on one side of the other, but the teams of mean kept the dray level. Without any sudden stops or jerks, the dune fell away, hundreds of yards of sloping sand passed beneath the dray and the team reached the bottom without incident. As the dray reached the base of the slope, Jamison removed the pole from the wheels to limit placing undue strain on the spokes and took the dray to a clear, flat area.

The ropes and pole were removed from the dray, and the camels removed as a harnessed team. Everyone retuned to the top of the dune, then descended to the far side, the camels slowly towing the poles and ropes behind them. Charly sat on her camel a little way to the side of the activity, watching intently. She suddenly understood that she was no longer required for these transits. She had chosen wisely when employing her men, especially the two teamsters, and that she should leave them do what they were very good at doing. She very much felt as a spare waterbag, available if required, but in reality, not needed, just an added weight to the process.

Charly smiled as she thought about Jamison's words the previous evening; he had been trying to tell her that her roles was not his, she was to organise, pick the best to do the jobs, and let them prove their worth. As she watched the men and camels descend to the sandy slope, she knew this would likely be one of her last transits for the years to come. She would come again, but only as a passenger, not as the caravan's leader. That role would be left to those she employed.

The thoughts sat heavy in her heart but also gave her great pride; she had achieved what she'd set out to prove; that she, as a woman, could live this life, prosper and be respected by the toughest of men.

The second crossing with the engine followed the exact course as the first attempt with the dray. The supply caravan and Patterson's almost empty wagon, drawn by the four camels, followed in short order, bringing all the equipment and stores required for the next crossing. They arrived at the base of the dune as the sun was low in the sky. All the men were exhausted, but the air was full of energy. They had bested one and had learned how to better the next. The next dune awaited them on the other side of the long wide valley, ready for their activities in two days' time.

The following day they crossed the flat valley, a long convoy of animals but with without any complications, they drew to the other side without effort. They set up the camp as they had previously at the foot of the dune, allowing the camels to rest for the next day's crossing. The crossing of the second dune flowed in practiced ease, the men in particular knowing their roles, lessening the orders and commands. The camels had also learned; the pace was maintained with ease both up and down. By evening the second dune was conquered and in two days' time they would arrive at their destination.

'You should be riding ahead, Mrs Khan,' noted Jamison as he sat with a pipe in his mouth, quietly puffing away like a small locomotive.

'At your camel's pace you'll arrive before sundown. Save yourself an extra night with us smelly old farts.'

Charly laughed at the very apt description. The smell in the camp some still nights was a little thick, even for her as a cameleer.

'What? And miss one more day watching the best two teams in a thousand miles?' she said, shaking her head. 'I think you know what I am thinking. I want to enjoy the last two days that I will be on the trail as a team boss. It may be the last for a long time.'

Jamison sat, and slowly nodded his head. What she was saying was true, her role had passed, the men around her had made the change, they had proven their worth. He knew they had a goodly number of further large loads to bring on this transit, and when it was done, then they would move on to some other role and place to show their skills, but till then they would not fail.

'Yep, girly, things change,' he growled. 'Be proud of what you done, this be one of the best crossings I've ever done, and you made it happen.' He stood, puffing away as he walked into the grassed area where the camels were hobbled before the evening light disappeared.

Late on the second day after leaving the camp at the base of the dune, Charly rode her camel over a slight rise and looked down at the windblown valley below. The supply caravan slowly filed past her, the lean cameleer calling a short phrase in his native tongue, words of praise and congratulation. Charly smiled and called back, praising his skill, knowing that this man was another well-chosen leader of future caravans who would not be requiring her daily directions.

Charly looked back at the changes that had occurred. the preparations for the equipment she carried were completed, the large shed that would house the stamp battery and mill partly built. The land of the valley was now better organised, with a number of permanent buildings replacing the flapping canvas tents. The mine works had changed, the surface scratching had evolved to a small number of well-formed pits and shafts. The biggest sat on the area of the quartz reef, a small mound of waste rock that lead from a slightly angled hole in the ground on the upslope of the ground that rose to form the edge of the valley.

In the distance was a frame surrounded by a few men and their favoured animals, donkeys and asses pulling the cutting head that was chopping a hole in the ground, the site of her well diggers. She pushed ahead of the first team of camels, moving quickly down the slope to the mine office, now three times as large as she remembered that auspicious day when she'd done the deal.

She stopped her camel at the front of the office building and forced it to drop on its haunches before she dismounted. The mine manager pushed open the door and stood on the verandah deck, watching with a barely suppressed smile on his face. Charly took the few paces across the dry dirt before taking the couple of steps up onto the deck, reaching out and shaking Derek Burrows' hand. His eyes glittered in almost religious fervour, which Charly knew was the last thing she would expect from the man who was as dry as the sand around him and rarely showed any emotion.

'Well, Derek, ya either tell me or you are going to explode,' Charly said, avoiding the usual pleasantries of arrival.

'You, my young lady, have arrived on a most auspicious day! You will never be the same again, we struck lucky at the mine.'

'What is it with you men? Ya all get excited and talk in babbling riddles.' She snorted, thinking of Jamison's word games.

He laughed, the excitement had put him a slightly silly mood. A little lightheaded he picked up Charly and spun her around, her slightly loose kameez blowing up, revealing a lot more of her body than she was prepared for. He placed her back on the deck and impulsively kissed her on the lips.

'My word, this is a welcome for the ages,' Charly said, a little breathless, her heart thumping in her chest. 'You're either very happy to see me or something is addling your mind my dear friend and partner.'

Derek took a few deep breaths, suddenly realising what he'd just done to the young unattached woman. 'Oh dear, that was unacceptable, my apologies. You are right, I'm losing my mind.'

'So, it must be crazy, you are one of the more sensible fellows I know.'

'Come into the office. It is almost unbelievable,' he asked her, trying to keep his head. 'As I said, we hit something yesterday in the mine, and this changes everything.'

Once inside Derek poured a glass of whiskey from a bottle that Charly had bought him after signing the agreement. As she sipped the fine liquid, enjoying its flavour, Dereck explained the reason for his excitement.

'We've been driving along the line of the vein, trying to get a feel of the grades before we invest in the shaft as you know.' To which Charly nodded, remembering the plans discussed three months before.

'Well, the grades are not bad, some up and some down, but generally steady.' He sipped on a little more of the liquid in his glass. 'Well, five days ago we hit the first of the cross veins. We hit the second one yesterday, and we proved what it holds this morning.'

Derek casually handed over a chuck of rock for Charly to hold, almost totally yellow, the size of his fist. '…And it holds the gold, Charly. It's massively rich, maybe over fifteen yards long and a foot or so thick. Runs a little on the cross vein too.'

Charly sat stock still. The amount he was talking about was insane.

'You, my dear girl, even at five per cent, are now a very rich person.'

'So all we need is water,' Charly said softly, knowing that this was what was controlling what they did in this valley.

'Yes, you are right, all we need is water,' replied Derek flatly, deflating somewhat. Without it they could not expand. He then laughed, his words holding a very serious edge. 'You find me water and then you have ten per cent stake plus all standard transport rates back, no arguments.'

The talked a little longer about the situation and possibilities, but the concept of water supply had exhausted Derek's earlier headiness.

The little they had from the original soak, now a shallow well, was managed with critical care. What they had was barely able to support the miners and the mine. They had noticed the levels dropping slowly, even with a number of good rains in the last couple of months.

Charly finally stood, the news of the rich strike a little too surreal to take seriously. Maybe some other time. She placed her empty glass next to the bottle.

'Well, I guess I better find out what my water digger is doing,' she said quickly, making to depart the office. She smiled. 'Oh, and Derek? I enjoyed the kiss, and it – well, you know – but I still sleep with my camels.'

Derek laughed at her words, the longstanding boundary between them. He also sat down his glass next the bottle, knowing both would have another drop or two while she was here but it would never lead to anything.

'And I need to get the guys unloading what you've brought, and, yes, you've fulfilled that part of the agreement better than I ever expected.'

As they left the building they knew that their futures were tied to each other and the small hole over by the head of the valley where the slope of the land rose gently.

Chapter 16

Charly quickly checked the teamsters, and was told all was in order and they would be ready to return in two or three days. This was followed by a quick assurance by the cameleers from her supply caravan that they would have the stores unloaded and ready to leave within a day or so. The men smiled at the slightly annoyed expression from Charly, as she again realised she was not really needed at this point in the process.

Patterson and his team were off getting a few basic supplies to take back, knowing their main resupply would be provided from the Springs on the next caravan. Charly hoped to see him before they headed back but if not, she would be able to provide her thanks when they crossed paths on the trail next. Knowing there was nothing left for her to do here, she mounted her camel and rode the mile or so to where the well was being driven into the dry sandy ground.

She pulled up slightly short and watched the large metal spike being dropped down, the steel pipe sitting deep into the earth. The sound of wet dirt being disturbed as the metal spike drove just a little further, loosening the solid ground driving a little further each time. The wet loose dirt and sand removed as required, the hole slowly getting deeper. Every foot was a foot closer to possible water.

A man slowly walked from the timber frame of the derrick, muddy, dirty and greasy, a slight scowl on his face. Clarence Guthrie, or Clarrie as everyone other than his mother called him, was not the nicest or friendliest man on the surface of the earth, but he could find water. Or more accurately, he once could find water.

'Hey, Clarrie, how's progress?' asked Charly, hoping for good news.

'Drove two holes over yonder, place looked likely but hit nothing,' Clarrie replied. 'So came over here where you said but thinking it's no better than before.' Clarrie looked around at the dry windswept valley, dust devils lifting in the distance where a gust flowed over a small crest of land.

'I thinking no water here, Charly girl. You gunna git nothing but dry bottoms.'

'How deep are you with this one?'

'About thirty-five feet. Can't go much past fifty in this stuff, then we likely hit rock anyways.'

'How long to get to fifty feet?'

'Three days, I guess, might be more.'

'Okay, Clarrie, I'm here about that long, let's see what happens,' Charly replied. 'We keep driving till I leave. Who knows what we might hit.'

Clarrie shook his head. He'd not hit water anywhere for over two years, his luck had ended, he knew his days were finished, he had lost all confidence. But if they paid, who cared if he was driving in a waterless waste; it wasn't his money. He walked back to his two dirty men. If possible, they were even more unkempt than he was. The thud of the heavy iron driving pole as it smashed into the fresh ground at the bottom of the hole echoed around them. Fifteen feet to go and he could return to his life on the bottle, an activity he'd missed. He hated that water driving and being a drunk did not mix out in these parts.

Charly watched the men for a while, then rode back to the mine. The next few days would be telling for the future of everything around her. She knew she would need to finalise a number of plans with Derek, and bring Jamison into the discussion; he would be taking charge of the transport to this valley, and there was a lot of equipment to come. It was time she stood back a little, let someone else deal with the everyday issues.

Charly rode back down to the tall timber frame where the hole was being driven deeper into the ground with every drop. It was her last day at the valley, tomorrow she would leave with the rest of her camel caravan and teamsters. The stamp battery was standing and the stationary engine in place where the big shed would one day be completed. There were still works to be done to connect the two pieces of machinery and have the battery operational, but that would be for others to finish.

As she rode towards the water driving operation, she thought about yesterday's incident, hoping that the aggravation between her and Clarrie would have softened. She still shook her head remembering the slight madness of yesterday, after she had ridden down in the afternoon to find Clarrie starting to pack up the water driving equipment.

'Hey, Clarrie, I thought we'd agreed that you would keep driving till I left tomorrow,' she had asked in a mix of annoyance and surprise.

'Yeah, well, maybe, but I hit rock, so it's stuffed. Nothing here,' Clarrie had replied insolently, refusing to look up from what he was doing acknowledge her. 'No water in this valley, about time ya stopped dreaming, girl. Look around, dry as one the dates your blokes eat.'

'So how deep are you with the hole?'

'Forty-five feet, seven inches,' was the reply. Clarrie stopped. 'Seriously, lady, you and me are wasting our time. We hit rock and it's all over.'

One of Clarrie's men walked over behind him, a frustrated look on his face. He looked at Charly and gave a quick shake of his head. Charly at first thought it was an action in agreement with his boss, but then she saw the annoyance and knew it was the opposite.

'So tell me, Clarrie, is the rock hard or can we still drive through it?'

The man behind Clarrie nodded, affirming she was on the right track.

'Hard or soft, girly, it's rock.' Clarrie snorted. 'Make no difference – there be nothing below it!'

Charly bit her tongue at the insolence. She was paying this man good money and he was acting like so many others before him, as if she knew nothing. She looked back to the young man standing behind him, noting the anger building on his face.

'How much for your rig, Clarrie?' she quietly asked, the tone slightly ominous. 'I will pay you and you can go.'

'I not selling.' He snorted in anger. 'Piss off and feed the chickens or something a girl like you should be doing.'

Charly smiled. He had done the usual thing, failing to take her seriously, thus providing her the options she needed to fight the battle.

'Thank you for your wonderful advice… but I remind you that you have three options: finish the hole, sell me your rig, or pack up.' She smiled up at him in the sweetest feminine look she could muster. 'Do the first two and I will get you back to the Springs free of charge. Do the third and you'll need to find your own way, but not on my camels and wagons.'

She turned and walked back to her camel, knowing that the now very angry man behind her could do anything, but she could not turn to face him. It would show her fear, provide him with the power.

'Ya be a hard bitch, Charly Khan,' Clarrie called after her in angry voice. Then he almost laughed. 'And bloody tough at negotiating. Alright, we keep driving till tomorrow evening.'

Charly did not stop, climbed on her camel and had it lurch to its feet and stand upright. Charly looked down at Clarrie, still standing at the same spot, the young man barely concealing his smile.

'Goodo, mate,' Charly said in a friendly tone as if nothing happened. 'See ya later tomorrow. Hopefully we have some water, hey?'

She'd ridden off then, knowing he would fume and snort and yell at his blokes, but he would keep driving.

Now, nearly a full twenty-four hours after the stoush with Clarrie, it would be interesting to see what progress they'd made. Her morning had been full of finalising new transport agreements and a quick trip underground to see the fabulous bounty mixed bright yellow in dirty brown rock. She had commented that the quartz had changed as they got closer to the intersection of the cross veins, moving from a nice white to a dirty rusty colour. Derek had laughed, explaining it was a good indicator, and they would find those other minerals lower that had oxidised just below the surface making the quartz rusty brown.

The sight of the mass of gold in the quartz still filled her head as she slowed her camel. If only they could get enough water to process it, let alone have enough water to supply the men to dig it out of the ground. The water in the soak was close to finished; they had no options but bring it from the Springs in the water carts, and that would not work for long.

Charly looked at the timber framed derrick as the drive head was dropped one more time, a dull thud emanating from the pipe. As she climbed off the camel, Clarrie slowly walked over. His face was downcast, a look that needed no interpretation as to its meaning.

'Nothing, still dry as a witches...' He let his voice trail off quietly, not willing to approach the issues from yesterday. 'Another hour and we pack up.'

'How deep are you now?'

'Fifty-two feet or thereabouts. Same ground, softish rock.'

'Do you know what it is? Maybe I can ask Derek.'

'Nope, but there is some laying up against the stem. Ya can go and have a look, just don't get in the way of the drive head.'

Charly walked over to the cast iron stem pipe, sticking about four feet out of the ground, and bent down to pick up a shard of dark grey rock. It was slightly layered, flaking in her hand. A shout caught her attention, causing her to step back as the drive head dropped one more time. She felt, as much as heard, the impact from where she was standing.

Charly was about to walk back, when she heard a strange groan and a sharp squeak from deep in the pipe. The cable lifting the drive head suddenly went slack, then tightened and went slack again. The cast iron stem pipe gave a shudder as another groan emanated from deep in the pipe.

Without thinking, Charly took a step forward to have a look down the pipe, as something smashed into her shoulder. One of the drillers heard the change in the noise of the winch with its telltale outcome of the driver being pushed back up the stem pipe. He rushed to knock Charly away from the danger, driving her off her feet to fall on the ground. The impact caught the kameez on the edge of the stem pipe, tearing it from top to bottom. It the instant she fell, the top of the stem pipe appeared to explode. The drive head and fifty feet of wire cable spewed upwards to smash into the timber frame. A powerful column of water followed, flinging the metal head as far as the wire would allow it, water spraying up over the timber, falling on everything around the shaking timber frame of the derrick.

A stream of water hit her, defected off one of the cross timbers, further tearing her old worn kameez, the frayed cloth notwithstanding the power of the water, washing it off one arm. The stream of water pushed her backwards as she tried to sit up, sliding in the wet dirt and mud that had formed around her. The pressure from the bore fell slightly, allowing Charly to crawl aside and lay on her back, the kameez now laying in the mud.

Charly slowly picked herself up to a sitting position, mud dripping from all parts of her body. She started to wipe it off, but the brownish mud just spread, as if she was painting herself. The young man that had crashed into her to push her away from the cast iron pipe quickly stood up and rushed back towards the pile of equipment, unconcerned by Charly's predicament. He joined Clarrie and the other men already dragging out large iron parts, spanners and other equipment.

Water and mud ran from Charly as she stood, as she noticed that the flow of water was lessening to a steady flow, but still pumped a column well above her head. Charly walked over and stood under the falling water, soaking her like being in a torrential downpour of rain. She was now totally soaked through, her remaining clothes stuck to her skin as she lifted her hands to feel the water falling on her. The sticky whitish mud slowly washed away, uncovering Charly, cleaning her of the weeks, months and years of imagined dirt and grime.

The realisation that she wore nothing above her waist failed to register concern. The ecstasy and relief of hitting water overwhelmed all other thoughts in her mind. She felt as she never had before, cleansed, refreshed, almost reborn from the soaking from the waters beneath the earth. A sudden fire burned through her body, an exhilaration she had never felt before, almost blinding her with flashes of light in her eyes.

Charly slowly walked out from under the spray of water, catching some of it in her cupped hands, tasting its sweetness. She watched as the three men pulled a big steel clamp and a massive open valve over the flow, placing it down over the pipe and fastening it. The water sprayed everywhere, soaking everyone to the skin, but no-one cared. The water still shot upwards but now through the open valve. A second clamp was attached, locking the valve to the cast iron stem pipe.

Clarrie turned and waved for Charly to walk over and join them, semi clothed, muddy and soaked as she was, water running out of the bottom of their britches. When she arrived to stand beside them, Clarrie bent to her ear, shouting against the noise.

'It's your well, Charly Khan! You have the right to close the valve and tame the beast.'

As she slowly turned the steel wheel, the power and excitement of the previous moment took over, her energy sapped. The very action of turning a steel handle was difficult. She waved back to Clarrie, pointed at the steel wheel, directing him to join her; this was his moment as much as hers. Together, they slowly closed the valve, gently as possible putting pressure on the clamps, letting them take the strain and force themselves into the pipe stem.

Slowly the flow lessened and then suddenly the water was finished. The derrick was silent, until they exploded with shouts and yells.

Charly felt she would erupt with the emotions that had taken over her. She slowed her breathing and looked at the others. All had massive grins on their faces, their eyes wide with a madness of ecstasy as they hugged and slapped each other on the backs.

The men suddenly stopped and looked at Charly, feeling slightly unsure as to how to react. Their eyes were on her body as much as her face. Charly instantly knew the issue, she tilted her head over slightly, spreading her arms She cared little of her lack of clothing, the excitement of being part of a team that had done the nearly impossible overwhelmed any self-consciousness.

Clarrie grabbed one of his men, dancing in a circle in celebration, shouting in the madness from the release of stress from the last weeks of hitting dry wells. They all slowly calmed down, the cheers and laughs slowly easing. Clarrie sent his men to untangle the mess of cable and drive head, before they started to organise the packing of the timber derrick.

Clarrie looked at Charly one more time, enjoying the sight of the young, carefree woman that had driven him past his fears and reluctance. One of the men walked over and picked up the muddy remains of her kameez, bringing it back to Charly. She felt no shame, the moment was so special as she flicked it to remove the worst of the mud and then pulled it on, tying the front together to provide a small amount of modesty.

'Getting one of these wells to give water is better than a good root,' Clarrie said, then realising his comments, turned red. 'Ah. Shit, sorry, forgot that—'

'Nothing to be sorry about, Clarrie. Let's hope your next one is as good as that moment,' she replied, laughing as the ecstasy still flowed through her, removing all self-consciousness, all her doubts she had in herself. She felt as she had matured, a woman who could hold her own in any company.

She knew her world had now changed again, it slightly frightened her, the power that this dry windswept valley had provided, but she had taken the smallest of opportunities and succeeded.

Charly climbed onto her camel to ride back to see Derek Burrows. She had fulfilled all her obligations to this place, now it was time to talk serious business.

Chapter 17

C harly slowly closed the door to the hotel's private side entrance, stepping out onto the main street. She smiled at the memory, it was three years to the day from when they had struck water in the windswept valley, opening every opportunity known to work the vein of gold. The vein had brought her riches that could not be considered, and provided the security that had opened up endless opportunities.

She looked at the buildings down the main street of the small town where she lived. The town had grown a little in the last three years. The Springs was now blessed with a new bank, general store and a new police station. The main offices of the gold mine, now officially called the Defiance Mine in respect for the issues that needed to be overcome to bring it to operation, were located at the end of the street, not far from her old compound.

The old, ramshackle rail terminus had been enlarged; this was now the drop off point for the whole district. Plans were being made to extend the line, but no works had yet commenced. The land was changing, new people, new activities, more cattle and sheep stations. But the same old issues remained. Only camels fared well in these parts, providing ample opportunity and income for Charly.

The compound had been moved, taken over by a scattering of housing for the new residents, including an area for the men and women who drove her camel caravans to all parts. The compound was being rebuilt towards the river, some twenty minutes' walk from her present location. She'd laughed at the new resident's reaction to a few hundred camels. The noise, activity and smell was a little much to tolerate on their back doorstep. A large community stockyard had also been built close to her compound to hold animals in transit or to sell on the occasions an organised sale was conducted.

As was her want, Charly still wore the kameez and shalwar that had become part of her life, even when not on the trail with her camels. Which, to her annoyance, was now nearly all of her working life. Her operation had grown too large for her to spend weeks and months trampling through the wilds of the surrounding lands. Her adopted father, Abdul, had pushed more of his business in her direction, scaling back on his own activities in the district as he and Mary enjoyed the fruits of their energies and the new, preferable routes to the west, the ones with less cost and better returns.

Charly was planning to spend the day reviewing a number of contracts that were about to be renewed, but as she reached the compound gate, she was drawn to the stockyards. She always liked to keep an eye on what animals, mostly camels, were being offered for sale, mostly by transient men such as prospectors, sometimes explorers or government men. The other interest she had were the horses brought to the district by people that found what they really needed was a slightly different, slightly uglier, four-legged animal with a hump that would thrive where a horse could not. These horses she would buy and ship back to her agent in Adelaide for resale. It was rare to not make a small profit.

Charly walked over to the stockyards, standing for a while just watching the animals as she leaned on the three-rail fence, the top rail slightly lower than her shoulders. The perfect height to relax, leaning on her arms. She observed two well-built stallions, maybe a good options for the streets or the countryside around the city, but not having the toughness and sturdy statue of the outback ponies that mostly filled the yard. Charly could understand why they were being sold, likely much to the great disappointment of the current owners.

She climbed through the rails and into the first of the yards and quietly walked over to take a closer looked at two possible targets for her plans. As usual, none of the animals considered her as a threat, allowing Charly to calmly walk up to the first of the horses, a beautiful black stallion. Softly rubbing its flank, she checked the condition of the chest, legs, hooves, all of which showed the animals quality. Charly quickly did the same to the second chestnut coloured stallion, again a fine animal. Not quite as good as the black, but clearly worth a few more pounds to be spent than she normally would.

Thinking about speaking to the stock agent, seeing if she might do a bit of a deal, she walked back towards the main gate, deep thought. Suddenly there was a gentle push against the middle of her back. Charly turned, expecting to see one of the stockmen she had noticed earlier, but it was a rather dusty and relatively old horse. With her mind on other things, she returned to where she was walking, but again was pushed gently in the middle of the back. This time, the bump was accompanied by a soft whinny.

Charly turned again, looking with a little more interest. Recognition suddenly hit her.

'Misty, is that you? My word, how the hell did you find your way here?' Charly said softly as she recognised her old horse from all those years before.

Misty pushed her head forward, demanding a rub around her ears and muzzle. Charly instinctively reached out and gave the offered parts what they'd once received. After a few minutes, with her emotions about to overcome her, Charly gave one final pat and rested her forehead between Misty's eyes.

'I have to go, but I'll find out about you too, promise.'

Charly gathered her thoughts with a shake of her head. Misty copied the action, much to Charly's mirth. One more pat and then Charly walked to the gate, where one of the stockmen opened it for her. She paid no attention, not looking at his face. Other than providing a quick thank you, she kept walking towards her compound. Her mind was spinning as to why her old horse would suddenly turn up in this town.

'Hey, lady, ya got a moment?' came a voice behind her. But Charly failed to recognise it was for her. No-one called her a lady.

'Charlotte, Charlotte Hendricks, is that you?' demanded the voice behind her. This time the words cut through, driving a sharp spike into her being, reaching deep into her heart. She stiffened and missed a step, but tried to mask her reaction, knowing that any acknowledgment to that question would lead to a road she did not wish to travel.

She increased her pace, but it was not sufficient. A very powerful, masculine hand dropped on her shoulder, slowing her and turning her to face him.

'Oh, sorry, but is that you, Charlotte?'

Charly looked at the face under the dirty felt hat, recognising it immediately, although older and weather-beaten from years in the sun. A good bit taller than she had last seen him, now slightly more than her height. But the boyish innocence remained tucked just under the weathered face. It was a difficult face to ignore.

'The person by that name died years ago. Please leave me alone,' Charly snapped as she drew her shoulder from his grasp with a quick shake, turning to continue her walk.

The hand again dropped in her shoulder, slightly firmer, demanding an answer.

'Piss off, Harry. Your Charlotte is gone! I am not who you knew, so bloody well piss off.'

'Ohhooo, aren't you a cracker,' Harry said behind her. 'Hey, so have you changed that much you don't even care to know what happened to your own brothers? Not even your own blood.'

Charly stopped dead in her tracks. As much as she'd pushed her previous life into a closed box, she could not ignore that comment. Her brothers had done nothing to her, they had loved her intensely, devastated they could not fight in her shoes. It would be wrong if she rejected them. And as for Harry, while not her brother, she'd known that he'd always loved her a little more than a brother. He'd treated her as the sister he'd always wanted and maybe a little more. Charly slowly turned and looked at his face again.

'Bugger it, Harry. Alright, you win,' she quietly replied in surrender. 'You always had a way to get under my skin.'

A broad smile split the dirty face under the hat, the impish boyish look enveloped his face. The look affected Charly slightly differently from how it had in her youth, much to her annoyance.

'Come on, lets wander down near the river,' she said. 'You can tell everything about my brothers and then ya can piss off and leave me be.'

They both slowly walked down what had become a well-worn laneway, both keeping a subtle distance between them. Charly waited as they walked for some minutes, but Harry was suddenly lost for words. The unexpected meeting of a long-lost friend had confused his thinking, the moment almost too much.

'So, Harry, what bring you to the Springs? It wouldn't be that you lot still looking for me,' Charly asked to break the impasse.

Her words shocked Harry out of his confusion. His first words were little halting as he slowly started explaining his activities over the years, working for any number of cattle stations as a stockman. At present he had brought a small herd of steers to the Springs to be sold to the local small meat works and butchers that serviced the town and surrounding small farms.

They finally arrived at the riverbank. Charly looked upstream a small distance where she'd met the aunties. That had not happened from many years after the last meeting, when she'd demanded to know about her mother. Thoughts of her mother led to her brothers.

'Well, Harry, what of my brothers?' she asked, clearly not interested about her father. She'd prefer the memories of Jed Henricks stay deeply buried.

Harry reached out and took her hand, an action Charly did not fight, finding it strangely comforting. Harry saw a big fallen log and suggested they walk over to sit down up against it, looking down at what remained of an almost dry river.

'Well, they are both still alive,' he said suddenly. 'But Bryan shouldn't be.'

Charly gasped. Her eyes looked at Harry, pleading for more information. Harry slowly explained the weeks after they arrived back at the burnt-out property. He left out her father's demise, before quietly describing the time after Jessie left, the weeks of sickness the tortured Bryan, twisted his body, leaving him a bent shell of the fit young man he once was.

'You cared for him for weeks. Oh, Harry,' Charly mumbled in horror, tears flowing down her face. 'How is he now?'

'He doesn't get around much. He rides fairly good, but walking is a bit of a bugger,' he replied. 'The spasms tore his body to bits. He snapped a few tendons and such, bloody near well crippled him. He'll use a cane for the rest of his life.'

Harry paused as the memories of those two weeks smashed against his skull, hurting as much as all those years before. A wave of distress built in his body, so he waited a little before continuing when he felt able.

'He still lives at the flats with Jessie. Does most of the business type stuff, mostly leaves Jessie to work the cows and such.'

'And how would Jessie be? Married with a heap of kids yet?' Charly asked to find more comfortable ground for both of them.

'Well, you're right there, married and kids.'

'To that Cunningham girl. What was her name? Ellie, I be guessing.'

'Well, it is one of the Cunningham girls, but not Ellie, he be married to Rachael.'

'Nooo... really? But him and Ellie always had a thing happening. I be sure they had a fair bit of practice at making kids too if I be remembering,' Charly replied in amazement. 'So how did he get the other one?'

Harry laughed knowing the voraciousness of the three sisters when it came to be enjoying certain activities. The subject lightened his thinking, his words suddenly stronger, the memories happier.

'Well, I be thinking using the same type of practice,' Harry said, still laughing, which increased in volume when he looked at the totally stunned look on his companions face. 'Well, after we arrived back, one thing lead to another and Jessie had to ride over to Cunningham's place. He arrived after a few days of hard riding, but the old man and Misses Cunningham and Ellie had travelled to town but were expected back in a few days. Jessie decided to wait for the couple of nights instead of heading on to town himself as his horse was about worn-out...'

Harry waited as Charly caught up. She gave a small shake of her head as let the information sunk into her mind. She moved closer to Harry, leaning on his shoulder and enjoying the old feeling of belonging to someone.

'So what happened?'

'Well, he got her up the duff as some say,' he chuckled, remembering the discussion that occurred between the men of the Hendricks and the Cunninghams. 'Old Cunningham gave Jessie two options: married or shot. So Jessie married.'

'But he and Ellie were mad for each other.'

'Yep, and that never changed, still are. Them two, they had something that would never calm down,' Harry said, nodding his head.

Charly remained silent simply knowing this was all about to become even more confusing.

'After we built a small rough old place on the Flats near where the old trappers hut was, Ellie moved in with them.' Harry smiled at the stunned gasp from Charly. 'Need to say no more, but they all happy. In the end, Racheal started up warming Bryan's bed.'

'Nooo, how does that work?'

'So Bryan married Ellie, all above board, and they sleep in other beds.' He laughed again. 'Confused yet?'

'And what about you?'

'Too much hanky panky on the property for me. I lived down at the old trapper's hut for a while but ended heading off myself a couple of years ago to do other stuff. Still see them, and that third Cunningham girl, Maggie, she still wants to rip me pants off every time I see her.'

This brought a massive laugh from Charly, remembering the third sister that was her age.

'Ya should have stayed, Harry, made it a fine family arrangement.' Charly chuckled as she struggled for breath from the laughter. 'Saved figuring out on in-laws.'

'Nah, that one's a little crazy,' mumbled Harry as much to himself as to Charly. 'Rode that pony once, knew it wasn't for me.'

Harry suddenly looked around in embarrassment, but Charly had a knowing smile of what that young woman was like. Harry took a breath, about to ask Charly about herself, when he was cut off quickly.

'So, Harry, you still have not answered my first question, did ya ever stop looking for me?'

Harry leaned back, then took Charly's hand and hung onto it. The question brought difficult memories. How could he explain that her brothers had always thought she had died, and still did. Everything had pointed to that conclusion.

'Charlotte, there are some questions I find really hard to deal with – that is one of them,' he said slowly, his emotions evident. He was speaking from his heart. 'There was no reason to believe you had lived, everything pointed to the opposite. So none of us really looked for you. I just hoped that one day, maybe who knows, the impossible might happen.'

Charly could hear his troubled breaths. She knew she'd entered a place of agony, of deep loss, in the heart of the man beside her.

'So when I saw you today talking to Misty, it was like... it was...'

Harry did not finish. Charly had reached up and pulled his face towards him, then softly kissed his lips. At first it was a gentle embrace of their mouths, then the hard crush of two people who at that moment they had found what they had been searching for in their lives. It was the missing element they both needed.

The moment took control of their actions. Charly knew exactly where she wanted this to go. Her heart was pounding as she slowly pulled Harry over as she laid down beside the log. Harry followed as if he was tied by a string, his love finally finding where his heart had been all those years before. Charly slowly squirmed, pulling up the loose kameez until it sat just below her breasts. Grasping Harry's hand in her other, she slid it up until his hand covered her hard nipple, pressing his hand down to show her intent.

A look of surprise suddenly flowed over Harry's face, bringing a knowing chuckle from Charly.

'I don't wear underwear in this weather, mister. Make of that what you want.'

The moment became endless, the emotions and passion taking both of them to a new place. They knew they had found something that they were frightened to lose. Harry slowly moved his hand down Charly's bare midriff, slipping his fingers under the waistband of her trousers. Charly sucked in her stomach, widening the gap a little, the sign of agreement to his desire.

As his fingers slipped among her tight curls and up the hardening mound, Charly suddenly reacted, slapping her hand hard down on the wandering hand in her baggy trousers. She sat suddenly, her shoulder catching Harrys face, and splitting his lip. She pushed him back.

'Stop, no stop, I can't... I can–I can–you must stop, pleassse no, stop please!' Charly suddenly shouted in madness, shaking in agony and fear of the moment.

Harry quickly withdrew his hand, fearful he had hurt the one person he cared for over everyone else, the person he had hoped to find one day, the person missed so much even when he had not realised what she truly meant to him. In his heart, he had never given up on finding her one day. And now he had destroyed everything.

Charly turned and looked at Harry, tears in her eyes. She reached up and touched the blood slowly leaking from his lip, wiping it away.

'I'm so, so sorry, Harry, it is nothing you did. It's me, it is just that it is something that...' Charly started saying but was unable to finish what was destroying her, had destroyed her, eaten at her for all these years. 'Sorry, I can't… I can't control what happens to me.'

'I know, Charly. I think I know,' said Harry softly, with power in his words. Charly was about to argue when he continued cutting off her interruption. 'It was him. It was what he did to you.'

'You don't know.'

'But I do, I saw what he did.'

Charly did not answer, fearing he was about voice the thing that had caused her shame. If he truly knew, she suddenly felt she could never face him again.

'I came to the stables that night, to see if you wanted some food,' Harry started, knowing he had to finish or they were finished. 'I saw him whipping you. The blood splattered on the ground, on your clothes… I saw when he bent you over the workbench. I saw him. I saw what he did to you.'

Charly sat dead silent, her breathing short and sharp, the panic she had felt so many times from that memory. She desperately wanted to run, but the fear that she would lose the person next to her held her in place.

'Charlotte, you did nothing wrong, he raped you… and he is dead. I buried him, he can never hurt you again.'

Charly sat wordless, unsure if Harry knowing of, seeing what happened in that one of many moments of revulsion in her life meant anything, it certainly did not feel it mattered that much, not as much as she had feared. She felt the beginnings of threads that held strong, but she was not sure. She stood silently, dropping Harry's hand and walked slowly away, unable to see, at first unable to think.

As Charly walked away, she let thoughts run through her mind, not as much thoughts but accusations. She thought of her brothers, they had done nothing wrong and yet she had closed herself off from them. The easiest way to eliminate the pain caused by her father, was by simply cutting off all memories of her family. Although she knew her brothers had loved her, treated her as much as a mate than as a sister.

Jessie had taught her to manage horses and work the cattle much more than her father. And Bryan had taught her all the ways to survive in the bush. Introduced her to the ways of the local people through his friendships with the children who lived by the billabong.

And now, just when the moment had presented itself to find a way back to them, she again rejected them. As for Harry, she knew she'd always had a soft spot for him, but had pushed him away because of what her father did to her. And now, when she had a man she knew would care for her as no other, she pushed him away again.

As Charly walked she got angrier with herself. The same accusations bubbled, building till she stopped an screamed to herself, and anyone in earshot.

'For fuck's sake, girl, get a grip,' she muttered to herself. 'Will you finally stop punishing the ones you love? It's about time to find a way past the shit. Stop making others suffer for what the old bastard did.'

As she stood, she understood it was now that she had to take actions to heal the family, and cement her relationships with the three men. A sharp whinny cut through her thoughts. Blinking, she looked up and in amazement realised she had walked back to the corral. Looking at her was the horse she so loved. An animal she knew understood her better than most people.

Misty whinnied again, stamping a hoof in the dry soil, a small cloud of dust rising around the horse's legs. The horse gave Charly a look that could almost be considered accusing. Charly looked at her old horse, knowing what the answer was. She suddenly smiled, yes, now was the time.

Harry sat still for a long time, his heart smashed, to have the highest of ups and now the deepest of lows. It was a moment worse, far worse, than when he found her nightdress in the flooded tree. Harry sat where she had left him, touching the ground where she had sat beside him, his heart suddenly empty, his mind unsure on what to do next.

Suddenly, he was aware of someone standing beside him. It was Charly silently watching, tears in her eyes. She held out her hand, dropping a key into his hand.

'Clean yourself up, come to that room this evening,' she said in a voice that broke with a sight tremble. 'I am not giving up on you, Harry. Can you not give up on me? I will try. It might take a little, but please don't give up on me.'

As Harry's hand closed around the key, he saw a small wooden tag indicating the place and room. Charly walked away again. This time Harry knew, it would be up to them, they were both scarred from life, young, but carrying in their heart things that stopped them being able to love and commit to another just yet.

Harry sat against the log, looking at what little water remained in the river, sub-consciously allowing Charly the space to walk at her own pace. He did not wish to rush her, and finally stood, walking back to the yards. He looked at his clothes, knowing what Charly was saying. He still had three weeks of trail dirt and dust on him, he really did need to wash. He hustled back to his basic accommodation, dragging out some slightly cleaner clothes from his saddlebag. He stuffed the rest of the filthy stuff back in the saddlebag and headed down the street to one of the back-lane bath houses. He smiled, knowing from experience it might take an hour or two and more than one lot of water to get his skin clean of the dust and the stink of man, cow and horse.

Chapter 18

H arry opened the door to the reception foyer of the Imperial Hotel, the grandeur a little worn, but still the place in town to stay. He walked past the unattended reception desk, a little confused at the lack of staff to assist latecomers looking for a room. He walked along the passage a short distance before finding the stairs. A sign showed where the rooms were located, either on the ground floor or up the stairs. The number on the key tag was not listed. His heart missed a beat, then a second, unsure if he was confused or had Charly found a way to brush him off.

Harry walked up the ground floor passage, finding nothing that aligned with the number he was looking for. He then quietly strode up the slightly worn, carpeted stairs, searching the upper area passageways for a room with the number wanted. He noticed that the number he desired was one more than the highest he could find.

Harry slowly walked back along the passageway, finding nothing that satisfied his search. Knowing he was done, he turned and walked quickly down the stairs. He strode purposely down each of the twenty treads to turn and walk past the reception, now manned by one of the staff who had their head down in the register. He passed, not interested in discussing his foolishness, but a voice cut into his funk.

'Hello, sir. Can I be of service? You appear a little lost.'

Harry slowed and looked around at the man of Chinese appearance, unsure what to say.

'No problems, mate, I was looking for a room with a number you don't have.'

'Please, let me see. I may be of assistance in these matters, I am rather good at puzzles.'

Unsure what to do, he handed the key to the man who quickly looked at it and then smiled warmly.

'Ahh, Mr Harry, I understand your confusion,' the registrar said with a knowing smile. 'Mrs Khan's room not numbered. She be a long-time resident, we take number off door.'

Harry was stunned by the term Mrs Khan. So was she or was she not married? He really didn't need another mystery to mess with his mind.

'Come with me, Mr Harry, I show you way. Charly tell me you coming here this evening.' He smiled again. 'My name Zhou Lee Xia, but everyone call me Jimmy Lee.'

The man quickly stepped around the desk and walked at a serious pace to the base of the stairs, ascending quickly before turning right and walking towards the end of the passage. Some ten feet short he stopped, pointing to a blank door off the end of the hall in a small alcove.

'That one, Mr Harry. Use key. She inside, she be waiting,' Jimmy noted and quickly walked away before he was asked anything that he really did not wish to answer.

Harry walked to the door in the alcove. The door, lock and handle were of the same quality as the others, but unworn, almost as the door was rarely used. He pulled the key out of his trouser pocket and slipped it into the lock. A strange feeling wafted through him, a feeling of excitement and fear mixed. The key fitted and the lock smoothly turned and with a gentle push the door opened, a sharp squeak right as it reached the full extent of the hinges.

Swearing under his breath, Harry stepped inside. He was standing in a small entryway and beyond looked to be a good-sized sitting room.

The furniture was of good quality but totally unused, as if someone had purchased it to furnish a room, but a different person lived here and hated what was installed. A small lantern hung from the ceiling, it provided just enough illumination so as not fall over the furniture.

'That you, Harry? In here, my darling man. I've been expecting you,' was Charly's voice from an adjoining room. 'Drop ya stuff out there, and come in.'

Harry had nothing to drop so he simply walked through the sitting room to the doorway that cascaded light on the floor. As he reached the doorway, what he found was a bedroom, a very large bed up against the decadently wallpapered rear wall, again beautifully furnished, this room slightly more lived in. Charly sat up against two enormous pillows, her nightdress buttoned close to her neck, her black wavy hair flowing down around her shoulders. She placed the book she had been writing in on the bedside table, placing the fountain pen onto of it. Two large lanterns hung from gimbles off the rear wall either side of the bed, spilling bright light to all parts of the room.

Charly provide a subtle up and under look as she unbuttoned part of the nightdress, opening the top to show the rise and swell of her chest.

'Take them off, Harry. I want to see you before you come in here,' she laughed suggestively. 'I've been waiting far too many years to see the man I so wanted from another time.'

Charly stood by the bedroom window, the heavy drapes pulled back, allowing the first soft light of the day to flow into the room. A mixture of excitement and panic thrummed through her. The evening before had not gone as well as it could, she'd had a panic attack again at that pivotal moment and could not find the way to provide what she and Harry so wanted. They'd found a way past that moment, but it'd stolen her enjoyment, allowing a darkness to sit over their bed.

Charly pulled the collar of the nightdress tighter around her neck. What if she lost the man she was discovering she so wanted to share her life with? Why, she asked herself, would any man want her? The light increased, the first rays touching the window, providing the silhouette of her tall muscular figure to the man in bed behind her.

'Take it off, Charly, it is my turn to see the woman I love,' said Harry's quiet voice from the bed behind her.

Charly jumped, not expecting that he would be watching her. Turning, she looked at the ruffled head.

'I can't. There are things I am ashamed of on the outside as well as inside.'

'You crazy woman, how can you be ashamed of anything? There is nothing about you that gives shame, nothing.'

Charly looked intently, suddenly knowing part of her issue was that she refused to believe that Harry did not care. In reality, very few people cared about what happened to her past. In total defiance to her feelings, she unbuttoned the top of the nightdress and let it drop slowly to the floor. Standing without shame, she felt his eyes trace her body, every curve and dip; she held her head high, she stood with pride.

She slowly turned. It was now or never. Time to get past the scars and puckers skin on her back, buttocks and legs. A sharp intake of breath emitted from the bed.

'Bloody hell. You were wearing it,' Harry breathed.

'Wearing it? What are you talking about?'

'The nightdress. The one in the river, the damage it had, the burn marks, they match.'

'Harry, dear man, you speak in total riddles,' Charly said as she walked to the edge of the bed, climbing in beside him. Harry touched the old scars and marks on her shin, the last signs of the terror of that day.

'When we got back, we searched for you. The river was in flood, a tree had fallen near to the top of the gorge. I saw a torn cloth in the branches and climbed out. It was a badly burnt nightdress. One of yours,' Harry slowly explained, struggling with what he was seeing, the emotions of the moment returning in a flood. Charly snuggled in closer and pulled the blanket over her lower body, watching the pain in her man's face, as he relived the moment.

'I nearly drowned, but I got it. I was dragged to the bank by Bryan, but I would not let go,' he said slowly. 'The burns on the nightdress match your scars. If I had only known.'

'Well you couldn't and didn't, so there. I lived. Ran like a mad rabbit, a little scorched, but I lived,' Charly responded, trying to liven up the moment. 'And, pray tell a silly girly like me, where would this burnt cloth be?'

Harry snapped out of his clouded brain, looked up. 'In my pack, been sleeping with it since that day. Bloody hell, Charly, I was never going to lose it, especially as I bloody near died getting it.'

Charly dropped her chin, looking at Harry in amazement. His quiet words crashed into her, then melted something in her soul. Although they had both suffered over the years, she knew right now, in this moment, she could offer Harry the comfort they had both longed for over the years. Her hand reached down and grasped his, sliding it between the top of her legs. She wanted to give her all to repay his devotion. Whatever fear and panic had ruled, it had disappeared, much to her pleasure.

Harry awoke a little later to the abrupt sliding of the curtains, knowing that he had been in a deep sleep. The excitement of a few hours prior had erased the previous evening's difficulties. He blinked at the shaft of sunlight that flowed into the room. An older woman walked to the second window and pulled back the curtain before placing a tray on small stand on the bed beside him.

'Mrs Charly Khan tell me to bring you big breakfast as you been working very hard,' the elderly Chinese woman said with a supressed giggle. 'Make me happy to know she been working hard too.'

Harry did not know what to say. Lifting the lid over the plate, he found a well-cooked steak, cooked eggs sitting on top and some freshly toasted bread that smelled amazing and some spicy chutney. He looked up at the woman, a little red in the face, embarrassed to know the obvious odour in the room was not overwhelmed by that of the food.

'Charly Khan say to me to wash your clothes. I take now.' She smiled in conspiracy. 'She says you to meet her at compound at midday, she say want to have lunch with you.'

'Thank you, but if you take my clothes, I will have nothing,' Harry protested.

'I leave you new shirt and pants in sitting room, they fit good. My boy, Jimmy Lee, he know good tailor, he get some this morning.' The lady smiled again. 'Oh, Charly Khan also say to tell you, you live here now, this bed. So you better get them other things of yours so I wash them too, okay, Mr Harry.'

Harry was overwhelmed by the orders the woman gave, but she was obviously a trusted member of staff, to be allowed access to the room.

'Okay, yes I can do this, I will get me things after. I thank you.' A thought hit him, this was not normal for even a long-time resident. 'Please, if I may ask, tell me, this is not a normal suite, really the manager's rooms, how is it that Charly lives here as if it is her home?'

The old lady smiled, enjoying the moment of knowing something that someone else did not, a moment that would be wonderful gossip later.

'This Charly Khan's home. She own Imperial Hotel. All this is her place, you sleep in her bed.'

Three hours later, still recovering from the surprise of what he'd been told, Harry was walking down to the end of the main street, a large calico bag in his hand, lunch freshly made for two, wrapped in crisp white paper within. He remembered the smells sneaking out of the top of the folded top of the bag, exotic and enticing, from lands he did not know. The shirt and trousers were an amazing fit, high quality material. Clothes he had only seen on the rich buyers at the sales. He had a feeling his hat and boots might also go very soon, but for now he would try and keep something of his previous life.

He still could not get his head around the fact that Charly was the owner of one very big, very expensive hotel. That made no sense to him. Had it been given to her? No, that was sillier. His thoughts flowed back and forward, missing the point of her transport operation, the many dozens of camels and the staff, failing to understand she also owned it too.

The compound was just before the yards, a solid fifteen-minute walk to get some unusual aches from his bones. He still could not get the smile from his face, laughing at what a crazy twenty-four hours it had been. First the horse he'd lived with for so many years was accidently grabbed and put in the sale yard, then as he was organising to get it back, the one person he'd so desired to meet just one more time had walked past him. He smiled again. And now he had spent the night with her, and a few more to come, he was hopeful he had found the person that would provide him the love and comfort of a true partner in life.

As he walked into the compound, he observed a high fence that defined the boundary of the area and held the camels securely as they were prepared for travel. Two large drays stood side by side near one of the buildings, with some smaller wagons nearby. There were what looked like two massive warehouses and storage sheds, stables, men and women everywhere. Harry let it all sink in. He had never been inside the Charly Khan transport compound and its size stunned him. It could not be hers, Jimmy Lee's mother must have been pulling his leg.

A smaller building sat to one side. A barely legible sign, worn by sun and blown sand, suggested it was the office. He walked over and stepped onto the timber verandah, enjoying the shade. He looked back at the bustle in the compound, but not one person stopped and asked who he was or what was he doing.

'They all appear to know about us already. Typical of this town, can't do nothing and some else knows,' said a familiar voice from the doorway.

Harry turned to face Charly. She wore peculiar, knowing smile on her face, and broke into a soft chuckle.

'So far, I have been congratulated five times, been asked if I am having a boy or girl two times and told once that if you can't ride a camel, you're not worthy to have me.'

Harry didn't know what to say. Charly leaned forward and kissed him, then took his hand and led him into the office.

'This be Lachlan Goodwood, good at numbers, organising just about anything that moves and most things that don't, but bloody average at stopping slugs from a Sharps,' said Charly as Lachlan came out of his small paper-laden office.

'Great to meet you Harry. And about time too,' he said fervently. 'But do me a favour, keep her busy, she couldn't organise a flea to find a mangy dog.'

Charly laughed and drew Harry to the next room, about the same size but with less paper but more odds and ends from her last five years. The wall facing the door had two large, soft chairs with a small table between them, Charly indicated that he put the lunch down on the table.

'Sit yourself down, beloved man. I'll get a cool drink,' she said as she strode out of the building and down the verandah.

Harry walked around the room, picking up the numerous oddities that had found their way into Charly's life. A slightly worn Winchester leaned against the corner of the cupboard, the cupboard holding two other rifles in an upright rack. A beautifully embossed silver cup caught his eye. Picking it up he was surprised at its weight, clearly solid metal, the metalwork and engravings of the highest quality. As he placed it back, he knew this was not of local make, but something exotic. A few other items were clearly from her travels. He continued until he saw a rusty coloured rock, yellow showing in large areas, sitting in prominence on her desk.

He picked it up, its weight staggering to what he expected. The rock was about the size of both his fists but weighed four or five times what it should. He had been picking up rocks all his life, this was strange experience.

Harry was about to replace it when the footstep sounded on the timber floor. Charly walked through the doorway, two tall glasses in the hands, a light amber liquid filled nearly to the top. His mind said beer, but the fragrance from the glasses said something else, different, new and slightly enticing.

'Ah, that would be one of the chunks from the small bonanza we hit a year back. A very exciting few days that was, I can tell you,' Charly said with a surprising level of disinterest. Harry had a fair idea what the yellow metal was, but why a piece sat on her desk, and using the term 'we' in the sentence confused him. Before he could ask the question, Charly headed in a different direction.

'This is tea, but not like anything you have ever had,' Charly said as she put the glasses on the small table and sat down. 'Qadir's wife makes it for me, it has spices mixed with the cold tea and it seriously quenches a thirst. Please try it, I promise you'll be surprised.'

Harry put the glass to his lips, the fragrance now clearly able to the appreciated, the smells different, a little scary, but he knew that he could not refuse. He took a sip, letting the liquid wash around his mouth before swallowing. The aftertaste changed his mind, he instantly wanted more. A grin spread across his face as he took a second mouthful.

Charly opened the bag and withdrew a flattish bread filled with cold meat and pickles and a stiff, soft white yoghurt. As Charly took a bit of hers, the second was handed to Harry who looked at it with a raised eyebrow, the exotic aromas now confronting him.

'Come on, Mr Cattleman, ya not gunna let a bit of cold cow put you off,' mumbled Charly, her mouth full, a cheeky smile on her face.

'It ain't the beef. That bit I can handle,' he responded with unease at what was in his hand. 'It's the bread, the pickles and whatever that white stuff is.'

'Ha! You want to share my bed? Well, mister, you'll have to share my tastes too,' she replied, a mock threat thrown in for good measure. 'This bolani is the bread of my world, the tastes of my family.'

Harry took a deep breath and took a bite. The bread was slightly spiced, light and seriously flavoursome. The coating on the meat tasted totally different than the smell, an explosion in his mouth, then finding the soft, white yoghurt cooling, balancing the other flavours. He chewed, swallowed and took another bite, this time bigger and with confidence.

The experience overshadowed the comment she'd made, though he thought he would ask a question. What did she mean by a 'family'? Certainly, a different group of people then what he knew of.

'Right, Harry, I guess you and I had some fun last night,' Charly stated, again changing the subject as Harry was ready to speak. 'You appear to have enjoyed the softness of my bed, and a few other things too.'

Harry looked carefully at Charly, not sure if she had enjoyed his attentions for a serious relationship. After a few hours of normalcy, perhaps she'd decided it would not happen. He waited for his life to be crumpled again as Charly took another bite of the bolani, chewing happily.

'And I want you to stay, Harry, as long as you do. I mean it, you are welcome in my world, in my life,' she finally stated with decisiveness. 'So, is this what you want?'

Harry did not have to think, he had found what he needed, wanted, did not want to lose. He responded quickly in the affirmative. Not that he had any idea what that would mean for him, like what would he be doing. Charly took a long sip of the cold tea, washing around her mouth, enjoying the spices doing their special tricks to her tongue.

She looked at Harry, taking another bite, chewing in bliss, a smile on her face. She didn't mind keeping Harry waiting just that little longer. He likely had a thousand questions for her, and she was not quite ready to surrender that information just yet. She had willingly given him her body, the rest could wait.

'That makes me so very happy. So what do we do with you?'

As they finished their lunch, a few basic plans were made to organise their lives as a couple. Not that Harry had much to put together or change in the way of plans.

'I got a standing offer to work at a couple of cattle stations, and Jessie will always have me around down at the Flats but that can be more than a little complex,' Harry explained without expanding on his final comment. The mention of her old home twitched Charly's ear, 'So I guess I'll try and find a bit of work around here.'

Charly smiled, she had already planned a few roles for her long-lost friend and now very much lover, in fact that is all she had done all morning, ignoring a few pressing contract matters, to find an answer. Lachlan Goodwood provided his support as she threw her ideas over his head. Her gut feeling had always supported her, her feelings about Harry would not desert her, she knew it would work out.

'Well I need a couple of things done, starting tomorrow,' Charly said seriously. This was now business. 'I want you to buy me a few horses at the sale.'

Harry's eyes popped as she described the ones she was after, not quite believing she had the funds as she described the six best in the yards. The prices might be lower but were still eyewatering to the average person.

'And what about Misty? I can't believe you want to sell her. Seriously, if you only buy one bloody horse, I want that one,' Charly snapped, her slight icy tone surprising him.

Harry suddenly laughed, realising how all the parts fell together, the gods finding a way to conspire to bring them together. His laughter continued, bringing a slightly concerned look on Charly's face, as she was not totally sure what he found so humorous.

Harry stopped, wiping a tear from his eyes as he explained how Misty ended up in the sale yard, the problems he had trying to get her out. The only reason he was at the yard's main gate when Charly walked through was simply that he'd got a little drunk the day before and Misty had wandered down the road looking for him. One of

MacDonald's police found her and thinking she had been discarded, as some older horses were, took her to the sale yards.

Charly looked at him, stunned at his story, but knew that Misty had done her proud.

'Fine. Buy the best two stock horses you can find, they'll be for you,' she directed. 'Misty needs to retire though, she's done enough, she brought you to me. And I would like my horse back, if that be okay with you.'

Harry smiled, remembering the last moment they'd been together before the world had gone mad, there in the stables, Misty between them, watching while they'd argued in the stall that evening. Misty had never been his horse, he'd only looked after her till he could give her back. He smiled at the edge of toughness that would pop out from Charly's femininity, a hardness that had allowed her to survive, an edge that slightly frightened him.

'Most certainly, my good lady, I was looking for another horse anyway, simply to give Misty a break. I would be glad to give her back, she being yours anyway.'

Chapter 19

By the end of the following day, Harry had showed his skilled knowledge of horse flesh, purchasing five of the six horses Charly had wanted, rejecting the last one only over concerns over its health. Two stock horses were also in the bag, not the best looking, but Harry saw they had the toughness to live in dry country. All this was accomplished after he'd recovered from the shock he experienced when Charly took him to the one and only bank in the town and organised for him to have a staggering amount of money made available in his name.

The treatment provided to both of them was one of reverence and total respect from the staff, with only the manager handing her affairs. Charly dressed as per her usual working attire, looking more like a tidy and clean cameleer than anyone who'd have more than two pounds to their name.

This added to the now long list of questions that filled his head, questions he needed answered before he went much further into their blossoming relationship. He didn't want to be thought of being little more than a useful, but otherwise worthless, assistant.

The purchase of the horses was followed by organising their transport back to Adelaide for resale. Again, Harry saw reverence from the tough and experienced agents as Charly did business and introduced him to her relevant contacts, both locally and by telegraph. By the end of the day he was exhausted, happy to ride back to the hotel instead of walking. Charly quickly said that walking was her blood, noting she had likely walked most of the way around the world by now if the miles she did were joined together. Slowly, one riding, one walking at the rapid rate that amazed Harry, the two made their way home, till Harry stopped his new horse halfway to their destination.

'Come on, get up behind me, this looks stupid.'

Charly laughed, also thinking at the oddity of the sight as they returned to the town. She was swung up behind Harry with a sharply lifted interlocked arm, and wrapped her arms around his body, snuggling closer to him. Harry urged the horse forward as they resumed chatting about their day, building the love that would be required in the future.

The next two days bumped along rapidly for Harry, the agenda and activities were driven by Charly to help him fit into her life and business. But to his growing frustration, Charly used every trick to avoid, and delay any conversation about her recent past, all the years since the fire at the Flats. He slowly realised that while she loved having him in her world, she preferred not to open that particular box of memories. But it was a box Harry needed to be opened to allow him to take the final step in their growing relationship. He hated secrets. That was the world of his mother, a world he detested more every day.

Harry started to plan a way to put Charly in a situation where she would feel obligated to open up, provide him the part of the person he loved but did not know. On the third day, as had become the norm, Harry rode to the hotel to get their midday meal. Just one secret, he just needed one, and the rest would be easy. He knew that the heavy rock on her desk would be the trigger he needed, he had seen her pick it up effortlessly, belying its weight. He knew what to do today.

As he rode back, he saw the cloud of black coal smoke and white steam billowing just a few miles outside the rail yards as the powerful small locomotive dragged another load of freight and a handful of passengers into the bustling town. Harry smiled slightly as the whistle blasted a long note, alerting everyone who needed to know that the train from the Port had arrived for its weekly trip. With its arrival the small town would soon become a bustling centre.

Harry kept riding, arriving at the compound at a slow canter. Eating food was a process that did not really need to be linked on the time of a clock. Charly had smiled when he'd raised that yesterday, adding that on the trail, they stopped a caravan when a good shady site was available, so an hour early or an hour or two late made little difference. Again, she'd let slip another comment that provided a question to be asked, noting that the prayer time for her cameleers was more likely to dictate the specific timeframes, depending on where the sun sat in the sky.

One of the Afghan children run over and took the reins of his horse, one of the new dry land breed stock horses. He carried the bag of meat-filled flat breads and sat them on the small table as usual. Charly got up, giving him a passionate kiss on his lips before sitting down.

'Hey, Harry, can you quickly go and ask Qadir if he needs any extra camels for his caravan to the valley next week?' she asked quickly. 'I'll be finished what I'm doing by the time you get back. We can eat then.'

Harry smiled. It was not a discussion, and there were no other options; it was Charly's way when at the compound. Harry had met most of the key Afghan cameleers in the last few days. Every Afghan male treated Charly like a revered and cherished younger sister and were exceptionally protective. It had taken a few sharp words in their language by Charly to break the ice. Now all treated him like a brother, as Qadir stated loudly to all, 'Harry is a brother'. From that moment, Qadir had become a close friend, a person he knew he could trust. His final comment in clear English confirmed it. 'Do Charly Khan any wrong, you better ride a long way. We find you, okay?'

Harry walked across to the warehouse, but not finding Qadir he was directed to the goods store. Again, not finding his quarry, he eventually met him walking back from the camel enclosure. Once the message was passed on, which provided a smile and laugh, indicating kindly that Charly should leave this to him, Qadir thanked Harry.

'She be like a mother hen, she need to let go a little, hey, Harry.'

Harry nodded. It had only been a few days, but already he could see that Charly struggled to let go totally of the world she had built.

'Hey, Harry, when you coming with me to learn to ride the camel? Just long-legged horse with funny nose and a humpy.'

Harry smiled and shook his head. He was a horse man, camels just felt wrong. The responding laugh showed Qadir's good humour, knowing the answer before he asked. Patting Qadir on the shoulder, Harry walked back to the office, meeting Charly at the door, eliciting another quick smooch.

'Can't get enough of them, mister.' She chuckled. 'Now, just wait for me, I'll get the drinks from Zannah, they should be ready by now.'

Harry sat on the chair, then stood, picking up the brown and yellow rock, again amazed by the ease at which Charly picked it up. He sat it down again. Well, he thought, maybe his questions would have to wait until tomorrow. He settled back, knowing Charly was only a few minutes away, when the face of an older Aboriginal woman, popped into the doorway. She was very well-dressed, her black hair wrapped in a colourful band of wound cloth.

'The girly be right, you be one really good-looking bloke,' the woman stated dryly. 'Well, shit, I been ten year younger I be thinking I might have given her a run for it.'

Harry had no idea who this person was, or why she had some level of knowledge of him. The fact an Aboriginal woman had the audacity to speak in this manner to a white man, in good English with little interest in his feelings on what was being said, now *that* stunned him.

'Matter of fact, had I known a good-looking youngster like you would arrive back at them billabongs, might have asked the old man to wait a bit longer,' the woman continued.

There was a shriek from someone behind the door and the crash of a glass breaking on the floor. The woman looked back into the next room, then turned and disappeared. Harry started to rise when another face, one obviously belonging to the same race as the men who worked for Charly looked in. He was dressed for travel in the harsh environment, but of quality rarely seen in the Springs.

'You be Mr Harry, I am thinking so. I am Abdullah Rahman Khan, the finest cameleer this side of the magnificent Murray River,' he proclaimed, then winked, laughing quietly. 'But Charly better, just no tell her that, okay?'

The man was pushed aside, and the woman looked in again, giving Harry a very intensive up and down look, clearly pleased when was she reviewed his evident masculinity.

'She chooses good, Abdul,' she said to the man beside her. 'He looks like he will give our girl lots of strong boys and beautiful girls.'

'Mother, that is wrong, you stop that. I know what you're looking at in that way of yours, leave him alone,' Charly's voice called from behind the two people in the doorway. 'Father, for goodness sake, get your woman under control, she is incorrigible the way she speaks.'

Abdullah laughed lightly in dismissal of Charly's comments. Mary could say the best things that ticked his humour, and embarrassing their beloved adopted daughter was a prime objective at any time they met after being apart for a length of time.

'Harry,' called Charly urgently from the other room, a slightly rattled tone in her voice. 'Ignore them, they mean no harm. They are becoming a little crazy as they age.'

The woman and man burst out giggling at her words, knowing they had hit the required nerve. As the woman turned to face Charly, the man stepped forward and offered his hand to be shaken. He suddenly had a serious look on his face.

'Mr Harry, ignore us, we love Charly like our blood child. She special, so when we hear she finally find a man for her bed, we had to come and check,' noted Abdullah quietly. 'So far, we think she had done exceptionally good.'

Meeting these two people, the cacophony of noise, activity and the total unknown had thrown Harry off balance. The use of 'Father' and 'Mother' by Charly as she addressed them totally hurled him down the last step. More questions popped up, he suddenly knew that in those short few years she had been away from him, Charly had filled the years with things he could never consider off the top of his head.

Charly finally calmed everyone down and ordered the two older visitors to 'stop and behave,' which caused a few additional giggles, but they smiled at each other and turned to face Charly.

'Harry, well, I guess this will likely tip you off your feet, but this is my mother and father,' Charly said calmly. She had no choice but to open the gate of her life, now that they were here. 'Abdullah Khan, and his wife, Mary. They adopted me many years ago, I am their daughter, both in love and in law.'

'Call me Abdul, everyone else does.' Abdullah pushed in before Charly could continue, then turned to everyone in the room. 'So we here, we now go and eat a good lunch at Imperial Hotel. I buying, okay, Charly?'

Charly had a funny look on her face, the concept of her father buying lunch for her at her own hotel. That made no business sense, but she knew he had to fulfil cultural standards. He was the powerful and very wealthy head of the extended family, and still provided a subtle influence on her business.

A quick decision was made. Lachlan Goodwood was sent ahead to let the staff know that they were to prepare the other private suite and dining room. Lachlan and Abdullah had developed a close relationship in the previous years, working closely to manage Abdul's affairs as well and Charly's. Abdul insisted that Lachlan should also attend.

As was the custom, what commenced as a late lunch, turned into a larger evening feast. Qadir, Mohamod, and a little later, Ishmael joined them with their wives and children. A number of the other Afghan men and their wives also attended, viewing their relationship to Abdullah Rahman Khan a thing of importance. The private dining room was soon bursting, flowing into the rest of the dining area. The few people staying in the hotel had the option to stay and join them or leave and eat elsewhere in the hotel.

Finally, Sergeant MacDonald dropped by, giving Mary a quick hug and then spending fifteen minutes with Abdul and Charly in earnest conversation before they all returned to enjoy the festive occasion.

Harry was surprised by the level of respect and courtesy displayed between the Afghans and Europeans in the room, but it was obvious that others were not so forthcoming, leaving the hotel without greeting or comment. As they dined, Harry noted a slight shift in the balance of the group. The food was spicy and tasty, his tongue slowly adapting to its flavours, but it had been taken up a notch in spice. As he ate, he watched with interest at the interplay in all the persons in the group.

He remained unsure at the roles of the two older persons that had arrived on the train, still failing to understand circumstances as to how Charly could end up an adopted child of an Afghan man and Aboriginal woman. But those answers were for another time; tonight was a time to celebrate. He was not sure what they were celebrating, but not having a reason did not appear to be an issue.

By the time the last of the participants headed for their beds, the night had crossed into the next day by an hour or so. Charly finally demanded that everyone go to bed, so she at least could get an hour or two of deserved sleep before dealing with work tomorrow. As Harry followed her up the stairs, he noticed that a tall waterpipe had appeared and Mohamod, Qadir and Ishmael sat on the floor on bright scattered rugs with Abdul, leaning back on with a number of back rolls, enjoying some peace and time for a gossip.

'Leave them, Harry. They have religious things to discuss, the four of them are the main heads of their peoples in this area, they are planning to build a house of worship for their community,' she said as they reached the top of the stairs, after Harry had asked if he should have stayed. 'They are the cleanest, loyal men I know. I trust them with everything. So should you.'

As they walked slowly to their suite at the end of the hall, Charly slowed, stopping to hold Harry's hands, then reaching up and giving a soft, loving kiss.

'You have been so patient with me, you must have so many questions and I know I have been a bit difficult,' she admitted softly. 'But maybe tomorrow, when I get a chance, I will tell you a story that will be worth telling to your children and your grandchildren.'

In her tired mind she suddenly realised what she had said.

'Oh, if you think you may be mistaken, don't be, mister. You and I will make the first ones you can tell the story to,' said Charly with a tinkle in her eye. 'But not tonight, I am truly buggered and need sleep.'

The following two days day were remarkable for Harry. He had gone from the sleepy morning on the first day Charly's parents had arrived, to a maddened rush to board a train leaving on its way back to Adelaide on the second. The visit by Abdul and Mary confirmed their support for Charly. They had checked her choice in men, but the vist had also allowed some time to do business. The day after their arrival was spent in casual meetings and discussions of the projects they shared an interest in, and future issues.

The participants were limited to Lachlan Goodwood, Charly, Mary and Abdul, with the odd invitation to others to provide information or their thoughts on a subject. The main room of the office had the furniture pushed back and rugs and back rolls placed on the floor in a rough horseshoe shape. A short-legged table was placed in the centre with a steady supply of food and cooling drinks.

Harry felt a little left out until late in the day when he was called in by Abdul to join them. He gave a look of surprise as he put his head through the doorway, coming in from the horse yards where he had been working.

'Harry, we have a few questions that you may have information on,' he was asked by Abdul as he sat on the woven rug, leaning back on the embroidered back roll. 'And I will apologise that you have not been involved, but much of what we say is of little interest to someone who knows little of what we do.'

Harry nodded, not sure if the words were accurate or a basic ruse, but it was true, he had little knowledge of the transport business. He was foremost a cattleman. He looked intently at Abdul, who was leading the discussions as the elder person, and the clear leader of the family business.

'Harry, on a few occasions recently we have brought cattle to the Springs and other outlying places similar to this where we provide supplies,' said Abdul with a tinge of concern in his voice. 'But they have fared badly, not surviving for any length of time as expected.'

'From where and how did you send them?' asked Harry, suspecting the answer.

'From cattle stations past the Ranges, down south along the Murray River, and usually by train to the Springs and then they are driven to other places from here,' was the reply.

Harry sat back and considered his answer, wondering if this was a small test or a serious question from a problem that beguiled them. He leaned forward. Everyone in the room was watching him, an experience that was a little overwhelming.

'The answer is actually easy: you are getting the animals from the wrong places,' he replied. 'They are not desert born and bred.'

'Meaning what? If I may be asking boldly,' asked Abdul. Charly already saw the point Harry was making.

'Okay, I've been to the stations near the Ranges and near the big river. The climate is dry and may appear similar, but with one big difference: desert cattle are not concerned about having no water for days. The cattle from down south would get stressed if they could not find water. Desert cattle would just start looking, they'd know it was around, and be content to wait a few days, even longer, till it was available.'

The words resounded around the room, the simple answer to a question that had confounded them, thinking dry country animals were one and the same.

'We are good with camels, but cows, we have very much to learn,' muttered Abdul. He leaned to look over at Charly. 'You have picked wisely, beloved child. This one, do not throw back.'

Abdul laughed as he nudged Mary. 'If my much-loved daughter unwisely returns you to the wilds of the sands,' he laughed some more at the indigent look on Charly's face, 'come to my tent, young Harry. Your knowledge and wisdom will be most welcome.'

'Bahh, Father, you will await another three lifetimes and even then it still will not occur.' Charly snorted in annoyance as she grabbed Harry's arm. 'This one is mine.'

Harry blushed at the interplay, feeling a little like he was chattel being bartered, but loved and appreciated at the same time.

'Hey, Harry, old mate, ignore the two of them,' said Goodwood, a smile on his face. 'Those two always need to have a little push and shove, one trying to better the other, but still wishing the best.'

Charly looked up at Harry and silently mouthed a quick 'sorry', knowing that she and her father had slightly overstepped in how they had bantered without consideration of Harry's feelings. She pulled a face like a naughty child, dropping her head in submission. Harry looked at Abdul, who returned a wink and nod, providing the assurance to Harry of his position.

'Harry, the words discussed on the cattle are important to know how we will proceed in plans. Charly has business in supplying food to a number of distant places, working places. These need fresh meat; I have helped but I am thinking she has found better.'

He looked at Mary, who gave a supportive nod, knowing that Abdul was taking another small step away from his businesses.

'Charly Khan will discuss this with you after we go, but where you need help to find... What it is called again, Lachlan?'

'Logistics.'

'Yes, yes, logistics,' Abdul repeated, the word he was not totally familiar with. 'Come to me. Telegraph if you need this, I have much information to help. Okay?'

Harry nodded, carefully watched by Charly. She knew that her man had just been taken into the greater family, one not entirely accepted by the English, but a wealthy and powerful family nonetheless.

'Okay, good. Harry, can you get Qadir, Mohamod and Ishmael?' Abdul asked. 'There be one more thing to discuss, something spoken to Charly Khan and myself by Sergeant MacDonald.'

The others were quickly gathered, as they'd been sitting, drinking tea in the next building. Knowing this was a critical issue, they sat quietly waiting for Abdul's comments. However, it was Charly that started.

'Macca spoke with us last night.' She indicated her adopted father and herself. 'He has warned that there are reports of men attempting to break into old customer trade routes and contracts. They usually bully and threaten but have been known to kill both men and camel.'

Her words chilled the room. Trade route raiders were not new, but to kill both man and animal was unusual and frightening.

'Macca has suggested we travel well-armed and be cautious as we approach and stop at water sources.' Charly finalised her comments. 'We travel with two extra men per caravan. We must be careful. Remember, we have the prized routes much valued by ourselves and so desired by others.'

All in attendance nodded their agreement, discussing the plans to protect both caravans and also the compound. The meeting slowly dissolved into smaller groups, finally melting into the individuals completing the day's activities, leaving Harry, Charly, and her adopted parents. Harry started to rise, thinking the three of them would like to have some private time together before Abdul and Mary left tomorrow morning.

Charly placed her hand in his arm, pulling him back down to sit close beside her. 'Wait, darling, Harry. I said I was to tell you a story as you have never heard. Well, a better storyteller wishes to start this story of mine, especially as she started my journey.'

Abdul leaned back, always enjoying hearing the telling of a fine tale. Mary smiled and nodded to Charly as she cleared her throat.

'Well, Harry, it all starts a few days before we arrived at Hendricks Flats. Something was driving me, something was urging me to push Abdul here to keep moving,' she said quietly. The room itself felt oddly still, as if the walls themselves were almost captivated by the words, 'It was this that drove us to find a young woman in the last moments of life.'

The story that unfolded stunned Harry. The words and power provided by Mary and Charly, first one then the other, adding detail of comments as they spelled out the days at the billabong, the first travels, Charly's encounters, her adoption, the first years working as a cameleer, the starting of an arm of Abdul's business in the Springs and finally the development of her own camel transport operations as responsibility and then ownership was transferred.

The only details missing were the days immediately before and after the fire. Harry knew this was a sensitive place, one that even Mary stayed clear of.

'Charly, dearest daughter, you have left the finest part out. I am thinking he is wondering about a rock on your desk, you should tell him your greatest journey.'

Charly shook her head slightly, as if denying she was going to follow the prompt.

'No, Abdul, the greatest journey was with you and Mary, but yes the rock has an interesting journey.'

Charly the briefly discussed a mine, many weeks journey into the desert, the insane gamble, the risk to lose all she had made and then the rewards when the risk tipped her way. Harry failed to understand the consequences of what ten per cent of a gold mine meant, until Abdul snort at Charly's obscure comments on her financial status.

'Harry, she never tell an untruth, but she is close to the prophet's displeasure with her words,' growled Abdul, annoyed at the lack of pride in her own achievements. 'She own all the camels here, the compound, the hotel we sleep at and other buildings in the Springs.'

Some of this Harry knew already, some was new, but the final comment stunned him.

'Charly could buy my business, and still have moneys to celebrate.' He laughed in almost shame, hanging his head in mock disappointment. 'She better business lady than me, the once great Abdullah Rahman Khan.'

'Ignore his comments, Harry. I have a little savings, I put what I earn in what I do,' retorted Charly to the description of her wealth.

Abdul almost choked in disbelieving laughter. 'The prophet now knowing she over the line.'

This ended the story. Harry felt he had twice as many questions, even after so many had been answered in the story. Yes, it was an amazing tale, but there was much more to find out. But he knew he had a lifetime to glean the facts, no rush.

Chapter 20

I t was a good three weeks since Harry had stood on the platform, waving farewell to the two most interesting people he had likely ever met. Charly had been close to him, his arm around her waist. She slept quietly beside him now, enjoying the last few moments of sleep before their next adventure. The next adventure, it all had started a few days after Abdul and Mary left, when the reason for the questions about the cattle became truly apparent.

'We take stores and vittles to a few outlying stations, a number of telegraph stations, but most of what we do is supply the Defiance Mine,' Charly explained. 'They basically live off corned and salted beef, and any food that takes a while to perish. They rarely have fresh meat.'

'No kangaroo they can kill? When we were droving, there was always that meat to survive on.'

'No, travel only a few days from here and they start to thin out. Out there, where the Defiance Mine is, there are none,' she replied providing a small education to the well-travelled stockman. 'Well, a few rock wallaby perhaps, but they are near impossible to hunt, and harder to retrieve in the rocky outcrops.'

Harry was stunned, he'd always believed that the one native animal he had seen everywhere he travelled was around to some extent, yes less numbers in the drier parts but still available if you knew where to look.

'Even the local people out that way don't hunt the kangaroo for food. They live off a lot less, mostly lizards or such.'

'So, not much grass and a lot less water.'

'Now you are understanding the issues with where the mine is located,' Charly acknowledged in agreement. 'Not enough grass and water, and the cattle we tried to get out there did not survive. So I want your opinion if we can get cattle to the site on a regular basis to supply fresh meat for short periods of time.'

The discussion flowed back and forth on available native grasses, and water, until Harry knew that the only way he could understand the issues was to travel out there, check the route, understand the conditions. The biggest drawback he was immediately told was the mode of transport: horses no, camels yes.

'Can't ride a camel. I'm not like you, I only do horses.'

'For really bright bloke, you, Harry, can be downright stupid,' she retorted in mock anger. 'Your horse will likely die, even now in the cool season.'

Harry said nothing, allowing Charly's grumpiness to settle down.

'You that keen on walking back next to my camel? It's a long way, mate,' was her final comment, waiting for another equally annoying response.

Harry got off the chair in her office and walked to the doorway, stopping as if to say something, then thought better of it. He walked outside, knowing his words could cause offence to the person he loved.

Charly let him go, hoping she had not said something that would make the first crack in their relationship. She returned to the papers on her desk, planning the trip out to the mine that she did as part of her regular routine to check for developing problems in both parts of her business.

Two hours later Harry poked his face in the door, a strange look on his face. The look changed as he observed Charly sitting at the desk, blank paper in front of her, tapping the fountain pen on the timber desk with a certain amount of force.

'Hey, what's the problem? You look all flustered,' he said.

Charly gave a snort and dropped the pen on the paper, a spray of fine droplets of ink leaving a fan shaped pattern on the page.

'You would think I might be able to right a few words to my brother, but shit, Harry, I can't,' she growled in frustration. 'What do I say? "Sorry boys, I ignored you all these years, but here I am can we be mates again?"'

Harry sat in the chair across the desk to take the weight off his leg, gave a shrug, then waved his arms wide. 'So the woman who has built all this, dealt with grumpy old men and prospered, can't write a letter to her brothers who still love her and miss her? If you don't, I will.'

Charly sat for a bit and looked at Harry. She said nothing, then gave another snort of annoyance and picked up her pen. Screwing up the spoiled pages she threw them across the room.

'Okay, you win, I will try again. Alright, already, I will, I promise.'

'Good and don't forget, Jessie and Bryan only go to town once every month or so, so it might be a fair time before they get your letter, and who knows what might happen in between time.'

'Okay, Harry, enough already... I will do it, for them if not for me,' Charly noted with a slight sour tone. 'You arrive back in my life for a week and you are getting to me already.'

They both sat for a few moment in silence. But the look of smugness on Harry's face finally caused Charly to soften her annoyance, letting out a chuckle at how she had so quickly accepted Harry into her life.

'And, pray explain, good man, what were you going to tell me when you arrived? 'Cause you had that silly boy look on your face I remember rather well.'

'Spoke to Qadir, he told me off too, looks like I am a bit hard-headed for my own good,' he replied with a knowing smile. 'So, miss smarty pants, you better show me how to ride one of your humpy animals.'

Charly looked at him dumbfounded, almost speechless at the sudden change, her head providing a slow deliberate movement from side to side.

'Typical man, need another bloke to tell ya before you believe a shelia,' she replied, then laughed. 'We better find you a bloke camel, wouldn't want you to spend a trip arguing with a dumb sheila camel, now would we?'

Charly quickly ushered her still reluctant man out the door, walking towards the camel enclosure, providing a few basic ground rules to avoid the real dangers from these generally placid animals.

'A bit grumpier than a horse, but every one of them is different. They tend to snort snot and dribble everywhere and do the odd bit of biting,' Charly explained. 'Worse is when a cow is in season, the bulls all go a bit mad, especially the big old dominant males. Need to watch them then. They been known to near rip off an arm or ya hand. But I'll keep an eye on ya around them nutters.'

'Yeah, Qadir told me as much a while back, guess you'll start me on a nutter to see how I go,' replied Harry, indicating the usual process in testing a new cowhand on a slightly wild horse to both see how they reacted and have a little fun along the way.

'Nope, can't do that. Camels are a bit different to your beloved horses,' was the quick answer. 'Anyway, I actually do like you a lot, so I am keen not to break you just yet.'

Harry answered with silence, looking at the animals he was about to encounter.

'Last thing I need is you propped up in my bed, and me needing to do all the work.' Charly completed the sentence with a suggestive chuckle as they arrived at the enclosure.

Qadir had already picked the best of the available camels: one of the sons of Charly's beloved Sheeba. Qadir was provided with an approving nod from his boss, settling the camel to allow Harry to climb onto the saddle. A second camel was already on its haunches, another of Sheeba's offspring, ready for Charly to ride.

Harry warily climbed onto the saddle, taking a strong grip with both hands on the saddle as directed by Qadir. A quick tug of the halter lead by Qadir and the camel lurched forward, then lifted it rear. Straightening its legs, then one leg at a time lifting and adjusting it front legs to suit. Harry was thrown forward, then back, then slightly forward again. Harry fought the movement, not quite prepared, almost losing his grip and seat. He looked at Charly as her camel stood, the same movements but Charly smoothly swayed in rhythm of each phase of the process.

With that complete, Qadir slowly walked the camel around the enclosure so Harry could get a feel of the animal's movement. It was immediately clear to everyone else, Harry was fighting every move, stiffly being jerked back and forwards, left and right. Then, ever so slowly, the jerking was lessened. His years of riding horses started to tell, his body winning the fight over his brain.

'Relax, Harry, watch me. Slump a little, flow with the rhythm,' called Charly as she rode slowly up beside him.

'Ah, relax you say,' snarled Harry in dismay. He felt like a child hanging on for dear life. 'How do you relax when every step it takes, you feel like you will fall off?'

Charly only laughed and stayed slightly in front of him as Qadir calmly walked the camel in a large circle. Suddenly confidence built, changing Harry from worrying about falling to understanding the movements, his body pre-empting each sway and roll, relaxing, flowing with the rhythm.

By the end of the week, circling the enclosure, first walked by Qadir, then given the reins, Harry could slowly ride around the enclosure by himself. After two weeks, Charly allowed him to follow her outside the enclosure, around the buildings of the compound. Harry was as amazed as everyone in the compound, especially the Afghan cameleers, with so much experience watched and cheered him on, not mocking but enjoying his excitement at learning. By the middle of the third week, Charly and Qadir were satisfied at his progress and took Harry for a long ride into the bush, along small tracks just outside of the Springs, returning late in the day.

'Good, Charly Khan, he know enough with you and I watching, he ready for the mine trip next week,' noted Qadir, suggesting that the planned small caravan should be planned for the trip to the Defiance Mine within the week.

And now, on the day of departure, Harry woke early, just as the first light filtered around the edge of the heavy curtains, a worm of worry wiggling in his stomach. He lay silently, hoping he would not fail, his pride as a horseman on the line.

'Will you stop worrying, my darling man. I can feel your unease through the bed's mattress,' muttered Charly half-asleep. 'After the first hour it will as natural as being on Misty.'

She slowly reached over, lovingly rubbing his arm on top of the blankets. Her love for him now unquestionable, his place the last part of the puzzle she believed that fulfilled her life.

'If I even had a small doubt about your safety we would not be leaving. So get another hours sleep, Qadir has everything in order, it will be a long enough day as it is.'

The following days made Charly's comment a fact of truth. The first day on the trail had allowed a body and mind to become part of the animal below Harry. These days, the road to the Defiance Mine was well-made, especially so close to the Springs. Qadir led a small caravan of supplies, taking some critical mining supplies in the form of boxes of dynamite, a little black powder, detonators and other parts of the underground blasting process. Due to the nature of the freight, it had always been considered too dangerous to take with a full caravan. If an accident happened, only four camels and a couple of cameleers would be lost, better than twelve or more camels and six or eight men.

Charly and Harry rode ahead, Charly leading one camel with everything required to set up camp for the caravan. Harry could see it was the typical open bush of the area, small areas of grassland and the rocky outcrops. The road to the mine now had well-defined places for overnight stays. Areas set up to hobble the camels for the night, cleared areas for bedrolls and a number had steel frames set over fire pits to allow quick set up of camps after a day's travel. While the road was a public project, in the main it was Charly's caravans that used the facilities and so she and the mine had funded much of the rest camp works and facilities.

The first three days were routine, with Harry learning the process. It was not much different to a stock run, only without having to chase cattle all day and eat their dust. He soon realised that Charly became a different person on the trail, a calmer and happier soul. She relaxed, smiled more and returned to the person he'd known as a young man.

'I do love being with the animals, the slower pace and rhythm of the camels, it is what I loved doing for all those years before everything else got in the way,' she smiled, a sparkle in her eyes, 'and you look a little happier too.'

Harry was quick to agree, being stuck in the Springs had not been to his liking, being on the trail, even if on a camel was better than sitting inside a room most days. He was sure he would enjoy the next weeks.

At the third camp, the fire pit and steel cooking frame had been smashed and badly bent. A few logs laid as backing for the sleep areas had been rolled to clog the open areas. Charly and Harry dismounted and walked around, looking in dismay at the effort required to repair the camp site.

'Who would be so stupid to do this?' asked Harry, slightly dumbfounded. 'It goes against all the rules of outback travel.'

'Route raiders. Not a good sign so early in the trip,' Charly replied, cautiously walking back to her camel and pulling the Winchester from beside the saddle. She walked back to his side. 'We might be watched right now, but I doubt it.'

She calmly handled the rifle to Harry, indicating for him to keep watch as she cleaned up the fire pit and as best as she could straightened the cooking frame. By the time she had finished, Qadir had arrived. The cameleer shook his head as he looked at the damage, knowing the reason before words were exchanged. Harry handed the rifle back to Charly, then assisted Qadir in placing the logs back in place.

Charly confidently held the rifle ready for use, then looking at her experienced Cameleer said, 'We will ride close tomorrow, Qadir. I am concerned when the raiders will show themselves.'

Qadir agreed, nodding as he unpacked his Camel with his fellow cameleer Ishmael. His concern was that he and Ishmael were riding on a camels loaded with explosives. One misplaced shot and they would become nothing but small bits blown around the rocks and trees. He asked if they should still keep going or head back and travel in a larger caravan.

'We keep going, they want to change our schedule,' Charly replied. 'We will keep close watch, but we will continue.'

The night passed without issue; the following day was the same until they arrived at the next campsite. Again, it had been badly disturbed, the damage similar. This time Charly walked further out into the bush as the three men tidied up the camp as best they could. The Winchester loaded and ready in her hands, she searched for any sign of the people who'd done this.

About twenty yards from the camp she found what she was looking for, the ground providing signs that could be only made by man. Charly quickly turned and walked back. the information was concerning. Hoof prints. The men were using horses, so whatever was going to happen would be in the next two or three days, before the serious desert sands started the horses reached their limit.

The horses had been there within the last forty-eight hours, the edges of the sandy soil still sharp. This, and the destroyed campsites were not a series of random actions. They were sending a message: continue and face what was coming. Charly stopped outside the camp, deep in thought. Continue or go back? She was certain the people doing this were serious in their intent. She finally let out a snort, she had not survived this far running away, but a little planning was required.

The discussions that evening around the fire were blunt. A number of arguments were provided in turn. Most were discarded as unworkable, one appeared to be an option with limited risk. The dangers were undeniable but they knew if they went back, the mine would likely run out of explosives, an outcome that would hurt them not only in reputation but also hurt the income of the miners. It also could mean that the next full supply caravan in around two weeks' time might also be delayed.

Ishmael said little. He sat and listened, considering all the comments, all the options and then carefully thought about where an advantage could be found.

'Tell me, what is these unknown people's greatest advantage?' Ishmael finally asked the other three as they sat around the fire.

'We know nothing about them, but they know much about us,' replied Qadir wishing to ensure his thoughts from experience were considered by Charly.

'Yes, but there is a greater advantage they have,' Ishmael answered, waiting to see if anyone could see what this was. 'It is that we do not know what extents they will take. Is it threats, or will they willingly take our lives?'

Before anyone could comment, he continued. 'What is their greatest disadvantage?'

'That they do not know to what level we may respond,' answered Charly, suddenly knowing what Ishmael was saying. 'We prepare to be bold. Ignoring them will provide them the advantage. Do we have any other advantages?'

'Yes, and they have horses, they must act quickly. In reality, the first opportunity they have they must force themselves on us,' said Ishmael with a smile. This was his world, he was pleased to allow the warrior in him again to be valuable. 'I learned many things in the battles against the English in the mountains.'

'Okay, Ishmael, it is clear to me you have already formed a plan,' noted Charly. 'So explain your thoughts.'

'The land is too open till we meet the first of the dunes. I would consider this the place as the road swings to run along the base of the dune for some distance. They are likely carrying some water for the horses, but it will not be much. We could try to arrive before they are prepared, but with the loads the camels cannot travel much quicker,' said Ishmael. 'So we delay, place pressure on them, make their horses uneasy.'

'What the word you say, Harry?'

'Skittish, flighty.'

'Yes, the horses will skittish as you say, not like our camels,' replied Ishmael, his smile getting broader. 'So we delay here. Two days, no more.'

Charly was surprised, not expecting to give them more time to prepare for whatever their adversaries has planned.

'But Ishmael, that will alert them that we know they are before us.'

Ishmael shrugged, clearly unconcerned of this situation. 'They have destroyed our camps, a child would know we have adversaries before us. They do this to disrupt, force us to choose to return or be uncertain in our advance.' He gave a short, dismissive laugh, patting the Sharps rifle he had acquired during the last engagement. 'But they have not met Ishmael, the terror of the English in the mountains. But they will. So Charly Khan, which is the quickest camel?' he suddenly asked, knowing the answer, but using the question to redirect the discussion.

'The one Harry rides... Why?' Qadir supplied before Charly could respond.

'Because you will ride back to the Springs to summon MacDonald.'

'Why me?' replied Qadir, startled that he be chosen to leave the potential fight.

'Charly Khan never leave, Harry too slow, I fight, and you the best cameleer in the compound,' was the response. There was enough adulation to Qadir's skills to soften the moment. 'You ride long days with no load, you will return to the Springs in two days.'

'Why do we need MacDonald, Ishmael?' Charly asked, knowing the answer even as she finished her words. 'Oh, yes, because if we succeed, we still require the law of the land to approve what we have done.'

Ishmael's plan was simple, the only concern was that Harry was to lead a train of four camels, but thankfully, the camels brought to carry the explosive loads were the best trained and of the calmest dispositions. Charly would ride to the front and Ishmael would ride to the rear.

A few final detailed parts of the plan were discussed, Charly saw it was likely the best and provided the greatest opportunity and lowest risk, if dealing with route raiders ever provided low risk. Qadir quickly prepared what he required in the morning, packing a small pouch of food and a full water bag. A second water bag was drained, the water provided to his camel to provide additional stamina, then the empty bag was placed on the leather panniers, ready to be turned into their advantage.

Chapter 21

Three days later, the small caravan moved slowly through the last of the open bushland, the few remaining eucalypts fighting to find enough water to live, their roots down deep in the red sand between rocks and hollows under the sand, sucking up what water was stored there. Ahead lay the endless tuffs of grass and spinifex that prepared everyone for the first dune, a small sandy bank, not thirty feet high, the dune that signalled the start of the desert. The dune was only a handful of hours ahead, maybe three or four.

They had planned to reach the dune in the later part of the afternoon, to allow the heat of the day to condition the four-legged animals, some negatively as in the horses, some it made not much difference, their camels. They took their positions, Charly riding some fifty yards before the caravan, Ishmael some ten to twenty yards off the rear of the last camel. They moved at a steady pace, the usual rhythm of a moderately loaded caravan, nothing in their approach appeared abnormal.

They had watched the dune grow before them as they approached, then turned to run parallel close to its base. The dune was not high and well vegetated with clumps of waving grass and the small, isolated stands of mulga that grew on its lower slopes. It was perfect cover to set an ambush, something discussed by the group earlier.

They had moved some five hundred yard along the side of the dune when they noticed a large stand of eucalypts and mulga sat in a slight hollow ahead of them, spreading a small distance up the side of the dune. Charly was within shouting distance, approximately fifty yards from the stand when a tall full bearded man, a wide brimmed felt hat shading his face rode out of the trees. Though she had expected the ambush, his appearance still provided a moment of shock, stopping her camel still.

Three men of similar features followed a short distance behind the man. Their horses were obviously desert bred, moving quickly through the long grass and spinifex clumps without concern. The first man rode onto the worn wheel tracks of the roadway and stopped, holding a rifle in his hand, the butt against his thigh, the barrel facing upward.

He slowly moved towards Charly as the three men moved onto the road, fanning out on either side of the roadway. Charly quickly turned her camel, moving slightly off the roadway in a small arch to head back to be alongside Harry at the head of the caravan. As she turned, she loosened a small package, the canvas waterbag, and with the body and legs of the camel obscuring her actions dropped it on a tall clump of grass.

She suddenly felt the cold hand of fear grasp her chest, a flaw in their plan was evident. She desperately hoped that Ishmael had seen where it lay, the plan would fail if he had not seen it land on the grass from where he was at the rear of the caravan.

A shout from behind her slowed her. Turning her head she saw the tall bearded man increase his pace. She pulled the Winchester from the saddle scabbard to show she was armed, then rode the last ten yards to stop slightly before Harry on the lead camel of the caravan. She faced the rider, holding the rifle in a defensive manner across her lap, working the leaver to show it was ready for use.

The man on the horse stopped some twenty yards short, surprised by the weapon in the hands of the lead rider of the caravan. The three men behind also stopped, some twenty yards behind him. They also held rifles in their hands, the reigns loosely looped over their laps.

'You be the woman called Charly Khan?' he shouted in a strong voice, power and authority the tone of choice. 'I be wanting to speak to her, business, I be thinking.'

'I have no interest in business with men who hold rifles and block the roadway I am using!' she shouted back. 'Leave us to pass on our way, I have no interest in your business.'

'These are dangerous roadways,' the bearded man replied, moving his horse slightly forward, then stopping as the barrel of the Winchester pointed in his general direction. 'It be time you left the roads to us men and filled a house with screaming brats. I be offering to purchase the rights to this contract you be having with the mine.'

'Nay, I be satisfied with my lot, leave the screaming brats to others,' she replied in disarming voice, playing for a little time, lowering the barrel of her rifle. 'So you be thinking the owners of the Defiance Mine be in agreement to your arrangement?'

'Aye, I spoke to them. They all satisfied at your leaving,' he replied as he pulled a paper from his bag. 'See here, they provided me with a signed contract, they being concerned at a woman be doing a man's work.'

Charly smiled, the man obviously knew little of the ownership of the Defiance Mine and little on the relationship she had with the other owner. She hoped that Ishmael was ready, the time was close. She moved the camel slightly with a gentle tug on the halter lead, putting her body slightly sideways to the dune where the men had ridden from, expecting that a man had been left to cover the four riders.

'I be thanking you for your concerns on my wellbeing,' she stated slowly again pausing as if considering her options. 'But I be satisfied with the protection I have on this route. I be asking you leave us be to be on our way in peace.'

The tall, bearded man instantly changed. He had allowed a little play with the woman, knowing he had the advantage of well-armed men who had no feelings for a person's life, especially those who crossed their paths and ignored well-presented advice. But he preferred that they simply signed the sheet of paper and handed him the contract. Death, even in the desert, was a complex matter to manage and hide.

'You be a foolish woman, I be offering a good deal,' he growled, annoyed at her calm dismissive refusal. 'I will leave you the other routes and you be protected by my men at a cost.'

'So read it out to me. Read what the paper says, to allow me to understand its words of your generous offer,' replied Charly with slightly sharper tone. She suspected that the contract would be nothing more than a fake produced at the hands of some lacky he'd met in a pub. But it would buy a little more time for her plans.

The man turned the paper to look at it instinctively, then his eyes flicked back at his intended victim. It seemed, by the flush of his cheeks that he was illiterate. He slowly dropped the paper, moving his second hand to his rifle, making the intent of his actions clear. He guessed while she was armed with a formidable weapon at close range, she lacked the fortitude to shoot at another human in cold blood.

'Ya last chance, Charly Khan. Do we have an agreement or no?' he shouted for his men to hear. 'Or we be taking it from ya with no reward.'

'The answer be no,' she replied. She lifted the barrel of the rife directly towards the sky, hoping that all things now went to plan.

The tall bearded man on the horse was momentarily confused. Charly's actions were of a person surrendering their weapon, but her words defied the actions.

A rifle cracked on the top of the dune, the shot coming from a small clump of grasses. The sound triggered unexpected consequences, as the solid large calibre slug tore through the canvas of the old waterbag, then smashed through the soft putty like filling of the waxed cardboard tube before smashing the delicately packed detonator.

The sound of the shot was momentarily heard before the dozen or so sticks of dynamite, stuffed carefully in the waterbag, exploded in a massive blast. The blast provided a physical force that reverberated off the wall of the dune, destroying the peace of the land. The blast removed all thought from every living creature within one hundred yards.

The three men sitting casually on their horses were the first to feel the force. The man closest, no more the five yards from the waterbag was blown off the horse, the horse knocked down. The man beside him on the other side of the roadway was thrown as his horse reared, his feet releasing from the stirrups, landing him on his head and neck. The man furthest away had time to react, but slipped as his horse bolted, falling to one side, his left boot caught in the stirrup. The man was dragged through the grass clumps and spinifex, bouncing along, unconscious or dead from the fall.

A cloud of sand, dirt and fine gravel enveloped them, slowly falling back to earth as a fine fog of debris; blown back towards the length of the dune by the slight breeze, obscuring those hiding on the dune.

The tall, bearded man was almost thrown by his horse as it jumped at the sound and force of the blast, but his skill as a horseman was extraordinary, keeping both his saddle and the rifle in one hand as he controlled the madly jumping, lurching animal.

Charly had her own problems. Her camel also reacted in a violent manner, almost throwing her, but thankfully she had prepared for the reaction. But she had dropped the Winchester in the dust of the roadway. Her greater problem was that Harry had been thrown, landing heavily, not moving. The four camels in the linked caravan had bolted a small distance, then become entangled in the lead ropes that linked them together. Her fear was the one would fall, triggering a much greater explosion. One that would end all their lives.

She ignored the tall, bearded man. He remained a risk, but one was greater than the other. She urged her camel towards to the four entangled animals to calm them and slow their madness. As she rode towards them, she heard the thumping of horse hooves on the harder packed roadway through the ringing in her ears.

A man yelled. She ignored it; her focus was on the four animals in front of her. A shot ran out, but where it went, she had no idea. Suddenly a second shot and her camel stumbled, throwing her forwards into the dry gravelly sand and thick grass.

Charly sat up slightly concussed; her camel lay lifeless beside her as the sound of hooves stopped slightly behind her.

'Ya mad stupid bitch, what did do that for?!' he shouted as he raised his rifle, pointing it at Charly's chest. A maddened anger had taken his mind. 'Beg, ya sticking bitch. I wanna hear ya beg for it.'

He sighted along the barrel, his finger tightening. Charly could see his eyes; she knew that her last moment of life would be looking into the face of the man who would kill her. She refused to give him what he wanted, refusing to show fear in her face. A shot sounded as the man pulled the trigger, but the tall, bearded man slumped forward on his horse. His shot snapped past Charly's ear, tearing the lobe, ruffling her hair and scarf before burying itself on the soils of the land behind her.

The tall bearded man slowly fell, thumping lifelessly into the ground, his horse slowly moving away. Behind it she saw her man, her beloved Harry, sitting in the dust and sand of the roadway, her Winchester in his hands the barrel slowly dropping from where it pointed in her direction.

Charly picked herself up and ran over to him, a mess of emotions, tears and laughter finding a crazy mix coming from her being. She reached him, falling to her knees, hugging him wordlessly.

'No way was he gunna do that to you. I waited too long for your love,' he growled. 'But ya might take a little care, I be thinking me arm be a little bit bent and broken.'

Before she could reply, the sound of another horse came riding towards them from where the ambushers had hidden in wait, emerging in the slowly clearing cloud of debris. A fifth man, holding a large handgun, rode towards them.

Harry and Charly scrambled to get better positioned to face the threat of the rider, Charly trying to take the Winchester out of Harry's hands but getting it tangled in the process. The rider closed the distance, took aim and fired once. The bullet tore between them, lodging in the ground just past them.

He aimed a second time, closer, not wanting to miss again when he simply lurched backwards off the horse, as if pulled by a rope. The sound of the Sharps rifle, a rifle wielded by the skilled marksman, Ismael, filled the area, leaving the lasting sound in all their ears, the sound of survival. Harry sagged to the ground, the pain and stress catching up. Charly sat beside him, cradling his head on her lap, knowing how close it had all come to being a disaster.

Some two hours later as the evening light started to descend, the shadow of the dune moving down its flanks, the sound of more horses sounded up the roadway. Charly and Ismael lifted their rifles in response, but quickly lowered them as they saw the uniforms of the territorial police.

The survivors sat in the shade of the small stand of eucalypts where the ambushers had waited. They were still exhausted emotionally and physically from the stand-off, the loss of a camel had hurt the party. They needed rest before they could plan their next move.

Sitting with their back to small trees were two of the attackers, hands tied together behind their backs, the tree not allowing them to move or stand. Neither could not hear, blood trickling from their ears due to the blast. Three horses were tied to the trees, the four camels hobbled, contentedly chewing the cud nearby.

The six riders, five uniformed, and one well known resident of the Springs pulled up before the three survivors. The six men slowly rode up on the almost worn-out horses, lathered in sweat, tongues and muzzles parched, before standing exhausted as the men dismounted.

The leader of the men, the gruff sergeant of police, looked at the dead men laying on the ground, the two well restrained attackers and then the three other persons sitting beside the small campfire.

'There be one more out there somewhere,' said Charly nonchalantly, a high level of disinterest in her voice. 'Likely still bouncing along behind his horse.'

The response was not what Sergeant Angus MacDonald expected but it made him laugh, from the mental picture as much as his relief that the young owner of the camels he dearly had affection for and respected was alive. Blood from her ear had soaked the shoulder of her overshirt, but other than that, she was her smiling almost childishly. He gave a quick response with a nonchalant salute to his brow, that was equally irreverent before he checked the two dead men and the two prisoners.

Harry sat back against a small log, pain blanketing his eyes, his arm in a crude sling, a rough splint holding the forearm stable. Ishmael said nothing as he sat next to the rifle that caused the devastation for the attackers, as usual he was cautious of white men in uniform. One of the men who rode with the police walked over to Charly, squatting down to look at the rough blood-soaked bandage around her head.

After checking the torn and slightly missing lobe, he quickly rebandaged it with fresh white linen.

'Young lady, this one might be your last warning,' he said in concern as he picked the small black spots of burnt powder from her face after she explained the circumstances of the wound. 'You may wish to take that man over there, love him to bits, bed him a lot and then settle down with some kids.'

'Doc, ya know what?' she replied, smiling at the thought. 'You might just be right.'

'Seriously, Charly, I don't want to be wrapping you in a calico sack like them two.' He pointed at the two dead men being wrapped up by the policemen.

He rose and stepped over to check Harry's arm as Macdonald sat beside Charly. The sergeant looked over to Ishmael. 'I be thinking right that Ishmael punched the stonking great big hole through the chest of that one with that cannon of his?' He nodded to the wrapped body next to the tall, bearded man.

Ishmael provided a single nod in partial agreement.

'Rightio. And this one, slightly smaller hole in his middle of his back, say a Winchester?' asked MacDonald pointing his toe the second man being wrapped in calico. Again, a small responding nod, this time from Charly.

'Okey dokey, I be thinking you need to explain yourselves. I was told you'd be waiting for me. So how is it as I am riding along, wondering just where you would be, that I hear this fucking great explosion in the distance? And then I find this mayhem with you sitting in the middle of it all big eyed and innocent... again,' growled McDonald. Yet again he had to explain two, maybe more, deaths in his district.

Charly, with a word or two from Harry but nothing but a blank stare from Ishmael, explained what had happened, in a broad-brush shortened version she thought MacDonald was wanting to hear. She left out the planning, and the use of explosives, providing just a short description of the exchange and violent ending.

'Nah, come on, Charly, from the beginning. Don't do the old, treat the copper like he be a dumb fool crap. I know what you be telling me is missing a heap of stuff I needs to know.'

Charly looked at him blankly, the message was clear: she wanted to protect her employee and beloved man from any possible complications.

'Look, I need to know the truth. I can then do a report that clears the air if I see any issues,' MacDonald grumped. 'Can't protect you if I don't know something.'

'What about them?' asked Charly pointing to his fellow police.

'They remember what I tell them. And as for Doc, he forgets more than he remembers.'

With his assurance, Charly provided the detailed description that MacDonald wanted. He stopped her on a couple occasions, once to congratulate Ishmael on his shooting skills and then later, Harry on shooting with a broken arm to save Charly's life. The final details were on finding two of the men still alive but suffering from the explosion and falls from the horses, semiconscious and bleeding from the ears.

By the time they were finished, the first darkness of night had taken its hold on the land, forcing everyone to prepare for camp. The first moonlight pushed across the grass, providing a silver light that Charly so loved.

'Ya know, bloody Qadir never stopped. He rode through the night, just enough moonlight he said,' muttered MacDonald as they finished a cup of sweet black tea. He nodded towards where Ishmael was cooking a spicy stew with one of the policemen. 'Ya gotta believe it, those blokes will die for you Charly, so it might be a good idea to avoid these situations in future. I be thinking you're not gunna enjoy living knowing they did that for ya with them dead and you living.'

Harry, laying on his bedroll, slightly groggy from the painkiller Doc had provided him, reached across and took her hand, providing support and showing his agreement to MacDonald's comments. Charly looked down. She now had to think of someone else; she had also put their love in danger.

Late the following day, Qadir arrived with replacement camels, additional supplies and large water bags, along with two Afghan drivers, knowing that whatever the task, the shipment of explosives had to be delivered. Charly had decided the previous day that she would continue to the mine; there were serious things to discuss on improving safety for her teams and these came with costs.

Harry said he had ridden with a broken arm before and so would continue with his beloved partner. He still needed gain an understanding of the challenges of moving cattle in this country. The Doc decided to join them, thinking a visit to the mining area would be beneficial for the workers. Having become proficient in riding a camel some years before, he gladly accepted a fresh animal to ride.

MacDonald loaded the dead and prisoners onto the spare horses, with one of the Afghans being provided with two spare camels to carry needed supplies and additional water for what would be a slow trip back on exhausted horses. One of his Aboriginal constables would ride with the caravan, providing a level of authority for the remaining trip.

'Not much will happen for a fair while, hopefully nothing. But I know Commissioner Sommerville will want to investigate. There have been a few of these incidents and most don't end as well as this,' said MacDonald as they parted ways. 'Time to love your man, Charly, ya know what I be meaning.'

Chapter 22

The remaining trip to the Defiance Mine was uneventful, and they made the remaining transit in surprisingly good time. The cooler weather and a small amount of rain had left unusually good fresh grass and some useful small water catchments. It also allowed an understanding where water gathered, to sit just below the surface in hollows. Harry kept a detailed diary on mileage, conditions and issues until they arrived in the windblown valley. The area surrounding the mine was now organised with roads, laid out streets for rudimentary housing, a small grocer and an ever-increasing number of mine buildings.

They stayed for three days. Charly discussed the issues of ongoing security and its future cost with the mine's operations management and all agreed to bring it to the next budget meeting. The Doctor spent his time fruitfully, setting up a small clinic with the support of the management to treat the many ailments and injuries men endured in these environments, but as usual, he spent most of his time pulling the odd rotten tooth.

Harry took the time to look at the bareness of the valley. The almost lack of grass and vegetation would be an issue to keep cattle for any length of time, but there was enough water, the driven well was providing more than what was required. He rode over to the small store and spoke with the men who ran the supply chandlery and grocer, discovering that one was the butcher, all they needed was fresh cattle and sheep. They discussed where holding pens could be positioned and what time of year they were to avoid transporting to the valley.

On the return journey, Harry checked, revised, and considered the decisions made in his head, drawing and redrawing plans. As they rode along the last leg just outside the town, Charly had enough of waiting for Harry's conclusions, her patience exhausted.

'So am I to be provided with your considerations, my beloved? Or has the incessant chattering by Ishmael and his new friend driven you to madness?' said Charly, referring to the close friendship that had developed between the Aboriginal constable and Ishmael. 'And what is with them two? Ishmael went shy when I asked.'

'I can answer the second with ease,' Harry replied with a small chuckle. 'Well, Jacko is the son of a lady that Ishmael would like to meet, you know what I be meaning, and Jacko thinks the whole idea is grand so they have spent weeks planning this meeting. Every time they agree to the plan, Ishmael gets cold feet and makes changes, driving Jacko insane.'

'Rightio, that makes sense. Well, sort of,' expressed Charly with a smile. Ishmael had not had a woman companion since his wife died some years before coming to this land. 'And the first question? Or is that just too hard?'

'Well, no. But I might need a favour or two along the way,' Harry replied thinking through his half-finished plan. 'We need to drive some wells, two or three maybe, and then I can get cattle out to the mine for most of the year. Less say one or two months when it is too hot.'

The discussion flowed back and forth for the last two days of their return, picking points apart, then putting them together before testing something else. Eventually, as they rode into the compound to the cheers and chanting of the people gathered to welcome them back, Charly agreed to let Harry progress with his ideas.

'Okay, speak with Lachlan to cost up the infrastructure. I also agree to you finding the desert bred cattle you want and bringing a small herd to the Springs, speak to Lachlan on what funding you need,' Charly said. 'Oh, and Harry? Well done. I think that is one smart plan. And I love you very much, never forget that. You mean more to me than anything now.'

As she said the final words, they were rushed into a cacophony of noise and activity. Excluding the possibility of further communications between them, for now.

The next four months passed quickly for Harry, hurriedly being provided the green light to develop a full plan to be costed and then implemented. A meeting with two station owners provided the small amount of cattle he wanted, having them shipped by rail to the Springs, first to be run on a small, enclosed allotment that was located downstream by the banks of the river, before driven to the Tamimi field. Harry was able to lease the small holding paddocks from the owners, with an agreement to purchase after one year if it suited.

It quickly became apparent that feed would need to be shipped in, to be stored in a new shed built at the rail yards. As the early spring season arrived, they took twenty-five cattle to the mine, all desert bred, all in good condition. One of the wells had been driven, in the location where Charly had a soak hole dug, next to the roadway. The well had good water at shallow depth, allowing a small windmill pump to be installed that fed a long timber trough.

An old water cart was refitted and taken behind two camels, feed in grain bags on four more to be delivered to the small holding area at the mine site. The small herd was driven to the valley in good time, the conditions just right. One of the cattle had died but the remaining had arrived to be consumed by the happy miners under the care of the butcher and grocer. The cost of the beef was excessive, but the provision of fresh meat provided immediate results, the workforce was happy, a happy workforce works harder and makes money.

The investigation by the commissioner into the ambush found that no fault could be found of the party heading to the mine, though the content of the story differed in certain areas, allowing that the deaths to the attackers was due to misadventure. The third body had been found by some local people, his leg still attached to the saddle on a dead horse via worn and battered leather and steel stirrup. As he provided the outcome of the inquiry to Charly, MacDonald suggested that the Sharps rifle find a quiet home for a while, but not before Ishmael taught a few of his constables how to shoot long and straight as part of the deal.

Harry sat up in the bed, the hotel quiet, a soft wind rattling a loose weatherboard he needed to fix very soon. He was enjoying a quiet few minutes before he had to rise and face the activity of another day. His life was acceptable, but it was not what he enjoyed.

Charly rolled over, stretching her arms, as she looked up at her man, content but also worried that she had to make some major changes very soon. Circumstances had crept up on her that demanded these decisions. Harry reached over and took one of the outstretched hands, bringing to his mouth and giving it a small kiss in appreciation.

'Charly, darling, I do enjoy being in the Springs doing all those jobs you need done, but it is not me, I am a cattle man, I am not doing what I enjoy.'

Charly saw the pain Harry suffered just saying this, she knew it would have taken many days to build the courage to say what he did.

'Oh. Well we can't have you being unhappy,' mulled Charly. 'Let me see, how about I buy us a nice little cattle station? My wedding present to both of us.'

Harry initially misheard, failing to pick up the last part, confused about the first part of the comment. Suddenly it came to him, hearing the words again. 'Seriously? Are you serious? Swear you're not pulling my leg.'

'Yes, I know things need to change,' she replied calmly. She'd made up her mind some weeks prior. 'I've agreed to sell the controlling percentage of the camel transport business to Lachlan Goodwood.'

'Hey, wait a minute, did you just propose to me?'

'Guess so. And it is about time, you needed to make me an honest woman one day.'

Harry reached down and patted her tummy through the blankets. 'And give this one a proper home too,' Harry said with a chuckle.

'How the hell did you know? I only worked it out a few weeks back,' Charly demanded.

'I'm a cattle man. We know these things, I saw the signs,' he replied.

Charly snuggled over, Harry giving a sensual kiss. As she came up for a breath, she slipped her hand down Harrys stomach, confirming her feelings.

'Mmmm, well, mister, that's one made. I do think we have time to practice on making a second before we need to get up,' she purred. She knew there would be no argument to that suggestion.

Chapter 23

Harry rode down the laneway to the well-appointed house. It'd been two years since they arrived in their new home, set on a few thousand or so acres of grassland in the eastern foothills of the Flinders Ranges, a pleasant ride's distance from Adelaide. A small river that had its origins in the Ranges flowed through the centre of the land, forming an oxbow in a few locations, providing small flood plains that provided good grass even in the driest months. The river flowed on to meet the Murray River a good distance past the edge of their land.

Two years had changed how he and his wife lived, as they'd learned how to fit into the surroundings, what life now required from them. Two years building a family had been a wonderful experience but having a safe place to do what he knew best and provide for his family was the ultimate satisfaction. Two years being what he so enjoyed: a cattleman.

A mile to be home, he thought, a mile before he could enjoy his two children and wonderful wife of two years and six months. He still had to laugh at the speed of their marriage. Well, they'd to move quickly before she showed what nearly everyone at the Springs already appeared to know. Four weeks after the enjoyable morning where he agreed to her proposal, he'd stood before the local priest, awaiting one seriously gorgeous woman. She had been dressed in a stunning dress, attire not of her first love, but worn to fulfil the customs expected. She was helped from a coach by two of her special men and her adopted father, dressed as a king of his tribe, and sergeant Angus MacDonald of the territorial police.

MacDonald, in full dress uniform had strode before the two occupants of the coach. Charly her hand on her father's arm. She could not wait till this was over; churches were not a natural thing to her, bringing back unwelcome memories. But she had relented to the advice of her closest advisers, both Goodwood and MacDonald, and finally agreed to be wed inside one. She wore a grin the width of her happy face.

The man in the robes completed the age-old words, stating that they before God and man were now husband and wife. Charly slightly baulked at being pronounced Mr and Mrs Hendricks, a name she had buried on the bank of a billabong so many years before. But what was done was done. It was Harry's surname, and she had agreed to accept it once more. With the dull stuff completed, it had been time for the evening's entertainment, organised by Abdul and Mary. No cost was spared, the whole town was invited, as was everyone that had done business with her for all those years.

As they made their way up the crowded aisle of the small stone church towards the door, two men suddenly stood before them framing the open doorway, both newly arrived, slightly dusty, one leaning heavily on a walking stick. Harry stopped, knowing them well. He'd invited them as Charly had been more than a little vague about the whole thing even after the first agreement. Charly, who now stood stock still and stared at the newcomers. As she recognised them she knew her letter that had taken so many attempts to finish, and then send, had arrived in time, the invitation had been accepted. She squealed in utter disbelief and surged forward, leaving Harry behind, throwing herself into their arms. Jessie and Bryan caught her at full flight, holding her tight as all three could not stop laughing in the joy of a long-delayed reunion.

It took over two days for the festive activities to finish, with Harry and Charly leaving after the first day to enjoy a few days together in a small town on the coast near Adelaide, before meeting with the agents looking for a new place to make their home. On the last day before they were due to return to the Springs, they rode in a gig down the laneway that Harry was now riding on. At the time, they'd not known that their new home, a classical single story, solid red brick house of the district, sat at the end of the gravel laneway. The sign at the gate read 'Riverstone Vale.'

It took many months to finalise the deal. Abdul took over the negotiations, declaring that Charly would not pay a silver coin more than she should. In this he was successful, finalising the deal with a gift of a small gold and silver camel to the owners in appreciation, costing him a fair value but he'd enjoyed the process immensely and that he'd saved his daughter a good number of pounds.

The final two months before they left the Springs were absorbed in the sale and transfer of fifty-five per cent of the transport business to Lachlan Goodwood, with both Charly and Lachlan making as many concessions as possible to make the deal happen. The lawyers of both sides finally declared they were obviously not needed, as the parties ignored any advice given in protecting their financial positions. Charly declared that she was done, she would be happy if Lachlan was happy, and he should contact her if he needed someone to take a caravan anywhere, but not in the next few years because she had other things on her mind.

With those enjoyable memories fresh in his mind, Harry rode down beside the end of the house, to the large stables at the rear. The only darkness in their lives was the sudden loss of Abdullah Rahman Khan, who at a family business meeting stood to make a point of conjecture to an issue raised by one of his sons. As he'd stood, he'd suddenly reached to his chest. He was dead before his head impacted on the table. The response was swift, Abdul had been buried before Charly knew, following the custom of his beliefs.

Mary then disappeared from their world; her presence not appreciated by Abdul's sons as they argued over the inheritance. Dismissing her advice and directions as unwanted woman's talk, they finally banned her from having a say in the family transport businesses. The once successful business was broken into conflicting parts, doomed for rapid failure.

Two days later Mary had left. Her daughters came to see her in her home, expecting to join her in mourning the loss of the one she so loved, but found no-one. The home was unlocked, but nothing was taken, her clothes undisturbed aside from one old kameez and shalwar tunic, thought to be missing, or maybe thrown away, but no-one was sure. The horses were stabled, the wagons in their place. Mary's location was unknown.

Charly was unaware of her missing adopted mother, until a single page in an envelope arrived by mail. Only a few words were written by her adopted mother, the message clear and uncompromising. Mary could not live if she did not have her beloved, she would do what the women of her people had done for years, return to their lands to die. Charly immediately knew where Mary was, what she would do, knowing that their lives were now so tied together, a place she once lived, her beloved Mary would die.

When a second letter arrived from her stepsisters, she considered telling them of her thoughts but then stopped. Why add to the grief? A person who had shown her so much love surely had the right to choose her own manner of passing. She wrote back, expressing grief but little more. She encouraged continued contact but knew that the links were ending as they had been with Mary and Abdul, not with their children. For Charly it was as if a full page of her life had ended. A new one was to begin as she put her hand on the very large bulge where her child lay.

Six weeks later she was a mother, a son, Myles, was added to the happy couple. They were now a family, it was time to grow together. And so, over the next year or so, a second child was added, obviously the early practice was beneficial. This time a daughter, Lilly, joined the family, increasing the families hold on their world.

Harry quickly stabled his horse, knowing the house master would check his work after he entered the house. Having a small handful of servants was an interesting experience, helpful, but it annoyed him nonetheless. He was still a cattleman, his best and happiest days were on the land, sitting on his horse watching his black cattle feed on the thick grass. He smiled again, remembering the response from their immediate neighbours, old, titled families, after they'd purchased the property. 'Bloody colonials, old chap. Riffraff, bloody place is gone to the pack letting them live here.'

For the neighbours, seeing Charly ride astride her horse, mustering as she had done in her youth was bad enough, but when a handful of camels appeared on the property, with Charly in her best Afghan kit riding them, it was just too much. The local constable visited, acknowledging Charly and Harry's rights but explaining the neighbours had complaints and they needed to take them seriously. This enounter left Charly in a fit of laughter, causing deep embarrassment to the very nice policeman.

Harry still chuckled at that incident, which had required a discrete ride to the neighbours to discuss the vagaries of the wealthy woman with a fascinating background. But in the end, he'd agreed that the camels would find a different home in the near future.

Not entirely mollified, the locals finally accepted who lived in their midst; they were a little shocked that a youngish couple with no wealthy family to support them could purchase such a fine property. Harry ignored the attempts to find the source of the wealth, knowing that they would be the gossip of the district for some time to come. A wealth that increased just a little more when after twelve months missing, Mary was pronounced deceased, and Charly was one of the beneficiaries of the Mary's surprisingly extensive holdings.

Harry crossed the back verandah and opened the back door, walking through the rear mudroom and into the kitchen. His steps walked him back into reality; it was time to stop thinking about the past few years, times were changing again, it was time to consider the future.

'Hey, gorgeous, that you? I'm in the sitting room with little Lil!' shouted Charly. 'Did ya get the mail?'

Harry stopped at the wood-fired range, sitting tightly in the masonry alcove that formed one of the building's four chimneys. He opened the lid of a pot on the range, smelling the food they would eat in a few hours. Now, having a cook was one benefit he *did* enjoy, Charly immediately noting on their arrival that she cooked on the trail but not in a building.

'Hey, Mr Hendricks, please be letting the pot lid alone,' muttered Mrs Janice Baker, the cook. She was a grumpy person, yet had the skills required for making the most basic staples very tasty, only the spices brought home by Charly surpassed her skills. 'You may be the master of the house but you will be eating in the stables if you be spoiling me stew.'

Harry let out a small snort of glee to have received the response he had hoped he would receive, but lowered the lid and walked on to the sitting room. Myles was on the floor, playing with colourful wooden blocks, Lilly was attached to Charly's breast, clearly enjoying one part of his wife that he also had an affection for.

'You tell that child of yours to be careful with that tit, that side is my favourite remember,' growled Harry in mock annoyance. He smiled as Charly blushed slightly. 'Okay, I like both sides equally.'

'Settle buster. Saying stuff like that will get me in the mood and then we'll have three,' responded Charly, still enjoying their mateship after the years together. 'So, any mail? I was expecting a letter.'

Harry handed Charly two letters, one a business update from Lachlan Goodwood, which no doubt needed little reading, he had a knack for improving business to both their benefits. Charly opened the second, it was from her sister-in-law Ellie Hendricks, the one married to – or was it sleeping with? – one of her brothers, not that she could ever remember.

The Hendricks family reunion at their wedding had also included the two sisters, who had waited by their carriage. The reunion had blossomed into wonderful, close friendship, especially with the third sister Maggie. The reunion provided a final opportunity grasped by the four young women, now connected in some way in marriage, the want to write, communicate and express the joy to each other as each individual family grew and matured.

'Hey, Ellie writes that she is in child again. Problem is she is really not sure which one of the boys is the father, again,' snorted Charly, reading from the letter. 'Those four need to move to different parts of the farm, gunna confuse the shit out of everyone when the kids get older.'

Harry was also reading a letter as he sat in one of the upholstered high-backed chairs, lost in the words on the page, failing to provide the required response to the irreverent comment by his wife.

'Oi, you deaf, ya bugger? You listening to me?' she grumbled in exasperation.

Harry lifted his eyes from the letter he was holding. 'Sorry, got a little lost in this stuff.' He lifted the letter from the light horse regiment he had volunteered to join some time back when he arrived in the district. After a few attendances, his riding skills ensured Harry was quickly accepted, now a valued member for his contacts and knowledge of horses.

'Rightio, so what's got your beard? You look a little razzeled, my darling one.'

Harry put down his letter. 'They want me to muster together some bush bred horses. It looks like there is a bunch of the boys heading to South Africa. You remember that insurrection with the local farmers over there that kicked off a few months back?'

'Bloody hell, Harry, you even speaking like them. Good thing I had Mary teach me some words, so I know whatcha saying, mate,' sniggered Charly, playing up her countryness.

She lowered her tone as she noted his quietness, seriousness taking the place of flippancy in her previous words.

'So what does that mean? You just selecting the horses, or you going too?' asked Charly cutting to the chase. The days had been too light in her life of late, dark clouds needed to form over their lives again somewhere soon.

'Not sure from the letter. I'll ride to see Cecil in a few days, he'll know,' was the slightly uncertain reply. 'Good thing it's the quiet season, a few days away shouldn't cause too much problem.'

The room sank into silence, both adults slipping into deep thoughts resulting from the letters in their hands. Finally, Charly tapped her letter on the edge of the small side table as she moved Lilly to the other breast, feeling a sense of relief as the pressure lessened.

'You know, Harry, the one thing I have never found out, and with Mary gone I likely never will,' muttered Charly, 'is where the hell my mother and my baby sister are.'

She paused as she softly brushed her daughters head. 'I would give every bit of coin I have to know that one thing, just to know they be alive, just to be able to say gidday one time.'

Harry set down his letter and looked at his wonderful wife. He knew that as she got older, as she became the very able mother she was, this one hole in her life was beginning to eat her. He only wished he could help but without any knowledge, he knew that he had no hope. He knew where his mother was, and he had no interest in visiting that spot ever again.

'We'll keep searching. Never know what might just pop out one day. Just need to keep hoping,' Harry replied. 'Sometimes the information comes from the darndest places, just look at us.'

The following days confirmed that Harry was required to source good bush bred stock horses for the regiment, horses that would survive the hardships of a dry and hostile environment. The men had learned from a previous military action some years before of the harshness of the environment in that other southern land, conditions so similar to theirs. Harry had his ideas and knew enough people to start the process quickly, bringing the first few horses to their property to be held in preparation. By the end of the third week he had sufficient to bring the senior commanders to review the horses for quality and suitability.

'Look a bit short in the leg,' mumbled one of the older men fresh from England, with a slight sneer. 'Seen better horses pulling milk drays.'

Harry smiled. Many of the senior officers based their concept of a good horse around jumping hurdles or seating cavalry with lances on smooth, grassy paddocks. But there were enough that knew what was really needed. He had been told what the conditions were to be, and their manner of use. Racing stallions would not suit.

Harry explained the skills and abilities these horses had, bred to be light on the ground and swift on poor country, but happy to survive on the poorest of grass and water. He then had two of his stock men ride a few of the horses around a poorer section of paddock, not that the property had much of that, Harry mused, not quite the back of the Springs or out in the rock country past the grassy plains at the Flats.

The demonstration sealed the deal, Harrys wise actions and choice of animal acknowledged. The funds to obtain the remainder were provided with directions from the senior officers. As they sat enjoying a delightful cup of tea and fresh scones of the rear verandah of the house, the commander cleared his throat, bringing the quiet chatter to an end.

'Harry, without any doubt what you have so quickly accomplished is a credit. Our regiment has been a bit of a voluntary arrangement where we all tend to enjoy the company and interests of like-minded men.'

The other older semi-retired military men with a collection of rank and decorations all nodded sagely. The comments by the commander having been previously discussed and agreed on before the visit was undertaken.

'Look, Harry, not to beat around the bush, I'll get to the point. We would like you to take on the management of the horses, train the riders we recruit and generally make sure when our men ride, they ride in a manner to make us all proud. Hopefully not to fall off at the first battle.'

Harry waited, a little surprised at the expansive level of the engagement.

The commander continued. 'We need to tidy up a few small things, but we're asking if you would volunteer for both jobs before we leave, and continue your role in South Africa. We'll authorise your role and also the rank. We're thinking captain for now. See how we go. Can you give Cecil your answer by the end of the week?'

Harry smiled. He, just a stockman, now not only accepted into the ranks of the titled and powerful – mind, the wealth of his dear beloved helped in that regard – but given authority and rank, the road to status. A need to be acknowledged and held in good opinion by these men sat strong. What was being offered fed that need, and there could be only one answer.

'Save you all the wait, count me in. Be my pleasure to take that role,' he replied. In the back of his mind he speculated a little what Charly would think. She was opposed to the warrior madness the affected the minds of sane men.

Charly took the news with a slightly raised eyebrow and an understanding sigh. She'd long observed the boyish enthusiasm for battle by a few of her closest friends and workers in years past. She had a small chuckle, knowing she too had fallen for that with some of the decisions she had made in her own history.

Sitting in her upholstered chair that evening, Lilly on her breast, she contemplated the words from Harry. Charly knew that Harry had to go; he would be unbearable if he stayed. He needed to go and do what he thought was his duty. She would survive without him, the financial position, her business support, and the ability to hire a skilled man to manage the cattle station would ensure that she would not suffer. However deep in his mind was the knowledge that she really would miss him more than she could ever have known.

'Okay, I will not say a word against your decision Harry, but I will miss you, so don't stay away longer than you need.'

Chapter 24

Harry and the small group of his men from the regiment rode down a slight incline between two large outcrops of massive boulders, locally called kopjes in this foreign place. They rode carefully to limit the dust from the hooves, so as to not give away their position to anyone within sight. The sparse stands of trees, the clumps of grass were all so familiar to him as they rode, only they were half a world away from where he had lived before. The fawn-coloured uniform he wore was soaked in sweat and well-worn, a few holes on places that would require patching soon. His felt hat was sweat stained, the leather band stuffed with a new cluster of colourful feathers, lucky omens to help him find his way home.

Between his legs was one of the extraordinary bush horses he had found in the outback of his youth, they were an inspired choice, they were perfect for the condition. It carried him down the slope with ease. The horses under his six companions equally as good; if anything was going to get them out of this situation, the horses would.

Four days ago, there'd been ten of them, but three lay somewhere back on the trail, dead, their horses collected, their packs raided, their weapons taken. There was no time to bury them, for Harry and his men had become the hunted. It was only their superb skills as experienced outback horsemen that kept them ahead of the following danger, as they tried to find a way back to their lines, a place of safety, a chance of life.

Harry's role had quickly changed after arriving in the land of these African famers of Dutch and German descent. His skills as a horseman demanded the role as he did now, riding deep into uncontrolled areas, observing and reporting. Harry was in command when they left, ten men, a two week reconnaissance of a relatively safe area, free of the main Boer forces. Their role, was considered to be minimal risk, entailed observing and reporting back on possible threats,

For the last three months this had been a simple task, riding with men who also knew the bush, on horses of quality, enjoying of simple hardships of the trail. It was surprisingly agreeable. It had all changed when they'd found a large encampment of Boers. They'd tried to furtively move away as a Kommando of riders chased after them. They were ambushed on the second day, then again on the third day by a party twice their number.

They had to return and deliver the sensitive information. With a under one hundred miles or so to go, they were moving as softly on the ground as their skills and experience would allow them but as quickly as possible without destroying their horses.

The men following knew how to live in this land, they too could ride as well as his men, and could outshoot them by some distance. After the first two skirmishes, the second killing Harry's junior officer by the name of Jones, they all knew that to live, they needed to ride as quickly and safely as possible.

'Captain, how long till we rest? The horses don't have much left,' asked his sergeant, his arm bandaged from a slight wound.

'Harry. Just call me Harry, okay, Ollie? Leave the formal shit till we get back.'

'No sweat, but what do ya think? I thinking we need to rest in the next hour.'

Harry knew he was right, but they had stolen a few hours lead with a shifty move this morning and he was loath to give it back. But he also had to balance the condition of the horses. Hopefully tomorrow they could make a hard run for it and finally escape to their lines. Harry looked up the longish valley, looking at another large rock outcrop in the distance.

'I be thinking there is a soak or spring down there. The trees just look a little greener, up near the base of the really big outcrop. We will stop there, set some pickets and rest for an hour.'

'Yeah, works for me, the stop will be good for Simmo, he's looking a bit peaky,' Ollie noted, referring to one of the horsemen who had a wound high on his chest that had amazingly missed all the vital organs.

'He has to make it. Can't stop to give him the rest he needs till we get there. He's a tough bugger,' replied Harry, still amazed that the toughness of the man from New South Wales. For anyone to ride through this type of rough country with a hole in his body was seriously tough

They rode on as before, finally finding a small waterhole at the foot of the kopje among a tall stand of acacias and remarkable similar eucalypts to those he knew from home. The small waterhole provided a thin trickle of water flowing down a shallow crevasse in the granite plates, feeding the vegetation further down the slope. The trees provided good cover from being observed from adjacent smaller outcrops, the closest about three hundred yards back from where they had come.

Harry set two pickets some twenty yards out on the edge of the tree line. A few random boulders about head height provided the cover they needed. As the pickets kept watch from where they had come, the rest of the men took their fill of water and food, refreshing the horses, filling the water bottles. They had eleven horses, a mix of those ridden, spares from the dead companions and two pack horses. Each horse thirstily sucked up its fill, happy to be able to give their best for the next hours if required.

The men stretched their legs, most lying down to enjoy a little shade. While it was not as hot as some parts they came from, the dryness still sapped their energy. Thankfully the water and shade revived them a little. Sergeant Oliver walked around the men, checking each, making sure they took in some food, now little more than dried meat jerky and hard biscuits.

Harry stood and with a nod to Sergeant Oliver, he walked out to bring back the pickets, preparing to swap them over so they too could get a little rest. He planned to take one's place, while Sergeant Oliver would come out when the men returned. Harry walked through the trees; it would have been a pleasant enough location if not for the pressing circumstances. He stopped beside one of the pickets, now sitting on the front of the boulders, his Lee-Metford rifle across his knees, comfortable that his uniform melded well into the background.

Harry was not particularly happy with the place he sat, it was a break from their training, but as they were about to leave, he held his tongue in his head, quietly beckoning the man down to stand beside him. The man climbed down and stood, facing the valley below, Harry stood beside him, slightly side on. Harry was about to open his mouth the provide the direction for this young man to return to the waterhole when the sound of a something solid hitting something soft and wet filled the air.

There was not another sound for a moment as the man was flung off his feet, grabbing the top of his chest, his rifle clattering to the rocks. Harry stood in shocked silence as the sound of a rifle discharge sounded across the valley. The second picket fell backwards off the boulder he was sitting on some fifteen yards away, landing with a lifeless thump in an untidy pile of limbs, blood seeping onto the rocks from the wound in his forehead. The sound of the distant rifle shot was instantly recognised coming from the very accurate Mausers of the local fighting men.

Harry bent slightly, squatting to grab the wounded picket by his leather braces, when a third shot smashed into his leg, low on his thigh, just above the knee. The bent leg slightly covering his chest. Harry fell forward, the impact of the heavy slug taking away his ability to stand. He landed over the man who he was preparing to pull to safety, scuffing his head slightly on the granite boulder. He sat up, took another hold of the man and started to drag him backward to be behind the boulders, using his good leg as propulsion. A fourth shot slapped into the chest of the man in his hands, who instantly dropping his head onto his chest. The man's body went limp.

Harry did not stop, finally getting close when strong hands dragged him the safety. Chips of granite flew where bullets hit the boulders they sheltered behind. The two other men quickly took position and replied with rifle fire, not quite knowing what they were aiming at, but the responding fire it quickly slowed the fire from the adjacent kopje.

Harrys eyes blurred as the first serious wave of pain flowed through his body as Sergeant Oliver tried to straighten his leg. The pain almost caused him to blackout; the bullet had obviously damaged the bone and tendons that ran up his leg from the back of the knee. With the leg straight, the trouser leg was split longways with a sharp knife, allowing the wound to be seen.

'Fuck, it stayed inside. Musta hit the bone,' growled Oliver. 'Shit, that gunna be bad, real bad, Captain.'

'I know it, Ollie. The bone's likely smashed to bits, the pain is telling me what the problem is,' replied Harry. Oliver tied a bandage around the wound, stopping the blood dribbling out as the flesh swelled around the hole.

'Rightio, boss, I'll get you to your horse. We'll make it, the boys can cover as I get you on her.'

'No Ollie, we all die that way. You blokes leave now without me.'

'Wadda ya mean, Captain? You're coming with us.' His words were shattered by another fuselage from across the small valley. 'We're not leaving you, we would all rather just fight it out.'

'No, Sergeant Oliver. I rarely give orders, as you know,' said Harry through gritted teeth. 'But this is an order, and you will follow it. The information of the large formation of the enemy we found must make our lines. Nothing else matters.'

Sergeant Oliver was about to argue, when Harry lifted his hand.

'Your orders are as follows,' said Harry, his voice now cold and totally commanding. 'Get me a couple of the rifles and enough ammunition to hold them off for an hour or so. You and those left that can ride will leave without delay. You have watered and rested horses. Dump what you don't need and ride fast and don't stop.'

Sergeant Oliver said nothing. The boy already knew that Harry could not ride; the pain would kill him as quick as anything else. Without a word he rushed back, bent down to avoid the sporadic but increasing rifle fire, and quickly returned with two loaded Lee-Metford's and a near full box of ammunition. More than enough for what Harry wanted.

Tears were in Oliver's eyes he gave a salute and called his men to stop firing and prepare to leave. Harry wiggled into the firing position and left fly with the first of his shots at the Kopje in the distance. Not a word was said, everyone knew they were deserting a respected man to whatever came from across the valley. Harry was using his life to give them a small chance.

Harry heard them ride out, leaving him with two dead and one living. But he knew they would all be dead by nightfall. These local Burghers had a reputation; very few men ever survived to tell the tale of being taken prisoner, especially if they were wounded.

Harry could see the men who had been pursuing them slowly moving by foot across the gap between the granite outcrops. They darted from tree to bush to tree on the semi open country. He fired random shots, making it appear that there were more than one in defensive position. Shooting and loading with good rhythm he slowed them, their movement became well timed and careful, they knew they had enough time and the shooting from the rocks was good.

Tears slowly filled Harry's eyes as the thoughts of Charly and his two children filled his mind. He was angry at what he had done, saddened by his decision. Not for himself, but because he knew that his death would cause great pain to the one person he so loved. The one person who he'd sworn he would never hurt. Now he was doing the worst, and all because he never considered the risk, the very likely outcome of what he'd agreed to do those months back.

The afternoon drew on. The first hour passed; the men had reached better than halfway, still careful, not providing much of a target. Not that Harry cared. He had lost the want to kill, the want to injure. He suddenly could not do to someone else what was about to be done to his beloved wife, his darling children.

Bullets still impacted on the granite boulder, but he was perfectly protected, tucked into a small gap between the rocks. After reloading again both rifles and brushing the many dozens of empty brass cases away from him, he looked up, wanting to get one last look at where the men were when the granite to the left of his face exploded into small shards. A bullet had hit solid rock that had been cracked from previous impacts, spraying sharp shards of granite into Harry's face, slashing, and imbedding in his skin.

For the first time, Harry screamed in agony. Blood filled his left eye. He emptied a magazine across the valley, not an any target, just to relieve the intense pain in his face. He reloaded again, quickly lifting his water bag to wash some of the blood away, but finding it empty. Time was getting short.

He fired for a little over a half hour more, then with the last round dispatched, he collapsed over the Lee-Metford, the pain shuddering through him in waves of unspeakable destruction. Harry almost blacked out, closing his injured eyes, he was ready to finish his days. He knew he had failed his beloved, but at least he had not failed his men. It was done; they had escaped.

He lay still, his breathing slow, exhausted, his mind lost. Harry sensed someone beside him. He rolled slightly, lifting his head, the low rays of the sun blinding him. As he raised his hand to block the blinding light, the stock of a rifle smashed into the side of his head. For Harry, all there was now was darkness, nothing but darkness.

Chapter 25

A well-polished coach slowly rolled down the lane behind two matching black horses. The rider well-appointed as he sat on the raised seat, the man inside wearing clothes in the costly style of the day. Cecil Richardson was not enjoying the recent days; the circumstances of his visits to a number of homes in the district was not a situation he'd expected he would need to undertake.

As the coach stopped at the front steps of the verandah, he lifted himself slowly off the seat. The door to the coach was opened and he was helped down, waving away the offered help to walk up the verandah steps. The last month had aged him. All the youthfulness he had been able to keep well past the sixtieth year was gone, he was simply an old man, and knowing what he was about to do just aged him further.

The front door to this stately house was opened by the house maid shortly after he knocked. She took him to the parlour, sitting him one of the soft upholstered chairs. He would normally lean back and enjoy the soft supporting comfort, but on this occasion, nothing was further from his mind as he waited for the lady of the house to attend.

Charly breezed into the room, grabbing his hand and giving his cheek gentle kiss, the soft caress of her lips hinting at the excitement in her heart.

'Hello, Cecil. It's a pleasure to have you attend our home. I hope you bring good news on Harry's return.'

The words stung the old man as nothing else could. It had been his badgering that had pushed Harry to make the decision to go to war; just another soul that would be on his conscious.

'Nay, Charlotte. I have news, but it is not of that kind,' he said, barely able to meet her eyes. 'The words I have are dire. I council that you get your maiden to be at your side.'

An evil coldness crept through the room, a thief of the happiness that had bubbled in Charly's heart when she had been told that Cecil Richardson had arrived.

'Garbage, Cecil. No words you have to say require that from me,' she snapped. But her heart raced, fearing what was to be said. 'Say the words and be gone.'

'Harry has been lost from the regiment.'

'What in God's name do you mean lost? Missing?... Captured or dead?... Or what?'

'Of that, we are not certain. He was wounded in action, saved a number of his men but has disappeared, we know not where he is.'

'Not captured?'

'Nay, of this we would have been told. He is missing, and I fear deceased. The action of his wounding was deep in the wilds, no body or grave has been found.'

The words chilled Charly. In the months since Harry's departure she had read up on the Africa that her man was to wage war, learning that the environment and the animals were as dangerous as the men he fought against. Tears were building but she refused to cry. She would not show her weakness to one of the men she blamed for this darkness.

In the moment of silence, Cecil pulled out of his coat pocket a long, thin box and folded paper in an envelope. He held it in his hand looking down.

'Charlotte, I know that his loss will bring much pain but I give you this which may provide a little relief,' he said as he handed over the box and envelope. 'Harry acted with valour rarely known among men, he saved five lives by his sacrifice. He allowed five men to live. His actions also contained a counterattack that would have cost hundreds of lives. He truly is a hero to the nation.'

Charly looked at the box and folded paper, hating it even before she had seen what was inside. Tears formed at the corners of her eyes, tears of deep loss and grief.

'Cecil, I would prefer my man back. That he is a hero does nothing to lessen that loss, I simply wish for him back to be a father to his children, a husband to me.'

Charly dropped her head, unable to stop the tears now. Her resolve was fracturing; she wanted to run but that was one impulse she could not surrender to, not right now.

'Charlotte, many good men have lost their lives, many good wives have needed to find strength from people around them. You are young and of fine features, you will easily find another man to provide the protection and support you and your children will require in this world.'

Charly was unsure if she had heard right. Her fracturing instantly repaired back to the solid, power of her old self. She lifted her head and looked at Cecil's face, a slightly bemused look on her face.

'Fuck off, Cecil,' Charly said in an icy tone.

Her next words were slow, a sign of the controlled woman of power and authority that she had become. 'I have lived and survived unspeakable matters as little more than a child without the assistance of a man. I will again. So be so kind and leave my house and never return. I say again, kindly fuck off and leave us alone.'

Charly rose and walked from the room, her spine stiff, her demeanour a mix of disgust and anger. Cecil was in shock, the words she had said he knew, said by working men at the wharves and rail, but not from a woman of such stature. But what pained him the most, was not what was said in a manner of contempt, the words used to abuse, but that they were spoken by a woman. Yes, a woman. To his face, and simply to humiliate him. Cecil rose and walked to the open front door, then across the verandah, stumbling slightly on the timber stairs. His days had been called out, as he sat in the coach, he felt had aged again but this time it felt mortal.

He looked at the woman now standing at the verandah steps, a child at her hip, another holding her hand. There was nothing in the woman's eyes that betrayed her feelings, but he felt the empty coldness directed at him nonetheless. As the coach moved away, he felt a slight pain in his chest. He hoped it would be swift but knew that was not a benefit he would enjoy, he had brought too much pain and suffering to the community around him. His time would come but not until he was punished a number of time more for his actions.

Charly walked back into the house and called the staff to meet in the kitchen. She presented the news of the likely loss of their master of the house but assured them that they would remain a close family unit, working to support each other. Crying, tears, and moans of pain and grief emanated from the staff. They loved Harry, he had been their finest master ever. The senior house maid walked over and took the children from Charly.

'Charlotte, we know you well enough, leave the children with us. Go ride, take his horse and ride. Celebrate him where both of you loved life, then return and grieve with us.'

Charly did as suggested. It was what she wanted most, to be in the open air, enjoying so much what he had loved, what they loved together. The horse was saddled for her and she rode out, carefully, but with things that needed exhaling from her soul. The anger needed to be removed, chained and left behind. She had done this once, she would do it again.

It was a little over a week later when the first of the visitors arrived: a lovely older lady and her granddaughter. They arrived in a nice coach pulled by good horses, bringing a very tasty sponge cake for afternoon tea. Charly had not really met either before, though had a slight memory of them at one of the regimental functions she had attended with Harry. They both expressed their sincere condolences and provided assurances of support should matters become more difficult. The few hours were sightly confusing and a little difficult, but Charly allowed a deal of generosity given that they had concern for her wellbeing, even if they'd visited unannounced.

This initial visit was followed by another a day or so later by another lady of reasonable status within the community, then at an increasing rate more visits from women of the upper echelons of society. Sometimes middle aged, often elderly, accompanied by daughters or granddaughters. Their kindness and concerns were exemplary, their interest in the future for Charly and her two children unquestionable. The darkness of the loss clouded the reasons. She simply enjoyed the company, taking away the stabbing pain she felt from the emptiness of her home, of her bed.

After many weeks and many visits, close to two months later, the same ladies and women returned, this time with sons, brothers, nephews or cousins. The reasons for the visitations quickly obvious thereafter. Due curtesy required that Charly meet them and entertain them as before, again they were expressing interest in her and her affairs. Hints at prospects and possibilities were annoying and condescending, provided by the attending gentlemen. Both subtly and a little more direct, bluntly delivered by the female attending when the male was too embarrassed to speak.

Charly stood on the edge of the verandah and watched another coach leave, a haughty grandmother sitting across from a very embarrassed young male filling the opposing seat. Their words were not only heard by the driver as they left but also clearly by Charly. 'Speak up boy, she will never notice you if you simply sit and say nothing.'

This was just another moment; another fishing trip, as she now called them, the men's faces, the names and their undoubted wonderful qualities simply a blur. She struggled to understand how the women failed to notice that they portrayed their men as weak, lacking the strength she'd so enjoyed from the one and only man she loved. Turning, she observed Jenkins, her house master. He stood between the house and stables, his arms crossed, a slightly annoyed look on his face. Charly started walking towards him as he turned and shook his head in her general direction, then looked back at the disappearing coach.

Jenkins had become a trusted confident, a clear and truthful speaker of his thoughts. Charly had developed a strong relationship as to his worth to her life. He was so like Goodwood, the same balanced and calm personality, willing to callout a foolish endeavour before it occurred. His words had become her strength.

'Will this ever end, Jenkins? I feel I am on show, to be poked and prodded and my pockets searched.'

'Nay, Mrs Hendricks, this be only the beginning.' He chuckled at the unashamed activities of the rich and titled. 'They all be positioning themselves, waiting for the starting gun to sound.'

'Positioning themselves for what? My Harry might be alive. I not a free woman yet.'

'Agreed, but they don't want to miss out, so they are all pushing to be at the front, the chance needs to be fought for.'

'And what, may I ask, brought that on?'

Jenkins laughed a little, thinking about the conversation he'd with a fellow man of his employment type, head of the servants in a large city house. A house from where the womenfolk had visited a number of times, piquing his interest and subsequent questions.

'Now do not take offence, Mrs Hendricks, but you are a great prize. If not the *greatest* prize in the colony.'

Now it was Charly's time to laugh, a sound rarely heard in the house of late. 'You speak a nonsense, Jenkins. I am a worn-out woman with small children, I am no prize.'

'Nay, it appears that a certain man has released information on your holdings and wealth.'

'Seriously? Now how would that happen?'

'I spoke to a colleague in the business, he had been made aware that when the old fool left here those months back,' noted Jenkins. Charly knew he meant Cecil Richardson. 'That fool went to speak to a friend, asking about your situation, on behest that you not be left without coin. The second man, a greater fool, burst out laughing at the comment and suggested without great thought that you could purchase all he had and much more besides, again foolishly stating your financial means in detail.'

'Ahh, that idiot. There's a reason I do not disclose such matters. I pay my taxes without concern, but it is not knowledge that allows my safety and privacy if widely known.'

'Ayee, you be right in your thinking, but your health is not the reason for all the interest. Most of the families and houses who have attended here of late once had wealth, but now they have property and costs they cannot fund. They see you little more than as a bag of coin to be swallowed and spent to support their heritage.'

Charly indicated that they should continue the conversation over another cup of tea and the last of the cake brought by that infernally painful woman earlier in the afternoon. The words being discussed brought to the fore thoughts she had mulled over for some weeks. The cook, Janice, now the much-loved wife and bed mate of Jenkins – a marriage being agreed after a long courtship – prepared the tea as the two sat at the kitchen table. The two children played on the flagstones under their feet.

The kitchen had become a place of comfort to Charly. While Jenkins was her confidant in business and the running of the property, the now Mrs Jenkins was her confidant in matters of the home, of children, and of being a woman.

'What do I do? I cannot undergo this for much longer, they are becoming more persistent.'

'They be doing that Charly,' noted Janice. 'Jenkins and I have discussed this. They will push till they break you, the prize is too great, to lose would be a humiliation.'

'So what do I do?'

Jenkins sat forward, knowing that the moment had arrived for the young woman to take a step that would take her away from her inner pain, the time was now.

'I think you already know, Charlotte,' he said, using her formal given name rarely. 'Your head wants to hear a message from your ears that your heart already holds as confirmed knowledge. Return to the things that give your soul joy.'

Charly sat still, the fine porcelain cup in her hand. What she really wanted to do was drink from an old enamelled tin cup, stained black on the inside with tannins from the sweet black tea, the smell of wood smoke through the water.

'You are right. I know what I want, there is only one place that can give the peace I need.'

Her mind raced through the ideas, the issues they provided, the consequences that might occur. It would change many things for people, but remove her from the pressure and anxiety she faced.

'But if I close the house, what of you two and the other staff?'

'Do not let us be the reason for your decisions. We have many opportunities, we are not your family, we are your employed servants,' replied Jenkins, looking at the question without understanding some of the issues.

'No, Jenkins, you are my family, the ones I love and call on for assistance. The property must keep working, my not being here does not stop that, the house must be able to be opened at short call.'

Janice also knew that Charly could not leave the house, the property, unattended. This was where her man might return; someone had to be here if that occurred and a bed and a table with food ready within short notice.

'If you so insist. We will run the land for you. Jenkins can manage it with Williams, your head stockman. Patricia and myself will ensure the house does not go to rack and ruin. I do not need my wage, as I will not be your cook, but please think of young Pat. She requires the coin you provide.'

'Oh, Janice, the coin is the least of my concern. I agree in principle to your thoughts. Let us make solid plans on the morrow after we have slept on them.'

Three weeks later, one of the offshoots of the planning arrived on the seats and the tray of the horse drawn wagon. Two slightly bedraggled Afghans, the ever-reliable Mohamod and Ishmael sat beside Simon Williams, the head stockman. On the back of the wagon, slightly unusual saddles and padded timber frames and small leather panniers, the basic everyday equipment for cameleers.

As the wagon slowed, the two Afghans jumped off and held Charly's clenched hands, providing it a kiss and salutation of warm welcome. Charly knew their love for her as a cherished sister remained strong. They had missed her for the previous years, Charly only having short visits to the Springs by train to enjoy the old camaraderie of people who have endured and survived hardship together. The two children became instant favourites to both men, Myles immediately hugging Ishmael's long beard and pulling on the ends of Mohamod's wonderful green turban.

Lilly looked at them from her mother's arms, a wide smile breaking out, then reaching out to be held. She liked them, and she had decided they were hers to order around.

'My goodness, by the word of the prophet, these two are their mother's children and show the wonderful calm of their father,' said Mohamod quietly to Charly as he observed Myles and Lilly. 'We are the protectors of your two children. Always, without question, as long as Allah wishes.'

Charly smiled, laughing inside at the slight grumble for Jenkins at Mohamod's words, a smile that resulted from knowing that this was part of what she needed, the simple and contented truthfulness of these people, the people of her life.

By the end of the day the equipment was stored in the large warehouse and four of the six camels that had arrived some days before were brought to stables. Her surprise was complete at the end of the day, when Mohamod handed her a well wrapped bundle, a little weighty but of a familiar shape. Unwrapping the canvas on the kitchen table, she withdrew her old rifle scabbard, the top capped tight by the leather straps, the leather scarred but sound.

Charly untied the straps, her heart a little excited. Lifting the top, she slid out her old companion, the slightly marked and scuffed Winchester that had been provided as a gift long ago by Angus MacDonald. She worked the lever, hearing the familiar metallic double-click as it worked the reloading mechanism. Knowing it was unloaded, she slipped it back in the case, and shut the top, smiling at the slightly concerned look on Jenkins's face.

'Thank you, Mohamod and Ishmael, you have thought of everything.' She glanced at Jenkins. 'Without this weapon, I would not be here. It has many stories to tell, and all of them are a little set in the madness of what I once did with these men.'

Charly went to bed excited, feeling lighter than she had for months, knowing the plan was under way. Now to test if it could be accomplished. Only the next few days would provide that answer, but she cared little as she drifted off to sleep, Lilly on the other side of the bed, Myles in the next bedroom.

By the end of the next day, the camels had been saddled, and three adults and two children toured the house, yard, and then they all wandered down towards the river, returning later in the afternoon. The children were tired, hungry and excited. Lilly rode with her mother, Myles on Mohamod's camel, sitting on a small seat behind the main saddle.

By the end of the week, the plan for the future had a solid foundation. The only concern was how the two children would manage the large animals, but as Charly thought, they had fit in quickly. The camels were also a concern; they had not been from her own stock, rather obtained from a by dealer in transport animals a short distance from the property. But after nearly one week it was clear that they were of good quality and mild temperament. They were ready for stage two of the plan.

Chapter 26

I shmael slowly walked along the well-worn path, with a large rock mass of sandstone becoming evident before him as he crested a small hill. In his hand was the lead from the camel's halter. Myles sat happily on the saddle; the small boy had adapted to this form of travel as if a lad from his own village. Behind him were the camels of Charly and Mohamod, each leading a camel loaded with their camp necessaries and other supplies. All moved at the even rhythm so common to cameleers, a good walking pace, the sway of the camels mesmerising.

'Do we camp soon or push on through the pass, Charly Khan?' asked Ishmael, using Charly's old name without thought.

'No, Ishmael. We camp at the stand of trees near the first rocks of the range, there is a fine camp where a small spring from the ridge provides sweet water.'

Ishmael nodded as he continued to lead the small caravan. It was fascinating to watch his boss as she moved closer to her old home, a place she had explained in great detail over the last week to the men and her children. The men were intrigued by all the twists in the story, while the children preferred to play in the sand and dirt of each camp.

He could see the stand of trees, estimating another two maybe three hours travel, arriving with sufficient time to allow for a considered and relaxed set up for tonight's camp. It had been this way for the two weeks travelling on the trails, roads and tracks towards the property at the end of this path. It was clear from the first day that Charly had requested the two men that she had total confidence in to provide the assistance and protection to her but most importantly her children.

Each night, Charly sat and told stories to her children of her life, then a few stories of original people of the land as she had been told by Mary some many years before. When she slowed and ran out of words, the two Afghans started, but their stories were of an ancient culture, where storytelling was a cherished artform. Charly knew quickly that she had much to learn as Myles and Lilly were mesmerised by the two cameleers.

The clear night skies allowed the stars to shine; Ishmael was the master with his knowledge of astronomy. Night after night, he told tales that allowed them to learn about groups and clusters and how he used the constellations to navigate. He had stories of how these celestial group interacted with each other, how they had arrived in these lofty places. Myles sat, his mind locked to the words, his eyes locked to the stars above, Charly knew that Ishmael had opened something in his thinking. It was a most special moment for her, but made the terrible loss of her man so much more painful.

As they had approached the rocky gateway to the gorge that led to her old land, the place that set her terrors and pain so long ago, Charly worked on her mind, keeping herself calm. She remembered the moment when she'd known that part of her healing involved finally facing the pain she carried from her youth. As they prepared to leave the wonderful home at Riverstone Vale, she had written to her brothers, alerting them of her arrival. Charly knew, that returning to the land would be a critical moment to her future happiness.

As they arrived at the camp, a calmness that had been growing through the day flowed through her, a strange feeling she remembered sometimes from being with Mary. The feeling was deeply spiritual, as if the land was speaking, saying all would be good. Under the shade of the eucalypts, with the sound of a billy starting to boil over the fire, and the smell of spicy meat being prepared by Mohamod as the base of a sumptuous curry, Charly finally relaxed. She knew in her heart that everyone that caused the pain, the horror and humiliation of her childhood was gone, dead, buried under the ground.

Tomorrow, she would reclaim the relationship with her brothers, something that had been stolen from her so long before. Tomorrow would be the start of something she needed. As she watched the happenings around her, Myles ran up to his mother, carrying some shiny rounded pebbles.

'Mummy, look at these, they very pretty.'

Charly smiled as old memories filtered back. As a child she had found pebbles like these occasionally in the old gravel beds, deposited well before the river had started to cut the valley in the range, or the old trees were seedings.

'If you look very hard, you will find shiny black and purple ones too. When you hold them up to the sun, you can see all the way through them.'

Myles rushed back and kept scratching in the gravels. After a few minutes he held up a small, rounded pebble, the sun reflecting a deep purple glow. He rushed over and gave it to his mother.

'For you, Mummy. You keep this and one day Daddy will come home, okay?'

He rushed off again. Charly knew he was missing his father. While he didn't remember much about him, he knew there was something missing, there was hole in his life. Charly looked at Lilly as she sat on a patch of dry leaves. Ishmael with a handful of red and black feathers in his hands was getting endless giggles from her daughter. No, she would not remember. For her, there was no hole, only a missed opportunity. Charly sighed.

The sight of her happy daughter allowed an old memory to crash itself into her mind, a memory of her younger sister, sitting by the billabong, laughing as Charly used feathers to imitate the raucous black cockatoos that visited, feasting in the grubs that lived in the black wattle trees. The thought took over everything else, filling her thoughts until it fermented into something greater, an understanding of the past, a feeling she could not release.

Charly had never been able to accept that she'd been left by her mother, been left to the repeating emotional pain and humiliation of her father and later the actions of that rock spider of a stepmother. Deep in her need to find her mother was the desire to express the pain she had suffered, and ask why she was left behind on that fateful day.

As she watched her daughter giggle at the performance of one of her protectors, Charly began to understand her mother's thoughts. Her reasons, and after a time, the decision. As the smell of the curry floated around the camp, setting everyone's tastebuds on edge in anticipation, it was then that Charly knew the pain her mother must have suffered in making that final choice. The choice was heartbreaking but actually quite simple; to save one, or lose both. To allow her youngest, Cassandra, the one that had not been exposed the evil of the twisted mind of her father, to survive, then the other must be sacrificed. Charly finally accepted what she knew in her mind was the truth: her mother did not leave her, her mother did what she did to try and save one of her daughters when she could not save both. The dice must have rolled to the youngest, it was that callous: one or none.

Charly approached the answer from other angles, looking for a reason her own thinking was wrong, then taking the final step: what would she do herself?

It was then she knew she had to forgive her mother, accept what occurred had not been because of a hate for her. She had to forgive in order to begin to love her mother again after all these years.

As Lilly finally tired of play, she crawled over and snuggled next to her mother, wanting the warmth of love, knowing where the true place of contentment was. It was then that Charly knew why Mary and the rest of the aunties refused to tell her where her mother was. Her heart was not ready, her anger had not left, the love had not returned. It was then she also knew that the aunties had never spoken to her mother in recent years. Rather, it was their feelings that dictated their actions, a relationship that they had once with her mother that was so close, they felt, rather they knew, her mind and thoughts. They were protecting mother and daughter.

Charly picked up her daughter and bounced her on her lap, getting more giggles and chuckles, the deepness of the voice a little too adult for a child less than two years of age. She then looked at Mohamod and Ishmael, knowing that both of them had come at her call without delay, knowing they needed to be at her side as she found her feet again. These people were her strength and something more than family. She thought a little longer about her future, knowing that there was one man she had not relied on for guidance and she would need to very soon, if matter turned in the way of darkness: Lachlan Goodwood.

She smiled grimly at the ring on her finger. Not only was she still missing her mother and sister, she also had lost her beloved husband. She wondered how long it might be before she one day found the strength to remove it. Perhaps on the day when she knew in her heart that he would not be returning. Charly snorted in disgust at where her thoughts were heading. Well the time was not yet, she refused to give up hope. That day was some time away in her mind.

The following day started early. Other than Myles and Lilly, who snuggled deeper into their blankets, the three adults rose and prepared for the final days travel of their journey. The breakfast was light and quickly completed, the camp packed and the camels moving well before they had on previous days. The two children were slightly annoyed at not being able to enjoy the camp a little more, this camp being a clear favourite over many of the others.

By mid-morning, the small caravan exited the gorge, slowly walking from between the sandstone walls out into the land that Charly knew so well. She stopped, looking down the length of the river, then around the grassy plains, dotted with cattle calmly grazing on lush feed. She slowly turned and looked where her home had once been. A new building stood, partially built, but clearly abandoned. Remnants of the burnt buildings had been cleared, as if her home and other buildings had never stood on that slight rise that she had run down to reach the river, her clothes aflame.

Charly moved the camel forward, following a clear track that ran to the north, and also between the abandoned building and the base of the sandstone range. She knew where the track led to, it had been explained by her brothers on the day of their reunion, the new home of the owners of the land. The track wound down through the eucalypts before opening out into a new clearing. It took nearly thirty minutes at a steady camel walking pace, but as much as Charly had a desire to break into a trot, she wanted to enjoy the place of her birth.

Before they reached the edge of the trees, they heard a call that was directed to anyone close by the house, a sharp 'Cooee,' followed by 'Come and get it.' Charly smiled, the strong voice of Ellie, calling the men or the children.

As they entered the clearing, Charly saw the house, slightly ramshackle, clearly built in steps and stages with some new and a good amount of salvaged materials from the fire. A house built from want to satisfy need rather than comfort.

A woman stood on the verandah, her hands to her eyes, looking at the approaching small caravan of camels. She walked inside and was soon followed back onto the verandah by another woman and a man leaning on a cane. Charly waved, but there was no response. She then realised, dressed as she was in her favourite sandy coloured kameez, shalwar and a green band of cloth wrapped around her head, they must look like a group of itinerant cameleers.

A number of children started to arrive from around the outside of the house, all ages and genders, standing with their parents. Suddenly one of the women let out a shriek and started running up the lane towards them, shouting Charly's name. Charly urged the camel forward gently with a flick of the lead in her hand, accelerating into a solid trot, with Lilly letting squeals of joy as they rocked and rolled down the lane.

Charly pulled up as she met the running woman. Ellie had a massive smile on her face, her eyes glinting in excitement.

'You've made it, Charly. It is so wonderful you are here. The boys will be beside themselves.'

'It took a while, but it is truly delightful to be back,' replied Charly as she handed down a bundle still making giggling noises. 'Say hello to my youngest, she's a bit of a crazy for fast camels.'

Once Lilly was handed down to a grateful auntie, Charly urged her camel to kneel, finally dismounting, and giving her sister-in-law a hug of joy. The sound of soft pads on the sandy track made them turn to look at the rest of the caravan as it pulled up beside them.

Ellie looked at the two men dressed as Charly was, dune coloured over shirts and voluminous trousers, tightly bound turbans, with trailing ends that were beautifully tessellated with beading.

'These are my two best cameleers, Mohamod and Ishmael, and my son, Myles.'

Both men gave short bows in greeting. Myles let out a brightly crafted, 'gidday miss,' much to the laughter of everyone.

'Let's go and meet the others down at the house,' suggested Charly impatiently. 'Say, Ellie, you ridden a camel before?'

'No.'

'It's really easy. After I get on, hand me little missy and climb up behind me, then hang on tight, and I mean really tight.'

Both women climbed on Charly's older bull camel. Ellie shrieked, partly in fear and partly in excitement as she was flung forward, back and forwards, hugging tightly to Charly's waist. Once up, they all moved slowly down to the house, with the man placing his arm around the other woman, the children stepping up on the verandah as the camels got closer.

'Hello, darling sister. Welcome to our home,' said the man leaning on the cane and Charly urged her camel to kneel, again eliciting more squeals from Ellie.

'Bryan, as I said to Ellie, it is just so wonderful to be back, and even better to return to my family.'

Rachael stepped down and also hugged Charly, followed by Bryan, who hadn't seen his sister since the wedding day at the Springs. The eldest boy was sent off by Ellie to get Jessie, who was checking some stock in the yards about two miles further on from the house. The rest of the camels were settled, and the riders dismounted to be introduced to Charly's family.

All the children were introduced. There were too many names for Charly to comprehend, she smiled. It was obvious what kept the four adults occupied in these parts after the lights went out, or maybe even well before.

'Rightio, we might not be a big house of grandeur, but we have a welcoming house to all visitors, especially a long-lost sister,' said Bryan. 'So with Rachael and Ellie, I be welcoming you all. I hope you be staying for a little while.'

As they had arrived when the midday meal was about to be served, a little extra was prepared to cover the newcomers. Mohamod and Ishmael quickly showed their skills at preparing food from what was quickly accessible from one of the panniers. Jessie arrived shortly after they had started, a new set of introductions, the family and a few additions filled the very large kitchen and dining area that was dominated by a long trestle table and simple benches on either side.

The table was filled, both with food and people sitting around its edges, a few of the older children sat on the flag-staffed floor. Sitting cross legged on the cool sandstone slabs, plates with a little stew and fresh damper, the common largest meal of the day, they chatted together, the subject being camels and cameleers.

The discussion was on everything and anything other than Harry and what might have happened to him, where he might be. Ellie and Rachael were determined to keep the atmosphere happy and light. When Jessie appeared to be building to ask a question about Harry, Rachael touched his arm and noticeably glared. Jessie and then Bryan apologised softly to their partners. Charly saw the moment from the corner of her eye, knowing she was in the right place. Her close relatives, the girls from up the track, would keep an eye out for her.

After the midday meal and a long afternoon spent on the verandah, sleeping arrangements were discussed and decided on. The stables suited the two cameleers from tribes of the lands of Afghanistan, who looked forward to the deep, fresh straw under their swags. Ellie and Rachael decided to evict the children from one of their bedrooms, giving it over to Charly and her children. Charly refused, saying they would be fine in the stables, but Jessie shook his head.

'The boys can sleep on the verandah in their swags, they do it all the time in the bush.'

Charly was horrified that she was causing such disruption, at that her family were kicked out of their beds because of her and her children. She was even more stunned that young children as these boys and girls were working cattle.

'But they aren't much more than ten, Jessie, they are riding with you.'

'Yep, no choices out here, sister. We don't have the money for help, and the local people will not come back, so if they can ride, they work the cattle with me.'

Charly suddenly knew why everything was so ramshackle, so second hand, but with good cattle prices, she failed to understand where the money was going.

'Have to buy the station back. Our stupid father left it to that religious mob your stepmother was part of.' He snorted in anger in response to her question. 'We've slowly been paying for it, a little every year.'

Charly lifted her hand to her mouth in shock, the ownership had never been discussed with her before. Harry either had not known or was too embarrassed to tell her. She suddenly felt sick, knowing that money she had at her disposal, doing nothing but keeping her accountant happy, while her brothers lived in near poverty.

'How much have you got to go?' she asked quietly.

'About a third, maybe a touch more,' replied Bryan, lifting his hat from his face and waking from a short sleep. 'And sorry, I drop off sometimes, the body still struggles, but in five or six years we might have enough to get it all back.'

Charly sat still, her mind in thought as the two brothers threw around some ideas on shortening the time frame, but five years was as close as they could get. Charly thought about those five years where they would be dirt poor and have nothing.

'But we eat good.' Jessie laughed. 'Best beef in the country and the kids grow great vegies, like you did, sis. Excellent food out here.'

'So what if I buy your third? Be shares three way,' asked Charly quietly.

'You planning to sell Harry's cattle station? Well if you are, we will not have it,' growled Jessie. 'That's pure dumb, and he ain't gone yet.'

A wave of anger built in Charly and she clenched her teeth at the mentioning of Harry and their property east of the Flinders Rangers.

'Hey, Jessie, settle brother. Charly looks ready to bite your head off, so just leave it.'

Charly quickly calmed as she heard the words. They were said in naivety. She let out a slow breath as Ellie came outside and sat down beside Jessie. As Charly was about to answer, Rachael sat on the other side of Jessie, both sisters leaning in on him.

'Righti,o mutton heads.' She looked at Jessie and Bryan to make sure everyone knew who was being addressed by the derogatory term for cattle men. 'First, it is my station as much as Harry's – it was my wedding gift to him. Second, there is one hell of a lot you do not know about me, so listen before ya speak. Third, don't treat me like your baby sister, them days died when the fire ripped this place many a year ago.'

Her words had hit their mark. Both of the men went silent, before Ellie asked what the question was that caused the sharp words. She shook her head in disbelief how in what had happened.

'Okay, my darling Bry, you be the man of the books,' Ellie asked, 'Tell Charly what's left.'

'A bit over eight and half hundred pounds and a bit of change to square it away.'

Charly nearly said, 'That's not all that much,' but bit her tongue in time. That would have been disrespectful. She knew she needed to wait, let them think it over. But for her, it was helping not just the two brothers, but also the two women and that bunch of children sitting at the edge of the verandah.

Before she had time to respond, the eldest, James if she remembered correctly, turned and looked at Charly.

'Auntie Charlotte, can we go see the camels? We not see them up close before, only when the mail man comes and he got real angry ones and we have to stay away.'

'Well, James… did I get that right?' she asked, receiving a nod confirming the name. 'Good, you are right, camels can be very dangerous. Sometimes they'll want to bite you and that can be very bad. If you want to go near the camels, you must ask myself or you can ask Mohamod or Ishmael, they are my very best cameleers.'

James nodded, he was now joined by two of the other boys, all listening carefully, excited but not wishing to upset their new auntie.

'Okay, all you kids, go see Ishmael in the stables.' She looked at her son. 'Myles, can you tell him I asked him to show you kids the camels.'

With a cacophony of shouts, squeals and yahoos, the six local children ran with Myles to the stables, excitement bubbling out of their skins.

'Will the children be safe? I'm not sure I like the look of your man, Ishmael.'

Charly laughed at Jessie's concerns, again understanding that their exposure to these people was distant and only when one arrived with supplies or mail.

'I agree, he is a tough man and has an interesting reputation. But like most of the men of his people, they just adore children. Your kids are safer with him than anyone you know, that I promise.'

Charly did not add that he also was her protector, and a fearsome killer of men who had threatened her. A wicked thought crossed her mind, but some things were best left unsaid, she thought. Well, for now anyway. Maybe she'd tell her brothers what he done at the dunes just before she was to leave.

The talk turned to other mundane matters as the children spent the next few hours before dinner was called in the barn and holding yard, the six locals being introduced to the large smelly animals that had served Charly so well.

The following day Charly and her brothers rode over to the abandoned building where their house once stood. What she really wanted to see were the graves, the final confirmation of her yearning to clear her heart of the pain she had endured. They stopped by the side of the building, constructed in sandstone external walls. One end wall remained open, the roof not built.

But it was the four head markers that immediately caught her attention. They sat in a row some twenty feet from the building. A small white picket fence surrounded them, missing a few pickets, the whitewash fading to a gentle grey.

The two furthest down the slope were crudely marked, the original boards replaced by simple crosses, a knife cut name and date of death but little more. The second two were of more opulent standards, time taken to carefully chisel the same details as the others, but now in thick cut boards with fancy trimmed edges and tops.

The first two were her father and stepmother, the second two were two names, one of which she recognised as the cause of much of her pain, the other unknown.

She stood before her father, tempted to spit on the head marker but held her mouth shut, then looked at the last known location of the hated rock spider. Her emotions were tightly held as she looked at both of them, a coldness in her heart, as if they were nothing to her. Charly knew that Wazir and Abdul buried her stepmother, not knowing who and how she had affected the person they had rescued that day.

'So how did the reverend and other bloke die? Accident in the building works or something?' she finally asked her brothers.

'Nope, really bizarre,' noted Bryan. 'The reverend had taken to baptising his new followers down at the billabong. He claimed that he wanted to desecrate the old local beliefs, so he decided that this was the way to do it. We warned them, but they being holy and all, just ignored what we said...'

'And they got bit.'

'Yep, got the other bloke first. He didn't make the water. The reverend lost it and grabbed the big king brown, claimed it was the devil and he had the Lord's power and he would destroy it.'

'And he got bit too.'

'Yep, you be right... You telling this story, Charly, or me?'

Charly and Jessie laughed. The situation described was likely to bring an obvious outcome.

'Go on, Bry, your story.'

'Rightio, okay, so them two became really sick. Now they were told how to treat them brownie bites, but no, they started to chant and call down power from above as the two blokes started to writher and shake in pain. Then after more calling and chanting, one then the other died within the hour.

'After the other members who were building the mission buried the two that had died, including their leader, they had a bit of the meeting and decided that God was against them and they just pulled out the very next day. Only problem for us was we did not know who the owner now was, or that part of the agreement was that we could live here and run cattle still stand.

'So we finally found out who the legal man was that was dealing with the estate and we all confirmed an agreement to buy back the station. We already had been saving a bit and were able to put down a good amount, but it's kept us poor.'

'And left you with a half built stone building.'

'Well, we don't own this part yet, the legal man is not sure he wants to sell this part or the parts with the billabongs. You see, he was one of the followers and he has some funny ideas of his own future grandeur.'

Charly thought for a bit, then made her decision. This was her moment, she had the one thing the boys just could not provide, the greatest power of all, great enough to cut through the holiest of men: money.

'Okay, you get me this guy's name, I will sort it out. No person is gunna take our waterholes away from us, not now, not ever.'

'Well, if you think you can, be our guest. He appears to take delight in making it difficult for us, stringing us out as much as he can,' answered Bryan, who had done most of the negotiations.

'Right, if I can, we own the station three ways in share. You two happy with that?'

Both brothers looked at each other, knowing that what Charly was proposing was likely not to happen, so why not try. Both nodded. Charly smiled, spat on her hand then offered it to shake both their hands.

'This is how I do business boys: a handshake first, paperwork later, we agreed?'

Both answered in the affirmative, then shook their sister's slightly sticky hand. They were back together, but not quite sure what that meant for them.

'I might be thirds, but you boys grow the cows and sell them. I don't want nothing, but my third goes back into the farm, like building a nice house for yourselves and the ladies.'

'Seriously? But you have to get something.'

'Oh, but I do. I get my family back, and that is priceless.'

The next few days were spent looking around the station, checking the cattle, the work the two men had done in the previous years. As she expected, the cattle were in great condition, and Charly found herself wishing she'd had access to these animals a few years ago, they being nearly desert bred and hardy to the lack of water.

Bryan rode with them. When Charly asked about his injuries, he noted that he was affected by the damage to the tendons that affected his walking, needing a cane. His bemoaned that his back provided a few niggles when digging or similar, but riding a horse, doing the odd bit of stockwork was not issue.

'I am still a cattleman, not quite like Jessie, but I can still ride.' He smiled. 'Mind you, we had a really good one, but it appears that you stole him for other purposes.'

The words were an opening that finally allowed the three of them to discuss the loss of Harry. A chance for three siblings to express their feelings and sadness. Charly was surprised how much it had affected her brothers.

'He became one of us that first drive. He worked so hard to prove himself, never complained, never asked for favours, just worked his butt off,' said Jessie with a tinge of sadness. 'I miss him. He was more than a mate.'

Tears filled the corners of Charly's eyes, and she stared ahead, unable to say anything for fear of bursting out in sobs.

'He ain't gone yet, little sister. Till we know, he is still part of us, we expect him to come back to us on day.'

The days on the Flats meandered past at a slow pace, allowing Charly to find peace in her soul as a world of activity flowed around her. Myles and Lilly were absorbed into the cluster of children, being dragged to all the places they played or did their chores. The two cameleers became engaged as very willing guardians of the troop, as Jessie called them after returning home to be overrun by small feet as he opened the rear door of the house. Very quickly the camels became transport for them, a small caravan of multiple riders, two men leading the camels in a long train.

As they disappeared up the track to investigate the rocky gorge one morning, Charly sat back on the verandah with Ellie and Rachael, enjoying a hot tea before starting their housework for the day.

'Now the men folk and kidlettes are gone, I got a question or two that needs answering to clear my head. Who the hell is with who?' Charly asked.

'Oh, we wondered how long before you asked that,' chuckled Ellie, as she looked at her sister, providing a lifted eyebrow and smile. 'It is a bit complex, but let's put it this way, we tend not to fight too much, and sharing is caring.'

'Rightio,' replied Charly still unsure. 'So no set arrangements?'

'Ellie is married the Bryan, as I am to Jessie,' replied Rachael with a slightly stern tone. 'We have our rules and they work for us, not that the people building the mission agreed to them, but they left us alone.'

'And the kids?' asked Charly.

'We know who belongs to who,' responded Ellie, knowing where Charly was headed. 'We thinks that Bryan can't have kids, so likely they're all Jessie's, but it don't matter much, they are all just our kids, and we all love them equally.'

Charly smiled at the two sisters, appreciating their openness. They seemed to know no offence was meant, and were happy to answer a fellow female's inquisitiveness. The conversations moved onto other matters, the two sisters having questions of their own.

'When you arrived, we thought you were another of them Afghan blokes the way you were dressed. And we've noticed that you rarely don't wear the big overshirt and baggy pants. So what gives? You a bit of a bloke at heart?'

Charly laughed, knowing that usual response to the same question.

'Because they are comfortable, dear sisters. Cool and keep nearly all the dust and dirt off me.' She then smiled, knowing that the next part would have an impact. 'And I don't need to wear anything else if I don't want or need to, if you get my thinking.'

The two sisters blinked in shock. 'Nothing else? Like nothing but what I can see?'

'Yep, and tell me, who would know but me?'

The two sisters nodded, as they thought of the ends of their long skirts and shifts trailing in the dirt, dust coating their legs and underwear. They considered the wisdom of baggy trouser legs closed tight at the ankles. Ideas converged as they looked at each other, and Charly suspected that a change to their clothing would happen very soon.

The discussion continued, finally falling to her future and that of Charly's two children. Ideas were discussed, Charly appreciating the input from her companions.

'I think I know. I just need a few more days to get it set in my mind,' she finally replied, then remembering the words by Jenkins, no, she already knew the answer, just was not ready to agree to what her mind was telling her. She twisted the ring on her finger without thought, then completed her thought. 'I will decide soon, I know the kids need a father, but I need a bit more time.'

The next day she rode one of the stock horses to the middle billabong, the place where she had spent so many pleasurable days in her youth, and the place that had saved her from the flames. It was her place of sanctuary, the place she had left till last to ensure she was ready to say goodbye to one person. Jessie had noted in conversation that they had found a dead Aboriginal woman lying in a rough bark shelter a number of months back.

They found it strange as it looked as if she had been killed by a bite from a king brownie, an almost unknown situation for the local people. Charly asked no more questions, knowing who and why, only asking what had happened to her.

After she stopped the horse and dismounted, Charly pulled the Winchester from the scabbard, feeding a live round into the breach after she dismounted, knowing the king browns were particularly aggressive at this time of year. Charly tucked the rifle under her armpit, then withdrew two small, hardened sticks from the pocket of her kameez, tapping them together as she slowly walked down from sandstone slab to sandstone slab. She knew a small part of the song in Mary's language, and struggled to say the words.

A feeling of loss overcame her. Mary had saved her in so many ways, given her a reason to live and enjoy life again. The feeling continued, then lifted, becoming one of lightness. Charly knew that land had called her back, to settle the account, to finish that debt. Charly bent down, placing the Winchester on the rock slab beside herself. She dug a small hollow in the dirt beside the rock, placing the sticks in the hollow before closing it over. Mary was at peace, the land was at peace, the people of the land could now return.

Suddenly, she sensed as much as heard a movement behind her, the sound was chilling. Charly slowly reached for her rifle, cocking it as it was picked up. As she turned, a large brown snake had moved onto the end of the slab of sandstone, semi coiled only four feet behind her. It lifted its head, flaring slightly. The sun glinted off its moist tongue. Charly knew it was preparing to strike, and this one was the big dominant creature of its species in the area, this one was a killer, one bite would be deadly, Charly knew she would not make the top of the riverbank.

Not moving too quickly to spook the snake, Charly balanced her feet, twisted and from her waist, lined up the long brown creature with the barrel of the Winchester. With no warning, it struck at Charly, the rifle jerking as the trigger was smoothly pulled. The creature impacted hard on to Charly's thigh, then bounced lifeless, its long thick body writhing in convulsions on the rock, its head missing.

Charly let out a slow breath, knowing that that was moment that could have provided terrible consequences to the lives of her children. It also solidified in her mind what she needed to do now, where she needed to go. The creatures of the billabong were no longer hers to play with, she was as all others, the spell of her youth had been broken.

She carefully walked up the grassy bank, stopping beside a small mound covered in rocks beside one of the large river gums, knowing who was here. She nodded her head, gave a word of thanks and walked to her horse, the land and herself had found an arrangement; she was content.

On the second last day before she decided to leave, Charly organised to take all the children down to the bottom billabong, the place where her mother had taken her children to play. Well away from the long grass and sandstone slabs, but on a sandy area between before the river flowed down the gorge. The idea was taken onboard by all, changed and revised, the final outcome was that everyone would attend. It became a family picnic, a celebration of renewal of the family's bonds, it almost appeared to be the start of a family tradition.

The camels were brought along, Jessie and Bryan forced by the children to ride. Their two camels were led by the two now much-loved Afghan cameleers. Everyone else either rode on the horses or on piled onto the wagon with the provisions for the day.

As evening started to close over the land, they all prepared to leave, memories made that would be repeated for many an evening. Charly stood and thanked her family, then thanked her cameleers for their patience. Turning to the four other adults she asked, then almost demanded that this gathering would now occur once per year. All agreed, with a few shouts and squeals by the children before she completed her words.

'I know where I am going, where my children will grow. There is a man I need to consult in dry and dusty place. My world wants me back, but I will return. We are again a family.'

Chapter 27

The man slowly shuffled himself across the seat of the gig. His movements were awkward, affected by the injury to his leg and the lack of vision on the left side of his body. He tied the reins on the top of the handbrake, knowing that he no longer had the ability to chase a horse and gig that might wander off.

Before dismounting the man looked at he house in front of him had a quiet stillness he did not expect, as if it had been deserted, closed up, left unused, unloved. He remembered many such from his years in South Africa, fine farmhouses, left empty, deserted by fleeing owners, desperate to survive the passing wind and fire storm of war.

The man lowered himself to the ground, pulling a crutch from beneath the seat and tucking it under the armpit on the side missing the lower part of his leg. Slowly he lurched across the weedy gravel to the foot of the verandah. Brown fallen leaves lay on the steps and timber floorboards from the deciduous trees. He climbed the four steps slowly, crossing to the front door and knocking loudly, one, twice, three times.

The man looked at a bundle of papers and envelopes, tied in rough string, sitting against the glass of the colourful leadlight panel beside the door. While waiting for a response to the knocks, the man bent and picked up the bundle. Envelopes, and a telegram, the dates a few months old. The man knew the contents of the telegram on the top of the tied bundle very well. He should, he thought, as he had sent it.

'Wadda ya want mate?' came a call from a young man stand at the corner of the house.

'The lady of the house, Mrs Hendricks, is she around?'

'Nah, mate, she left about ten months or so back, then Jenkins went to Adelaide a month ago. Mrs Jenkins being poorly, left me in charge till he returned,' was the laboured reply.

'Rightio, so would you be knowing where Mrs Hendricks would be living at the moment?'

'Nah, mate, not my business to know. Jenkins might but he not being here, can't ask him.'

As the man stood up straight, leaning on his crutch, his hopes deflating, his energy seeping through the open boards on the verandah floor. He placed the bundle back on the floor, not interested in what was in the letters.

'The missus, she took the kids and left with a couple of them Arab blokes, had camels too,' came a little more information from the corner of the house.

The man finally smiled. He knew exactly where his wife was, where his children were. Of course, they would naturally go there, they would return to where they had support and protection, her world, not what he thought had been his at this wonderful place, Riverstone Vale.

Harry thanked the young man, hoping by the time he returned, the house would still be standing, but that was not an issue for now. He hobbled to the gig and climbed back on the seat. He had a little more travelling to do, just when he thought it had finally ended. Not that it was an issue. Just being in his home country was satisfying, smelling the things he so missed for months calming his soul. He flicked the reins, accelerating up the laneway from the house, the hooves cutting deeply into the gravel. He had some hours to travel before he found a bed in a rest house, and then tomorrow he would return the gig and horse he had borrowed and find the train north.

He could have argued for a place to sleep at his house tonight, but an empty house, without his family, and his beloved wife was not what he needed. He drove the gig on faster, he had places to go, he was a man on a mission again.

Harry stepped onto the platform from the worn passenger carriage. The amount of dust inside had not changed in the years he had known previously. The locomotive was new, but the rest was close to its end. The Springs was not much different from what he could see, just a place to stop and then move on to your next destination. It was still a town for doing business, the only other reason to live here, not a place to live for the enjoyment.

His bag was dropped beside him by a young porter, standing waiting for a few coins for the effort.

'Say, son, could you get this bag up to the Imperial? I'll pay.'

'Nuah, the imperial don't do casual stays now. If they got a booking they send a bloke for ya bags.'

So something had changed since he was last here. Harry pulled out a pound from his pocket, an exorbitant amount of money for the task. He waved it in front of the face of the boy.

'It's yours. Get my bag to the Imperial, and find someone to take me to Khan compound.'

'Don't call it that no more,' the young porter proudly said, confirming that the crippled man was not from here, then snatching the pound note from Harry's hand. 'Okay, I'll take ya money, mate. Ya can pick ya bag up from the Imperial when ya find some lodging.' He started to walk away.

Harry called after him. 'Oi, what about the transport to the compound – I paid you.'

'Nope, cobber, ya walking. Don't have a wagon for ya.'

The young man sped up his pace, knowing that there would be no repercussions. He doubted that the cripple knew anyone here that would worry him.

Harry watched the porter disappear with annoyance. Something had changed, the lad's attitude would never have been accepted before they had left. Hoping that his bag was safe and would be delivered, he straightened his eye patch and brushed his well-shaped beard. Harry pulled his hat down to shade his eyes and slowly limped towards the end of the platform, leaning on the crutch. It would be a long walk in the sun.

The train pulled away, moving in the opposite direction, slowly accelerating further along the line from where he had come. Something else had changed: the Springs was no longer the end of the line, the reason for its existence was less, the chances for its demise increased.

Harry limped through the gate at the enlarged compound. The storage buildings were larger and there were a few more of them. The small old timber-clad office had been replaced by a substantial masonry structure, but the lack of camels and other transport equipment surprised him. He limped across the yard, his armpit a little raw from the extended walk from the train platform. Suddenly a horde of children rushed from the back of a smaller building, nearly bowling him over. One of the boys stopped.

'Sorry, mista, hope you okay.'

Harry looked at him, the facial features familiar. 'Your name Myles?'

'How didya know that, mista?' the boy replied, but he didn't wait for Harry's reply, running off and chasing the others. Harry watched him disappear, knowing he had a little ground to make up.

He limped to the steps of the masonry building, reaching the front door. He opened it and looked inside. There was no-one, he checked the door with his good eye, it said 'office' and 'enter' in a finely painted letters on the glass of the door.

Harry limped inside and looked around. There was a small counter with a bell. He hobbled over and rang it a couple of times. An elderly face popped out of an adjacent doorway, any eyebrow lifted, not much interest in his face.

'Yerss, can I be helping?' said the face, the tone clearly not thinking that helping was an option.

'Yes, I would like to know if Mrs Hendricks, or maybe it is Khan, is available to see.'

'Nope, she be in a meeting, not available,' replied the man, now standing in the doorway, his arms crossed dismissively. 'What would be your business?'

'Oh, that would be a personal matter, something I would prefer to discuss with her.'

'Look, mate, we got no work for likes of yourself. I'm sorry for what might have happened to you, but we can't help.'

Harry dismissed the words; his missing leg, the eye patch, scars on his face and crutch often provoked this response from people. He took a deep breath to calm his nerves and lower his annoyance.

'Not looking for work, my friend. Look, can I wait somewhere, I know that Mrs Hendricks would be very upset if I left without saying hello.'

The older man looked at him, past the injuries, the missing lower leg, the eye patch and saw the cut of the cloth, the likely price of the hat on his head, a well-trimmed beard. Being a cautious man, and not wishing to taste the fabled cutting tongue of his employer, he decided there was no problem with the man sitting in the waiting room for a while till he got sick of it and left of his own accord.

Harry was shown to a soft chair and provided with an old newspaper; one he had likely read a few days before. The older man assured him that he would call him when Mrs Hendricks, or be it Khan, was available.

Harry sat for an hour, having scanned the paper a couple of times when he heard a very familiar voice thundering through the building.

'Bloody hell, Herbert, get in here! These numbers don't add up, you been cutting me out again.'

Harry watched through the open door as the older man rushed from his small office and entered another door some way down from the entry foyer. Harry lifted himself up and slowly moved across the room towards that door, hearing the last part of Herbert's comments.

'He be well-dressed but just another grifter.'

'Alright, I got no time now, can you–' said Charly.

Harry cut off her words form the doorway. 'You're not going to tell me to piss off for a third time.'

Charly looked up, seeing the face familiar but changed. The full beard, the crutch and missing leg causing her mind to jump around. But the voice could only be from one person: her man, her Harry.

'Harry!... Harry!' was all she screamed, jumping from her chair, sending papers flying. Herbert was knocked sideways, catching the sideboard but knocking a bottle of amber fluid onto the floor with a crash. The liquid slowly spreading over the boards, dribbling down the cracks.

None of this mattered to Charly as she threw herself at the man in the doorway, crashing into him without care for his stability or her dignity. They fell backwards, landing with a crash on the floor of the foyer. Occupants came running to various doorways to see what had happened, arriving in time to see their employer straddled over a man's waist, bending down and kissing him with total abandon.

Sobs of joy and gurgle of passion filled the room until the man lifted the woman's face by pressing his open hands upwards on her breasts, feeling the sudden points of hardness in the palms of his hands.

'Hello, darling, missed me?'

Charly placed her hands on his; two people in a world of her own, disinterested in anyone else but the man she was straddling.

'Too bloody right, Harry, and I can feel you might have missed me, hey?'

The words caused a few blushed faces as her employees withdrew, a little confused until another man opened the door to his office.

'Well, bugger me, it's you, Harry! What a bloody beauty, boy aren't you a sight for sore eyes,' said Lachlan Goodwood. Goodwood looked at Charly's beaming face, tears dripping onto Harry's slightly torn open shirt and continued in a sotto tone. 'Charly, ya can't be doing that here, woman, folks will get the wrong ideas what the office is being used for.'

The next suggestion from Goodwood was considered about as best as could be thought-out for the afternoon. 'You two can bugger off, leave the kids with us. Just come back and get them before dark,' he said. No other words needed. Charly was incapable of working now anyway, all she wanted was her husband, her prayers answered, her fears destroyed.

Harry lay back in the bed, memories from the first night they'd been together running through his mind. At that time, he'd thought it could never get better, now he knew that it very much could. Charly lay snuggled beside him, crying again, Harry knowing that her tears were for years of pent-up emotion and if he asked if she was alright one more time, she would likely belt him. They lay together for nearly an hour, not speaking, just listening to each other breathing, enjoying the knowledge they were together again.

'Darling, how was it that no-one knew where you were?'

Harry had started to explain the circumstances earlier, but both had other more pressing needs that expressed the deep feelings and desires they had for each other. It was their time and only their time, and there had been only one way to express it.

'As I did try before, but you know,' Harry started to explain to the sound of Charly chuckles. 'I'll leave the detailed stuff till later but was due to the way I was taken prisoner, the injury and person treating it. I didn't really even get into a real camp, even in the last week before I was released.'

'So no-one knew where you were the whole time?'

'Yeah, well I did. And the people where I was staying did, but they were disinclined to tell anyone.'

'You've lost me again, Harry. Who are these people?'

Harry signed, knowing that there was no way to do this in a very shortened version, the various steps to his capture, recuperation and finally his release. Harry sat up, knowing there was no option. The story needed to be told to Charly first anyway. She deserved the full explanation as to his disappearance and lack of information as to his survival.

'I was captured by one of the Boer Kommandos, which were organised groups from towns and villages. Well-trained and armed, they work within basic military rules. We stumbled on a big lot of them and then we took off to let our troops know. They sent one of their teams to chase us, well basically hunt us down and kill us before we told our people

'About a day from home, we were ambushed a third time. I got injured and the only way I could get the information back was to delay them as the rest of my blokes headed for our lines. I couldn't ride anyway, my leg was stuffed, and then I got hit in the face, which took my eye.'

'I sort of know that bit already, it's the other stuff,' said Charly impatiently.

'Yeah, yeah, anyway, I held them off for a bit over an hour, and finally ran out of ammo. When they found me one of the buggers smacked me with his rifle, breaking my jaw. I don't know much from then. I woke up to a big argument, but I could not understand their lingo. I was lying next to the other guys that were killed, thinking they would shoot me and piss off after the others. I blacked out again as one of the blokes started getting bits of the rock from my face and eye and when I came to, there was only three of them; a couple of men and a woman, the rest were gone.

'My face felt a lot better; it had been cleaned and my jaw set and bandaged, but he could not get all the bits stuck in my eye. The younger bloke man spoke a bit of English, telling me that they wanted an officer to interrogate, and I would be taken back to their camp. He then told me that the other bloke was a doctor who patched my face. The doctor and the younger woman cleaned my leg, put a splint on it and both of them put me on a horse. Now things go a bit funny from here. The three of them had a short discussion, the young bloke gives her my reins and then rides off, likely following the others. The older bloke and the woman are nonplussed and ride the other way. I realise fairly quickly they weren't headed back the way we came. We skirted small towns and villages, staying of any roads and stuff, all a bit funny but I did not care.

'It took about three, maybe four, days – I was a bit hazy from the pain – and we arrived outside this middling village. We waited until night fell before we went into the village and old bloke and the woman helped me into this really nice house on the edge of the village. Turns out that the young woman was his daughter and had been living with him after her husband was killed in a skirmish with our blokes.'

Harry stopped speaking for a short time, the pain he suffered coming back. 'My leg was a mess and the pain in my eye was crook to say the least. They tried really hard to help, but nothing would work to knock the agony. I'm not sure I could have ridden much further anyways.'

Charly was now sitting up, turned slightly leaning on the head of the bed, two fat pillows supporting her. 'Come on, and?'

'Yeah, rightio, so it turns out that the bloke is a bloody good doctor and knew how to treat gunshots and such. Ya see, most blokes with my type of injury had a good chance of dying. The bullet stuck in the bone, the bone smashed, ripped the crap out of my knee, being poisoned from the inside. The old bloke knocked me out and got the bullet out, and the bit of rock, but my eye was stuffed. He told me next day he was worried as infection had started and there were bits of bone everywhere. He was right. About four days later he had to remove my leg, the damn thing would not heal, and the infection had spread into my knee.'

'So why did he and the woman do this for you?'

'Well, her old man said because she was the one that shot me. She was one of the best marksmen, errr girls, they had, but stuffed up, her shot being a bit low. When she saw me and how I had fought for nearly two hours, well her words to her father were, "He has the heart of a lion, he deserves to live". So live I did.'

'Right. A nice, shortened version, darling, but why not send you back to the camp when you were better?'

'Well again, a bit odd, but they did not want to. They were happy to keep let me stay. My leg took ages and the eye longer, so I was stuck anyways. The old bloke said that he didn't want to risk my wounds. Fair enough, but once I was able to be sent to a camp the old guy just said that he did not trust his own blokes anymore and staying in his house might be a great idea. His daughter agreed, so there I stayed.'

'How old was his daughter?'

'Wondered when you might ask that. Well, her name is Gretchen and she is about your age, maybe a touch older.'

A silence followed that bit of information, Charly considering the likely scenarios that might've happened between a wounded soldier and the kindly woman tending him. She gave a small huff, finally deciding Harry and this woman deserved a bit of latitude.

'I hope she had a pair of nice big tits. You were deserving of that much,' responded Charly calmly.

Harry remembered the blond hair, the soft rounded parts of a very athletic body sitting on him, no clothes, no sounds that would wake her father. He cut his thoughts off quickly.

'And now you can forget her, she is over there and you, my man, are here,' Charly said.

Harry lifted his hand and encased the small firm breast on Charly's chest, looking at her eyes. 'I am with who I want to be with. The war was total madness, nothing was real. You are, I am all yours for as long as you want me… And these will do me just fine.'

Charly snorted, not happy with what was a slight admission by her man, but understanding enough. For her own part, she had made her decision to remove the ring from her finger, wanting someone to ease the pain in her bed. But the man she'd tried to bed had told her to wait; it was something she had to be sure of before he would agree. She was now glad of his direction; Lachlan Goodwood was no fool.

'Anyway, when our troops got close, the old doctor, that would be Alois Hochman, rode out and told them they had one very bunged up Australian in his surgery. Well, the silly idiots arrested him. It took two days before he could convince someone where I was. Gretchen was seriously stressed.'

'I'd prefer if you just called her "the woman",' grumbled Charly, a shade of jealousy creeping in the tone of her voice.

'Darling, she saved my life. Had I gone to a camp, I would have most certainly died. They didn't care for badly wounded prisoners real well. You and I owe her my life.'

'Oh,' Charly said, suddenly knowing she had overstepped. She supposed having Harry back came with accepting certain issues. 'Sorry, I should not judge. I am very glad to have you back.'

'Well, the next problem was what to do with me cause our regiment had been put under different controls. So they registered me and simply just sent me home. I'm guessing they forgot to tell anyone I was alive, and they had a bit on their plate, so home I came on a nice steamer, arrived at the Port not long back, and here I am.'

Charly reclined, thinking how different things would be if any of those things changed just a little, knowing that Harry would have been gone from her forever. She rolled over and provided Harry the view of two very firm, slightly scarred buttocks, as she checked the pocketwatch on her bedside table. She clicked the top shut, then rolled back, her breasts wonderfully exposed, her head slightly lowered, the eyebrows suggestively lifted, a small smirking smile on her face. The message was very clear: there would be a short delay before they walked back to get their children.

As they rode the small gig back to the compound, with just enough time to fulfil Goodwood's request to pick up the children, they chatted about what had happened in their lives in the last year of more.

'This town has changed, feels a bit different,' noted Harry.

'It has. The rail line was extended, opened about three months back, so passengers and goods travel to the next town. The work from here is falling, we still have enough contracts, but the bigger ones have changed.'

'I noticed the lack of wagons in the compound and there did not appear to be as many camels and drivers.'

'You're right. We moved a lot to the next town up the line, we have another operation from there, more costs, but that's what we needed to do to keep the work.' Charly paused, thinking about the main issues she faced. 'But that hasn't been the biggest challenge.'

'Oh, I would have thought that would be enough.'

'Nope, the reason there are almost no camels here is that the Defiance Mine has closed.'

Harry was in shock. It had been their biggest money earner, constant weekly supply transport, long distances and high returns.

Before he could reply, asking the problem, Charly explained. 'Water, would you believe it was water that stopped it?'

He almost laughed at the irony.

She continued. 'They had a small amount of ground water for a while, the pumps worked, then one day it was as if a plug was pulled, flooded the bottom two levels.'

'So what will happen?' Harry asked.

'Not sure. Depends on costs to reopen, pump out the water and put in new bigger pumps. Derek is working that out at the moment. Still plenty of gold, but the costs right now exceed its recovery.'

'And if not, if it does not open?' Harry questioned.

'Harry, my dear man, I have you back, let's enjoy being back together, without adding to our pain.' Charly then laughed. 'I do think we may now realise that everything can end at any time. It might just be time to become full-time cattle famers on a little place I know called Riverstone Vale.'

Harry looked across at her in surprise, knowing the ironic smile on her face, suddenly understanding that she had spent an hour or so planning their future as they lay together on the bed. He looked forward; the compound was not far away.

'Oh, there is something I found out on the steamer back that might interest you,' Harry said quietly. 'Something that will surprise you very much.'

'On the steamer? I doubt it, I don't do water much, I don't like boats.'
'I think you will.'

'Well, tell me or you will be walking back… without your crutch.'

'Ooooe, touchy.' He sniggered in glee, knowing he had found the famous small kink in her armour. 'It was a bloke I was speaking to, injured, a prisoner like me, fairly young. Ranked a little above his years that told me he had good connections, came from a snotty family in Sydney.'

'Okay, okay, get to the point,' growled Charly as they were about to enter the compound, the children running towards them.

'I think I found your mother.'

Before Charly could respond, they were surrounded by yelling children. One was Myles. He stood and looked at his father, unsure what to do. Charly was totally flustered, torn between finding out more and the confused look on her son's face.

'Up ya get, Myles, my boy, look what I found. This is your long-lost dad,' said Charly, prioritising what was needed now and what could wait a little longer.

Myles climbed up and sat next to Harry. 'Are you my dad? You look very different.'

Charly suddenly burst into tears, the emotions of the afternoon too much. She had tried to ignore the wounds; ignore the pain her beloved must have suffered.

'Mummy, don't cry. I do think it is Daddy, he has come back,' he said as he pulled a purple pebble from his pocket, handing it to his father. 'I told Mum that if we kept this one, we would find you one day.'

Harry pulled his son close, tears in his eyes, the occasional sob of joy. Charly looked at the small purple pebble as Lachlan Goodwood brought their daughter out of the office and handed her up to Charly.

'For goodness' sake, don't come to work tomorrow, don't come for the rest of the week,' Lachlan said as he smiled that almost boyish smirk, the "I know and don't care if I say it" look. 'Actually, maybe just piss off. Don't come back, Charlotte Hendricks, it's time you lot were a family again.'

The words caused both Harry and Charly to laugh, tears in their eyes, knowing the truth of the words. It really was time to hand it all over.

As the children were fed and put to bed, Harry realised why there were almost no people staying in the Imperial hotel; Charly had taken over most of the rooms on the upper floor as her house for herself, the children and a couple of staff.

Earlier in the evening, Harry had sat with his two children and explained with remarkable ease the things that had happened to him in that other land below the equator, leaving out one German descendent of fine figure, but including lots of other stuff that was ugly and horrific.

He wanted to leave the horrors out of the story, but Charly said that the children need to know why his leg and eye were missing, so keeping it simple, he told them of his injuries. Myles was intrigued, but Lilly was simply fascinated, standing and walking over to her father sitting on the floor. She reached out and lifted the eye patch. A raw closed eyelid, scarred and torn still existed covering the hole.

'Ooooh, look, Myles, it is missing. Wow that must have hurt, Daddy,' she said calmly. 'I got some dirt in my eye a few weeks ago, and it hurt terrible, so I know exactly how you must have felt.'

By nine o'clock, it was time. The two were nearly asleep as he took them to their beds, encouraged to tuck them in by Charly. It was special moment. He had never done this before, but he knew this would be his role from now on, the connection he wanted.

As he climbed into the bed next to Charly, she sat up, fluffed her pillows, and crossed her arms in mock annoyance.

'Right, mate, you got thirty minutes. I know you delayed earlier, fluffing about, so spill the beans, tell me more. You think you have found my mother.'

'And sister. Well, it is your sister I can be certain of.'

'Yeah, yeah, on with it.'

'As I said, I met this bloke on the steamer, he was a few years younger than me but had made captain. So we got talking. It's a long trip, so we covered some areas, war, then home, then wives.'

Harry could feel the pressure building beside him, deciding if to spill it right out or risk a little delaying tactics. He decided that he was excellent at delaying tactics.

'So we started on where we had grown up, him on a fine property outside of Melbourne. Turned out his father had some title, so he got a fast rise to officership.' A smile built as he saw the annoyance creeping over Charly's face. 'Anyway, I described where I grew up and where we moved to at the Flats, and that bit in a fair bit of detail. When the bugger stands up – lucky cove had two legs, but anyway – he tells me his missus, well, she came from a place just like I described.'

'Yeah, but there are a hundred places just like that around the country,' noted Charly, almost dismissing the comment.

'Maybe, but he then said really quietly that she had told him one day that she had run away with her mother after her father had done bad things. A group of black women took them across the desert, and she had left her favourite sister behind.'

Charly was stunned, unable to think. One item was possible coincidence but five, six facts that lined up, all made it highly possible. Well, it was so possible that it could not be discounted.

'And her name is Cassandra.'

And that pinned it. The name matched too, it was just impossible for it to be anyone else.

'So, where is she?'

'Not sure, he never told me where he lived, but I do know where her mother is, sort of. Places don't change that much, married to an interesting bloke not far from here. Matter of fact, your mate Macca knows him real well.'

When he told her, Charly went pale. The consequences now added more problems, the issues maybe a bit too great to get past.

'Oh. Well, maybe now I know, I can be happy. I know that... well it would be, look we...'

'Shit, Charlotte Hendricks-Khan, you of all people, someone who never gave a rats about title and power, don't back away now. That would be unacceptable, to me but mostly to yourself,' growled Harry in almost disgust.

He rolled away from Charly to face the side of the bed, then pulled the blankets over himself, smiling ironically. Only his first night home and they'd already had a tiff. A hand suddenly run down his arm, then pulled him close. A face pressed against his hair, and her breath was warm on his neck.

'Sorry, darling, it is a bit of a shock. Who would have known?' Her hand then slid down his side, onto his thigh, reaching for something he knew would lead to other things. 'Once more, big man, then we can sleep.'

Charly bit his earlobe, then chuckled, a feisty tone to her voice. 'I bet your Gretchen didn't have my stamina.'

Chapter 28

C harly slowly walked up the short pathway towards the wonderfully
cut stone steps, she was clothed as she rarely did for anyone, in
a dress that belonged at a ball or opening night of the opera. It was
extravagant, but this was a special day for her. She wanted to impress,
not to be immediately rejected by some interfering servant. Harry
walked carefully behind, stairs always requiring special concentration
with his crutch and one eye. Clothing for him was a good quality suit;
he'd found one hanging in the wardrobe at the farmhouse which still
fit perfectly. Harry looked at the brass nameplate on the front of the
building, a little unsure if this was the way for them to gain access.
Charly looked at him as she saw the big hanging handle in the slight
recess that would ring a bell inside the solid double front doors.

The house was a statement of power, of authority over the
community, close to the centre of the capital, its lands running down
to the banks of the Torrens River. A house to intimidate, its sandstone
slabs standing two stories tall to limit its access to the common folk. Its
power had the intended effect on most, but was lost on one Charlotte
Hendricks-Khan.

A smile crossed her face, a face that had swiftly washed away the
tight muscles and puckered frowns that had crisscrossed her face as
she arrived in the coach. It was amazing what a few small decisions

had done for her demeanour. As she reached for the handle, a mischievous look crossed her face. She was tempted to cause a slight riot by ringing it endlessly till someone opened the door. Harry knew what was bouncing around that almost childish mind. he shook his head, wobbling slightly as he leaned on the crutch under his armpit.

Charly gave a slight shrug of her shoulders and pulled the handle once, holding it for a moment before letting it jump back to its position. A loud double clang reverberated through the door, as much physical as audible. Charly lifted her finger, indicating one more. Another shake of the head from Harry knowing that his wife was loving the moment, still herself under all that fluff and cloth.

As Harry waited, he thought back to the last month or so after his arrival in the Springs. The rapid changes driven by knowledge it was time to simplify, not just because of his injuries, but they had a family to raise. Charly sold her stake in the Defiance Mine for a pittance of what it was worth six months previously. It had closed, now unlikely to ever open again in the near future. She kept the stake in the transport business but handed all operations to Lachlan Goodwood, simply now being a shareholder.

A number of her holdings in the Springs went the same way as the mine, sold but missing their previous worth. Charly knew that operating and maintenance costs would very quickly eat up value. It was time to cash in her chips, only keeping the Imperial Hotel. By the time all had been sold or put on the market, they packed and shipped everything back to their home on the cattle station by the Flinders Ranges, Charly had become a cattle farmer at Riverstone Vale in earnest.

Once settled, it was time to follow the leads to find her mother and sister, which was what had led to them standing on the stone portico outside an influential house of a very powerful man in the freshly proclaimed State of South Australia. Harry's thoughts returned to the present as the door creaked as it was opened. A small, balding face popped around the edge, looking at both of them in disdain.

'Yearrsse, how can I help?'

'Would Lady Sommerville be available to have an attendance?'

The man's face froze, this request was totally unacceptable. No-one, absolutely no-one arrived unannounced and asked to meet the lady of the house.

'I am terribly sorry, but you will need an appointment. Speak to the masters office in the city, we do not allow such intrusions,' said the clearly insulted balding face, slowly withdrawing, the door creeping shut as if an unstoppable force drive it.

'Tell her ladyship her daughter is here to see her. Tell her that her daughter's name is Charlotte,' snapped Charly quickly. 'And if you don't and she finds out you haven't, she will not be pleased.'

The face said nothing, the door slowly creeped shut, the lock making a solid thunk as the bolt slid home. The message was clear: go away, you are not welcome. Harry went to leave but Charly put her hand on his arm, cheeky grin on her face.

'Just think how he feels, knowing that he only wishes to treat us with contempt, and does not wish to disturb the mistress, but the threat is now burrowing into his mind, he is driven to do what he does not want.' She gave a little giggle. 'Ahh, the power of suggestion from a beautiful woman in expensive clothes can do great things.'

They waited for some minutes, stretching to ten, then fifteen. Harry's good leg was aching, looking for somewhere to sit, when the door suddenly creaked as it opened with a lack of haste.

'Please, follow me,' said the balding face, puckered and annoyed to acknowledge he had been beaten. The door slowly creaked shut behind them as they entered the ornate foyer, closed by unseen hands as they walked down a long hallway, then turning left, down another, till they arrived at a side door. The man with a balding head stopped them with a hand movement, then knocked once. That done, he opened the door and directed them inside with a curt wave of his hand, closing the door behind them.

A woman stood in the centre of a light-filled room, rays of sunshine of glittering across the polished timber floorboards. The woman stood stock still, her hands cupped on her face, her hair slightly dishevelled, greying at the sides but clearly once black and wavy, flowing over her shoulders. Her hair was the exact match for the woman who walked through the doorway; it was clearly Charly's hair.

The two looked at each other, unable to respond, unsure on the situation, then the slightest movement by one caused the identical reaction in the other. They rushed together, catching each other in their arms, words lost in sobs of anguish, sobs of happiness, sobs of joy. They held each other, their faces buried in the black hair, now a single mass of waves and curls. The odd word of apology could be heard but it made no sense, words did not count, only contact, person to person, mother to daughter.

Finally, Charly's mother lifted her head, brushed a few strands of the black hair from her daughter's face, then wiped away her daughter's tears with a gentle brush of the back of her fingers.

'Oh, my darling Charlotte, what did I do to you? I am so sorry, so so sorry. What did I do to you?'

She dropped her head again, tears flowing from her face, soaked up in Charly's hair. They stood until Charly leaned back, a typical childish grin as she repeated her mother's actions.

'No, that is not important. Only being together is important, being with each other that is important,' Charly quietly stated without any blame in her voice. 'Mummy, I have waited for this day for so long, but only recently have I wanted to do this with love not hate. I love you. I do.'

Charly's mother smiled and kissed her long-lost daughter gently with deep love, she then leaned back slightly and saw a man behind her daughter, knowing at once who it must be.

'And you must be our rather famous Harry,' she said. 'I am so glad to meet you too finally, I have read so much about you in the papers.'

Lady Sommerville put her hand to her mouth, knowing she had let something slip, then smiling and giving Harry a wink.

Charly was about to ask the very pertinent question as she realised that her mother knew things that maybe she should not. But her thoughts were interrupted as the door pushed open and a well-dressed man walked in. He immediately filled the room with his presence, he was undoubtedly the Master of the house and all its surrounds, as if the house and everything in it needed to give due respect to his arrival. Lady Sommerville smiled as he entered, his uniform sharp and crisp, the many bars of his service medals above the right pocket.

Harry stood upright as best he could, almost overbalancing.

Lord Sommerville turned and quietly stated, 'At ease young fellow,' to allow Harry to slightly relax. Charly held her position with her mother, untwining on one side, still leaving her arm behind her mother's waist.

'My deepest apologies, my dearest wife, those idiots in cabinet have no idea,' he grumbled, as much to himself. 'About time some of them went past the edges of the city and saw what the bloody police have to do in the scrub… Idiots.'

He then looked at the stunning young woman standing arm in arm with his wife, a striking similarity. 'And, pray tell, who do we have here?'

'Charlotte, darling, please meet my dear husband, Lord Basil Sommerville,' said Charly's mother as she turned to face her daughter, 'and my darling daughter, please meet your father.'

Charly slowly awoke from her daze, her brain still fuzzy, her head still swimming, the room slowly spinning. She was laying on the couch, Lord and Lady Sommerville sitting in dining chairs beside her head, Harry in a very soft occasion chair at her feet. Charly looked up, the room was not familiar, then she remembered the shock, and her head spinning, the words, the meaning… Then she remembered what caused it… Her father.

A large, powerful hand gently brushed her forehead. The touch was light, loving.

'Ahh, the young beauty awakes,' Lord Sommerville said with a light lilt in his voice. 'My darling wife, I did warn you to break that one with care if the occasion was to arrive.'

'Ah, damn it, Basil, and how does one do that with care you great lump? Now go and get the cranky old butler of yours to organise some afternoon tea. I think we have a little explaining to do to our children.'

'Most certainly, Amelia, I think we do,' said the ex-Commissioner of Police, now minister of the government, as he stood and walked from the room to organise what his wife had commanded.

They all sat under the large and ornate pergola in the rear garden. The lawns ran gently to the edge of the river, a soft from the water breeze cooled the skin from the heat of the afternoon. Two servants ensured that every need was fulfilled. Harry felt very misplaced, and Charly was simply in a daze.

'Harry, young fellow, I take it you have not been demobbed yet?' asked Basil

'No, err, Lord Somerville, I have not. But it will happen soon as we get back, I would expect.'

'Mmmm, that is interesting. And please, it's Basil, I do so get sick of the formal shit,' he replied, inducing a curt, 'Darling' from his wife. 'Yes, yes, but I am sure Charlotte knows a few words that would make me blush.'

Charly blushed. Again it appeared the older persons at the table knew a little more than they let on, it was time. She lifted her eye in query as she looked at her newly minted father. Her face now providing the look that demanded an answer or two.

'Right you are, Basil, but I think the explanation is required. Firstly, about you two, and then about a lot of knowledge of us that appears to be known,' Charly asked.

Basil Sommerville laughed. It was the pleasant, happy laugh of a man very much at ease with himself.

'Well, Charlotte, I do think your mother has the right to explain the first one. I most certainly can do the second, but not till the first is explained, so... Amelia, darling.'

Lady Amelia Somerville cleared her throat and took a sip of her tea. It was as if she was clearing the air to allow the story to be told on her terms. As she started, it was clear that she was speaking only to her daughter, but allowed the others to listen in.

'Charlotte, as you know, the flats could be a lonely place, and the man I married could and was to be somewhat difficult after the first years together. But I truly do not wish to discuss Mr Hendricks at the moment. I am fairly sure that you know enough now to understand we lived together as husband and wife, and I carried his children, but not because of love or devotion. It was simply expected. After the second year, when I carried Jessie, things changed between us and they were never to return as before. In those years he had strayed a number of times, mostly with that woman who lived on the adjoining property.'

'Cunningham.'

'Yes, her. She provided him a soft bed on many an occasion, but there were others too, like that harlot that he finally married after I left.'

'He knew her all those years before...?'

'Knew her? He was besotted by her, that idiot of a man. She had him in her hand and would never let go. But I digress, and that is not the story you wish to hear, I am sure. Well, it was during one of his whoring episodes when he was away in the city, that a small team of surveyors and government supervisors came through the valley. The man leading the support team of police constables was the son of a fine gentleman who was directing the process from within the government of the day. That young police officer made quite an impression on me and as they say, one thing led to another.'

Lady Amelia Sommerville smiled at her husband, who nodded his responding affection.

'Well, as luck would have it, young Basil here left me with a small surprise.' She looked at Charly. 'And that was you.'

Charly sat up, her hand on her mouth, shocked at knowing how she was conceived. In one way, she was glad it had been in love, but was also horrified at the disfunction in the family she'd entered into, knowing now why it had felt like an endless war in the house.

'Jed, the old mongrel, knew very quickly. He could count, I guess, but I was not going to get rid of you. Never. Anyway so you made it into the world. I knew I could not leave him, there was some misplaced loyalty, but also maybe madness. You were my children, I loved you all and I tried to stick it through. Jed kept his habits, likely half the Cunningham girls are his. I simply kept the house and brought you children up. His bastardry saw no limits, enjoying explaining his exploits in great detail and when I no longer reacted, he went and took the next step...'

Amelia began to sob, gasped as she struggled for air. Finally taking a breath she looked at her daughter with the reality of what how occurred all those years before, and then sobbed from her heart, tears beginning in her eyes before she continued. 'He started on you.'

There was a stunned silence. Charly felt as there were no others listening, just her and her mother finally exchanging these words.

'I'd had Cassie a year or so before, through a series of brutal acts by Jed, really little more than rapes that it was but he got what he demanded. But when I came to know what he was doing to you, my darling, my heart broke. I had no idea what to do. I looked at Cassie one day and saw the next victim of his hate for me.'

'So how did you plan to get out?' asked Charly, her voice trembling, the memories harsh, the pain felt in her body.

'I had remained communicating with Basil for some time, very secret and very infrequently, but very special. It kept me alive inside.' She gulped back another sob, wiping the tears from his eyes, a little guilt still sat in her heart. 'It was the aunties that stayed at the billabong. I needed someone to speak to who would not judge me or my actions, anyway, they knew that one day he would kill one of us. So they started planning with some of the local people to find a way to get me and a child out, to make us disappear.'

Lady Amelia Somerville sat for a moment, her head down. Silence filled the room, a silence that demanded respect to the person telling the story, demanding that she be allowed to continue when she was ready.

'A few of the aunties found a way. I will not say much, but we travelled by foot a very long way. It was harrowing, Cassie nearly died. But it was the women from the deserts that got us through, they knew the soaks and the springs. Ironically, I had to leave Basil's daughter behind and bring the one bred by the mongrel. Not that I loved either of you any differently.'

Charly put her hand on her mother's arm. An acknowledgment that there was no resentment.

'Basil was told of my disappearance, and quietly come to my side when he knew where we were hiding. So, we did a few shifty things that I cannot speak about. Cassie and I disappeared to a different land to the north, then ceased to exist. One day we became different people as we arrived back on a boat, and as time allowed, I was married to this man.'

Amelia smiled uncertainly at her daughter. The response was a loving smile of acceptance without fault. Then Charly started laughing, and laughing, tears of madness trickling down her face. Her parents looked on slightly in concern, unsure what it was until she slowed and finally stopped. Charly looked at both of them and laughed even harder, until the mirth eased allowing a word to be said.

'What a totally mad bunch of people in my family. So my mother, and that would be you, my dearest mother, was married to two men at the same time. The man I thought was my father was married to two women at the same time, and my oldest brother, who is my half-brother is likely sleeping with his sister.' Charly looked at Harry, starting to laugh again. 'And somehow, for that should have happened but didn't, the father of my children is somehow not my brother.'

A silence sat over the table for the remaining three, before the meaning of the words were unravelled, the madness of the intertwined structure contemplated. First Basil, then Charly's mother and finally Harry started laughing.

Lord Basil Sommerville slowly tempered the laugher to a chuckle before he banged his hand on the edge of the small table. 'Children, you will be remain for supper, and a rather sumptuous bed will be prepared. My child who I have desired to meet for many years will not be staying in some flea-bitten hovel. I demand, no order, that you and your beloved husband will remain with us.'

Charly looked at Harry in shock. They had arrived at the elegant house, knowing that in all likelihood they would be shown the direction back down the steps.

'Your offer is beyond consideration, but we have a room... well a suite... and our bags and clothes,' stammered Charly, rather unsure.

'Oh, Basil will get Jarvis to have your things brought over and cancel the booking. Not an issue at all,' Amelia said as a direction to her husband. 'If you think that I will let you out of my hands after all these years, my dearest girl, that will never happen again. we have so much to discuss.'

Charly smiled as she looked at her father, her heart busting with emotions she never knew existed. And things to discuss, she thought, damn right there were. Especially about her baby sister and her family, and maybe her children. She looked at her mother. It was time to love and forgive, what had happened in the past was in the past, the future should be for happiness.

'Yes, Father, we have much to discuss,' were her only words as tears ran down her face.

As was so clearly inferred, the young two visitors became captives to very interested parents. After an extraordinary supper, mother and daughter sat close in the parlour, a hand from one on the hand of the other, the need for touch important as important as words said or heard. The two men sat watching for a short while before Basil stood and beckoned Harry to follow him outside. Harry stood, unsteadily from a little too much wine and followed, his crutch tapping on the polished timber floor.

'Let the girls to have some time to themselves. I will get a chance to chat with Charlotte later,' Basil noted quietly as he lit a fat cigar. He offered another to Harry who shook his head. 'Ahh, good thing, young man. Now, Harry, I have friends that tell me things about your service record that impress me. I have an idea that may assist both of us.'

Harry smiled. He knew that a man did not reach Lord Basil Sommerville's position without asking a question when it required asking, like now.

'Certainly, Lord Basil,' replied Harry, picking a halfway point between formal and relaxed. 'But I am a little banged up these days to be much use in anything active.'

'Bloody hell, Harry, ditch the title crap, you young bugger,' growled Basil with a smile, knowing what Harry was doing. 'And as for the other, it is the brain that wields the more powerful sword, and I am thinking you have a reasonable brain.'

Lord Basil Sommerville led the way back inside, heading down to the smoking room and a crystal decanter of fine port. Once seated with a weighty cut glass filled with a deep purplish red liquid in their hands, he explained the rough detail of the proposal. Harry listened, knowing his cattle mustering riding days had ended. This was an opportunity to keep an active brain and keep doing something that would provide satisfaction.

'I will consider your idea, Basil. But now, and before Charly asks, tell me how the hell do you know so much about us?'

Lord Basil Sommerville smiled and then touched his nose a few times. 'Sergeant Angus MacDonald,' he replied with a conspiring chuckle. 'Really it was Charlotte that came to my attention first, with her, well, let's call it her exploits. But Macca is an old friend, and after we figured out who Charly might be, his job was to keep a bit of a watch over her.' He smiled again. 'Macca was to be a bit of a guardian angel, but for sake of all the saints don't tell her that.'

'And me, I guess with that one lot of information, my activities in the regiment were a little too easy.'

'See, a fine sharp brain, and for that I do not need to answer, as you have done so already.'

After nearly two days in the company of Charly's parents, it was time to return to their children. Mother and daughter delved into parts of their lives and digested all of the diverse activities undertaken by a strong-minded young woman. The older man became very impressed by the business mind shown to achieve what she had in such difficult circumstances. An open invitation remained, a room and beds always available for visits to the city. A demand from two older people to have the younger ones return with their grandchildren before the month was out. In return, a promise to visit the cattle station was exchanged before they rode away.

As they settled in the coach, Charly looked at her husband with interest, the closed-door discussions between him and her new father intrigued her.

'So tell me, what secrets have you and your new best friend conspired?' asked Charly in mock annoyance. 'It was as if we had become irrelevant to your interests.'

Harry laughed a little to himself as he wiggled back into the firm leather seats in the small, enclosed coach that had been provided by Lord Sommerville to take them to the train siding to commence their travels home. Charly snuggled over as he placed his hand on her thigh.

'Well, it was not as though the two women in the house were providing much opportunity to join their discussions,' replied Harry, indicating how mother and daughter had spent the best part of three days regaling their exploits of the previous years. Charly's stories at times dragging in the two men as she described the days as a cameleer and all that had occurred.

'True, true, but I did notice some seriousness in the discussion with the former Commissioner of Policing, him being our newly minted minister in the parliament. So pray tell, can your wife know?'

'The truth of the matter is that an offer has been made. While I have not agreed, my mind is leaning to an acceptance of the proposition,' Harry declared firmly, his mind almost locked down. 'My days being shot at in uniform, riding into small conflicts with my wife, mustering on a grassy flat paddocks or sandy hills are at an end.'

Harry paused, finally admitting to what he knew were to be the limitation of the wounds from Africa. 'Basil has a ministry in the government for policing the state. He asked if I was interested in being one of his assistants, being from the country and all that. Well, actually, he wants me to run a new department, looking at sorting out a bit of rustling and similar stuff.'

'And the rest? I am sure that man did not stop there.'

Harry looked at his wife, a person he had thought he had lost more than once from his life, and he was never going to let that happen again.

'Well you're right as usual, he also asked if I would be interested in putting my hand up to be a member in our area in the next election for the party.' Another pause allowed the magnitude of his comments to be considered. 'And with your agreement, I might be inclined to say yes.'

Charly snuggled in closer to her husband, smiling at how a near dead survivor of those horrible things in her childhood, a penniless cameleer who had battled to make a business survive, who had made a small fortune and handed some of it back, could one day end up as a respected woman in the community? She had not reached her thirtieth year but had lived through one, maybe two, lifetimes of excitement, sadness and horror.

She knew the things that had driven her to prove who she was and that she could succeed under her own power were no longer needed. For the first time since her mother left all those years before, she was at total peace in her heart. At peace with the world. It was clearly time to enjoy what her mother had so missed in her years at the Flats, a wonderful husband and beautiful children. The final message from the person who she had missed for so many years was clear: it is time to love your family.

She placed her hand on her stomach, wondering if it was time to tell her man the news. He was obviously slipping, not the cattleman of old she knew so well. Charly reached up and gently turned his head, providing a soft kiss on his lips.

'Most certainly, my darling, whatever my gorgeous husband wishes. I am here to support you, always.'

She suddenly started to quietly laugh, putting her finger on Harrys lips as he was about to ask.

'And just think, you and me, in the cream of society. A rough old jackaroo and a cranky sheila cameleer. Who would have thought?' Charly noted in conclusion, having another chuckle. 'And what will Jessie and Bryan say when they find out I am the oldest daughter of Sir Basil Sommerville, Esquire.'

Shawline Publishing Group Pty Ltd
www.shawlinepublishing.com.au

SHAWLINE
PUBLISHING
GROUP